The
FATE

Leigh Evans has raised two kids, mothered three
dogs, and herded a few cats. She lives in Southern
Ontario with her husband and a short, fat, black
dog. *The Trouble with Fate* is her first novel.

Follow her on Twitter @LeighEvans001
www.leighevans.com

The Trouble with
FATE

LEIGH EVANS

TOR

First published 2013 by St Martin's Press, New York

First published in Great Britain 2013 by Tor
an imprint of Pan Macmillan, a division of Macmillan Publishers Limited
Pan Macmillan, 20 New Wharf Road, London N1 9RR
Basingstoke and Oxford
Associated companies throughout the world
www.panmacmillan.com

ISBN 978-1-4472-3126-4

1 3 5 7 9 8 6 4 2

A CIP catalogue record for this book is available from
the British Library.

Printed and bound by CPI Group (UK) Ltd, Croydon, CR0 4YY

Visit **www.panmacmillan.com** to read more about all our books
and to buy them. You will also find features, author interviews and
news of any author events, and you can sign up for e-newsletters
so that you're always first to hear about our new releases.

For those who I call mine—Kevin, Chelsea and J.B.

Acknowledgments

There are so many people who helped me with this book. Deep thanks to Deidre Knight, agent extraordinaire and dear friend, who saw a faint glow and knew how to make it shine. A tip of my hat goes to my editor, Holly Blanck, who fearlessly pushed me toward a trip to Threall. My endless gratitude to Caitlin Sweet, both for her insightful comments and for the fact that she'll drink merlot even though she prefers white wine. A big cheer for Susan Seebeck's amazing ability to put her slim finger on the exact thing that's fouling the scene. A bouquet to Chris Szego who read a draft of Hedi and had the courage to write "TSTL" beside something that was truly dumb. A heartfelt hug for the lovely Rebecca Melson who was honest enough to tell me that Trowbridge needed some work. A smile and a bow to Charlaine Harris whose virtual home was the birthplace of my writing career. And many thanks to Angela Zoltner, a friend and champion of the missing word.

But the final hand-over-heart salute goes to my family. Thanks, my darlings, for the "Go Bear Go," for the Christmas rescued, for the trips to Creemore, for the Saturday-morning phone calls, for the notes and story reviews, for every movie missed, and for every job of mine quietly shouldered. You're the lights in my sky.

Prologue

We lived in a long flat bungalow in Creemore. It was a mixture of gray brick and faded blue aluminum siding. I can remember other things about that house—the pond, a tree outside, the bush that flowered in the spring with little tiny pink rosebuds that actually weren't rosebuds, but opened like them, and smelled sweet. It's not a common bush, but I've seen it here and there in the springs that have followed, and whenever I do, I think of that backyard, and the tree, and the little path that wandered between the bushes and the fence, made not by design, but by the constant patrol of two kids. I remember using that path to follow my best friend, a boy twelve minutes older than me, but two inches taller, with blond hair that curled. He was my brother, and I called him Lexi.

More facts. The ones that hurt. A Werewolf killed my father, and the Fae executed my mother. They took my brother Lexi with them across a portal I could never breach.

They left me behind.

Chapter One

What do the tree huggers call it? Karma?

No, wait a minute; that's not right. "Karma" is just a word for what goes around comes around, isn't it? And on the surface, Robson Trowbridge's only crime was to have been the hot guy in school who was totally oblivious to the bottom dwellers of his world.

Like me, Hedi Peacock, formerly Helen Stronghold, and still, unfortunately, a bottom dweller.

"Karma" isn't the word I was looking for. Should someone's life turn to crap just because he's handsome? Even I'm not that bitter. But still, I wish someone would even it out, make it so that everyone had the same luck and chances. If I created the world, you could bet there would be a set of natural laws, and one of them would be the Law of You Can't Stay Hot Forever. It would be stamped on the forehead of every high school heartthrob in ink visible only to bottom dwellers, just as an incentive to survive the ordeal of high school. According to my law, hot guys would age very badly. At thirty, they'd be thumbing through the yellow pages searching for a hair renewal salon.

I shifted on the back of my heels, and strained to peek over the counter. Ten years out of high school and Trowbridge still had hair. In fact, more than when he'd been the to-die-for son of the Alpha of Creemore. Back then, he'd owned a Jeep and had dibs on a crown. He'd have been considered cute even without the killer smile.

"What are you doing down there?" asked my manager, Mark.

"I thought I dropped something, but I can't find it." I stood and reached for the silver milk container beside my espresso machine. It had been a dumb instinct, dropping to my knees behind the counter. Most things are better faced when you're upright.

"You're slowing down again." Mark slapped another cup on the order shelf. "Now, you have four orders to fill." He lowered his voice. "Hurry. Up."

I nodded, teeth clenched, and let out a jet of steam to make him back up. He was going to fire me.

I may have broken a cookie here and there. Everyone knows that broken cookies can't be sold. Everyone knows that the person who notices the broken cookie gets to eat the cookie. These are facts. If people stayed with proven facts, work environments would be easier. Groundless accusations just stir things up, like the whole "Who hid the turkey breast sandwich behind the milk?" controversy. Did they think I did it? Well, prove it. Maybe I did do it, and maybe if you were an anal retentive asshole who counted cookies and sandwiches, you might feel those were two good reasons to fire your barista. Maybe.

But I was a goddess behind the machine. Normally, my fingers flew over the knobs, steam didn't bother me, and no one, I repeat, no one, made foam like I did. I was a good barista, who could usually keep up with a stream of empty cups appearing by her left elbow. I even found it comforting, that monotony of press the button, steam the milk, empty the shot glass, pass the cup. But lately the familiar routine wasn't automatic. Twice today, I'd come out of one of my aunt Lou's transmitted thought pictures—something of a trance—with steamed milk running over the lip of the silver container and my heart jackrabbiting in my chest.

People were giving me plenty of space this afternoon, which was good. Space is a nice buffer when you work a shift with the idiot tag team of Mark and blonde-from-a-box Jennifer. They kept batting back and forth answers to the really important question of "If you could save only one thing from a fire, what would it be?"

Come on, guys. It's not that hard. There's only one answer. *Yourself, dimwit.* When fire is chewing through everything you've ever cared about, and there is no one left to rescue beyond yourself, the decision is simple: forget your charm bracelet and find the door. I'd point that out, but that would mean getting cozy with a human, and I don't do cozy with the humans, which is providential, because as it happens, none of them have ever offered to extend the relationship beyond work hours. They keep their distance. Which is good, and bad, and maybe a little sad.

I can't say I blame them. If I had to share a shift with me, I might be leery of getting in too close. Even full-blooded Fae need sleep, and my lack of quality time spent with a pillow was starting to show. But as long as I had a choice between an acid stomach or dream-plagued sleep? *Pass the espresso.*

At least when I was mostly awake, I could fight the sickening tentacles of Lou's wandering mind reaching for mine. And if I failed, I could say to myself, *Okay, take a deep breath, you're all right, you're just seeing her dreams through her eyes, but you're still Hedi. You're just stuck in your mad aunt's head for a bit, witnessing how truly fucked up her brain is.*

But when I was asleep? Different. Scary different.

And now I had Weres in my Starbucks; my stomach gave a disapproving gurgle.

When Trowbridge had opened the coffee shop door—the second Were to enter in ten minutes—I'd dropped to my knees, stricken with the fear that I'd slipped into a hallucination of my own, and had done so without experiencing the usual shit-here-I-go slide that happens before Lou pulls me into one of hers. Then, just as quickly as it had swamped me, my fear eased. I don't detect scents when I'm dreaming and my nose had picked up an aroma over the brewed coffee that was Trowbridge's alone. Ten years ago, when I'd been a lovesick twelve-year-old, I hadn't been able to put my finger on that unique thing in his personal scent signature that my hormones interpreted as "Yum, Robson Trowbridge."

Even now, older and a hell of a lot more bitter, I couldn't find a word for it. It was just a truth, as tiresome and hard to deny as the notion that chocolate bypasses your stomach and goes straight to your hips. Trowbridge smelled different than the other Creemore Weres. He always had.

He was still pretty, if a bit unkempt. His jaw hadn't seen a razor in a good week. And his hair was different. Now it was long, dark rumpled curls that brushed his shoulders. The type of curls that say, "I just got out of bed after a night of really hot sex." Curls that don't need a brush, just some sated female to finger-comb them.

Annoying. A girl couldn't look at Robson Trowbridge without thinking about sex, even if she had reason to hate him. To keep myself sharp on that point, I checked out his neck, and sure enough, he had a gold chain hanging from it. He'd hidden the rest of the amulet under his shirt, but I knew it was there. Fae gold calls to my kind. I could feel its siren song, even from where I stood, half hidden behind the coffee machine.

Old history, and yet not.

"Double decaf, tall, no-foam latte." I placed the coffee on the bar and scowled at the man who reached out for it before I finished centering it on the tray. There's protocol, even at a Starbucks. You don't reach for it, you wait for it. I snatched my fingers back before his could brush mine. All this pent-up fear was making me cranky.

It had snuck up on me, this yearning for Trowbridge, around puberty. I'd taken one glance at his Were abs, and gone from kid to preteen so fast that Mum had gotten whiplash. Worse, it had clung to me, that desire. Even though I try not to think of him, I still call up his face for every dark-haired hero found in one of those romance novels I boost from Bob, the blind bookseller.

Yes, I steal books from a blind bookseller.

How screwed up is that? Imagining Trowbridge as Lord Worthington, complete with the spotless Hessians?

I really wanted to rub my eyes. Behind my glasses' magicked lenses, my eyes were sparking so badly it felt like a squad of Boy Scouts were competing to see who could start a fire with a flint and steel. But if you have a disguise, you wear it, even if it's inconvenient, even if part of you wants to do a pirouette on top of the bar and sing, "Hah, I didn't die after all, you scum-sucking dog."

As I reached for a new gallon of skim milk, Trowbridge moved from the doorway toward a white-haired Were who'd come in a few minutes earlier. Geezer-Were had looked as benign as an old Were could, but I'd been keeping tabs on him anyhow, ready to bolt if he looked at me sideways. By my rulebook, Gramps shouldn't have been there in the first place, not if he was a regular Were, doing regular things. Why? Because, basically, the stench of coffee is akin to the best doggone wolf repellent available. It won't stop the motivated, but will deter the average Were.

Which is why, when the old Were had entered the café, nose high, and snared the last free table, my stomach had tensed, and I'd shrunk a little lower behind my brewing machine, not knowing what to expect. But since then, he'd just sat there, slouching in his comfortable country clothes, one hand playing with a stir stick someone had left behind. My ill ease had flattened, because part of me figured I could outrun a fossil like him, any day, any time. But now my fight-or-flight instinct was tapping me on the shoulder, telling me to stay sharp. What would two Weres be doing in a coffee shop? Had the Weres of Creemore finally come looking for me?

Trowbridge took a quick glance around the room before pulling out a chair opposite Geezer-Were. I held my breath as his gaze skipped me and drifted over to a shapely brunette, waiting to place her order. So much for the "aha" moment. He didn't point a finger at me and exclaim, "Lo, there be the long-lost daughter of Benjamin Stronghold!" I wiped the counter while the steam did the foam thing, considering the implications of that. My features hadn't changed that much. I mean, if you searched hard enough, it wasn't a big stretch to spot the similarities between a kid named Helen and a girl named Hedi. Did the Creemore pack actually think I was dead? Unbelievable. After the flames and smoke had petered out, hadn't anyone pawed through the rubble searching for our remains? Two kids, plus two parents brought the body count to four, not two. Fools. No one scratched their head and said, "Hey, we're missing two corpses"?

Unless the fire reduced everything to ash? Could it do that? Bones and teeth too?

I'd never made their wanted list. It was a near sickening thought when one took in all the effort Lou and I expended hiding our tracks . . . oh hell . . . I could have gone to school . . . Without taking my eyes off Trowbridge and company, I pointed my finger and sent out a mental stream to the steam knob. It eased a fraction to the left.

His wedding band winked at me as he tucked a hank of hair behind his ear.

"Didn't stop the cheating dog from checking out the brunette, did it?" I muttered to my chest. In response, my amulet, Merry, twitched in her sleep, still hidden under my shirt where I wore her. Sometimes she roused to see what was up, sometimes she didn't—she'd simply twitch or flinch, sort of her version of a pillow over the head. In the end it didn't really matter, because I'd give her a blow-by-blow later. Unless Merry was feeding, she hung around my neck on a chain, making her a convenient audience for one of my monologues. The rest of the time I let her nap inside the cup of my lace bra.

Trowbridge sat a little straighter. Well, he was a Were; he'd probably heard me. But recognize me? That appeared to be another thing. I wasn't twelve anymore, and besides, I was supposed be dead, burned up in the fire.

"Peacock," said Mark. "Speed it up."

I spooned off a little foam and put the next order on the bar.

"That's nonfat?" asked the woman.

"Yup," I said with my toothy barista smile. When she

turned away, I began to clean the nozzle with the damp rag. Trowbridge hadn't moved much since he'd done the visual and slapped a "later" label on the brunette, but from my side of the bar, I could smell his growing unease over the coffee, warm milk, and humans.

That's right, something's wrong, I telegraphed. *What is it?*

His head tilted to the side as if he were searching for a clue. His nostrils flared.

Good luck on that. Faes don't have a scent. He wasn't following the script. He was supposed to haul me out from behind the bar, and stalk out of the coffee shop, with me a helpless, fainting burden in his arms. I'd be wearing kitten heels, one of which would drop off. My small fists would beat on his chest, and he'd look down at me and realize that his life was over unless he claimed me as his own.

Of course for that scenario to work, I'd have to be weak, blond, and at least fourteen pounds lighter. And he'd be Lord Worthington, not some no-account Were. I'm round and short. I don't wear kitten heels. I'd like to, but they aren't on the approved shoe list for Starbucks.

See, there you go, another lie. I'd never wear kitten heels.

My hair is brown. When it's freshly washed and the sun catches it just so, someone who's read one too many bodice rippers might use the word "chestnut" to describe it. That's a stretch. Most days it could be best described as mousy brown. I haven't worked out what to do with it, so I usually wear it pulled back in a ponytail—one of those slacker ponytails that conveniently hide the ears.

And I'm not in the least bit beautiful, which just goes to show what a contrary bitch genetics is. My mum *was* beautiful, otherworldly beautiful, with golden hair that swung in graceful waves to her hips. But then again, she was born a Fae—what most humans call a fairy. She didn't have wings, and she didn't go around in a belted tunic. She did have the ears though. Mine have a slight point to them, courtesy of her. Sometimes I find my fingers stroking their sharp, curved peaks. It soothes me.

What's on the other side of my gene pool?

Werewolf. From my moon-called father, I got a full upper lip, a temper, and my own personal inner Were. I have that bitch on permanent lockdown, buried so deep that she represents little more than a salivation problem when I walk past the deli. I do not turn furry when the full moon rises in the night sky. My eyes don't glow red with rage, my teeth don't elongate, and I can hear only a little better than humans.

Get over the myths. They're never accurate.

Trowbridge got up, and jerked his head toward the exit. Geezer-Were stood to follow. Trowbridge held the door open for him, his right hand spread wide on the glass door. It had three fingers; a thumb, a pointer, and an f-u. The pinkie was missing, leaving a rounded nub close to his palm. The ring finger had been severed after the first knuckle. *Who'd hurt him?*

"Did you get that?" hissed Mark.

"What?"

"The next order. Grande, two pump vanilla, nonfat, extra hot, latte. You're falling behind again, Hedi," he said, from the safety of the cash register.

The door swung closed behind Trowbridge. I bore down on the next orders with a ferocity that made all the other little baristas stay well clear as I came to terms with the thought that all my hiding had been for nothing. They really did think I had died in the fire. *Walk away, Trowbridge,* I thought. *Take your chewed-up hand with you.*

Fourteen minutes later, my beautiful silver coffee maker started to shimmer. I squeezed hard on the steamer's shiny silver handle, and concentrated on my fingers curled around it. Small hands, the knuckles four white sharp stones under soft skin. I could feel the pull, the sick slip of melting into Lou's thought-pictures.

A big fat red apple flashed through my brain.

"Easy, Lou," I said under my breath as I slid a bold one to a short guy. Fae tears, my aunt was lost today. This was the third time.

Concentrate. My hand. This handle, shiny, and silver bright. Concentrate on the sounds in the background. Someone was jiggling his keys. Use that as an anchor, cling to the sound, stay in the *here*. There was a sickening flutter of images as she overwhelmed my resistance. *A red apple, something flying through the air, a face angry and distorted.*

"Stay in the here, stay in the here," I whispered. I tried to focus on the feel of my hand on the handle, the distinctive reek of coffee, and the murmur of human voices in the background. Lou's telegraphed images started to get thin to transparent. For an instant I could see the lineup of cups on top of my machine.

Another flash, another push, and suddenly, she'd started to tow me helplessly back into the current of her thought-pictures. *The same freakin' red apple. A gravel path. A tree line, dark and somehow horrifying. The inside of Bob's bookstore, with midday light streaming weakly through the open space of glass. A natural pool. The water dark, but the trees so green, and the light so bright. A dark uniform, bulky and foreign. Lou's hand, her ornate ring too loose on her finger.*

The "here" was gone.

"Ow," I squeaked as sharp pain broke through my haze and shattered Lou's thought-pictures. I was back, staring at my hand on the knob again, with the smell of coffee pungent in my nostrils. Saved by Merry, once again. When all else fails, a well-timed pinch works just dandy.

Lou had never pulled me so quickly into the broken puzzle of her deteriorating brain, except when I was asleep. When I was inside her head that deep, I couldn't spit out the fear that lay heavy on my tongue.

"Hedi," my manager said carefully. "You're off the line."

The next customer had stopped jiggling his keys. I bit my lip at his carefully neutral face, and turned with a sense of inevitability. Mark was standing halfway between the cash register and my machine.

"Work the cash register for the rest of your shift." He didn't have the balls to come any closer. Jennifer was behind him, her brows pulled together. One day she'll be Botoxing the crap out of that vertical line.

Humans all around me.

"You know what, Mark?" I pulled the apron over my head and tossed it. It caught the milk container, ghosted over it, and slid to the wet ground. "I'm not feeling well. I think I need to punch out early." I pulled my backpack out from the cabinet storing the vanilla bottles.

"Wait a minute. I haven't given you permission to leave." He lifted a hand as if to catch my arm. "I'd like to look through your bag before you go."

"Kiss my ass, Mark." I shouldered past him, shrugging on my backpack.

"You walk out that door and you're fired. You've broken your last machine, and stolen your last sandwich," Mark snapped.

I searched for a good retort, couldn't come up with one, and threaded my way through the tables. I kept my head high even when I heard Mark claim I was the worst barista ever. A patent lie. My foam was the *best* ever. Period.

"She's on drugs," Mark said in a low voice to Jennifer.

"Crack," she said.

I paused, one shoulder holding the door open. The cool wind slid past me but it did nothing for my temper. I took my time, eyeing targets, before settling on the coffee machines. Affixed to the top of each machine was a plastic bowl. Inside the bowls were the coffee beans, waiting to be fed into the grinder. Two machines, two bowls each holding two pounds. Four pounds total.

Mark stood with one possessive hand on my favorite machine, his eyes all puffy as he narrowed them into a squint. That's what made it so easy. They never saw it coming.

I felt my lip curl.

I cocked my fingers backward, smiled, and with a flick sent my magic streaking through the air. Invisible to humans, its progress left a bright fluorescent-green trail to my Fae eyes. It hit the first bowl and stuck. I parted my fingers into a *V.* The stream separated into two trails. The second trail streaked toward the next bowl. "Weave," I said, tracing an *O* with my fingers.

"Grow." I fed a little more energy down the invisible cord.

I did four rotations with my hand until the rope of magic was swollen and hot and then I snipped the line.

I put one foot out of the door, and waited.

You know how you're not supposed to hold a lit firecracker in your hand? So what do you think happens when you tell magic to grow and send it to a place it can't expand? Uh-huh. Kaboom.

The lines around the base of each bowl swelled, until the contained magic looked like a sausage hooked too long on the meat grinder. The bowls began to creak with the pressure around their bases. The plastic lids began to shiver.

Jennifer backed up.

Abruptly, the lids shot up, hitting the ceiling-mounted water pipes with enough force to make them shatter. And then the fireworks.

Sweet to my soul was the Vesuvius of magically powered coffee beans spewing in one long sweet eruption of caffeinated hail to the ceiling. The stunned silence of the café was punctuated by Mark's strangled, inarticulate, "Ack, ack, ack," and the rat-tat-tat of the beans hitting the water pipes.

I waited for the last bean to fall. It clinked on the ground and then rolled until it hit the back heel of a suit.

Silence.

"Huh," I said. "That was strange." I smiled again, baring all my teeth, and let the door close behind me.

Merry, being Merry, was pissed. I hadn't taken six long jubilant steps out of the café before she struck in a fury of searing heat that just about took a strip off the tender skin of my left breast.

"Shit, Merry-mine, not now," I said, speeding up toward the corner of the building. "Cool down. Please, just cool down."

She was so red that the front of my white blouse glowed as if I'd tucked a flare into my bra. I hunched my shoulder protectively, shielding my chest from the customer who was staring at us through the front window, his mug of coffee suspended halfway to his mouth.

I rounded the corner of the building at a good clip. The dusk had already deepened into urban night, the sort of leached-out gray that passes for a night sky in the city. Immediately on breaking the corner, I bent over at my waist, pulled my blouse away from my skin so that I could jerk Merry out by her chain. I let her dangle from it, red, gold, and glowing.

Merry hung from a long length of Fae-wrought gold necklace that my mother had placed around my neck the night she died. You'd need a magnifying glass to see it, but Merry was more than just a smudge in a piece of amber. She was an Asrai. I knew that at least, even if I didn't know precisely what an Asrai was. I knew that she once had form: two legs, two arms, long hair. She belonged to the Fae world, but Lou had trapped her inside the amulet long before I was born. A horrible fate, I agree, but she wasn't completely powerless.

Fae gold is not to be confused with mortal gold. Fae gold snickers at titanium's relative weakness. It isn't some dumb inanimate thing that just sits there, forever frozen in the shape that the artist had hammered it into. It's alive. It can remold itself. It could, powered by the wrong Asrai's spite, literally twine itself around your neck and choke you.

That bore remembering when you were talking to an Asrai-powered amulet.

And as much as Merry sometimes pissed me off—say, like when she tried to burn a layer of skin off me—she and Lou were it. One crazy-ass Fae named Lou, and one amber-colored stone, mounted in a swirl of baroque gold, named Merry. That was my world.

"You can cool down right now," I said, flattening my shirt so that she could hang in the cool night air. I lowered my voice to a soothing tone. "My hand barely hurts. It's not red, well, not red like my freakin' boob is. You know, you've got to control your temper." One of Merry's unique attributes was the ability to heal my payback pain.

The red light turned a fraction purple.

"Okay, maybe I'm not the one to be talking about holding on to my temper. Trowbridge was in the shop tonight, Merry.

And I quit, and so yeah, I may have used some magic. Just a little bit. I was feeling stressed." I rubbed the soot off my finger against the rough grain of my khaki pants. "Look," I said, pulling my finger up so that she could see it. "It's barely red. I don't need healing. It hardly hurts." I was lying like hell, my finger was throbbing like someone had slammed it with a car door, but I held it up straight so that she could see.

"You don't need to heal me, and you don't need to have a hissy fit."

She knew as well as I that payback pain would get worse before it got better. Her color cooled to a stubborn claret. I don't know what claret is, but that's what the bored heroes in my Regencies always drank, and I always figured it was red wine. And sometimes when I was feeling mellow, a furious Merry reminded me of a glass of something vintage, held up to the golden dancing flames of a lit fire.

I kept walking, passing the last car parked in the lot, so engrossed, and still, admittedly, somewhat high with adrenaline, that I didn't even notice the red van idling against the metal fence until I was too close to avoid it. The vehicle smelled of hamburgers, Febreze, and car wash. The sweet bubble-gum smell of the latter twigged a scent recall. I looked, and saw Robson Trowbridge in the driver's seat talking to Geezer-Were. Eyes averted, I walked past the rear of the van, Merry tight in my fist.

Geezer-Were opened the window.

Were scent, fragrant as the woods that I was heading to, reached out to me. Silence as I passed. I don't know who would screw around with a pause, but this one struck me as pregnant. I held my breath, kept my gait casual, and wondered how fast I could run. As fast as a full-blood Were? I skipped over the barrier between this parking lot and the next, and made it onto the gas station's patched asphalt. I didn't change my speed until I had made it around the repair shop, then I broke into a light trot.

Lou's next flood of pictures came with no warning. *An aisle in the bookstore. A path with trees, leaves whipping out in the wind. A dark uniform. Something glinting gold. An*

*arm with a sword, raised high. Then bushes, and ground.
Lou's hand reaching for a rock. Booted feet passing the vegetation.*

As abruptly as they came, they were gone. No visions, no
pictures, no fear. I was back in the "here." I took another
lungful of air.

The entry to the ravine was another half block ahead. I
tightened the straps on my backpack and picked up the tempo.
Lou would be waiting for me at home. So would my bed, and
my dreams. I found my feet slowing. I was early anyhow. If
I came home too early, she'd ask why. I walked twelve feet
along the ravine path thinking about that before I stepped off
the trail to find a tree for Merry.

If anyone passed, it looked like I was just leaning against the
tree, thinking up poetry, and really that's what I was doing.
The tree-leaning bit; not the poetry.

I don't have to do much to feed Merry—there's no can-
opening, or big bags to lug—so I have plenty of time to think.
Once I find a tree and plop her on a limb, all I have to do
is stand guard as she chows down. True, I have to be particu-
lar about the type of tree. It has to be green, preferably wild.
She prefers hardwoods. Pines and spruces make her turn an
unattractive yellow-brown. In a pinch, flowers at a grocery
store will do, but they really fall into the fast food category.
She doesn't get much juice from them. Not enough to last
more than a few days, anyhow. Don't ask me to explain the
mechanics. She doesn't watch me when I'm soaping up in the
shower, and I don't observe her too closely as she sucks down
some tree essence. It gives me a chance to think, that half
hour while she's eating. Some of my best thoughts happen
then. Some of my worst too.

I'd cried for three hours the day Robson Trowbridge married Candace Temple. I might have gone longer, but my twin
Lexi bartered two of his *X-Men* comics for one hour of silence. So I stopped, but felt tragic and misunderstood, even as
I turned the pages and ate a brownie. But then of course, I'd
been twelve, and I'd thought marriages were eternal honey-

moons. Since then, I've seen enough human unions to know that's just another myth. Sort of sucks for Weres though. When they say "I do," they're saying it for life. If one mate dies, the other follows. Sometimes right away, sometimes it takes a few grieving months. I didn't need to be told that. I'd listened to my dad's heart stop, and then my mum's. That's the deal; the sour side of having a true mate.

"How am I going to keep Lou's dreams out of my head now, Merry?" I used the rough tree bark to scratch a spot between my shoulder blades, as I worried the problem. Without a job, I had no distraction from Lou. "I wish I knew how to keep her out."

The constant dribble of Lou's thought pictures and dreams was wearing me thin. I couldn't sleep without being overwhelmed by them, and the problem had grown intolerable since she'd taken to napping during the day. Thought-pictures I could handle. But when her nighttime dreams became my daytime terrors? I can't explain how equally repugnant and fascinating I found it. Prior to this, I'd needed no defense against Lou's fragmenting mind. We'd been two separate beings with a whole bunch of white space between us. We didn't even exchange thought-pictures like I used to with Mum and Lexi.

Handy things, thought-pictures. You can get a lot across with two well-selected ones. For example, imagine a picture of one twin batting the other over the head with something hard. See? Bet you have an immediate opinion about that. If you don't like your sibling, you may think, "Hah, good." But if you're one of those humans with delicate sensibilities—you know, one of those manual-reading mums who believe in naughty corners—well, your first thought might be, "That's terrible."

Now here's where the skill comes in. It's all about the next image. Pair the picture of Helen hitting Lexi with her shoe, followed immediately by an image of Helen's mother frowning fiercely. Neat, huh? You have an opinion *and* a lesson delivered in two quick images.

Merry signaled that she was finished with the tree by roll-

ing off the branch. "You done already?" She pointed to another tree; one with different-shaped leaves. "You know,
you're getting as fussy as a cat." I picked my way through the
knee-high vegetation and reached up to place her on the lowest limb.

I could live with Lou's thought-pictures, but increasingly,
the images were melting into dream fragments and that just
scared the shit out of me. The first act was considered nonthreatening; it was common practice among the Fae to share
a static mental snapshot or two with their blood relatives. But
sharing dreams? Those are dangerous things, aren't they?
Your unconscious is at the controls, and he's that bad relative
that gets drunk at the wedding, and tells *all* the family secrets.

Anyhow, for most Fae-born, the issue was moot. They
simply weren't born with the ability to send or receive another's dreams.

Most of them.

The first non-Hedi dream I ever experienced was Lexi's.
For want of a better word, I was dream-napped. My conscious
self was caught and dragged into my twin's unconscious
mind, as if it were something sticky on the aural plane that
got tangled in the trawling hooks of his dream. That's what it
feels like. Nothing at all like a thought-picture's discreet
knock. A slip, a slide backward, and then, that feeling, that
awful, dreadful wrongness, as if you'd taken off your skin,
and squirmed into another's. Once in, there was no out. You
were forced to stay in it until the dream ended—an unwilling
spectator to what they saw, an unwilling receptor for what
they felt.

Merry tugged her chain to get my attention. I opened my
palm and as my fingers closed over her, I felt soothing
warmth seep into my skin. "Let's go home, Merry."

I started walking again, following the trail through the
woods, but my mind was still on the first time I heard mention of Threall.

The morning after my first dream-walk, I told Mum that
Lexi had slid his dream into my head. Absolute horror twisted
her features. "Threall." She grabbed my hand, yanking me

out of the kitchen faster than you could say, "Lexi stole the last macaroon." Next thing I knew, I was sitting on the edge of my parents' bed watching her shut the door softly behind us. She rested her ear against it for a moment and then turned to ask me questions in that low, tense un-Mum-like voice, and when I was done answering, she was silent for a long time.

She sat down. Without looking, she pointed to the coins on their dresser. A penny lifted from its surface and floated gracefully to me. I reached for it.

"No, Helen, listen and watch." She waited until my hands were back in my lap, and then said slowly, "You know that there are two different realms. The world to which you were born." She made the penny jiggle. "And another, in which the Fae live, called—"

"Merenwyn."

A quarter flew across the air, and hovered above the penny. "Yes, Merenwyn." She made it spin so its bright silver surface caught the early morning light. Her eyes softened as she watched it. "I wish you could see it."

"Why can't you take us there?" I tucked my hair behind my ear. "You used a portal to come here, why can't we open one and go there?"

"I made an oath that I would never cross a portal again. It's an oath I cannot break." She touched my hair. "Even if I could return home, I couldn't bring you with me. The mages keyed the gates to open only for those with Fae blood."

"I have Fae blood." I fingered the bedspread.

"But you also have Were." She gave me a slight smile. "The gates would sense that and might not let you pass. I don't want you to ever try it, okay? Promise me?" When I didn't respond, her voice got sharper. "Helen, using one is not like walking through a doorway. Even for a full-blooded Fae, it's disorienting and dangerous."

"I could do it."

"Could you? When the gate is open, you see right to the other world, like you're looking through a round window. It tricks your mind. You expect to cross a flat plateau, but instead your body is pulled upward at a great speed. It's terrifying the first time, even if you've been told to expect it. If you lose focus of where you need to go, you can be pulled into the wind, and killed. They train your mind for weeks before you're allowed to even think of stepping into a portal."

"Who trains you?" I asked, my mind already wandering.

"There's something more important for us to talk about." She turned her head, and levitated all the coins sitting on the dresser into the air, squinting at them until she spotted the flat washer that Dad had put in his pocket and never returned to the jar in the garage.

"There is a third realm called Threall. It lies between this world and Merenwyn." The flat disk floated across the room. It slipped into the empty place between the Merenwyn quarter and the earthly penny. I studied the stacked coins floating in space.

"Threall looks like a washer stuck between a penny and quarter?"

The coins dropped to the bedspread. "No, Helen. It does not look like that."

"Then what does it look like?"

She sighed, but didn't squeeze the bridge of her nose like she usually did after some of my questions. Instead, she picked up the quarter and the penny. "It's said to be a land of mists and bad things. They say a part of every Fae lives in Threall, the dreaming portion of us." She pressed her hand to her heart. "It should be sacred, not a place anyone can visit."

I gazed dubiously at the dull piece of metal lying on the quilt. "How do you know Threall exists if no one has ever seen it?"

"There are some who can travel there."

I gave her the "aha" look. "So there's a portal."

"No, Helen. There is no portal. Only mystwalkers can travel to Threall."

"How?"

"With their mind. Once trained, a mystwalker can create a second body in the world of mists, and walk on two feet, just as she does in Merenwyn."

"Cool," I said.

"No. Not cool. Mystwalkers search for people's souls in Threall, Helen, and once they find them, they can do great harm."

"Huh." There were a few Weres I felt like harming.

"Don't look like that." Her fingers gripped mine. "There's a reason I'm telling you this. Look at me." Her eyes were so fierce. "Do you know how they find mystwalkers? They search for children born with the gift of walking into others' dreams. Those children are brought to the King's Court. Their gifts are tested. If they don't have enough raw talent, they're killed, and if they're not killed, they become wards of the court. The King's Court is not a place for any child. Those children, the ones who make it to adulthood, they become . . ."

"What?"

"Mad and soulless. The royal family trains them to walk in the mists, and do things there that Faes consider soul destroying."

"Like what?"

"They steal others' gifts. They plant seeds of madness in their enemies' heads."

"How?"

"Helen, it's not a talent I want you to develop. It's *not* a good thing." Her grip turned crushing. "It's a terrible crime to steal someone's talent. Mystwalkers are shunned by all except their trainers. The lucky ones die young before they are driven mad, or worse, disappear."

"Where do they disappear to?" My voice sounded small.

"Their souls stay in Threall. It gets harder and harder for them to come back, and one day they never do. Their body dies in Merenwyn, and the mystwalker is never heard from again. They say they float on the winds of Threall, crying for their home."

I bent my head to study the washer lying innocently on the chenille spread.

She lifted my face with mum-loving hands. "Don't walk in others' dreams. If you feel yourself being pulled into one, resist. Never travel to Threall. Ever. Never admit to anyone that you know anything about dream-walking. *Anyone,* do you understand? Don't tell your brother, don't tell your friends, don't tell your father. But most important, never mention it to a Fae. Do you understand? Helen, it's very important. Myst-walkers always come to a bad end. Threall is a bad place. It can hurt you."

She got down on one knee, gazed deeply into my eyes, and repeated the last sentence, but slowly, as if each word were an individual sentence, turning the comment into a four-word paragraph heavy with meaning. Dream-walking was bad. Threall was bad.

But it was like having something stuck between your teeth, and never being able to get it out. I didn't want to get her all upset, so I didn't point out that I had no friends other than Lexi, and that I was unlikely to ever meet another Fae. Instead, I rationalized that two out of three was good enough, and as soon as Mum and Dad fell asleep that night, I trotted over to Lexi's room, shook him awake, and asked if he ever dream-walked.

No horror on his face. He said, "Shut up." Then he rolled over.

Clearly, he never felt the terrible suck of his waking mind being pulled into someone's dreaming one. For once, I knew something Lexi didn't. And right there I decided it was one secret I wasn't going to whisper into his eager ears.

We already shared so much, a lot of it unwillingly. Does anyone really want to fight for elbow space in a womb? Be perpetually twelve minutes behind? Yeah, sure, there were probably advantages to being second—there were baby pictures of a pointy-headed Lexi—but the downside is that you start out not being first. And it seemed my legs were never long enough to catch up. For our first ten years of life, my brother plowed a trail ahead, leaving me to follow in his wake. Predictably, he was the first to walk. First to talk (and yap, yap, yap, did he ever talk). First one to dare to wander off the property and explore where he wasn't supposed to explore. First one to be brought home by the Alpha after that adventure, looking muddy and wet, and more pissed than a cocker spaniel who's been denied a treat.

Fae Stars, I miss him. It's not something a singleton can understand; the depth of grief a twin feels over the loss of their sibling. Except maybe if I explain it to you this way: once I stood on three legs. Now I wobble on two.

But the future wasn't something I thought much about back then. Like every other self-absorbed twelve-year old, I took it for granted that my brother would always be there; part best friend, part worst enemy. Mine to love and abuse. And so, I got mulish about the following. I got selfish about the sharing. And maybe Lexi did too. Maybe his heedless race through our short shared life was an effort to distance himself from me—the bobbing cork that followed the currents left behind him.

But still, even after Mum's talk, I kept poking at the idea of Threall. I wanted to see it, just once. The best way, I reasoned, would be to visualize "up." It's how I manipulate my magic. Think the word, and let her rip. And besides, I strongly doubted that you needed to create another body up in Threall. Why couldn't you just take your own up there, and bypass the whole "lost my body" problem?

So I sat there, cross-legged on my bed, and thought "up." After a bit, I tried a different thought. "Lift." Then I strong-armed it. I kept thinking "up" until sweat broke out on my brow and I felt queasy, and then suddenly, I felt a tearing inside me, so strong, it was as if a giant had my head in one hand and my toes in the other and was determined to stretch me like a piece of taffy.

At the onset of the pain, my concentration splintered, and took with it that horrible rending sensation. I curled up in a ball on my bed, held my stomach, and decided right there that I'd never try again. In fact, I added a codicil to my pledge: if dream-walking had anything to do with Threall, I'd resist being pulled into any vision. I'd turn away. I'd stay awake.

Scary stuff, Threall.

I exited the nature trail and turned down our street.

Funny how life works out. Pledges aren't so much broken as worn down. I'd gone from thought-picture deprived to dream overloaded. And even though the circles under my eyes were starting to look like purple bruises, I still wouldn't speak to Lou about it.

How could I tell her I was an untrained mystwalker?

And there was more. Stuff I didn't like to admit. There was something in the pull of my crazy aunt's unconscious that I liked. For all my horror, for all my fatigue, there was a part of me that craved being dragged into her dreams. Something in me enjoyed thumbing through her thoughts and memories. Sometimes—so rarely—I saw Merenwyn. Sometimes I saw my mother again. And sometimes I saw things that frightened me.

But it's like a Fae version of Pandora's box, right? You have the box, you're not supposed to open it, and then somehow it's open, and whooee, the stuff you find in there.

Fascinating, scary stuff.

Sometimes I wonder if it wouldn't be easier to be bat-shit crazy like my aunt.

Chapter Two

Raymond Street was a place that tried hard years ago to be more than it was—and failed. Some fifty years back, a few knuckleheads thought they could make another shopping district in our town. Considering that Deerfield is a small dot on the map between the cities of Toronto and Hamilton, they were being overly optimistic. They pulled down old houses to replace them with the square flat boxes favored by the sixties developers. The consequence of their planning were four blocks of flat gray brick storefronts leading depressingly toward the lake.

Now it was the street that sold dirty videos.

Home was the top apartment over a used bookstore called Twice Read Books, owned and operated by a guy whose vision had slowly eroded until he had to hold the books up to the light and squint through a magnifying glass to read the sales sticker. Bob came from money, which was good, considering how his life had run. He owned the building, so he never had to worry about paying rent for his money-losing business, while the rents that he collected for the two apartments over his store were enough to keep him in the black.

The entrance to our apartment was an anonymous brown door in the back parking lot. I started up the stairs feeling the bite of my backpack's strap. It wasn't all that heavy. I carried a change purse, two tins of maple syrup—the Fae-born's preferred food group—plus a silver travel mug, four books that had come into my hands during my tenure at the café, and a hoodie liberated from the coffee shop's lost and found. That and guilt made it feel heavier though. There was rent to pay, and syrup to buy when this lot was gone, and not a hell of a lot left in the kitty. I should have stolen something worth pawning.

The door to the apartment was unlocked. Again. Any thief could walk in and help themselves to our stuff. I thought about that as I eased the door shut, and tiptoed down the corridor past Lou's dark bedroom.

Safe in my own room, I toed off my shoes and tossed my glasses on the bed. Then I stood for a bit, rubbing my elbow.

How do you find someone to mind a batty Fae princess? Can you imagine that ad? *Wanted: Someone who can endure being called a pestilent mortal, will work for almost nothing, is nimble enough to dodge projectiles, and finds it easy to rationalize every weird thing she sees happening in our apartment.*

My fingers started stroking the peaked tip of my ear.

And then it occurred to me—I hadn't made it to my bedroom undetected in months.

Oh crap.

I pressed my ear against the back door to Bob's store. Okay, if I was a full Were, I wouldn't have to do that. I'd be able to detect the discreet blip of a mouse's fart right through the bricks. Hell, I'd hear a bird drop a feather as it winged its way over the parking lot.

I think.

There is, technically, a lot I don't know about Weres, even though I lived among them for the first twelve years of my life. When they're not tracking a flea with their sharp teeth, they prefer to live like humans—they have mortgages and jobs, pay their car payments and taxes—but underneath that, they're *different*. And exactly how much so is something they don't share with someone who wasn't 99 percent Were.

Secretive lot, the bunch of them. I know from experience that their ears could pick up just about anything. You could keep your face absolutely blank, so they couldn't read your expression, but the bastards could hear your heart speed up, and know that their insult scored a hit. It's why Lexi and I mostly traded thought-pictures during school hours at the private school in Creemore where the pack's young were taught human stuff. Our moon-charmed classmates couldn't read our minds, and considering what I thought about most of them, that was probably a good thing.

Bob wasn't doing much talking on the other side of the door. His son, loathsome Lyle, was though. Annoying stuff, like how to start the eviction process.

I pushed open the door and stood there, quietly taking in the damage left by Hurricane Lou. Not too bad at first glance. A lot of books strewn around. One of the flimsier book turnstiles was tilted, but that could be fixed by jamming a book under its front legs.

Bob turned when Lyle said, "You!"

He was old, Bob. I don't know how old, but he was really ancient. Maybe sixty. Usually you didn't notice his age because he wears Coke-bottle glasses that overwhelm his features. But now his face was naked, and his eyes were normal sized and tired. Where the glasses habitually sat on the bridge of his nose was a dent, and around that, a painful-looking scrape.

"Did she break your glasses?"

"No." He had another red scrape on his cheekbone. "But they're not comfortable to wear right now."

"We're going to sue," Lyle snapped. He might have gone on, but Bob lifted a staying hand, so Lyle ceased, lips clamped tight, his eyes narrowed on me like a thwarted cat. I'm pretty sure Bob still owned the deed for loathsome Lyle's house.

"Most of this came from tripping over my own books."

"Because she shoved him after she called him a troll," threw in Lyle.

"I'll do the talking, Lyle." He patted the air behind him

for his stool. "She came in the back way, and she was already angry. Babbling something about the evil ones and another word. Something to do with mourning."

Merenwyn. Not angry then, I thought. *Frightened.*

"I told her you'd be home soon. She started to leave and then she saw the book on the counter, you know, the new one on display by the cash register. The one with—"

"Fairies on the front of it," I said.

Bob offered me a faint smile. "She said it was an abomination."

"And?"

"She started taking books off the shelf and throwing them at me. I went to call for Lyle, but—"

"She pushed him," Lyle said. "We're going to file charges."

"Lyle . . . let me tell it my way." Bob finally found the chair and sat down on it. "My glasses had fallen off and I couldn't find them. I couldn't see well enough to dial his number."

"So you called 911. And they sent the police." I swallowed, imagining it all in my head.

"Before they even got here, she was out on the street. She got hold of that rolling display I put out every morning, and she was emptying it, throwing the books at passing cars, screaming insults at people. Plague carriers?"

"Mortals. Pestilent mortals," I said.

Bob nodded as he stacked a book on top of two others. His fingers felt for the edges, and set them in a perfect tower. "The whole street backed up. Two cop cars came."

"Did they touch her?"

"Yes. Then it turned really ugly." His lips flattened. "She started screaming 'It burns, it burns.' "

Skin-to-skin contact would have raised blisters wherever their mortal hands touched. It hurts worse than holding a curling iron to your neck and counting to five.

"The woman is out of her mind, Hedi." Bob's face was concerned and bruised. "You know that, don't you? She can't be left alone anymore."

"Where'd they take her?"

"To the hospital in an ambulance. There *were* burns on her

wrists. I sent Lyle up to check your apartment but he couldn't find anything left on, or signs that she'd scalded herself with the kettle. We don't know how she hurt herself."

Lyle in our home. It didn't bear thinking about. I pushed my glasses up my nose. A hospital. I could break her out of a hospital.

"Hey," said Lyle as I turned to go.

"If you total up the damage, I'll pay for it." Another lie. Maybe Karma was snoozing and wouldn't notice.

There is always someone who has control over the button. It's never wise to piss that person off.

In this case, it was a fat forty-something woman seated behind the reception desk at Beacon Memorial. I made the mistake of going straight for the doors to the treatment rooms, which messed up protocol in all sorts of ways, and ignored her importance as the guardian of the open-sesame button.

She made me wait. And wait. People went in, people came out. Two weary policemen escorted an agitated man cuffed to a gurney into the treatment rooms. For a moment, as the doors swung open, I thought about slipping in via their wake but she was watching me, so I sat, and waited and tried to look like every other person waiting in the waiting room. Bored. Inside I was contemplating flattening the receptionist with her own computer screen. I was fretting over metal handcuffs, and I was thinking about ties. Not the ties that handcuff you to a gurney, but the ties that handcuff you to a past, present, and future.

Finally, after forty minutes, she pressed the button and let me in.

"My aunt was brought in," I said to a nurse in the hall.

"And she is?"

"Louise Rogers."

"Ah." I was handed down the line like an explosive package, until her case nurse escorted me to a curtained cubicle. A note had been taped to the curtain: *Gloves only*.

The curtains rattled as she pulled them open. They'd taken Lou's clothes and put her into a blue hospital gown. The white sheet was pulled up to her waist. The hospital gown gaped at the neck. Her eyes were half open, half closed, exposing unfocused dead gray pupils. Up and down her left arm were burns, some livid red and some liquid filled. Someone had tied her wrists to the sides of the bed with white gauze. A needle had been inserted in one blue vein. A drip bag hung from a metal stand.

"What's in the bag?"

"She's dehydrated, so we've got her on fluids. She was given a sedative as well. It affected her more than we anticipated." She checked the fluid level and reached for Lou's chart. "Is there any immediate family we can call?"

"I am her family."

"She's your guardian?"

I shrugged my shoulders. "No, I'm hers."

"How old are you?" she asked, frowning down at me.

What is it? Is it because I'm short? Or because my face is baby-shaped? I'm going to be carded until I'm forty. I added a year. "Twenty-three."

She didn't look like she believed me, but she didn't ask for the fake driver's license I'd been forced to spend two hundred bucks on—it's impossible to get a job or even a bus pass in Deerfield without some sort of ID—which was too bad, because the new card was a beauty and I hadn't had a chance to air it yet. There was another piece of gauze taped to the inside of Lou's elbow. I tilted my head toward it inquiringly.

"We had to take some blood tests. We're waiting on the results. The sedative really knocked her out. Is she on any medication?"

"No." Except for the slow rise of her chest, Lou looked dead.

"We're concerned about her burns. Do you know how she got them?"

"I was at work."

"Hmm." The nurse made a note on her chart. "There are some older burns too. Maybe she got them a couple of weeks ago? Do you know anything about them?"

They just *looked* older. She got all her wounds at the same time, a couple of hours ago when the cop tried to subdue her. The touch from a mortal male burns a female Fae—the result of some Mage spell that kicks in at birth—all because some ninny on the Royal Court started worrying that humans might foul their gene pool. The truth was, she didn't heal very well anymore. The mechanism was still inside her, trying to heal her, but it was weak and fitful like her moods. It had healed some, already, but was slowing down on others, making it seem like she had a long history of being burned. Try explaining that to a human. Try explaining anything about my life to a human.

The Fae don't fade out in a logical fashion, as if someone had a checklist and a panel of switches. Do they all fade like that? I don't know. I've never seen one do it before Lou. And as far as I knew, Lou was the last Fae on this side of the portal to Merenwyn.

She hadn't been able to Call to the Seven in months. That was her talent—calling metals. In Merenwyn she was known as the Collector. She was able to call to precious metal with her voice and hands, and it would melt and roll right to her, to collect in a puddle by her feet. She could do that with all the seven: gold, copper, silver, lead, tin, mercury, and—this is where her talent came in real value for Merenwyn's royal family—iron. Gold was valuable, silver was pretty, but iron was deadly. Enough of it could render a strong ruler as weak as a drooling infant.

She told me she was one of only two living Fae who had the talent. I could never understand why they let her stay on this side of the portal, after my parents died, if her skills were so prized. Before they closed the portals that night, they must have sounded some sort of retreat before they slammed the doors. Humans blamed the horrific sound of the barricades coming down on a minor earthquake, but they were wrong. That loud earth-trembling boom was the sound of gates closing simultaneously, forever ensuring that this world and the other would never touch again.

Lou's hands were curled like claws on the white sheet. The skin on them was thin, but her nails still grew long and diamond-hard. "Where is her ring?" I asked.

"I beg your pardon?"

My voice was sharp. "She wears a small green ring on her baby finger. It's missing."

"Oh, that thing," the nurse said. "She scratched one of our nurses during admissions with it. We locked it away for safe-keeping."

"I want it returned right now."

"Fine. The receptionist has the key. When she comes back from break, I'll get it from her." Her tone was cool. "In the meantime, maybe we can get your information. And later, someone from social services will need to talk with you." She pulled the curtains wide and bustled out.

There was one blue plastic chair, jammed under the shelf with the box of gloves. I pulled it out and sat down. And then I leaned back to pull the curtains closed again. My last remaining relative was tied to a bed in a human hospital. I didn't have the right to feel sorry for myself. Not one bit.

As I worked at the knot on her restraint, I studied Lou. She was too thin, too yellow. I was losing her. I'd been losing her for the last half year. A year ago Lou could have passed for a thirty-five-year-old. Now, her scalp played peekaboo with what was left of her long hair. If you stared hard at her, hard enough to ignore the slack skin, you'd realize that her features were still handsome. But the fading was relentless. The fat had melted away from her face as fast as her muscles withered, leaving crepe skin and jowls. Without that padding to soften her edges, her nose appeared sharper and predatory, her mouth a thin, pale gash.

She wasn't an old lady. She was just a Fae on the wrong side of the portal, without a key to get back. There wasn't enough magic and maple syrup to keep her here.

Would I wither like her one day? I have my own measure of Fae blood, but it's diluted—poisoned, Lou once said—by the Were blood running in my veins. Sometimes I find myself thinking too long about whether I'll fade like Lou, or live long like a Were.

The nurse jerked the curtains wide. "Do you have her health card?"

I stepped outside the cubicle, pulled the curtains all the way until one edge met the other snugly, and then followed the nurse.

After some creative form-filling, I took a slow stroll through the hallways. The nurse still had me in her sights, so the best thing to do was to map out our escape. As far as I could tell, there were only two ways to get in; through the swinging doors at reception and through the back hall that lead to the imaging department. At first glance, the back hall seemed like the best way of moving her out of the hospital, but there was a long corridor leading to it, and leaning against the wall were the two cops, their belts bristling with things that could do serious harm. Talking to them was a couple of paramedics.

The cops' eyes flicked to me as I passed. There was a door ahead for the women's washroom, and I took it. I closed the door and locked it.

"Merry?" I pressed my hand to my chest. "I need to talk." Fae Stars. The washroom smelled even worse than the hallways. I pulled my white blouse away from my chest, looked down and tried again. "Merry?" Nestled between my breasts, Merry remained stiff and unyielding.

"Stop sulking."

Merry didn't stir, unwind, or even change color. That was the measure of her hatred for Lou. She was in her usual place, the inside curve of my left breast, tucked warm between the lace of my bra and my skin, pretending to be asleep. Somewhere during that anxious jog to the hospital, she'd reverted back to her original design. Golden strands of elegantly entwined ivy formed a protective basketwork around the cloudy amber of her stone. "Gone baroque, huh?" I gave her a disgusted prod. "You know, sometimes I feel like taking you off my neck, and leaving you hanging in a rack of costume jewelery at Zellers. All I wanted you to do was listen while I worked out a plan."

No response. No pulse of heat, no change in color. When she wanted, my Asrai could look as dumb as a rock.

I emerged from the washroom, pausing on the threshold to fastidiously dry my hands. The tally had swollen to two cops and three paramedics. All of them looked like they worked out.

The nurse stopped me on the way back to Lou's bedside. "Here's her ring."

I tore open the envelope and shook into my palm the only piece of jewelry I'd ever seen Lou wear. As befitting a ring designed to go on a woman's baby finger, the design was simple. A narrow strip of gold had been fashioned into a serpentine cradle for one dull, irregularly shaped green stone. Uncut and unpolished, the gem was unlovely, except for one little perk. With the emerald on her finger, Lou could lie— breathtakingly huge whoppers—and do so without a flicker of her eyelash to betray her deception. Which was a bonus as Lou was pure Fae, and was born handicapped by their natural inability to tell an untruth, something that could have posed a huge problem to us, considering that we lived a life on the margins of the criminal world.

Possibly we might have limped along without her needing it. Faes can't lie, but they can do wonders with misdirection. Still, I was grateful for the fact that somehow, somewhere, Lou had charmed a mage out of his ring. It made life easier. When I wasn't around to lie for her, she could do so on her own, providing she rubbed the gem before she spoke. Once, for payment to the ring's dark magic. The second time, to seal the lie. Sort of like a compound fib tax.

I slipped the ring over her knuckle and sat down beside her with a sigh.

I hate thinking. I hate that whole, contemplate your life, find your inner self, hug your tree, kiss your neighbor mind trap that comes from watching too much daytime TV. I'd rather be entertained. Give me a book. Show me a movie. Be a human. That's comedy enough. Don't ask me to sit and think. Don't ask me to come up with a plan.

Step one. Wake up Lou. From my backpack, I pulled out the maple syrup I'd bought on the way to work. I smeared some on my finger and put it to her lips. Her mouth softened, and the tip of her tongue reached out for it. Her thin lips opened wider. After the second mouthful, she shut her eyes against the artificial light. I was so damn grateful, I forgot myself and put my hand to her face.

There was no warning, no slow slip into her head: I was just suddenly in there, experiencing one of her memories. The colors hit me first. All of them were supersaturated, as if gray didn't belong in the palette. I couldn't have pulled my hand off her face for the life of me, for she was in Merenwyn, and she rarely allowed herself to think of home.

Lou is outdoors, looking at a man standing with his back turned to us. It's a nice, well-developed back in a gray T-shirt that has gone through the spin cycle enough times to get thin and tight on the shoulders. There's a painting of Champlain in the same pose, staring at the river that he probably thought was going to be called Champlain, but ended up being called the St. Lawrence. Change the boots for sneakers, and it's essentially the same guy. This guy's tawny hair is shorter, but he has one foot propped on a stony outcrop. Like the French explorer, his hand rests on his thigh, while the other sits on his hip. Even without seeing his face, you know this man understands his own attraction. It's something in the pose, something in the arrogance of that straight back.

Predator.

Beyond him, impossibly green trees grow upside down into a fluffy bank of clouds above a layer of brilliant blue. A breeze picks up a lock of his hair. A fish jumps in the pool, its scales glittering in the sun. Suddenly, it all made sense: the upside-down trees, the reversal of clouds and sky. The smooth surface of the natural pond is catching the reflection of the surrounding trees and sky.

Don't let him despoil that pool, I think. But in Lou's thoughts, the breeze plays with his hair like a lover, while the clouds slide across the brilliant sky.

"Don't touch me," Lou said peevishly, as her dream abruptly disappeared from my vision. My chair screeched as I bolted backward. For a second I gaped at her, horrified at my thoughts. *She could have dragged me to Threall and back again, and I wouldn't have tried to fight her. Fae Stars, I'd been so Fae-struck by Merenwyn, my only worry had been whether the dream would end.* I breathed carefully, willing my racing heart to settle. It had been running in my head, like the chorus to a ballad. *Stay, stay in the dream.* Damn, Mum was right: those dreams were dangerous.

"More," she demanded, without opening her eyes. Carefully, I stood to dribble another mouthful of syrup into her. She swallowed and then rolled her head to look at me. "There are a lot of mortals here," she said.

"I know."

She focused on me, her fingers plucking at her bed coverlet, her forehead creased. "I want to go home."

Chapter Three

Bob keeps the keys to his aqua '93 Taurus wagon in the drawer under his counter. That was the first thing I went for when I arrived home and found his shop empty. I left him four books from the café, my tips for the day, and a stethoscope, which had turned out to be kind of a one-trick pony. I relocked the shop's back door on the way out. My legs felt like lead as I climbed the stairs to our apartment.

Our home is nothing much. Four-room apartments that don't cost an arm, a leg, and a kidney are hard to come by in our town, so you don't bitch about niceties like new paint or better floors. You pay the rent, and keep your head down, and try to blend, blend, blend.

A good landlord doesn't notice that you never go to school. A great one is mostly blind and completely unaware that his tenant's kid uses his store like a lending library without due dates. Sometimes I wondered how oblivious one human could be. Sometimes, I wondered if Bob was just a nice man instead, which made me feel all kinds of squirrelly inside.

So, our home. Four rooms, all connected by one long hall. The kitchen used mostly by me, though Lou sometimes stepped inside, her lip curling fastidiously, to pick up a new can of maple syrup. Beyond that, two small bedrooms and a rectangular living room. I had furnished the living room slowly over time, exchanging lawn chairs for real ones as my muscles grew along with my ability to grab things before the garbage man got them. I had two mismatched armchairs book-ended by two beat-up matching side tables. In the corner was my entertainment center: an RCA and a $40 DVD player.

It had taken me a long time to find a working television that didn't need a remote, as they were problematic for Fae-born. Not only remotes, but cell phones, a computer when connected to the Internet, and weirdly, intercoms were just some of the things that worked on the maybe-yes, maybe-no basis around our kind. On the free wall was a faux-wood shelving unit from Goodwill. It was cheap and I could lift it, and it did the job of displaying my paperbacks and my growing collection of pirated movies that I bartered for with a high school kid named Melanie.

That sounds sparse, but it wasn't. I'm a thief with poor impulse control, a fact that would have surprised Mum and Dad if they were still around to register their disapproval, because of the two of us, it had been Lexi, not me, who'd shown a certain Fae-bent talent for acquisition. Relatively speaking, I had lived a virtuous life before the Fae stole my brother. Then, two months to the day after I lost Lexi, I stole a pair of salt and pepper shakers from a diner on Spadina. There wasn't any premeditation to it. I was thinking of my twin, and felt myself sinking downward into that awful, aching hurt, and then the neatest thing happened: I became Lexi. Not for very long. Just long enough to slide the condiment containers across the laminate table into my lap, and then from there into my coat pockets.

It filled the Lexi-sized hole left in me. Well, maybe not filled; nothing seemed to do that. But stealing stuff shrank the gaping wound until it was nothing more than a wistful, whistling tear in my armor. And that was good enough. That afternoon, I tossed my inconvenient conscience over my shoulder and became a thief. Now, whenever my nerves start to jangle, and that hole starts to widen, I take something. Other than a fascination for anything in pairs, I'm fairly in-

discriminate. Consequently, there were a lot of shiny things
in that room to brighten it up.

We needed to make tracks, and we needed money. It took
a lot of convincing, plus the threat of being left in the hands of
the pestilent mortals—nicely inserted into the argument after
another visit from the nurse—before Lou told me where to
find my mum's bride belt. When I think of all those hours I'd
spent searching her room for it, I wanted to smack myself.

I'd pinned a poster of four dogs playing poker to the living
room wall as a taunt to my aunt, who rarely let an opportunity
go by without making reference to my mixed blood. The print
had stayed there ever since, even though humidity had long
ago curled its edges.

Lou had quietly delivered her own insult, and I hadn't
even known it.

I ripped the poster down and studied the wall. There was
no dimple or crack to say "here be magic," which meant that
she'd spent good money purchasing the spell from the local
coven. Which, if I cared to think about it, was a double slap,
as my paycheck had probably paid for the magic. I repeated
the word Lou had whispered into my ear at the hospital, and
immediately, the illusion melted away, exposing a four-inch
hole in the wallboard. Inside the dark cavity, Fae gold
gleamed.

With a trembling hand, I pulled my mother's bride belt
into the light.

How many times had I seen this thin gold chain around
her hip? Ran my finger over the gilt embellishment that decorated the small leather pouch that hung from the sleek supple
links? The belt had been a gift from *her* mother, a token to
remember her Fae heritage, and an open acknowledgment of
Mum's transition from child to woman, on the occasion of her
marriage.

I drew open the delicate leather strings and peered inside
the pouch. Lou hadn't sold them, after all. Nestled at the
bottom were five tear-shaped pink stones. I inhaled deeply,
and caught my father's scent for the first time in ten years.

Move, I told myself, as everything inside me stiffened into want. *Move.* I fastened the belt around my own waist and let it fall low. Mum was taller than me, but I'm sure I'm rounder; despite my curves, the chain hung low on my hips.

Merry unfurled a strand of gold. The chain around my neck tightened with her weight as she slipped free of my bra. I ignored her, tucking the belt inside my cargo pants as I headed for my bedroom mirror. For the first time, the cost of the pants was justified. No matter which way I turned, the belt was invisible, the pouch nothing more than one more wrinkle amid a mind-boggling number of wrinkles.

Merry's head popped free of the V of my blouse as I made my way to the kitchen. If she wanted out, she could do it herself—I was still pissed about her silent routine at the hospital. I bent to retrieve some garbage bags from under the sink, and fast as a snake, she took advantage of gravity, snapping out another strand of ivy to catch the other side of the chain. She was already efficiently twining herself around both sides, each revolution hiking her higher until she was hanging from the hollow of my throat like a goth choker.

I crossed the threshold to Lou's bedroom. "It's too late to talk," I told Merry, tossing Lou's clothing into a bag. "I'm not leaving her there. So, we're going to take her, and then we're hitting the road. We'll start over again somewhere else."

Merry's stone slowly warmed as I found Lou's shoes and coat. I stripped the bed and threw her pillow and comforter in another bag. Then I did a slow turn. A bed, a lamp, curtains, and one chair. Lou wasn't leaving much.

My room had fewer clothes and more clutter. I was standing there, thinking hard, when someone knocked on the apartment door.

Shit. Was it Bob? Or Lyle? Or, just-shoot-me-now, the police?

I went up on my toes and squinted through the door's peephole. He'd been smart enough to tuck himself to the right of the doorway so I couldn't see him, but he hadn't taken the time to have a bath. The Were who stood out of sight in the hall needed to be spritzed with boy cologne.

I didn't know him, clean or dirty: his scent didn't trigger any recall.

So I had to ask myself, was this a T-rex situation—you're only on the menu if you move? How soundlessly had I tiptoed to the door? If I stayed frozen, with my nose flattened against the door panel, not making any noise, would he decide I wasn't there and go away? As my air ran out, I began hoping he had a short attention span.

He did.

I saw a flash of a gray shirt through the peephole; I jerked backward as his fist exploded through the door. A bloody hand shot through the jagged hole, showering wood splinters onto the carpet, and started to fumble for the lock.

I turned and ran. Behind me the door thudded against the wall. I sped up, running as fast as my size sixes could take me to the kitchen and its knife collection. I didn't make it far. Size twelve always trumps size six. He grabbed the back of my shirt, I heard a whoosh of air close to my ear, and then my head exploded.

I hurt. Merry felt hot and anxious against my chest, and the dog in the apartment downstairs was barking "danger, danger." I rolled my head experimentally, and then moaned at the resulting spear of pain.

Dimly, I began to separate the smells into three different cues: Rover's fear, seeping like natural gas up the stairs, cheap carpet, and Were. This one had an unpleasant layer of musk over the usual woods-and-fields smell I associate with Weres. His boots had walked through some nasty things. I kept my eyes closed and faked dead.

"Get up," he growled, unimpressed. I worked a little harder on being limp.

"Up." He kicked me. I curled tight as a hedgehog, one hand pressed against my ribs, as pain and shock ran up and down my side. Merry shot out an alarmed spike of heat.

"No," I grunted. Merry stilled but her tension furled her gold into furious prickling spikes that bit into my cleavage. "Not helping," I muttered to her.

Then he pulled back his boot and did it again. In the same freaking spot. "Don't make me tell you again, bitch."

When I got my breath back, I raised a hand. Past his scuffed heels I could see the curved leg of my easy chair. I crawled to the chair to brace a hand on the seat cushion. With its help, I heaved myself up as far as my knees. That was as far as I could go.

I'd been hit. By a Were. *He'd hit me*. And I hurt.

"All the way up."

One glance at him and I was inspired to stand. I wobbled to my feet, feeling my broken ribs scream. He'd hurt me. I'd never been hit before, unless you counted Lexi, but he was my twin. Twins do that, fully expecting to be hit back.

Lou was right. There was no upside to being around Weres.

A couple of days ago, when his clothing was still clean, and his eyes didn't look like he'd been smoking crack, he might have been hot. He was young, he was built, and he was good-looking, in a sort of studly, teenage way. Too young for me, but still, a great body is a great body, until the owner of it uses one of his body parts to kick you. Then you change your first impression, and start noticing things like red-rimmed eyes, and scent; in his case, a ripe, unpleasant combination of unwashed Were, male musk, and hot emotion.

Downstairs, Rover was trying to scratch his way through his door. "You stink of coffee and you live around dogs," he said, thumbing open his phone. Loser, his gaze said, as he waited for the phone to be answered.

It was short and sweet, his phone conversation. It went like this: he had the amulet. Some girl had it around her neck, but he'd encountered some problems taking it from her. Should he just take her head off or should he bring her in too? Both of us waited for the answer, but I bet his heart was still beating, whereas mine stopped somewhere after the phrase "take her head off."

"Right," he said, nodding as if he were right in front of the guy on the other end of the phone. "We're on our way." The man on the other end hung up first.

"What do you think you're going to do with my amulet? You're a Were. It won't do a thing for you."

"Doesn't have to do a thing for me. My Alpha wants the amulet, and I'm the Alpha's boy. His *top* boy. I get the job done," he added with a superior smirk. His phone chirruped again, startling Rover into another chorus of "danger, danger."

"What?" The Were's voice grew testy. He yanked the lamp cord out of the wall socket as he listened. "No, tell them not to wait. Take the old lady straight to the Alpha." Casually, he tore the electric wire from the base. "Rolled her right past the nurse, eh? And the cops? What did you do . . . yeah, that was smart. So, what about Trowbridge? Not yet?" He started advancing toward me, the wire swinging from his grip. "What's your problem? Just follow his trail." He stopped to adjust his jeans and roll his eyes. "Yeah. No problem. I'll toss this bitch into the trunk and swing by." He closed the phone.

"Good luck getting me into the trunk, asshole," I said.

He flexed his hands. The fingers on the right one were blistered, as if he'd seared them on a hot frying pan.

"You couldn't even get my amulet off without burning your hand." My mouth twisted into a smile I knew I was going to regret. He growled, low in his throat, and shifted on his feet. "And now you have a sore paw—" His hand swung out and slapped me hard, and I went flying across the room. It wasn't a big room; I didn't have far to go before I hit the wall and slid down it into an awkward heap.

Enough.

My power was waiting for me. It had been coiling inside of me ever since that first boot to the ribs, waiting for me to mean business. Waiting for me to use it in a way my mum never let me do. No more half measures.

I meant to hurt.

I gave that churning mass leave of its fetters, and it surged up my arm in an exultant stream to collect at the ends of my fingers. Hot. It was like I had fire ants trapped beneath my skin, which goes to show—malice burns hotter than mischief.

With a quick flick of my hand, I unleashed my talent and it sprang out in an invisible fat thread to attach itself to my television. Another twist of my wrist, and the old heavy RCA lurched from its stand, electric cord trailing like a serpent's tail as it flew upward to smack the Were hard on his head.

He didn't see it coming. They never do—they're always too busy staring at my hands.

His skull made a wet squelch, and then the back of his broken head met the wall behind him. For a heartbeat he held himself upright, until his eyes lost focus and he slid down the wall, leaving a long smear of bright red blood as he went. He didn't get back up.

It was almost quiet in the aftermath.

Silent except for my own uneven breath, coming quick and hard through my parted lips. *Don't panic. Don't panic. Hold on.*

Merry pulled herself free of my blouse, her stone turning orange with all the red shot through it, to slide down her chain like Tarzan on a handy vine. She had morphed again, this time into her favorite stick figure: two golden arms, fashioned from long tendrils of elegant golden ivy, and two legs, which ended in feet that looked like tips of an ivy leaf.

"We're in a shitload of trouble, Merry-mine," I said thinly. I couldn't pull my gaze from the trail of blood down the wall. I would not panic. I would not panic. Even if the sight of the red stuff makes me panic and think of things I don't want to think about.

In an instant, I was back in the kitchen of my old home, watching my mother's blood splatter the wall, smelling the sweet Fae scent of it mix with the Were and copper tang of my father's. That's the only time they smell, the Fae—when they bleed.

That was my last conscious thought before my brain shut down.

I probably would have just sat there, right by the mess of vomit I deposited on the carpet, if not for Merry. She found my ear, gripped the sensitive tip and squeezed the shit out of it. We went into the kitchen, and found blue plastic gloves which I slid over my shaking hands. I leaned against the wall to catch my breath. Merry gave me about thirty seconds' rest before she slunk up the chain to my shirt collar. She made a grab for either edge, then planted her feet firmly on my collarbone, and hauled on it backward as if she were the Pekinese with the Saint Bernard's leash in its mouth. I pushed away from the wall.

Turns out it's really hard to kill a Were.

Until I had touched his throat and felt the beat of his sluggish pulse through my rubber glove, I had been thinking more along the line of tarp than tape. You see whitish flecks of brain matter floating in a pool of blood and that's where your mind goes. Tarps and shovels and ponds.

I had no corpse, but I had a body. Damn Weres. They're a bitch to kill. Straight out of a horror flick, the freak started healing. His blood loss slowed to ooze instead of a steady drip, while underneath his skin the bones began to knit themselves back together. It's not something you want to watch, even if you don't get girly about blood.

I went back to the kitchen and got some duct tape. I circled his torso with it, binding his arms tight to his chest, until he looked like a twenty-first-century mummy. I did the same to his legs. As an additional precaution, I manhandled him into a sitting position, and then secured him to the old radiator near the window. It was hard to do. He was heavy and bloody, and yeah, he scared the shit out of me, even gory-headed and unconscious. I could smell my own fear leaking out from my sweating pores, and that was enough to turn my fear into a cold rage that gave me the juice to get up close and personal with that gory head and its sticky-sweet blood. I made a collar of duct tape around his neck, and then ran a loop of it around a radiator coil, so that he was drawn back into a pugnacious chin-jutting position that suited his sunny nature so well.

It took some contortions to get his wallet and BlackBerry out of his pocket. His wallet revealed eighty dollars, which I pocketed, and a license for one Stuart Scawens, age eighteen, living on Walnut Street in Creemore. I riffled through the rest; a health card, a Visa—*he's just a kid, how'd he qualify?*—and a folded-up piece of paper that turned out to be a grocery list written in a woman's flowing script.

Pretty thin in the wallet for an Alpha's "top boy." That used to be a prestigious title, filled by a guy who cracked a smile about as frequently as the woman in the pastry shop went on a diet.

I pushed my glasses up on my nose, and turned my attention to his phone. Before I had conceded that there wasn't any phone my woo-woo Fae genes wouldn't eventually screw up, I used to steal people's phones regularly, so I didn't have a lot of trouble navigating my way around the BlackBerry. Yeah, yeah, I know it's a nasty, terrible thing to steal someone's cell. All those contacts and phone numbers. Let me get a hanky.

I checked his phone history. Scawens's last call had been to Eric, who—judging from the thumbnail photo—was about twenty-five and spent a fortune on hair gel. The call before that was from the Alpha. Annoyingly, the Alpha was listed under "The Alpha" in his address book, without any additional info that I might find useful, like a name, address, or a picture.

They'd taken Lou? Where? And how in the hell had Scawens known where to find us?

Trowbridge. It had to be Trowbridge.

I kept scrolling, glancing up periodically to see how well Were-boy was doing in his slow crawl to consciousness. I was congratulating myself on my inner fortitude when I found the photos attached to the e-mail titled "Wanted." I opened the first image. Just like that, my anxiety spiked from tolerable to unbearable. I clamped down on it, before I did something stupid, like kill the healing Were just because he was there.

One thousand, two thousand, three thousand . . . I hit twelve thousand before my breathing leveled out.

It was a picture of an amulet. It appeared that someone had blown up a much smaller photo, because the details were indistinct and all the edges were pixalated. But I recognized it. I'd seen it once before.

"Old sacred wood," my mum had said as Dad secured the pine cupboard, with its fancy heart-shaped cutouts on the doors, onto the kitchen wall. "Keep it off the ground, and it will hold a spell." Fourteen months later, I was hiding inside it, safe from the Weres and the Fae, but helpless to go to her as she lay dying on the floor. I had hollered, I had shouted. I had beat on those panels until my palms were hot and puffy. Her protective spell still held. No one could see me. No one could hear me. Even after the Fae left, and the fire started licking the kitchen table.

When Trowbridge broke through the door, I thought I was safe.

It's a picture frozen in my mind's recall, seen through a heart-shaped hole. The kitchen wall was in flames. Dad's body was sprawled on the hooked rug, right beside Mum's. Blood still leaked from the red line cut into her throat, but her heart was slowing. *Thump, thump.* I could hear it over the flames. Robson Trowbridge was kneeling beside her, and he had that amulet in his hand.

She died. And then he left, even as I screamed, "Come back, come back."

Thirteen thousand, fourteen thousand, fifteen thousand . . . I took a deep breath, and scrolled to the next image. It appeared to be a screen capture from a grainy video of Lou, initially recognizable only by the clothes I had laid out that morning. Her hair partially obscured her face, but I knew it to be Lou in full rage, with a clutch of books held pressed to her chest, and her outflung hand frozen, as if they had caught her just after she sent a book flying.

The last picture was an old one of a young Robson Trowbridge, wearing an ill-fitting tux, standing beside an even younger-looking girl in a poufy white wedding dress. Why was he on the wanted list?

The Were came awake slowly, groaning and twitching spasmodically before blearily opening his brown eyes. "What the—"

"Duct tape. A whole roll of it."

"You bitch," he began, and then he lapsed into a string of increasingly frustrated grunts as he tried to thrash free.

"Where did they take the old lady?"

His reply to that was to try to spit a mouthful of blood in my direction. Not so smart, our Stuart. His missile of woe arced up and then fell, splat, on his shirt.

"I'm going to ask you again: where did they take her?"

He lashed out with his feet, but taped as they were, his flailing was as productive as a fish flopping on land.

I tried a different tack. "So, how's your eyesight? Any better than your IQ? Let me show you something." I pointed the cell phone in his direction. "This is the amulet you're searching for, right?" I tapped the photo. "It's got a round stone in the middle of it. Perfectly round. It's a light blue, not a brownish yellow. And around the stone, what do we have? Ah, let's see . . . it's got all this Celtic crap twisting around the stone. Kind of a distinctive piece of jewelry, right?"

Merry slid down the length of my chain to take a peek for herself. I almost palmed her, before remembering that Were-boy had already had an up close and personal moment with her Fae gold vines. She minced her way along my arm to perch at my wrist.

Scawens's gaze flicked from Merry to me. "What the fuck are you?"

"Ever seen it before?" I asked Merry, tilting the screen so she could get a better view. All of a sudden, her leaves flattened around her body.

"So I guess that would be a yes." I felt like I should pat her or something. I snapped my fingers at the Were, who seemed preoccupied trying to wipe blood off his chin with his shoulder.

"Okay, Fido, pay attention." I tapped my thumb on the screen. "This pendant is not *my* pendant. Take a look. Round stone versus oval stone. Blue stone versus amber."

Merry started coiling a strand around the BlackBerry. "A little space, Merry. Let him see." She was starting to freak me out.

"So what," he said.

"Okay, one more time for the remedial student. The stone on that one is blue. The setting is different. Different design, so therefore, different piece of jewelry." I dipped my head at Merry. "You've gone and chased the wrong prey. Bad Fido. Sit here while I find the newspaper."

The Were spat again. He glared up at me, his teeth all bloody. "What are you?" he repeated.

"Always the same question. *What are you?* Well, I'm a mystery, okay? I'm one big, fat mystery that your little, itty-bitty brain is never going to figure out."

"You're a fairy, aren't you?"

I rubbed my nose. "All right, let's try combining the questions. What does your Alpha want with an old woman and an amulet?" I waved his BlackBerry under his nose. He didn't like that; I did it again.

"I'm not telling you jack."

I sighed and reached for a hank of his hair. The sigh was baloney, just a gloss over something vile inside me, because down there, the part that grew malice so easily was saying, "Go girl, go." His greasy hair was short, and my blue rubber gloves slipped off when he twisted his head away. Merry quivered on her perch. I looked into his red-rimmed eyes and said in a low voice, "I'd rather you just told me. I don't need to hurt you."

Yeah, I know. Another lie.

Merry's patience broke. She sprang across the eight-inch gap, leaves extended like pincers. His head thudded back in a futile effort to avoid her, and then all three of us danced. Merry dug into his cheek muscles, he thrashed his head against his duct-tape bindings, and my neck, anchored by Merry's chain wound around it, echoed each of the Were's savage jerks.

"Get it off, get it off," he screamed, trying to scrape her off his cheek with his shoulder.

Merry dug in. Thin rivulets of blood streaked down his face in four distinct trails. Very red blood. Pungent and rich smelling. I readjusted my balance, both inner and outward, and came to rest on my knees beside him, so close his blood smelled like wet copper.

Merry was really freaking me out.

"I'll ask, you'll answer. Okay?" I took another deep steadying breath through my mouth. "What does your Alpha want?"

He braced for pain. Merry obliged, and tortured his cheek. Scawens held out until Merry sprouted another arm. It positioned itself a quarter of an inch from his wide, blue right eye. There it swayed, back and forth, its sharp tip promising a world of hurt and disfigurement. He stopped moving, maybe even breathing. She tightened the distance between the tip of her ivy leaf and his pupil. A spasm of pure horror rippled across his face.

"Okay, we'll start with a smaller question. Which pack do you belong to?"

His jaw worked. The tip of Merry's leaf brushed his eyelashes with all the tenderness of a ditched girlfriend. He said, "Ontario."

"Which *pack* in Ontario, Stuart?"

"Ontario," he said, carefully enunciating each word, "is only one pack."

Not when I was a child. Back then the Alpha of Creemore had ruled his small fiefdom with vigilance and pride. If one of the Danvers kids tossed a ball through a glass window, he knew of it before the glazier had a chance to back his truck out of his garage. Yeah, Jacob Trowbridge had been Big Daddy all right, but his eyes had never strayed beyond his own turf. In a wolf's world, personal territory was everything. It meant you got squinty-eyed with visitors, careful with your words around humans (even around those half-Fae mutts), and humorlessly insular. Possessive to the extreme. Put bluntly, you peed on every bush in your parish, and that pungent flag said, "Hey, don't go any farther. This is my woods, my street, my woman." That's how they got along and avoided conflict—Weres respected one another's boundaries. I couldn't wrap my head around the concept of all of

Ontario being united. Why? Why would all those little packs living hundreds of miles from Creemere ever have chosen to relinquish their territory to another Alpha? Unless, of course, I realized with a start, it hadn't been voluntary. *There must have been bloodshed for that to come about,* I thought uneasily. *Lots of it.* "So then who is your Alpha? If he's so strong, it won't make any difference if I know who he is."

He weighed his answer before replying, but evidently his fear of his Alpha was greater than his fear of wearing an eye patch for the rest of his Were life. He clamped his lips shut.

"I'm losing patience," I said.

"Bitch, you are so done. You're so done. You've hurt one of the pack."

The pack, the pack. I'd lost a family, reinvented myself, gone from burden to breadwinner, supported my aunt and myself over the last two years—and come to think of it, Merry—all without the help of the pack, and yet, here it was. The pack used against me like some sort of acid against my soul.

Stuart tried to sneer but it was a sad, lopsided effort, with Merry embedded in his cheek muscle, and blood coating the gums of his white teeth. There was a light shadow of a beard against the lower part of his jaw. I felt tired, looking at him with his Hollywood tough guy smile.

"All right, last time. This woman." I shuffled back to Lou's photo, pausing to push my glasses back on my nose, before turning the BlackBerry toward him. "Where is she?"

"Why don't you look in the hospitals?" He shook his head as if I were the dumb one. "My Alpha's going to come looking for you after this."

"Merry," I said coldly. "Do your worst."

He wasn't strong enough to hold back a scream, or to stop his bound feet from drumming on the ground. If my parents had seen me watch him writhe, with that horrible little smile I could feel on my mouth, they would have disowned me.

"Stop," I said when bile started to rise in my throat as his shrieks became piercing. Scawens took a few harsh shudders of breath. Under that I could hear his heart beat, fast and hard, even harder than mine, which was trying to pull itself free from the monster I'd become.

"It can be worse," I whispered to him, trying not to look at the right side of his face. "She's nothing more than a frightened old lady. She has no power left anymore. She can't do anything with an amulet. Why don't you tell me where to find her? You don't have to suffer like this."

He swallowed and then looked at me, hate making his eyes too old, and too bright. "He's going to rip your head off when he gets you."

"You're very fond of ripping things, aren't you?" Merry's chain sawed on my neck as I lifted my shoulders to ease the ache between them. We were still tied together, Scawens and I, by an Asrai without human or even Were morals.

"Merry, let him go." She held on for five more seconds, and then released her grip to fall in a hard lump of gold and amber against my chest. I brought a tentative hand up to her, before cupping her in my cold palm. She was sticky with blood.

I picked up his phone and opened it to Trowbridge's photo. "Last question. What do you want with this guy?"

He spat again.

"So, not a friend."

He stared at me with silent hatred.

"I'm going to let you go, Stuart Scawens," I said. "Go back to your Alpha. Tell him that I don't have it, but I know where to get the amulet." I stood up, keeping my eyes steady on him. I could feel payback creeping up on me. You can't use Fae power in this realm without paying its price of pain, nausea, and fatigue. The adrenaline that had kept them at bay was wearing off.

I leaned into his face. "I'll call him in twenty-four hours or less. You tell him to keep Lou safe. No harm should come to her. We'll trade. She's a crazy old lady with no special powers to her at all. If he gives her back, I'll give him the amulet he wants. And Scawens? Tell him that you're my last messenger. After this, he'll be picking up body parts. Make sure he gets the message before anything happens to her."

Scawens braced his legs and heaved upward, fighting to stand upright. Stupid male, get a hernia, why don't you? The radiator was solid iron, pure enough that I couldn't have touched it without the gloves (even if its metal *was* coated with five layers of paint), and it was connected to yards of pipe.

"You don't have to run off now. Ladies first." I tucked his cell into my pocket.

He made one more effort, his teeth clenched, his muscles bunching, his thin lips drawn back to expose his bloody teeth. The pipe made a mournful betraying sound, and he lunged as it snapped.

Freaking iron.

There was no time for finesse. I called and my power answered. It hit him with everything in the room. Books, tables, DVDs, knitting work, chair, faux wood shelving, even the dog poker poster flew around him like the wings of a devil. He swung about, trying to use the radiator that dangled from him as a shield, but then something hit his unprotected head again with a thunk, and he slumped, slow motion over the twisted metal. It wasn't enough though. The mix of anger and fear sank low, picked up any remaining viciousness sitting deep inside me, and threw it back, bringing everything that had fallen airborne again into a terrible vortex that spun around him in a black cloud. His mouth was wide open when the cloud exploded over him in another smothering rain of debris. I didn't drop my hands until the last book dropped onto the heap piled on top of his still body. A knitting needle was impaled in his chest. It shivered when he breathed.

I snatched up my backpack and ran.

Down the stairs. Around the landing. Through the door. Across the parking lot. I didn't even bother with the flimsy lock on the garage's side door, I just strong-armed through it. Then I was in the driver's seat, fitting the key into the ignition of the Taurus.

I heard a loud "Bitch!" from the stairwell. I shoved the car into gear and hit the gas before the car door even closed.

The Taurus took wing, clipping the side of the garage in

one long tearing crumple of metal as we hurtled away. I made the turn onto the street, heart banging away under my bruised ribs, and then we were free, running straight up the narrow street away from the lake, and away from the danger that was still spewing curses from the parking lot of Twice Read Books. We blew through the first red light.

Halfway up the second block, I looked in Bob's rearview, fully expecting to see an angry wolf taped to a radiator charging after me. But the road was empty, save for a nimble pedestrian who'd leaped out of the way. He stood frozen on the pavement, his face a WTF pictogram. I lifted my foot from the accelerator, reached painfully out and snagged the handle of my car door. When it clicked shut, I hit the gas again, hard.

I'd convinced myself, during that white-knuckle drive to the hospital, that Scawens was full of crap, and that when I walked back into the emergency room, I'd find Lou sitting upright, her dark gray eyes alive and snapping.

What I found were three cop cars in the emergency bay. I drove past the hospital's parking lot in search of an empty space on a side street, since I didn't need spidey sense to know it would be faster to use the ER's doors, but smarter to go through the hospital's lobby and worm my way back to the treatment area. My rubber heels squeaked as I followed the signs for the radiology department. I walked past it, and found the unmarked corridor that led back to the ER treatment rooms. No cop gauntlet to pass this time. The hallway was almost empty, save for a couple of paramedics filling out paperwork.

All the cops were clustered outside Lou's cubicle. Her bedsheets had been discarded on the floor. One end of the curtain had been torn off its track. A cop nodded, fingering his belt, as he listened to an agitated nurse. Two more cops were beside an orderly, who was rubbing his shoulder while looking suitably heroic.

Scawens's goons had hurt her. I could smell the sweet scent of a woodland Fae blood over the ER's usual perfume of pain, illness, and disinfectant. Were scent was there as well, though the smell felt off to me, like a sweet piece of fruit that had spent too long in the vegetable drawer.

I turned on my heel. No one stopped me with a "Hey you." No one followed.

I don't remember getting into the car or driving past all those dark homes where families slept. For all I know, Merry drove. When I came back to myself, the car was in the middle of Sears's empty parking lot, and my foot was on the brake, while the engine rattled as it ticked over. My glasses were on the dash, beside the rubber gloves.

Adrenaline was gone, leaving behind shock and payback pain. I threw open the door and heaved. Technically, you can't throw up a cookie twice, but my stomach gave it a try. Each time I convulsed, my foot jerked off the brake pedal, making the car bunny-hop forward. We were going places, the Taurus and I. One hop at a time.

Eventually I stopped heaving. With a shaky sigh, I leaned against the padded headrest and listened to the Taurus's indignant ding. I tried, but it is virtually impossible to ignore a dinging door alarm, even if you know that it is going to hurt like a bitch to close the door. I wrapped my arm around my rib cage in a self-hug and then reached out, biting down on my lips as my ribs had a tantrum. I felt for the handle blindly, too afraid to catch a glimpse of my crispy fried hand. A few shits and fucks later, my fingers brushed pebbled plastic.

Shock was receding, but the throbbing misery in my hands was growing.

Geez Louise. Now I knew why Mum came down hard if we even flirted with using our talent for anything other than mild amusement. They could have spared us all the "stay low/don't show" lectures and told us the unvarnished truth: you stick your head out of the foxhole, and someone is going to take a shot at you. Use your magic with a dark heart, and it will turn around and bite you on the ass with teeth as sharp as a hungry shark's.

I hurt, really hurt. And the pain was worse, getting hotter

and more horrible with each breath. The black dots dancing in front of my eyes joined together into one huge black hole and I start spinning toward a place I dread.

Of all the dreams, my own were the worst.

I dreamed of the old cupboard and the last time I saw Robbie Trowbridge.

It starts with the memory of us doing normal stuff. That's usually how I slide into my personal nightmare, each time seduced by the sweet comfort of our family's routine. We eat dinner, the four of us sitting at the round oak table. Then it's homework, and some TV. Mum tucks me into bed, and tells me lights out. I can hear Lexi on the other side of the wall, playing with his G.I. Joes. He's making *chuh-chuh-chuh* noises for gunfire.

I fall asleep, listening to him.

I wake with a start, feeling frightened. "Mum?" She doesn't answer, so I get out of bed, and go down the dark hall to the kitchen. Mum's standing in her nightgown by the table, an expression of dread on her face. Dad has his arm around her. "Are you sure?"

She rubs her arm and nods. "I can feel it on my skin."

"I'll stop them," he says.

"Don't go out there. Promise me you'll stay here with us." But as Mum pulls out her ward stuff from the top drawer— some herbs and that long lariat that she uses to make her magic set—he takes the shotgun off the rack, and starts down the path to the pond. She bites her lip and begins casting protection spells on the windows, chanting so fast the words all run into each other.

When she speaks, I jump; her hands don't even pause. "Hedi, go wake your brother."

I don't. I should, but I don't. Instead, I follow Dad outside.

He's by the pond, with his weapon in his hands. I can feel a shiver running right up my spine and goose bumps rise on my skin. Daddy raises his gun and points it at the water.

The first thing I see is a mist, not a fog, but a mist that

curls upward. It's colorless at first, and then the mist tints to a purple that softens to violet. And I smell flowers. Sweet, like freesias. The air has cleared in the middle of the gate, so I can see the other side, shimmering through a thin veil. I hear a wolf yip from Merenwyn. Dad shifts his balance, and bends his head so he can squint down the site on his shotgun.

A gray wolf is running toward us, hardly breaking stride before he leaps through the barrier. From Merenwyn, I hear the shiver of bells, silver-sharp and sweet, and for a moment, just long enough for me to suck in a breath, he is frozen in the air separating this world and that, before he lands on our side. Dad lowers the gun, and swears. Paws splayed, the wolf skids right off the end of the portal's edge, and lands in our pond with a splash.

A Were falling into our swimming hole. Everyone knows Weres can't swim.

I cover my mouth, but don't laugh, because right away, Dad wades in after him. He pulls the wolf out by his ruff, and starts cursing him. "Do you know what this will do to Rose and the kids? Did you think? Did you ever stop and think?" The wolf wobbles over to a patch of weeds and collapses. Dad's shoulders slump. When he speaks his voice is flat. "If they come after you for breaking the Treaty, I won't stand in their way. I won't lose my family over this." He looks at the portal. It's daylight on the other side. I can see the sun shining off the water there.

"You just had to do it," Dad says, still watching the portal with narrow eyes. "Why'd you go there? Do you really think you're a better Were now? You don't even smell like pack anymore. It's not moon time, and you're in wolf form. You better hope that you can change back." He scowls at the Were. "You've crossed the line. The Alpha has to know."

Mum was wrong. The portal does accept Weres.

My foot slips on the shale. Dad turns. His face fills with blood, and he yells, "Get back up to the house. Now!" I don't like it when Daddy's so mad. It freezes me, like he's a predator, and I'm something with a soft white belly. He says it again, louder. "Now!"

Behind him, the wolf surges to his feet, taking advantage of Dad's divided attention. He charges, hitting Daddy square in the back. The gun goes off as they fall. Then, they're rolling, and grappling, twisting on the ground, churning up weeds and last year's leaves in a to-the-death struggle.

I can't make a sound. I'm mute as a hare.

I hear a scream, high and thin, quickly followed by another. The wolf scrambles off Dad, his jaws smeared with blood. Dad's fingers find the shotgun. I hear the gun go off, but I don't see the wolf fall. Instead, he pivots, and runs up the path that leads to the Trowbridges'.

For a few moments all I can hear is Dad's breath coming out fast.

"Daddy?"

Part of me cringes from him. He's dropped the gun, and rolled onto his side. Blood's streaming down his neck. He's holding his stomach together with his hands. "Help me to the house."

Mum's face crumples when she sees him. "Oh, Ben, oh, Ben." It takes both of us to drag him into the house. He leaves a wide trail of blood on the linoleum. She runs to the oak cabinet and flings open its door. "Get in. Hurry."

I hang back. It's too small. Impossible to imagine crouching in. Mum's arms are cruel with haste as she shoves me in. I have to duck my head and fold in two. "Keep this safe," she says, putting Merry around my neck. She shuts the cupboard door. I press my eye to the cutout, and watch her face twist with fear and desperation as she casts a protective spell on my hiding place. Then she turns, calling for Lexi.

The outer ward set on the kitchen door breaks.

Five Fae slide through the door. Three have short hair, while the other two have long, straight hair, black as their jackets. Their clothing is foreign. "You've lost much of your talent, Rose," the cold-looking one says.

The dream jumps ahead.

The same man says, "Roselyn of the house of Deloren, you've violated our law. You broke the Treaty of Brelland, and allowed one of the unclean to bathe in our sacred Pool."

Her face is as white as her nightgown as she denies it. One of the short-haired Faes glances down at my father and says, "He's dead."

Another Fae, very thin and dark, comes up behind my mum. He grabs her hair and pulls her head back. The knife in his hand glints under the overhead light.

"According to the laws of Merenwyn, and the Treaty of Brelland, your life is forfeit." Her gaze flies to my cupboard.

I say, "Mummy," in a little voice, but the sound echoes back to me.

The ward on my cupboard is strong. I am invisible, both by sound and sight, as he drags the blade across her throat. Her blood makes a noise when it sprays the cupboard.

I'm too scared to even breathe.

They drag Lexi out of his bedroom. He's fighting them with everything he has, but he's just so little. We're both little. I know I can't bear to watch what will follow, so I cover my eyes, but open them when I hear one of them say, "No, don't kill him. I'll claim him as payment for my loss." The long-haired Fae studies his new acquisition with a coldness that frightens me to the depths of my soul.

The man who cut Mum makes a ball of fire erupt between his hands. He tosses it at the kitchen curtains and sends another flying into the living room. Next, he purses his lips and blows. I hear a whoosh, and then the wall color changes from cream to red from the reflected fire's glow.

They walk out. Calmly. My brother is a squirming burden over the cold one's shoulder.

Lexi's gaze catches mine, as I squint through the hole. His eyes get smaller, and for a second, I think he's going to cry, but he slants them away.

I can hear Mum's heart, still beating. And so I hammer the cupboard door with my fists. I scream and call for help, and shriek some more, but have to stop to catch my breath. I keep it in my chest, and press an ear to the hole, straining to hear the slow thud of her heart.

She's still alive when Trowbridge comes through the door.

Chapter Four

"Merry, don't," I said sometime later, startling myself into full consciousness. Oh Stars, I wished I were out cold again. The shark had chewed its way through my ass cheeks and was gnawing on my bones. Merry had tunneled up and over my boobs to perch on my collarbone. A strand of gold ivy pressed against my cheek. It lifted, pressed, lifted, and pressed again. "Merry, don't pat me." She stopped patting, but stayed put, cupping an ivy leaf around the curve of my chin.

"You might want to get out of the line of fire," I mumbled. To prove my point, my stomach did one last housecleaning squeeze, sending up another mouthful of bitter bile. The Taurus windows were of the roll-up variety. No freakin' way. I looked for something to spit in, but Bob kept his relic clean. Merry skittered to my shoulder as I twisted around to spit into the backseat. I did it again, and then added "clean Bob's car" to my to-do list.

It was bad, this payback. Worse than anything I'd ever lived through. My body would gradually absorb the pain, given enough time. Headaches lifted. Fatigue was conquered by a good long nap. Finger soot got brushed off, revealing perfectly normal skin. But this was a first. I'd gone straight past soot to crispy. What would be revealed when the outer skin fell off? What do they call that? Degloving. Oh please, no degloving.

How long would it take to heal? Twenty-four hours? I
didn't have twenty-four hours. The digital clock read 9:53
P.M. I'd already wasted an hour out cold. The car was still
running. All I had to do was steer.

Put your hands on the wheel, I told myself. *You don't have
to look at them; you just need to use them.* They spat fire
when I moved my fingers. I couldn't help it—I held them up
for inspection. Oh Goddess. My fingers didn't even resemble
fingers anymore. They were swollen fat and bent unnaturally.
The skin had turned deep brown, and there were black spots
of charred skin across three knuckles, two of which were
nothing more than open red sores. Yellow liquid seeped from
the cracks. Suddenly, the charred odor that I'd been trying to
ignore was the only thing I could smell. Mother of Fae, how
was I going to heal from this?

*You're part Were. You'll heal. Don't be a coward, Hedi
Peacock.* I took a deep breath and tightened my hands on the
wheel. Then I screamed.

I woke up with a sense of déjà vu. Merry was patting my
face again. The clock read 10:27. And my raw hands had
fallen back to my lap. The pain was as bad as before, maybe
worse. I knew what she was going to do before she started to
move. Merry traversed my shoulder to the midpoint of my
chest. She slid quickly down it, the polished surface of her
stone sliding soundlessly across the fabric of my shirt, until
her chain pulled prematurely short. She pivoted to see what
was holding her back.

Me. I couldn't put my hands up to the chain, but I could
use my chin to pin a length of it against my collarbone. Stubborn foolish Asrai. She'd take all my pain away and kill herself doing it.

She strained and won another half inch. "No," I said. She
did her shimmy thing—the amulet version of a huff—before
turning back to strain in the direction she wanted to go.

"Give me a couple of hours, and I'll be able to steer," I
whispered.

One of her long strands disentangled itself from the nest
of woven gold that framed her stone. It stretched toward me,

the ivy leaves flattening back into the length of it, giving the searching tendril an extra inch to extend until its delicate point reached my jaw. She stroked my skin, once, twice, each stroke a soft caress. Then she pulled back and swatted me.

"What if you can't heal me, without—" I concentrated on keeping my voice steady, between my uneven breaths. "Without going too far? What if the healing of me is the death of you?" I stared through the window, noting the blossoms forming on the cherry trees.

Another impatient tug. There was desperation in the way she grappled with the leash of her chain. Why? She knew eventually I'd heal and she absolutely loathed Lou, a reaction not unexpected considering that Lou had enslaved Merry in a piece of amber. I'd never seen Merry so vengeful, so bloodthirsty, and now so frantic. As a rule, she was bitchy, but never mad-dog focused. I thought back, trying to pinpoint the moment her attitude had changed.

"It's the other amulet. That's when you got all ferocious. He's something important to you." I lifted my chin. She fell on her back. "That's right, isn't it?" She bobbed energetically, as if she were playing charades with a jackass who only now was on the cusp of getting the right word.

"Just once, I wish you could talk back."

A bit of red winked in her amber belly.

"Trowbridge has the amulet they're searching for. I saw it around his neck today." I shook my head. "It's just too damn coincidental. Of all the Starbucks in this town, why would he walk into ours? We're going to have to be so careful, Merry. It doesn't smell right." I thought for a bit. "All right," I said slowly. "Heal me. But only enough so I can drive."

The chain slithered after Merry as she rappelled to the end of it, hanging beneath the curve of my breasts. I heard a rip and then felt cold air on my midriff.

She found her spot, right over my heart. Her gold rippled and unrolled, pulling itself free of the braids and embellishing curls, until only a thin casing of gold surrounded her central core. The rest of it re-formed into four long slender limbs that spread out to hug my ribs. As they stretched and tightened across me, her stone remained flat, hard against my heart.

Merry's amber warmed to my body's heat until I couldn't feel the difference between her and me. As I watched, faint pinpoints of white started to flicker deep within her heart. A tiny dot of pure light here, another bright spark there, as mesmerizing as fireflies on a hot summer night. Those winking stars started moving, circling the dark smudge in the stone's center, and as they did, they changed Merry's golden-honey core to a brilliant orange-red, fierce as the sun before it slips beneath the horizon. Faster they swirled. White and pure, and so brilliantly incandescent I had to squeeze my eyes closed against their radiance.

The inside of the car began to get warmer. My limbs grew heavy. The shark released his grip on my bones tooth by tooth. Then he swam away.

When I woke, she was a cold dull brown. I held her tight in the fist of my healed left hand, and shoved the car into gear with my right. The back end of the wagon went up and over a curb as we sped out of the parking lot. She needed food.

At 11:43, there was no one on the heritage conservation trail, and thus, nobody to stop me when I maneuvered the Taurus up and over the sidewalk, around the vehicle barricade, and down the gravel path leading into the woods. I drove with my eyes trained upward, searching for a clump of trees that were already in bud or leaf. Twigs and dirt spun up in our wake.

"Hang on, Merry," I said, lowering the car window. The night air rolled in. My scent glands absorbed everything at once, overloading me with information. They noted the stagnant wetness caught between the fallen leaves, the rich earth, the trails left by the inhabitants of the woods—the rabbits mortals sometimes spotted, the foxes that were too sly, the mice and rats and moles—my nose sensed them all. I found one sweet note among all the others carried on the night breeze.

I followed it to a narrow pedestrian bridge spanning a small creek, then shoved the car into park and lurched out the door. The scent led me off trail. I sprinted up a hill, and there they were—a colony of serviceberry trees growing in rangy disorder under the canopy of oaks, beautiful with their showy clusters of flowers, in horizontal drifts of pure white.

I pushed aside some shrubbery, strained inward for one of the thicker trunks, and pressed Merry hard against it. There was nothing for the count of five. On six, she shuddered, her coils of gold rippling. First one coil flexed, followed by another, and then all of her unwound until each vine found a place to curl around the sturdy stem, until her heart was pressed close and tight to the source of life. The yellow-brown of her amulet flickered. A red light beat deep inside, small and rapid, like a baby's heart. The brown became orange tinged. Orange led to yellow, and then yellow to green, and then, her center was overtaken by a brilliant blue light.

Merry fed. And healed. And I came close to weeping.

The car was still there, the door wide open, the engine rattling reproachfully, when we returned a half hour later. Emotion always makes me hungry. I popped open the glove compartment. Another thing about Bob was that he was *always* prepared. He had an emergency stash crammed into the compartment. The bottled water tasted stale, but it was wet. It washed down the eighteen unsalted almonds that were meant to stave off starvation if Bob and his Taurus ever went off the road, slid down an embankment, and went undiscovered for three days. He had a flashlight in there too, and a CAA card that had expired five years ago, two months after his license had. Sometimes I could tell by the seat position that he'd visited the Taurus. I never caught him sitting there in the dark behind the wheel, reliving the years when he was the menace of 401, and he never queried me about the thick new steering wheel cover, or how the car never got dusty during all the years it had sat waiting for Bob in the garage.

While I chewed and Merry drowsed, I fingered my ear and worried over Lou. She hadn't sent a thought-picture or dream in hours. And that was plain worrisome. Nothing? During these last few days, her dreams and thought-pictures had constantly dribbled into my mind, and now nothing?

So strange, how quickly you got used to a turned-around world. For the first nine years of our life together, I hadn't needed a barrier from Lou's mind, because she never, ever shared it with me. Between us, there would be no easy communication of silent thoughts. Somewhere during that first terrible week after the fire, I sent Lou a thought-picture. Her response was a cheek-burning slap, right across the face. When my sobs wound down to hiccups, she said, "My mind is my own, just as your face is your own. I will not touch yours, if you do not touch mine."

Lou's version of child-rearing. I never reached out to her so intimately again.

Last summer, I'd been chewing on a peanut butter sandwich while watching a cop show. And out of nowhere, I got that feeling—like a nudge, but on the inside. Then I'd seen a thought-picture of a garden, clear as crystal in my mind. I'd never seen a garden like that, with so many intense shades of green. And the flowers—nodding, trumpet-shaped bells in shades of blue never witnessed in this realm.

Merenwyn.

At first I believed Lexi had found a way of contacting me. There are no words for the feelings I had. It was a cocktail of joy and happiness and relief and eagerness, swallowed down on an empty stomach. Rollicking glee lasted a night, maybe a day, before it fizzled out, and was replaced by a bitter sadness that made me want to weep. I spent an anxious month, replaying the picture in my mind, searching for clues about how to open the door from here to there. He wouldn't just send me any picture, would he? There had to be something important about that garden. And then one day, I got a deluge of thought-pictures, flickering and stuttering in my mind like one of those silent movies. A hand fumbled with the cupboard door in our kitchen and pulled out a can of maple syrup.

I walked into our kitchen. Lou turned and looked at me,

confused. "I can't remember how to open this," she said, turning the tin over in her hand.

As her mind softened, so did the grip on her thoughts. At first it was unpleasant, like reading someone's diary and understanding for the first time that you only knew them on the surface. Sometimes, there were tantalizing glimpses of the Fae world, dredged up from her memory, but most of the thought-pictures were increasingly depressing distortions of the world we lived in now. She brooded a lot about the Werewolves.

"Lou," I said experimentally, trying to search for her in my own mind. "You there?" The Taurus ticked over. I heard a small animal burrow under the leaf mulch. I counted silently in my head all the way up to twenty-six Mississippis. Nothing. Merry curled a tendril through my buttonhole, and pulled herself high onto my shoulder.

"I can't feel her, Merry. She's not around anywhere close."

I wished I were home, making Kraft dinner while Lou wandered the apartment sucking on a spoonful of maple syrup. I flipped down the visor. The face staring back from the mirror was too round, too pale. In the darkness, my light green eyes seemed to flicker. In terms of beauty, they were the only thing I got from Mum. Her eyes had been light like mine, almost translucent, embellished by tiny specks of yellow and blue, and a deep outer rim of soft green. But her eyes hadn't flickered. She'd had control over it. Averting my gaze, I pulled my hair out of its ponytail, and braided it, not looking at myself again until I fastened the end with the rubber band. I slipped on my glasses and flipped the visor back up.

They say when you're in a skid you should look in the direction you want to go. My life had hit the mother of all skids. I went looking for a curly-haired Were.

Chapter Five

I knew where to go. I'd done a lot of walking in this town. Some of it because I had to, some of it because there are only so many romance novels you can read, and so many hours of television you can endure, before you need to see real people, even if they're not *your* people. Watching them go about their daily lives makes you feel normal.

Which is how I knew what corner in our town has three different fragrances: car wash, Laundromat, and Burger King—the same scent signatures I'd noticed on Trowbridge's van.

The Easy Court Motel sat in the epicenter of all three aromas. It was flat, and long, and mostly brown, with a parking lot poorly hidden by a patchy growth of low bushes. The front office was lit, and an OPEN sign reassured all those with an itch that needed immediate scratching that the Easy Court Motel was ready for business.

Trowbridge's red van was parked in front of the unit closest to the manager's office.

The last time I'd spied on Trowbridge, it had been from the safety of the woods that bordered our home. I'd been twelve, and he'd been a guitar-playing eighteen-year-old, celebrating the last exam he'd ever have to take with his friends and a few bottles of cheap pink wine.

Mum had found me before my brief stint as a voyeur became educational. She'd pulled me back home, her long soft fingers hard on my arm, and then I'd had an argument with Lexi that had dragged on and off for two days. We fought a lot that last spring, my twin and I.

I drove slowly past the motel's entrance, eyeing the parking lot. I couldn't see any Weres but that didn't mean there weren't any. To be on the safe side, I drove past the motel, and pulled into the adjacent strip mall. The fluorescent light from the interior of the twenty-four-hour Laundromat shone through its plate-glass windows, spilling a weak circle of light onto the two cars parked in front of it. I went farther down the lot, until I found a dark place to park, and reversed into it.

I don't have large Were ears—I can hear just a bit better than the average mortal—but I do have a Were's nose, which I used to test the air. When I was sure that there wasn't a new scent to worry about, say that of a hair-gelled Were named Eric, I rolled the window back up. The sweat I'd broken out in during the healing had dried, leaving me feeling itchy and chilled. I'd be warm soon. Boosting something always made me feel warm and alive.

Merry climbed down to the vee of my white shirt and slid quietly into my left cup. I tightened my bra strap so that she was safe and snug. From my backpack, I pulled out the hoodie. It was too big, and I needed to roll the sleeves up twice, but once it was zipped up to the neck, I smelled of coffee and human.

There was a gap in the bushes between the two businesses. I pushed through it, chewing the inside of my lip as I tried to conquer my pregame jitters. The trembling would stop when it was go time. I had no plan. I never have a plan. Usually, I just count on opportunity.

My Fae Goddess was looking out for me. Just as I passed the first room on the end, opportunity hitchhiked on a stiff breeze that blew down the narrow catwalk in front of the rooms. Three more scents. Febreeze, cigarettes, and alcohol. I followed the trail to room 6.

He'd chosen the woodland version of the room deodorizer. By laying a sickly sweet commercial scent over his own pure wild natural one, he'd almost gotten away with it. Almost.

I kept walking, thinking. Trowbridge was obviously cautious. He'd disguised his scent in room 6, but he'd parked his van outside a room near the manager's office. He must have rented that room as well, and stowed something personal there because Were fumes were seeping from that room through the aluminum window frames. In the room, a television was flickering behind drawn curtains.

Two rooms. One as a decoy, and one for sleep.

The night manager wasn't in the motel's office. From the adjacent room, I could hear someone hawking exercise equipment; guaranteed to transform flabby bellies into rock-hard abs. The spare key to unit 6 hung from the brass hook.

"Be there in a minute," a man said. It took less than that to lift the key from the hook and pocket it. I wasted three minutes cooling my heels around the side of the building before the manager waddled back to his shopping channel.

Two people were having sex in room 3. I slunk past it, my nose crinkled against the scent. I put my ear to Trowbridge's door. Someone—hopefully Trowbridge himself—was breathing deeply, his exhales loud enough to almost qualify as a snore.

The curtains had been yanked together too enthusiastically, creating a slit between the window frame and curtain, which made recon easy. Not much in the room. A dresser, a chair, and one long lump on the bed, facedown, feet dangling over the edge. The television was on, but muted. A light had been left blazing in the bathroom. I could see a sink and an empty bathtub.

Measure twice, steal once. I did another visual survey of the room before putting the key to the lock. It turned with a little snick. The hand tremors were gone, and now I just felt that focused rippling pleasure I always got from taking something. As if everything else were gone, and nothing else mattered except that thing I wanted.

The thing I would take.

I put my hand on the knob and then paused, instinct hissing caution. Weres were almost as tricky as Faes. I checked the room one more time, straining to see into all the corners. No one was standing behind the door, waiting to bash me over the head with a baseball bat, but there *was* something strange about the door handle. It took three beats to figure it out.

The bastard. He'd balanced an empty liquor bottle on it.

Well, that's a roadblock. Driving here, I'd considered the probability that I'd need to use magic. Weres have ears, and they're possessive. I couldn't just tap him on the shoulder and say, "Can I have that?" I figured I might need to use my talent. But it was going to hurt. And to be honest—which I rarely am—I wasn't altogether sure how much of my Fae magic was left inside me. I rubbed my thumb over my fingers, feeling the new soft tender skin.

I counted to ten, stretching the eight, nine, and ten out as long as possible in case I could come up with a reason why I didn't have to use my talent, before I forced my two fingers into position and pointed at the liquor bottle through the window. "Lift."

It levitated, a little less smoothly than normal, but hey, working through glass was trickier than it appeared. The empty pint of Canadian Club swung gently through the air until it hovered over the dresser. I lowered my fingers. The bottle landed short and trembled on the edge.

I smothered a curse. "Up." The empty rose again. "Back." It slid backward. "Down." The brown bottle landed with a slight thump. I clipped the line of magic, and felt the sting on my fingers.

Sometimes I wish I had a personal remote control for my life; whenever things got bad I could just put my thumb on rewind. Instead of getting up and going to work, I would have rolled over and slept the day away. Lou wouldn't have wandered, the Weres wouldn't have found us, and I wouldn't be standing with my hand wrapped around the doorknob of a motel room, waiting for a bad-tempered Were to go all vengeful and possessive when he realized I wasn't there to make an Avon delivery.

I opened the door.

On the surface, the room smelled of air freshener, Were, alcohol, sex, humans, and cigarettes, but below that were other, more disturbing subtones of emotions that I couldn't decode. It takes training to identify scents into subsections of motivation, and I had no training. I toed aside a bottle of Febreeze. There was a debris trail leading to Trowbridge's bed. Jacket, shirt, boot, another boot, jeans, one single white sock.

He lay facedown on the bed, with his head turned away from the door. Some of his curls were smooched up onto the pillow, the rest lay draped over his shoulder. I picked up the bottle of Canadian Club whiskey by the neck. Swung it in my hand thoughtfully and waited. Thirty-seven Mississippis later, I came to the conclusion that if he was going to jump me, he would have done it by now.

It was a temptation to hit him with the empty flask, just to even up the score. Instead, I picked up the sock and tossed it at him. It landed on his hairy calf. He didn't flinch, nor did the slow, deep tempo of his breathing change. Each exhale filled the room with a little bit more recycled whiskey. Light a match in the room, and we'd both go kaboom.

The Were seemed to be out cold. I pulled my glasses down my nose and studied him. A man probably doesn't look his best when he's facedown on a bed, wearing a pair of shorts, a rucked-up gray T-shirt, and one sock on his foot. The gray T-shirt was half on and half off, as if he'd paused to reconsider taking it off halfway through the job, and then just gave up on it, once he'd got his left arm free. It was bunched up to his throat, which left three quarters of his back bare.

Trowbridge had the pillow hugged to his face, which didn't do much for his appearance, but did a lot to show his impressively lean and muscular back. Take off his head, and he was a perfect triangle—wide shoulders, tapering down to a waist probably only a little thicker than mine, and hips that were indecently narrow, and then, oh yes, all that leg. A single white sock hung from his foot.

His ass was covered by a pair of low-riding black briefs. Not tightie-whities, the other type—the ones I don't know the name for. They clung to his glutes, and the long muscles of his thighs. He had runner's thighs. All Weres have runner's thighs.

But like his? A traitorous thought. I gave myself a well-deserved bitch slap and moved on. His wallet lay on the dresser, along with a cell phone, an empty can of Coke, and a package of cigarettes. Beside that was what looked like a little black box camera. It was sitting up on its end like a tower, which struck me as strange. People usually lay cameras flat which makes them a lot easier to palm. When I picked it up, I felt a twinge of current. On closer inspection, it didn't have a lens, but did sport a weird little pull pin on top.

A new toy. I grinned at myself in the mirror as I thrust it into the hoodie's pocket.

Merry pulled her head up out of my neckline. Her gold seemed to pulse with nervous energy, which just felt all wrong. No one wants a vibrating necklace. The analytic part of me, that little tiny segment of brainpower that wasn't caught in the moment, earmarked her tension for later examination. She was usually bored or disapproving of my thefts, not anxious. Never so nervous that she hummed like a tuning fork.

Other than my half-naked Were, there wasn't much in the room. No luggage, no books, no iPod, nothing personal beyond the wallet and cell phone I picked up and examined. I'm never greedy. I put the wallet back. Then I slid the dresser drawers open and felt around inside them, all the time keeping an eye on the lump on the bed.

I checked the bathroom. He didn't even have a toothbrush. I came out and studied him again. A thick wedge of dark hair covered most of his long nose. His chin was scruffy with a beard, not the type that said metro, but the type that spelled unemployed. *What do you do for a living, Trowbridge?* I tried to imagine him wearing a Creemore Springs Brewery uniform like my dad's and failed.

The amulet was still probably around his neck.

I inched to the bed, crinkling my nose as I got closer, because the nearer I got, the clearer it was that he'd sprayed the entire bottle of Febreeze in a circle around it. It pretty much

obliterated his own natural scent, which was tangled up in the
air freshener, and the other things leaching out of his pores—
alcohol and some emotion that I couldn't place. It wasn't happiness and it wasn't anger. Those two opposites I understood
and remembered from childhood. It wasn't fear either. I knew
that smell. But the emotion scent was strong, and it tickled the
back of my mind, as if I should remember it, but just couldn't.

Enough. His emotions weren't my problem. I was bent
over him thinking that the amulet was probably underneath
all that swaddling cotton bunched up around his neck when
Merry suddenly high-dived off her perch on my bodice to
land with a plop on his pillow.

I reached for her, but she pivoted like a scorpion, one
stinging tendril poised. I shook my head, and tapped her
chain with my finger, but she obstinately hooked herself into
the cheap cotton pillowcase. She was going to get us killed.

I let her go. Her chain dug into the back of my neck as she
streaked over the thin pillow toward the folds of T-shirt
bunched by his neck. She worked a piece of gold free from
its coil around her setting. It thinned and stretched, until it
was no wider than a pencil lead.

Of the two of us, I was better at the sleight of hand because
I was the only one who actually had two hands. "No," I
mouthed, with a small shake of my head. What was *with* her?

She rolled the end into a hook and slid it smoothly under
the crumpled cotton. I used a hand on the wall to steady
myself, and concentrated on keeping my breath shallow and
light as the material quivered under her examination. If
Trowbridge sat up, he'd be discovering the ceiling was a lot
lower than it had been when he went to bed. Providing he
could remember going to bed.

I don't remember my father ever drinking. Or smoking.

Merry backed out, empty-handed. *Crap.* I reached down
to scoop her up, and as I did, my braid slid over my shoulder
and fell onto his pillow. For a comatose drunk, he was pretty
damn fast. Before I could stand up, his hand had snagged my
hair. Sure, an ambulatory amulet lands on his pillow and he's
out cold. A woman's braid comes within his reach and sud-

denly he's Freddy the Wonder Dog snatching a Frisbee out of midair. There were a lot of painful things he could do with my braid. I was working on the short list when he did something unexpected. He sighed into his pillow and rolled his thumb over the bristled end. Eyes still closed, he played with it for a few seconds, until the corner of his mouth pulled into a weary smile. He shifted onto his side toward me.

My hair fell from his lax grip. Straightening up, I held my breath and took a half step backward. I flinched as his hand reached out and surrounded my thigh. Panic started to flutter at my throat. Sleepily, he ran his palm up to the swell of my ass and then back down to the sensitive back of my knee in a gentle motion that probably was meant to be soothing, but wasn't in the least. It was distracting and uncomfortable, particularly when the Were-bitch inside me raised her head from her sleep, and said, "Is that a Were, fondling my leg?"

The bitch had been struggling to get out since puberty. She could keep on yipping until she was hoarse. I wasn't letting her out. Ever. *And not for him. He left me in a burning house.*

"Sorry," he said. He dug his head into his pillow and sighed. "Sorry I was so late. Come back to bed."

His hand slid slowly up to my bottom to cup its curve. *Stop touching me!* He gave my butt an affectionate squeeze. Then to my relief, he yawned wide, and rolled flat onto his back, the bedsprings creaking in protest. His T-shirt didn't roll with him, which judging by the scowl that turned his face from cover-boy pretty to something wolf-sharp and harsh, really pissed him off. Snoozing Beauty growled low in his throat—*and they called me a mutt*—then grabbed a handful of the offensive T-shirt and tore it in two. He tossed the shredded jersey onto the bed. I held my breath in my chest, scared to so much as twitch, but he simply cleared his throat, dug his head deeper into the thin pillow, and covered his eyes with his forearm. His neck was red from where he'd torn the T-shirt away, but his throat was bare.

He wasn't wearing the amulet.

"Don't be mad," he said drowsily.

What the hell had he done with the amulet? I was turning

to reinspect the room when Merry squeezed my thumb. She pointed to his fist with one trembling leaf. Well, bless my Fae Stars. He wasn't wearing the amulet. He was holding it tight in his palm, the chain wrapped around his knuckles. Merry scrambled for a handhold on my cotton sweatshirt as I leaned in to take a closer look.

"Everything's okay now," he said.

"Mmm-hhhm," I murmured, eyeing the prize. My blood started humming in my veins.

Trowbridge's heel rasped on the rough cotton sheets as he straightened his leg. Then he exhaled through his nose, and I found myself suddenly fascinated by the way the hand resting on his flat belly rose and fell with each of his deep breaths. A little trail of dark hair ran south of the dip of his belly button, in a straight, come-on-it's-this-way line that disappeared under the elastic waist of his underwear.

Okay, he *was* a fine specimen of Were. Bodywise, anyhow.

He hadn't been burdened with the excessive hair that made some of my father's kin look like extras for *I Was a Teenage Werewolf.* He had some fur between his two small nipples, but it was soft looking.

Temptation bit. I tested it with my finger.

It was soft. The hair on the back of my neck stood up.

His hand left his taut belly, and slowly traveled northward. Over the edge of his rib cage. Up, past his heart. Up, to where my finger lightly teased his chest hair. He touched my finger with one of the two calloused ones left on his scarred hand, and then circled my whole hand with his. I forced myself to let my fingers lie there calmly in his palm.

Warm. Rough. Large and gentle.

"Come to bed," he said, tugging on my fingers.

"Soon." I put a knee on the bed, and with that his eyelids flickered and began to lift. *No!* I yanked my hand free. His shredded T-shirt was by my knee, and then it wasn't; it was in my hands, and then it was stretched over his eyes. I'd gone and blindfolded a Were. With a T-shirt. *Now what?*

He reached for the T-shirt, but I blocked his hand with the first thing that was available. His palm slapped my forehead.

I turned my head and pressed a kiss on his warm knuckle. "Let's play," I whispered, urging his head up.

His face froze. And then the right corner of his mouth lifted. He gave a huff of laughter. "Cute."

"That's me," I said in that same toneless whisper as I tucked the tails under his head.

His long arm came out and swept me down on top of him. Heart, brain, breath, muscles—all of my vital organs temporarily forgot their duties and I froze rabbit-scared for one time-splintered second.

No one had touched me for such a long time. No one had held me in forever.

"Fun, but I'm tired," he said drowsily, rubbing his bristly chin on the top of my head. "I'm so tired."

A blindfolded almost-naked man pulls me into his arms, and all he can think of is his fatigue? I was so going to die a virgin.

But I wasn't in Joan of Arc pain, was I? Trowbridge's clutch was heated, because Weres are hot, that's just a fact. Hot looking, fiery tempered, and bone-meltingly warm to the touch. Your own personal hot water bottle in winter. A little too steamy in the summer, but air-conditioning took care of that. Trowbridge's embrace didn't hurt. For the first time since I was a kid, someone was cuddling me and I wasn't writhing in pain and breaking out in heat blisters. By a monumental oversight, Weres were exempt from the burn-her-flesh curse that some miserable sod of a Fae mage conceived to keep Fae travelers from mixing with mortals who had dangly bits.

I wished I were naked, just to explore how much this cuddling didn't hurt.

My right leg was between his. My breasts were mashed against his chest. So this is what it was like to be pressed thigh and hip tight with a man. I felt deliciously small, and decidedly feminine. There was no give to his muscles, no softness to the flesh beneath the skin. Unless you're talking that mound down there. Poor devil, he really was tired. Very softly I nudged his manhood with the inside of my leg.

Down there approved. My eyebrows rose as his penis

twitched against my leg. I gave it another coaxing rub, and it started to rise like the warning gate at a railroad crossing. Okay, I know—it's politically incorrect and probably illegal to tease a comatose male, but I'd never experienced the thrill of sexual power before and I'm not ashamed to admit I liked it. Suddenly I knew exactly what sort of smile Eve had when she turned to Adam with an apple in her hand.

I lifted my head to look at him.

Trowbridge had two deep lines running vertically between his brows, visible over the strip of T-shirt blindfolding him. Merry squirmed impatiently in my grip. "Okay," I mouthed to her and started to roll off Mr. Hard-body. His arm tightened around me.

Huh. I planted a forearm on his chest, and strained backward, but that just rammed the lower part of me harder into the lower part of him.

"Mmphh," he said, digging his heels into the mattress. He flexed his hips, and I rose with him. The guy had serious thigh muscles. The Were-bitch inside me anxiously whined—something she usually only did passing the food court. *Go back to sleep,* I warned her. I tried to slide off his body, but he wasn't about to let me go—he clutched my upper body like I was his favorite blow-up doll. Clearly his happy-stick was sad and lonely. He registered its discontent with a few pelvic tilts, putting a severe strain on the elastic waist of his tented shorts. With that, Were musk permeated the room.

Oh my word.

It was like someone flicked the switch to "on." I went from curious, to hazy-in-lust as my Were's mating instinct woke up with a start. Indiscriminate bitch. My fingers forgot all about the amulet, and slipped down to lightly skim the skin south of his belly button. He sucked in his breath obligingly.

I ran a fingernail along the elastic edge of his underwear, encountering something hot and hard. He pulled his belly muscles in so tightly that the vein running along his hip stood out. "Candy-girl," he whispered, a wealth of yearning in his voice. And there it was. The lick of lust faded as fast as a sugar high after an Oreo. I put my head on his hot shoulder for a moment and breathed in the deep mix of him: scotch, sex, and salt, woods, grasses—that indefinable combination of scents that spoke of a male Were—before I pulled my hand out of Candy's territory.

Even my Were reluctantly agreed. There is theft and then there is *theft*.

"I have to go pee," I said, feeling sad, my lips moving against his salty skin. His groan was more of a low growl, but he relaxed his grip on me, and I sat up. *Focus*. I said that to myself twice. The second time it stuck.

The tail of the chain still dangled from his grasp. I carefully teased it away from each finger, getting as far as his thumb before I met any resistance. Gently, I gave it a tug. He growled, low in his throat, and tightened his hand into a fist again.

If the Candy-loving Trowbridge wasn't going to give the amulet up on his own, I better make sure he was really out. I twisted my head to eye the room for a weapon. The light was bolted into the cheap furniture. The television remote was too small. There was a flimsy wooden chair with a truly ugly cushion, that would likely break into kindling over his tough Were head. There was the empty bottle, but it would shatter and then I'd be in a room with shards of glass and an enraged Were. I smothered a sigh. It would have to be the television again, but at least I could unscrew it from the cable before I sent it flying through the air. I brought a toe to the floor.

Trowbridge let out a sigh of his own. Not an I'm-waiting-and-ready sigh. More of an I'm-too-wasted-to-stay-awake sigh. I looked at his hand and smiled. It no longer clutched the amulet—it cradled it, leaving the necklace there for the taking in his open palm, with its chain hanging like a garland from his fingers.

See? Opportunity. I tossed Merry over my shoulder, and quickly leaned over to untwine the amulet's chain from his fingers. My lips were curving into a victory smile when his hand came up again, cupped the back of my head, and pulled me down for a kiss.

My First Kiss.

His lips were hot and his beard was scratchy, his breath was a trifle sour. I could get over that. Because his lips . . . oh Goddess, the feeling of them pressed to mine. Warm, heated by his heart. Soft and tender. A little damp. Larger than mine, but mobile and never still. A press, a lick, a little nibble on my lower lip. The bristles of his beard were not sharp at all—if anything, their tickle felt intimate and male. A soft noise escaped my lips. His hands suddenly moved—one to capture the nape of my neck, the other to cradle my jaw. My Were gave a food-hungry moan. A scent exuded from him, foreign to my nose, but it spoke of urgency and want. Sighing, I threaded my own hand through his curly mane. *So soft, and silky.* I mirrored his cupped hand against my chin.

Oh, he liked that. At the touch of my fingers, he made a noise in the back of his throat, part growl, part masculine hmm, and teased my parted lips with his.

I stopped worrying about my frolicking inner Were. I let go of caution, and common sense. I surrendered to the awesomely incendiary combination of me and him.

His tongue stroked mine. So strange, so . . . intimate.

Go ahead, for a minute or two wallow in the full experience of THIS . . . There was no pain, no need to grit my teeth as I waited for the hurt to pass. Tears built at the pure, simple freedom of it. *Remember this:* a man's chest under my body, lifting me with each of his heavy breaths. *Never forget this:* the scent of him—his whiskey breath, his shampoo, his wood-fragrant Were skin. See? No hurt. No pain. Just . . . him. Oh Goddess. *This* was what they talked about. So simple. Bodies lined up. Hip to hip, swollen breast to hard chest. Legs entwined. *This* was what everyone else had. Schoolgirls, grown-up women, even old ladies with their faded smiles.

The need grew inside me. I trembled on the brink of full capitulation, and then—as one does when their toes are hanging over a bottomless crevice—I took a mental cautious step backward. *If you stay one more minute in his arms, it's over,* common sense told me. *All those years of hiding from the Weres—both the Creemore ones and the little bitch buried inside you—they'll mean nothing. And soon—maybe in another second or two—he might discover that he's not holding just a woman, or even another Were.*

He might look at you like they used to.

My tongue withdrew from the cavern of his mouth. I slid my hand away from his tempting curls, forced my fingers to stop stroking his jaw.

"Baby?" he muttered, puzzled. I strained from his hold.

Trowbridge pulled the blindfold off and squinted blearily against the light. I knew what I was going to do—my knee was already poised—and yeah, maybe I was already regretting what was surely going to come next. Just before I let loose the knee-from-hell, the phone in my pocket chirruped.

His eyes shot fully open. Black lashes around sharpening blue eyes.

"Your phone's ringing," I said.

The two lines between his brows deepened into crevasses.

"You going to get that?"

He glanced at the side table.

Then I brought my knee down hard.

Chapter Six

"Jesus," he roared, rolling into a fetal ball of woe.

I made it off the bed and three feet in the direction of the door before he tackled me. "Ooooph," I said, collapsing under his smothering weight. Oh shit, I couldn't even inhale under him. It's those Were bones, you know. Think about it. All sorts of strange shit must be in them to allow Weres to elongate and reshape themselves monthly.

There was a frantic mouse squeaking in the room. Dimly, because—oh crap—the light was really fading, I realized *I* was the mouse. He was the trap, and I was going to die with my cheek ground into the floor, choking on dust mites. The scent memory I'd have before the trip to the other side would be whiskey, Were, and the musty odor of old sex.

And then, thank you Goddess, he got off me. I took a grateful breath, dust mites and all. His fingers bit into my shoulder as he rolled me over.

"You thieving bitch," he shouted as he straddled me. His beautiful face was ugly with rage.

I squeezed my eyes shut as he drew back a fist to hit me. Once again, air whooshed by my head, but this time there was no pain. Just a loud splintering thump right by my ear. "Fuck," I heard him say over my head. His weight lifted off me. I sucked in some air. With my bruised lungs, it was like sucking a milkshake through a tiny straw.

He was doing a boxer's cha-cha three-step by my head, alternately swearing and flexing his red knuckles. "Shit," he cursed. "Shit."

My heart was banging away so hard in my chest that I was sure he could hear it. I didn't want him to. I didn't want anyone to ever hear my heart like that—all defenseless and frantic. I rolled onto my side and curled my arms around my chest.

I could see him, standing by the door. Trowbridge had gone from nursing his hand to holding his head as if it pained him. He kicked the chair with his bare foot, and then limped over to the windows. He pulled the curtain aside. Turned his head to this side and that, searching for bad guys. Tested the air with his nose with sharp urgent inhales that made his nostrils flare like a racehorse's on its last lap. Managed to resemble a freakin' dog doing it.

When my heart settled down, the rest of my body started sending in damage reports. Lungs, functioning. Ribs, painful. Hip, being bruised by something hard. By what? I swept my fingers under my hip and felt the cool smooth surface of Fae gold. The amulet was larger and heavier than Merry. It felt dead. There was no intelligence to it, no response to my Fae blood. Trowbridge was still watching the parking lot. Quickly, I jammed the amulet into the hoodie's pocket while Merry scrambled over my shoulder, and tunneled down under its neck.

His head swiveled. While I'd been recovering, he'd been doing the same thing. He'd brought himself down from mad dog to pissed-off male. The frightening wildness had left his face. His cheekbones still had a flushed residue of heat to them, but his blue eyes were just dark blue now. When he'd pulled his fist on me, I'd fancied there was a light burning like a ring of blue fire around his black pupils. An Alpha's eyes do that. But he wasn't an Alpha, because he wouldn't be alone, he wouldn't have pulled back on his punch, and his eyes were just a dark, tired blue.

His gaze roved the room and then returned to me. "What are you doing in my room?"

"Maid service?"

"Be careful, kid, I haven't decided what to do with you yet." He stared at me, and ran the fingers of one of his hands through his hair, before he frowned. "Are you alone?"

"No. I have friends waiting in the parking lot."

His nostrils flared. "You're lying."

I shrugged. Weres. Some were like breathing lie detectors.

"How did you get in here?"

I pointed a finger to the door.

He went to the dresser. His balance was improving. "There was an alarm."

I pointed to the bottle lying on the floor and raised one shoulder.

He patted his side, as if checking for his cell phone, which looked ridiculous because he wasn't wearing anything other than a white sock, a pair of crumpled briefs, and an armband of shredded jersey. Absently, he rubbed his neck as he contemplated me, then his hand froze at his nape. "Where is it?"

"What?"

"My necklace."

I could have said, "What? The Fae amulet that you don't have any right to? *That* necklace?" Instead, I shot to my feet and streaked for the door.

I met the door, though a lot harder and faster than I planned. He crushed my five-two into the cheap-veneered door like a six-foot flatiron. He ran his hands around my waist, and then down the front of me. I shoved my hand inside my pocket, found the amulet, and tightened my fist around it.

"Give it." He fumbled for my hand and slowly pulled it out of the pocket. He didn't try to break my fingers or my wrist. The lazy bastard just leaned into me, squeezing the air out of my chest. I hummed through my nose, writhing between the vise of his body weight and the unforgiving surface of the door. "Let it go."

I nodded, but didn't let go.

He ground into me. Writhing turned into pure frantic wiggling.

"Can't breathe again," I choked out.

"Let. It. Go."

I held on until my vision got spotty. *Then* I let it go.

"Sit."

I stumbled over to the bed and sat on the edge of it. He inspected the amulet by the light of the television before placing it around his neck. It was incongruous. All medieval girlie pendant on a chest that was neither.

He raked his fingers through his hair. "Take off the sweat-shirt."

I crossed my arms over my chest.

"I could pat you down again, but the way I'm feeling right now, they may need to call 911 after I'm finished."

He had a loud voice that grated on my ears.

I unzipped the hoodie slowly, fussily, using both hands on the zipper, giving Merry enough time and cover to scoot into her cup. The sweatshirt made a thunk when it hit the floor. Probably broke my new toy.

"Hands up, do a three-sixty."

I rotated for him.

"Put your foot on the bed, then lift your pant leg. Show me your ankle . . . now the other." It was like a really bad game of Simon Says.

"Put your knife on the bed, very slowly."

I scowled at him.

"No knife? Silver, then?" His eyebrows rose, making his forehead crease into two lines. "You came in here without a weapon? Jesus, I didn't think anyone would be that dumb." He picked up his wallet to riffle through the cards and bills. With a snap of his fingers, he said, "My cell. Give it now."

It must be hard to sustain alcoholism as a Were consider-ing their fast metabolism. Fur-boy had been unsteady on his feet two minutes ago. Now he was all squint-eyed and evil. I tossed the phone. He caught it one-handed. "Okay, now give me yours."

Buying time, I brought my hands up to my eyeglass frames and straightened them carefully. I know it's a disarm-ing thing because it's worked on humans for years. I gave

Trowbridge my best Bambi through the frames as I said, "I don't have one."

He snorted.

Reluctantly, I pulled out Scawens's phone. I was going to have to steal it back before I left this place.

He flipped it open. "So, who's Eric?"

"My boyfriend."

"You're a terrible liar." He scrolled some more. Then his jaw got hard. He turned off the phone and took out the battery. "Stand up. Don't try it with the knee again or you won't be able to use your own." Yeah, all brave Were. He walked up to me sideways with one hand ready at his hip level. "Put your hands behind your head."

I clasped them loosely behind my neck, and thought really evil thoughts. My blouse had a two-button gaping hole below the apex of my boobs, where Merry had torn the shirt to get access to my heart. The underside of my red-lace-covered breast was exposed, along with a five-inch strip of white skin. I'd liked the bra when I stole it from one of the circular racks at Wal-Mart, but now the acrylic lace screamed scratchy, and the orange-red appeared unpleasantly garish against the contrast of my pale white skin.

His attention wandered off my face, roamed over my body, then slid to my cheap red bra long enough to assess my cup size. A muscle tightened in his cheek. I was still trying to figure out what that meant when he said, "Tell me you're not a teenage hooker."

The look I gave him was pure disgust. His body search was perfunctory. Up my sides, across my waist, down my arms to my wrists. The same hands that had caressed my ass a couple of minutes ago patted my butt, but this time there was no affection in it. Trowbridge reached for the hoodie. He never took his eyes off me as he searched through its pockets.

"Aha," he said. "The alarm." Then he pulled my new toy out, and all hell broke loose in room 6 of the Easy Court Motel.

* * *

Sound. Horrible, horrible sound blew through the small room. It was spine-cracking, eardrum-piercing, body-contorting noise. I screeched and fell to the ground, covering my ears. Oh Goddess, someone stop the pain. The pain, the pain. My ears.

The noise suddenly stopped. I trembled in the aftermath. "Up," he said, sounding grim. I let out a faint moan as he jerked me to my feet by my collar. I really was going to hurt him. I wasn't even going to mind the payback pain. Then my stomach—Hedi's emotional barometer—took care of any revenge fantasies. I threw up eighteen partially digested almonds and a bottle of water all over his bare stomach and my pant leg.

"Christ, you're such a kid," he said. Big on words, Trowbridge. He used my sweatshirt to wipe his stomach.

I could feel the vomit on my chin, and used my shirt's sleeve to wipe it clean.

He winced. "You are ruining my day."

"It's night."

"Detail." He blew out some hot air. "Come on, kid. I can't think past the stink of your puke." He wrapped his hand around my braid again, but this time instead of fondling it, he hauled it up high over my head. What do you do when someone tries to lift you off your feet by your braid? You go on your tippy-toes and hold on to it with both hands.

And that's how he frog-walked me to the bathroom.

The bathroom hadn't changed in the last five minutes. The white sink was still rust marked. The toilet seat was still up. The thin vinyl shower curtain still hung off a dull silver rod by metal hooks. There was no window. The only thing by the sink was a thin rectangle of cheap pink soap. There was nothing I could use.

He shoved me face-first into the wall between the sink and the bathtub and kept me there, his hand on the back of my head. "Keep your forehead on the wall."

There was a hiss of water as he turned on the shower. I rolled my eyes to the right. The dial was set on blue, not red. The cold spray started to wet the back of my leg and the floor.

"Don't move."

I watched from the corner of my eye, as Trowbridge leaned over the sink, let some water run and slurped up several handfuls before he was satisfied. He glanced at himself in the mirror, without doing any of the rearranging most of us do. He didn't widen his eyes, or lift his chin, or suck in his cheeks. His face was neutral, as if he were used to seeing himself hungover and needing a shave. Then he scowled down at his arm.

"Shit," he said, reaching for the armband of jersey left from his T-shirt shredding. "I liked that shirt." He rolled it down his arm. The last piece of his T-shirt fluttered to the floor.

I couldn't take my eyes off his hand. Could he still strum the guitar with a thumb and two fingers? I used to watch him, almost every night. He had a spot under the tree on his ridge; I had a spot behind the bushes on mine. He'd play the guitar, pausing every so often to take a sip of his drink or study the night sky, a brooding expression on his face. It used to bother me, that sad look.

Back then the cool girls had called him Bridge.

Heartless bastard had noticed my interest. He was glaring at me in a very unfriendly way as he tilted his jaw to the side, and reached into his ear and pulled out a small tube of pink foam. It landed in a clink on the soap dish. An earplug, the sneaky sod. He flipped his head to the other side to forage beneath his mane of curls for its twin. He really needed to shave. His heavy stubble ended in a rough line under his chin.

He stepped back out of my range of sight. A second later his vomit-coated briefs landed in the sink. I reached for one of the earplugs and squished it between my fingers. There was a cylinder of something dense inside the foam.

"Don't touch those." Now that he could hear himself, his natural voice was lower, quieter. Melodic. Bit of a rumble beneath the clipped sentences. Butter over what?

He inhaled. "God, what is that smell?"

"Febreze, booze, cigarettes, sweat," I said to the wall, my own sour breath bouncing back at me. "Unwashed man—"

"Shut up." He rubbed his hand over his stomach, frowning. "It's coffee. You smell like puke and coffee. And not much else."

My gaze dipped to his crotch.

"Into the tub," he commanded.

The cold water was pit-pattering against the acrylic tub enclosure. "Uh-uh," I said.

"I'm not asking, buttercup. Get into the shower." He reached for my hair again and then growled when I swatted at his hand. "Kid, I'm an inch away from taking your head off."

Losing my head sounded painful. I put a reluctant foot in and immediately wished I hadn't. It would have been warmer taking a dip in the Atlantic in January.

"No you don't," said Trowbridge when I tried to scurry out. He pushed me back in. Then, leaning away from the cold water, he forced my head under the shower's spray and kept me there, spluttering under its frigid deluge, until he was satisfied I was rinsed, if not clean.

I shrieked and skittered for the tub's other end as he twisted the dial to warm and got in with me.

"Relax," he said, letting the hot water cascade over his chest. He picked up the soap. "I only do teenage hookers on Tuesdays."

"Who sent you?"

"I thought we'd already established that I'm working alone." I was trying to wipe my face dry with his sheets. He'd taken the only towel, and dried himself off while I stood dripping and shivering in the tub. "Look, I made a mistake. You were drunk. I thought you were an easy mark. Either call the police or let me go." He'd never call the police. And somehow, even though he spent a lot of time growling at me, I didn't feel like he was going to kill me anymore. Fool. I was going to steal that amulet and *both* cell phones.

"What are you?" Trowbridge shrugged into his jeans commando, eyes steady and hard on me. He jammed his foot into one old boot, and then took the time to put his white sock on his bare foot before picking up the next boot. He picked up his shirt, and thrust an arm through the sleeve. "You don't have much of a scent, Tinker Bell."

I swear it was a cue. A car alarm went off in the parking lot. "What now?" he spat, whipping around to pull the curtains aside. I made quick like a bunny to the dresser, pocketed the alarm and Scawens's cell phone. Then I sidled toward the door. Unfortunately, it's next to impossible to move quietly in wet pants and squelching shoes.

He caught my arm and pulled me beside him at the window. He craned his neck to the left, flattening his cheek to the glass. "Not the van," he muttered.

"I can't see," I whispered.

He looked down at me as if he'd forgotten I was there, and tightened his grip, wrapping an arm around my ribs again, and lifting me up in the process. There was nothing loverlike in his cinch hold.

"Do you want to live?" he asked me, his eyebrows pulled into a scowl. I nodded with as much vehemence as you can when your feet are dangling above the floor. "I don't like liars. Think carefully before you answer this question: Are you with those guys by my van?"

I opened my eyes as wide as I could and gave the smallest nope-not-me shake of my head. His beard covered up most of his mouth. All I could see of it was a lower lip. It didn't look like a happy lip.

Someone's voice—a human's, judging from the high fear in it—yelled. "You better get out of here, I've called the cops!" Trowbridge's gaze returned to the window. He bent his head to see through the crack in the curtains.

"Oh, you bastards, you're going to pay for that," he said in a low voice.

Pay for what? I tilted my head to look.

His attention returned to me. "I'm finding it hard to believe that you being here is a coincidence." The thumb and pointer finger on the hand clamped down over my mouth came up and pinched my nose shut. What was it with the smothering? I lashed out with my legs, catching him on his shin. He didn't even grunt. Instead he waited.

My eyes started to burn.

"See how easy it is for me to take you out?" He let go of my nose. "It's that easy. Now, we're going out this door, together. You're not going to make any noise. You're not going to fight me. If you do, I'll snap your neck like a . . ."

Like what? I wondered, as he backed me up and opened the door. Trowbridge covered my mouth with his hand, and eased us over the threshold.

There was a drama going on by unit 1. The room's door was hanging on its hinge, its frame splintered. Light from the rental's ceiling fixture spilled through the open doorway, providing ample illumination to the vandalism occurring in the parking lot. A guy was crouched inside Trowbridge's van, tossing the contents out onto the pitted asphalt—mostly clothing, bedding, and books from what I could see.

Another Were—short, dark-haired with one of those spiky, emo haircuts—stood beside the van's open door, his expression glum, his hands shoved deep into the pockets of the black hoodie he wore over a graphic T-shirt. Closer to thirty than twenty, he was one of those oddballs who favored sneakers over runners, and green laces over white ones. He wasn't doing much in the way of helping, though he did wince when an acoustic guitar went shooting over his head and made a hard landing.

Trowbridge kept me pressed to the front of him as he silently backed us away from the danger. And we might have made it, had my foot not caught one of the white plastic chairs positioned outside unit 10.

It made a hell of a racket as it fell on its side.

"Shit," said Trowbridge, soft in my ear.

The van trasher's head popped out of the open van's door. He was a little older than me, with a wide jaw, and small

narrowed eyes. The type of face that spoke of hockey rinks
and beer. Light glistened off the pointed tips of his dyed yellow hair. *Eric.*

"He's here!" Eric pointed to us. Rocker-Were swiveled to
follow his finger.

"Shit," said Trowbridge again. Then everything moved at
fast-forward: I saw a girl step out of unit 1, just as Trowbridge
spun me around and pushed me into a run down the motel's
covered walkway. We came to the end, veered right at the
Laundromat, and pelted down the service road between the
motel and strip mall. Another left, and then he was shoving
me ahead of him, toward the end of the short unlit back alley.

Which of course, because God hates me, turned out to be
a dead end.

Chapter Seven

Trowbridge grunted in frustration and changed directions. The back door to the Laundromat was ajar, propped open by a milk crate. He pushed me in, then kicked the milk crate into the alley. The fire door closed behind us with a thick metal clunk.

The noise of the place hit me, the almost deafening tumble of clothes as they rolled around the metal dryer cylinders, the angry thrash as they were pummeled by the washers' agitator; it all mixed into a wall of sound that hurt my already tender ears. The place should have been empty, but it wasn't. There was a blond girl behind a narrow service desk to the right of the front door. Standing by the long table that split the Laundromat in two was a tired woman in purple pants holding a bottle of spot remover. Trowbridge motored us around her as smoothly as a speedboat around a buoy. "Hey," she spluttered in our wake.

Trowbridge's head swiveled as he made for the front of the Laundromat. In the three seconds it took for him to push and pull me down the length of the room, I watched him evaluate everything. The blonde by the door, the woman with the spray bottle, her laundry basket, the cash register, the video camera mounted on the wall, and the chairs. I case a room like that when I feel the urge to steal—he was casing it for survival.

"You got a car?" Trowbridge asked me as we came abreast

of the blond girl sitting at the service desk. Her mouth fell open, exposing a wad of gum sitting on her back molars as she took in Trowbridge's unbuttoned shirt, my gaping wet blouse and rattailed hair. Something heavy thudded against the emergency back door. Fist, foot, or body, I wasn't sure. But it was loud enough to make the blonde squeak.

"Station wagon," I replied. "There." I pointed to it through the glass. The Taurus looked gray under the weak light.

"Good." He pushed open the door, turning to me. "Keys?"

"In the ignition."

"Aren't you worried someone's going to steal it?" he asked with a twisted smile. He paused with his hand spread on the door, and gazed down at me. The shower had turned his hair into a mass of fat, loose, corkscrewing curls. I could have threaded my finger through the center of one and it would have been lost, covered with dark wet silk. Something crossed his face—not regret, not anger. It softened his mouth, and gentled his eyes. Then it was gone, replaced by a look of decision that thinned his lips. He opened his mouth and said, "Kid, this is where—"

I'll never be sure what he was going to say, though I can guess. Both our heads turned at a squeal of tires: a red racing Honda peeled into the parking lot, its rear end fishtailing as the driver braked hard. It skidded to a smoking stop a few yards from the Laundromat. Stuart Scawens had evidently detached himself from the radiator. He sat behind the wheel, and even through the windshield I could see his eyes burning, promising me a new lesson in payback pain.

"Shit, they're multiplying," Trowbridge said, pulling the door closed. "Just how many friends have you got, kid?"

"They're not my friends."

His head snapped to the left as Eric came thudding out of the alley. "Son of a bitch," hissed Trowbridge, turning the lock. "How many more?"

"I have no idea."

Eric didn't even see the red Honda. He ran straight for the door, grabbed the handle and pulled. The door shuddered and my stomach plunged when it seemed like the handle would give way. Trowbridge stood his ground, not moving a muscle. Impassively, he stared the younger Were down through the plate glass. When Eric finally broke eye contact, Trowbridge jerked a thumb to the video camera mounted on the wall. "Think about it, champ."

"Eric, over here," called Scawens through his car window.

Eric whirled around. "Trowbridge's in there."

"So's the bitch with the amulet," said Scawens. "Come here. You got a phone?"

"Kids. They're sending kids after me now," Trowbridge muttered.

Even through the glass, Scawens heard that. "Come on out, pops," he yelled. "We have to talk. You don't want to do that in front of the others."

"No, I think I'll stay in here." Trowbridge folded his arms.

"They've probably called the cops already." Rocker-Were came ambling out of the alley. "We should leave before we pick up an audience. He can't run that far now that we know where he is."

"When I want your opinion, Biggs, I'll ring your fucking bell, okay?" Scawens fixed Rocker-Were with a withering glare. "Now, shut up."

I didn't like the way they were eyeing the front of the Laundromat. "They're going to come right through that door."

"Depends." Trowbridge stared steadily at the three Weres. "On what?"

"How fast they think police will respond to the 911 call the woman at the back of the Laundromat is making right now. How brave they think they are. How much force they think they'll need to expend. But most importantly, it depends on what they've been told to do." He rubbed the back of his neck. "So, my little thief, you want to tell me what they want?"

I took a step closer toward the back door. "I don't know."

"You're lying again."

"You can take them, right?" My stomach wasn't happy at all.

"They're kids. They don't have the juice." Trowbridge's eyes flicked briefly in the direction of the blonde sitting at the narrow service desk. A couple of feet past the front door, she was positioned to greet the customers, and keep an eye on the clientele as they fluffed and folded. It was dead center in the kill zone. The blonde must have come to the same conclusion, because her baby blues were so wide that her thickly mascaraed lashes fringed them like clumpy exclamation points.

"Does that thing work?" he asked.

Her forehead creased in confusion. He surged sideways toward her, and she gave another mouse squeak as she scuttled into the corner. Trowbridge pointed above her head. "I asked, does that thing work?" Her eyes rolled up to the video camera mounted near the ceiling.

"Uh-huh," she said, with a vigorous nod. She cringed into the corner as he leaned forward.

"Where do you store the video?" he asked in a soft voice. Below the counter evidently, given the direction of her panicked eyes. "Got a cell phone?"

She swallowed and offered up a phone covered in candy-pink leather. "Let's ramp up the visibility," Trowbridge said, pulling the phone out of her shaking fingers. He dialed 911. His fingers drummed impatiently on the countertop as the phone rang.

Cell phones. Tibetan monks and I must be the only ones on the planet who don't own one.

Outside, Scawens sprang out of his car. His head looked mostly normal now, except for the dried blood caked to his hair, which flattened some parts, and made other sections stick up stiffly. He'd removed the knitting needle, but the blood trail still marked the place where it had been embedded in his chest. He squinted at me and then rolled his neck as if he needed to perform warm-up stretches before he exerted himself in the tiresome task of hurting me. "Come on out," he said. Eric stood right behind him.

Biggs dug his hands deeper into his pockets and rested his hip against Scawens's flashy red car. Everything about his body language screamed "not engaged."

Trowbridge passed the phone back to the girl. I heard the

operator ask what the emergency was. She had to ask twice, because a series of loud thumps on the back door distracted the blonde as the Were on the other side got impatient. With each angry kick the woman's eyebrows ratcheted up until they got lost under her bangs.

"Tell them murder and mayhem," Trowbridge prompted. "Total cluster fuck. Bad guys outside. Another bad, crazy guy inside. Really crazy, tearing the place apart." He gave her a lunatic's smile. "Altogether bad, okay? Maybe a gang war. Mortal danger, blood, real bad guys."

"There's a man here," the blonde said in a wispy voice to the operator. "He's scaring me."

Scawens paced outside, every so often pausing to make a Bruce Lee "come on" gesture. Except he did it with two hands, which made him look more like one of those guys who back planes into the hangers. "Come on out, you piece of shit."

Trowbridge walked over to a chair, picked it up, tested its weight, and brought it down hard on the nearest washer. I covered my ears, and the girl with the phone squealed, "Oh God, he's going to kill us."

"Trowbridge, stop," I warned.

"Tell them," he yelled over to the girl, totally ignoring me. "The address." He smashed the chair again. "And that the crazy guy has turned violent."

She did, adding a few "Oh Gods" at the end.

Trowbridge made a closing clam motion with his fingers, and said, "Hang up now." She whimpered, but closed the cell and then stood there shaking, holding it close to her heart.

"That's me, big scary bad guy," muttered Trowbridge, examining the splintered chair. He popped the plastic seat off one leg. The blonde gasped as a silver U-shaped leg fell to the floor with a clang. He glanced at the Weres on the other side of the door as he methodically disassembled the cheap molded chair. With about as much effort as I'd use with twist ties, he wrapped the two metal legs around each other, until they became one crude length of steel. Then he folded one end into a ball. When he was finished, he'd fashioned a club; I started to feel hopeful. If Scawens had that type of strength he would have used it to kill me. But he hadn't killed me, right? So, he couldn't be as strong as Trowbridge. Things were looking better.

From the back end of the place, I could hear the purple pant lady on her phone. "Things are getting bad in here, real bad."

"I do not get involved with other people's problems." Trowbridge ran a hand through his hair. "Forget that once and look what happens."

"Why aren't they coming inside?" I asked.

"The security video. YouTube and the Weres don't go well together. No one wants to be the first asshole featured in a video. We're not supposed to exist. Give the world proof we do, and you'll have the Were Council down on your ass, and then there'd be no place to run." He kicked aside a piece of plastic. "Which makes me wonder how you're running around with the kin, alive and unbruised. We aren't much for mixing with others."

"Can't you take them?"

"Three kids? Of course I can. But there are certain problems in attacking someone's pup, when you don't belong to a pack. If I attack first, I'll be on every bad boy list in Canada. It's better they come through here, with witnesses and video."

"They can kill witnesses."

He smiled. "Only if I let them."

I didn't realize I'd been taking steps backward until my butt hit a washer. I corrected my course, and kept backpedaling, heading toward the door. "Why don't you just call the pack?"

"What pack?" He made a minute adjustment to his club.

"Your pack."

"I don't have a pack," said Trowbridge, eyes on the Weres. Outside, Biggs passed a phone to Scawens.

"He's calling for reinforcements," I said, bumping into the purple pant lady. "Sorry," I said automatically. She frowned fiercely and planted her feet firmly in the aisle. She had a cell phone tucked between her shoulder and ear and a bottle of detergent hanging from her other meaty fist. A cornered woman could do a lot of damage with her bulk and a full bottle of scent-free Tide. "Sorry," I said again, sucking in my gut to get past her.

"Kid, stop heading for the back door," said Trowbridge.

He had to stop calling me a kid. Particularly as he kept calling *them* kids. He was by the door, watching the Weres through the long stretch of plate glass that fronted the place. I could see myself reflected in it. If I looked past my reflection to the dimly lit parking lot, I could see three Weres outside, clustered by the Honda. A scowling Scawens was punching numbers into a cell phone with sharp, quick jabs. Judging by the way Eric was bouncing on his toes, the dyed-blond Were knew exactly what he wanted to do, but a significant lack of balls was keeping him from doing it. Biggs worried a pothole with the toe of his sneaker. His hands were tucked into his jeans pockets.

When I blinked, the outside drama fell away, and I was looking at the reflection of the inside of the room again— the long row of dryers, and me, edging my way backward toward the emergency exit, and the lady in the purple pants and her towering basket of laundry and then finally, *him*. He was watching them and me, all at the same time, and suddenly I felt a flash of kinship toward him. Inexplicable and untimely. Like me, he was outside of the world, and inside all at the same time.

"No one would send just a trio of kids after me. There could be ten of them out there by now." He changed the angle of his head, and I knew he wasn't studying my reflection anymore. "You open that door, and you'll be letting in more than I can deal with." His deep voice was flat as he studied the two outside. "And if I can't deal with them, you're dead."

At the word "dead," the purple pants lady said into her cell phone, "You got that? You get your asses out here, right now. He said dead. Dead. I'm not waiting around to be killed. You get those cops out here now." She nodded, and then said to me, "You better get yourself gone, girl. The cops are coming. They're on their way."

But I didn't get myself gone—I stood there indecisively.

Trowbridge jabbed a finger at Scawens. "Who *is* he?"

"Someone who really wants to hurt me."

"Well, there's a surprise." He let out a huff of air. "His name?"

"Stuart Scawens."

Trowbridge closed his eyes briefly. "Repeat that."

"The guy on the phone is Stuart Scawens from Creemore." I waited for his reaction, one foot shifting behind, ready to haul ass when he smacked his head, and said, "Of course!" But he didn't.

"Stuart Scawens from Creemore," he repeated slowly. I could swear a bright blue light flashed in his eyes for an instant. His nostrils flared as he took a deep breath. "That," he said, jerking his head at the Were, "is Stuart Scawens." A muscle tightened in his jaw. When he spoke, his voice was flatter than the prairies. "Well, there goes killing them."

"No, you can kill them."

"Oh, you think?"

I'd hit Scawens with a fifty-pound RCA, and a number ten knitting needle and he'd bounced back like Wile E. Coyote. "Killing him seems to be the only way to stop him."

"Thanks for the blessing. But as it happens, I've got a problem with that. Right now, Stuart Scawens is the one person on the planet I can't kill. And I want to kill somebody. The longer I stay around you, the more I want to kill somebody."

Purple pants had thighs like hams, and they rubbed together as she crept backward toward the emergency exit. "Lady, don't even think about it," Trowbridge snapped. She seemed to shrink, and then she took herself to the corner where dryers met washers.

In the parking lot, the phone call had come to an end. Biggs pushed the cell into his pocket, and then glowered at nothing in general.

"Stay here, Biggs, and watch how it's done." Stuart sent us a feral smile.

"So it begins," said Trowbridge, softly.

Scawens didn't even bother with the locked door. With six bounding steps, he leaped. Glass sprayed inward in a showering arc as he came through the storefront. Momentum carried him into the first row of machines. Eric leaped through the same hole, a great deal less tidily, as he skidded on the glass shards littering the floor.

Well, so long, Trowbridge. I'm no idiot. I sprinted for the back exit as his club connected with Eric's flank. As soon as my hand met the metal bar of the emergency door, Merry started to writhe inside my bra. It barely checked me. I stuck a cautious head outside. I had expected ten Werewolfs to be outside, doing crosswords while waiting for me to come pelting out. There was nothing but a scrub of weeds lining the chain-link fence and asphalt. I put a foot out on the pavement.

Merry whipped her vines around my left boob and squeezed. I mean, *squeezed.* "What?" I shrieked in disbelief. "You want me to help him?" Bent in half, holding my boob, I squinted behind me. Trowbridge and the two Weres were doing a dance around each other. Mostly it seemed like Scawens and Eric were making increasingly infuriated swipes as Trowbridge danced nimbly out of their reach, deflecting each strike with his makeshift club.

"He left me in a burning house. A freakin' burning house. Did he ever stop to say, 'Gee, I think there were kids in that house too? Maybe I should check for them?' No. He did not. Let him take care of himself." Unappeased, Merry bore down on my flesh. "Seriously, help him? Let the Weres fight it out. Someone will end up with the amulet, and I'll follow them." She hung on like an evil twisted clamp. Through clenched teeth, I said, "It's the amulet, right? I won't lose sight of the amulet." She curled infinitesimally tighter, adding heat to the misery. "Geez Louise, knock it off. Okay," I whined. "I promise I won't leave until I get the amulet." Her vines fell away, and then she dropped off my boob to swing from her chain. Her stone was still shot with red streaks. Probably matched my breast. I breathed hard through my nose against the pain before I could tolerate straightening up. Ten years of no pain, and now look at me.

Trowbridge and Eric were dancing, unconsciously matching each other in an intricate pattern of nimble footwork.

Every second beat, the younger Were tried to slash Trowbridge's neck with hooked fingers, the Were-hard nails of
which had been sharpened into predator's claws. But Trowbridge was too fast. He was a feinting Beckham, all grace and
supple agility. Teeth bared, he brought the deadly minuet to a
quick end. He dodged, and then he spun, slamming a fist into
the kid's kidneys, following it up with a hard jab of his knee to
his opponent's midsection. The kid went down, but as he did,
he swiped his leg out and brought Trowbridge with him.
Trowbridge rolled and was up before Eric could leap on his
back.

Trowbridge was good. He was fast. He was strong. He
didn't need my help. He could clearly outdance Scawens and
Eric. What he couldn't outmaneuver was a gun. I heard a shot,
and gasped as the impact spun Trowbridge around.

I'd forgotten about the female Were. She shouldered
through the Laundromat door with the gun in both hands,
dressed in dark, fitted pants, and a tight black body-hugging
top. She was beautiful, with dark smooth hair that fell in
long wings around her face. Her face was taut, battle ready,
with brown eyes that flickered nervously as she watched the
two Weres circle the bleeding Trowbridge. She adjusted her
aim. The handgun in her pale hands was dull grayish-black,
pointed at Trowbridge.

"Don't kill him," Stuart said sharply. "But I won't mind if
you hurt him some more." His face broke into a triumphant
smirk at the sight of Trowbridge's bloody right shoulder.

The girl with the gun wasn't shaking out of fear, but out of
sheer adrenaline. I could hear the soft pants as she breathed
through her mouth. She lowered her chin, centered her balance, and held that ugly gun like she was posing for a *Char-
lie's Angels* poster.

"Don't do this," Trowbridge said slowly. "You add a gun
to this and someone's going to be dead. It won't be me." He
made a slow motion with his good hand, urging her to drop
the weapon. She raised the gun higher, but took a cautious
pace backward. It brought her closer to the washer.

Washers come with doors.

I pointed my hand at the machine, and said, "Open." The power sprang from me, whistled through the air, found the machine, and popped that washer door open right into the small of the female's back. She fell with a startled grunt.

When she bounced back to her toes, the weapon was pointed at me. I ducked and the bullet aimed for my head went whizzing by my ear to ping harmlessly into a washer. Me, apparently, they didn't mind being dead. I don't know what other people think when someone fires a gun at them. But all I could think was, *She shot at me. The bitch shot at me*.

Even as I dodged death, I was still attached to the line of magic. It stretched thinly between the machine and me, vibrating with tension. Rage fueled more power to surge up my arm, burning my fingers, swelling my hands. Sickening power. I felt my stomach knot with the tension of holding it, and then with a harsh whisper, I said, "Push." My Fae gift flew down the invisible cable of magic to hit the machine with such a cataclysmic jolt that it ran a savage reverberation right back to my hand.

I yowled as the machine went shrieking across the floor, pleating up linoleum as it sped toward the female Were. Fueled by my magic, the washer plowed into the girl like a freight train. Her gun went spinning up on impact, and then she became the hood ornament to the Christine of washers. Ornament and machine slammed into the corner with a bone-crunching smack. I didn't see it. I'd closed my eyes as she careened toward the corner. When I opened them again, the wall was decorated with a fanning spray of wet blood. The woman's arm stuck up over the top of the machine, like a white broken flag. I couldn't see her head, just blood. Red on a white wall. Three sprays of it, to be precise. And one long vermillion smear. Did she still have a head?

Don't think about the blood. Don't look at it. Don't smell it.

I was still linked to the machine, like some damned creature in a Poe story, tied to the scene of the crime by guilt and the supernatural. I couldn't detach. The power held on to me, and held on to the machine, and all memory of squashed boob was overlaid by the horrifying misery of being held between the push and pull of my tethered magic. I strained, as I desperately tried to cut myself off from it. Smoke started to curl up from my fingertips.

"Oh Goddess." I groaned, arching my back against the horrible sensation of being linked and pulled and torn and burned. Merry scrambled over my chest and maneuvered into a healing position. "Don't," I said, pulling her away.

I was deeper than I'd ever been before, practically bathed by the power that was no longer adequately contained. It simmered and swelled inside me, a hard knot of unnamed fury, ready to explode, multiply, and consume. The Fae part of me was lost. It was just a speck, being squeezed by all that venom. Hunched over that machine, with one hand holding Merry away from my chest, I let out a whine. I was burning. Outside and in.

I plummeted deeper and then bumped into something. Something *other*, which had been locked deep inside. Another identity—a hot hungry implacable hunter, one that liked being linked to that vengeful power—rose up, took a pitying glance at the weak half Fae who was floundering, and reluctantly snipped the link.

Oh Fae Stars, the Were-bitch was loose inside me.

My knees buckled, and I slid down the cool surface of a washer. In the background I could hear noises of men struggling. Grunts. The sound of bodies hitting the sides of walls, dryers. The squeak of sneakers on the tile.

There was something "other" in my body. It was running up and down my spine. It was stretching out my sore fingers, rippling under my skin. She was lean inside me, but foreign. So foreign. She was also strong. I borrowed some of her strength to rise to my feet, and then we three, the Fae that Lou had reared, the Were-bitch inside me, and what was left of Helen Stronghold, stumbled to the front of the Laundromat.

Scawens was on the floor, facedown, not moving. Dead, I hoped. Trowbridge was still on his feet, even though blood was dripping down off the fingers of his right hand. He was using his left to hold the club across Eric's windpipe. Eric was turning purple. It would be over soon. Then Scawens got back unsteadily to his feet. He looked around, grabbed a chair, and swung it in a clumsy arc down on Trowbridge's back. Trowbridge fell to one knee, but he didn't let go of the weakly struggling Eric. There was a long squeak of sneaker as Eric struggled to hold his balance. He lost it, and fell backward, choking, onto Trowbridge.

Scawens shook his head to clear it, and brought the chair up high again.

"No," I said. *Mine, mine, mine,* said my Were-bitch.

I pointed to the chair poised over Scawens's head. Fae magic spun out, stuck to the chair like a spider's web, and held. Scawens tried to swing the chair, but to his surprise, it seemed stuck solid to air. He looked up at the chair, and then behind him, before the penny dropped.

Anger mixed with fear slid across his face. As the sweet stench of his fear spread like a pool of dismay around him, the bitch inside took over my facial muscles. I could feel my lips stretching into a murderous smile. *Kill,* she said.

"No," I said. But my other hand was already reaching for the last chair. Magic caught it before my fingers could and brought it to the air. Scawens turned, but he was too slow. Much too slow. The chair hit him. And as he ducked to avoid it, hands defensively over his head, the other chair followed. They weren't much in terms of weight. The bitch regretted that. But it was enough. It brought him down to Trowbridge's level, and once there, he fell victim to Trowbridge's foot. The savage kick caught Scawens under the jaw, with enough force to snap his head back. He went down and, this time, stayed down.

I walked unsteadily to Trowbridge. Eric's legs twitched as he hung on to his last moments of consciousness. The bitch wondered why Trowbridge didn't crush his throat. The metal bar could do it. The bitch wanted him to. But Trowbridge just kept the pressure steady, enough to render insensible, not enough to kill.

Mine, mine, mine, said the bitch, feasting her eyes on
Trowbridge's snapping blue eyes. Lights were shining within
them. Blue irises surrounded by a ring of white-blue light.
So, I hadn't been wrong before. His eyes shone. Just like an
Alpha's.

Or a Fae's.

And with that, I remembered who I was. Hedi Peacock,
almost all Fae. I slapped the wriggling bitch's paws off the
controls.

"No," I said, reaching toward Trowbridge. "He's not yours.
He's not ours."

Trowbridge was leaning far backward on his knees, his
neck arched painfully as he held the bar grimly across his opponent's throat. I could smell Trowbridge's blood. The Were
inside me gave a wiggle that felt like butterflies under my skin
when I touched his hair. My fingers slid through it. It was dry-
ing at the ends. I felt around his bulging neck muscles for the
chain. I grasped it, and I looked away as I pulled the chain up
and over his neck. He tried to snap his head to the side, but
there was nowhere to go, was there? And then it was up over
his chin, and over his head. One long lock clung to the chain
briefly before it floated down.

"This is mine," I said, in Hedi's voice. "This is mine." I
held the amulet, and then jerkily put it over my own neck.

Merry surrounded the amulet with her gold, wrapping
herself around it with sinuous grace, until it was hard to tell
what was Merry and what was the other. I stumbled toward
the door like a drunk. My leg muscles felt odd. Weak, lique-
fied, like I'd run too far. With every step, I lost another fraction of my strength. It took too much effort to get to the
door.

Metal scraped as I pulled the door open. I looked over my
shoulder. The Christine of washers was being pushed away
from the corner by the dark-haired Were girl in a one-armed
display of power. She was alive, then. Maybe that would
mean more to me later. One of her arms appeared mangled.
I could see bone, and tendons, and other things I didn't want
to see. Her middle section was stained bright red. There was

more blood, red, visceral, disgusting, on her face. None of that seemed to make her pause. She didn't even do the "Oh my God, look at my arm!" thing that I would have done. She just stared at me, and then at Trowbridge, much like the Akita I once saw charge at a retriever.

I put one hand on the door frame to steady myself. Put the other into my pocket. Felt for it, found it. "Trowbridge," I called. His eyes were still on me. Had they ever left me? I could feel the heat. The squirm inside. "Here." I threw the alarm to him. He caught it in midair with his wet bloody hand.

A second later, sound blasted through the Laundromat. Horrible noise. I pressed one ear to my shoulder, and covered the other with my heated hand. And then I staggered out and away from it all. The door swung slowly behind me. I took a step. Another. Three lurching ones. I made it past a pothole. Past Biggs who didn't seem inclined to interfere. The Taurus looked farther away.

I put a shaky foot forward and fell to my knees. Then both knees sort of oozed away, and I was on my side, lying on the crumbling asphalt of the parking lot. My head was turned to the door, and so I had an unwanted hazy view of what happened next.

Trowbridge heaved Eric's limp body off. He felt around in his jeans for his earplugs. He jammed them in his ears. The girl behind the desk ran to the back of the Laundromat, bent over in a crouch.

Things got blurry. I blinked and they got clearer.

The Were girl had made it out from her corner. She was heading toward the door, half bent over, holding a broken hand to her ear. She was, in fact, glaring at me. I wondered how much more pain she could inflict. My vision went grainy again.

Another blink. Trowbridge was prying her fingers off her ear. He held the sound blaster right up to her head, and waited until she fell down. Then he grabbed the back of her pants, and threw her into the bank of dryers with the same dispassionate enthusiasm a baggage handler uses on luggage. Her impact made me swallow hard. And for a second I could see with cold clarity.

He was a Were. Furless, yes, but still a Were. Robson Trowbridge, the much loved youngest son of the Creemore Alpha, and beautiful Bridge, every girl's grade school crush, and even the Trowbridge of my recent disappointment—those guys weren't in the Laundromat. The Were was. His neck tendons stood out in long ropes, the lines beside his mouth no longer looked like laugh lines, but like lines carved for intimidation. He picked up the gun before moving toward Scawens.

I closed my eyes. There would be more blood. I waited for a shot that never came. I opened them a crack.

With a muttered curse, Trowbridge pulled back his leg and kicked him again. He must have aimed low. Scawens's shriek was as high as the alarm.

Things got dark.

I thought I heard Biggs say, "You've got to hit me, man." But that didn't make sense. Nothing in this day had made sense.

Then, Trowbridge was by me. I was too tired to lift my head. He stopped close enough that I could study his bare knees poking through the new rip in his jeans. There was a pause. He bent on one knee and yanked me up by one arm. I swayed. He had two faces, and both of them looked mad. I reared back. The double vision settled down to one very angry Were with gleaming blue eyes and black whiskers.

He looked furious enough to chew up fairies and spit out their wings. He bent down, shoved his hard shoulder into my stomach and hoisted me up with a pained grunt. My braid flopped down over my hanging head. In protest, Merry lightly bit my skin, as she became squashed between his hard muscled back, and my flattened breasts. She'd grown in size, my protective friend. What had once been a smooth warm lump was now a big fat hot one. Was I destined to be burdened with two amulets now? One for each cup?

I must have asked that out loud to Trowbridge, because I could hear him grunt something. "Never mind," I muttered to his ass, moving my head to the side so that I wasn't staring at the gun tucked into the hollow of his back. Things kept flickering in and out of focus. I made a fist around his T-shirt, and tried to pull myself more upright. Bad, bad idea. His shoulder pressed deeper into my stomach and the scent of his blood was already making it cramp. I sank down again to rest my bouncing head on the small of his back. With one eye, I watched his ass cheeks move in a smooth rhythm. He hardly broke stride for potholes. In the distance, I could hear sirens. The cops were coming.

He stopped in front of the hood of Bob's car. Roughly, he bent forward to roll me off. My head smacked down on the hood. "Watch the car," I said, but what came out of my mouth was all muddled. He pulled Merry's chain up from under my shirt, letting her dangle from his fingers for inspection. She spun slowly, one fat ball of crisscrossed gold protectively surrounding both amulets. He started to pull the necklace upward.

"Don't do that," I said, but was too late. Merry spat electric fire down the length of her Fae necklace. Trowbridge hissed and sprang back as blue sparks jetted between his fingers and her gold. "Ow," I said weakly, feeling the heated metal char my neck.

Stars winked down on me. I twisted onto my side and heaved, but my empty stomach only produced a weak dry retch.

"None of that," he said, and grabbed me around the waist. My feet dangled as he carried me around to the open car door. One slipper teetered off my curling toes and fell to the pavement. He shoved me into the car. My head and ass bounced as I made a landing. His hip followed mine before I even had a chance to figure out how to mount the obstacle of the console. My backside received another impatient shove over it as he settled behind the wheel.

"My shoe," I complained.

One swipe at the pavement and the shoe went flying over my head. It bounced off the window and fell between the door and the seat. "Put your seat belt on," he said, clicking his own in place.

"Huh?"

"Cops."

I tried, but my hands blazed trying to fit the two pieces to-gether. He muttered something uncomplimentary under his breath, and then batted my hands away. That hurt. I told him exactly why he was a misbegotten son-of-a-Were but my rant came out in another incomprehensible jumble of words. He clicked the pieces of the buckle together, then he turned the key in the ignition, and we were smoothly exiting the parking lot. We made a left at the first light. We were traveling at posted speeds as the cop car blurred past us, its roof flashing red warning lights.

Four stop signs and one light later, I tested my mouth. "Trowbridge?"

"Shut up," he replied.

Take the man out of the Were and what have you got? Were. I closed my eyes and let the darkness come.

Chapter Eight

The sun is shining on the water. Lou watches the same man, but this time, she's closer so that bud-swollen branches frame him. His hands are on his hips. His back is turned, as always.

But then the memory sequence changes. The fish doesn't leap out of the pool. The wind doesn't ruffle his hair. He twists around, glancing at her over his shoulder; his smile is full and satisfied.

Her lover looks at her and she knew. *All the light went out, the picture fading dark around the gleam of his feral smile.*

"Wake up, kid," I heard from far away. Deep voice. Harsh and butter-soft to my ears all at the same time. Black claws were reaching for me. I could smell the copper-rich scent of his blood.

I attack. "You stupid Were-bastard, you left me! You could have saved me!"

"You ungrateful brat! What do you mean I could have saved you? I *did* save you." He ducked a flailing fist. "Keep it up, and I'll glue you to your seat," he said. "And stop calling me a stupid Were."

He waited for me to explode again, and when I didn't, he used his two fingers on my forehead to ease me back into my seat. "You are one crazy-ass Tinker Bell," he said, returning his attention to the road.

I barely heard him because I had made another discovery. *Oh Sweet Stars, I'm blind.*

Everything was blurry and dark—except him. His outline had a yellow-white halo that made him stand out in a world that looked mostly gray. I looked about, disbelief churning in my gut. Everything was horribly out of focus. The buttons on my shirt. My hands on my lap. The view through the windshield was worse; everything outside was an indistinct smear of black and gray shadows.

I can't be blind. I can't be a half-Fae/half-Were, blind, homeless person.

"I should have left you to those Weres, just like you left me." I turned on him again, and got in a few good clubbing blows to his body—he woofed out some air once—before he brought the assault to an end by catching my wrists.

"Are you nuts?"

His touch felt pulse-hot on my skin. I wanted his throat, but settled for his shoulder. I leaned in and bit him.

"Son of a bitch," he howled. Undeterred, I bore down with the single-minded intensity of a pit bull coming off a long veggie kibble diet. The car went into a sideways skid as he grabbed my braid to haul me off. I heard the brief *rah-rah-rah-rah* noise as the Taurus tires bumped over the breakdown lane's skid-resistant grooves, and then the car dipped sharply to my side, and he let go to steer. The wheels caught hold on the soft gravel shoulder, and rolled to a stop.

I struggled with the lock, shoved the door open and tumbled out before the wheels had stopped turning. There was no firm footing, just a broken cable barrier, and past that a whole bunch of down. The ground gave way under my feet, and I found myself rolling down a sharp incline, picking up bruises and twigs as I flattened shrubbery, flew over a log, and finally came to rest, stomach down in the sludge of one of the town's protected heritage wetlands.

For a moment it was enough just to breathe. The door slammed. I heard him walk across the pavement, his boot heels clicking on the asphalt, and then heard the soft scuff of the gravel as he came to the lip of the ravine. There was a long pause. "Anything broken?"

It was tempting to pretend that I was dead, but you can't play possum with a wolf, and just the sound of his deep voice was enough to make my stomach roil. Nothing was broken, but my eyes were burning as if someone had splashed hot pepper juice in them. I pressed the heels of my palms against my watering lids.

"You going to sit there all night?" he asked.

"Go away." Somewhere, I had lost a shoe.

Where were my glasses? Hanging off one ear. I ripped them off, and concentrated on slowing down my breathing while I knuckled sludge off my cheek. Blinking didn't do much for the burning sensation in my eyes, but it made the world look clearer. I felt for the tail of my shirt to clean my glasses. It was wet. Ditto the other tail. After a brief search, I found a clean spot on my sleeve that would do. Once done, I held my glasses up to the night sky, and instead of a blob of goo on one lens, I had made a smear of pond slime on both. I hooked my glasses through Merry's chain.

Trowbridge's voice was damnably cool. "I'm not going anywhere until I get my amulet and some answers."

"Come down and try to get them, you stupid Were."

"I'm on my last pair of clean jeans, so I'll wait for you here." He moved and a pebble of gravel bounced down the hill. "Besides, there's nowhere for you to go but up, Tinker Bell."

My vision surged in and out, which felt kind of nauseating. But he was right. There *was* nowhere to go but up. I was at the bottom of a soup bowl of wetland. All around me was hillside. A thick wedge of bulrushes was behind me, and beyond them, a sharp hill covered by an impossible tangle of wannabe trees. The only feasible place to start climbing my way out was four or five yards to the right of where he was standing. I chose the other way, the one through the dense thicket of bulrushes.

Point of fact: bulrushes don't yield. They sway to the

wind, but they don't bend to the two-footed. One stiff broken end left a bleeding gouge on my cheek, before another's thick ball root caught my toe and tripped me.

"Hurry up, kid," he said. "We haven't put enough distance between us and the bad guys."

"I'm going to kill you when I get to the top," I promised.

"Well, there's something for you to work toward."

The top of the ravine was about three times my height. Not too much of a climb, but the mud-slick slope was steep, and covered in rough growth.

He'd stopped the car right on the edge, and I could make out the long, dark rectangle of the Taurus. Trowbridge was the candlelit ghost figure turning to open the passenger door. A burst of light illuminated the inside of the car as the overhead light kicked in. He sat down sideways, facing me, as the open-door alarm started to ping.

"When I woke up and found you in my bed, you had me stumped for a minute." Trowbridge lifted a foot and jammed it in the door spring. Immediately, the annoying pinging stopped. He slouched in the passenger chair, one leg stretched out toward me, and the other bent at the knee. "Were you a thief who likes to steal amulets? If so, who hired you? You knew about Weres, but weren't one. You wore a Fae amulet, but the last of them died a decade ago. My next guess was witch, but once I got that hoodie off you, I realized you don't have much in the way of a personal scent—"

I don't have any.

"I should have picked up on that before, but I was distracted by the lap dance, the puking, and the bunch of Weres on my tail."

"And you were drunk," I reminded him, jamming my knee in a hollow between a root and a flat rock. I tightened my grip on a root, and heaved myself upward.

"Detail." He paused and then continued. "You pick up aromas that you've been around, but it's all surface stuff. Underneath that, you're virtually scentless. You have the softest, whitest skin I've ever touched. It actually gives off a little *brr* of magic when you stroke it. So, you have to be a fairy." He stretched a glowing hand outside the car. "Is it starting to rain? Yeah, I think it is. I kept going back to the fact that you know about Weres and you're still walking and talking, so I ran my hand over your throat again. You're not full blood, but I can feel your Were answering—"

"You can feel the Were inside me?" I asked, horrified.

"Which makes you a half blood that no one has got around to killing. Considering your personality, that's this side of a miracle."

He can feel her *underneath my skin. Oh, someone just shoot me.*

"You're about the right age. What are you, seventeen? And there's your build. You're small and . . ." He consulted his brain for a suitable word. "Curvy. A short, chubby kid could grow up to look like you. I lifted your eyelids at a stoplight. You've got exceptionally light green eyes—"

"It's too dark to see the color of my eyes."

"Were vision." He pointed to his own baby-blues. "And then I knew. The last time I saw eyes like that, they were staring at me from the face of this little blond-haired kid who was crushing on me. Every time I looked up, there she was, staring right at me. Spooky little kid."

"Why don't you just f—"

"That is when I knew you were one of the Stronghold twins. Hilda? Helga? Hermione?"

I craned my head to glare up at him. He was sitting in Bob's passenger seat, his dark hair shimmering with its bright white halo, his head bent as he buttoned up his shirt. I'd always thought the big reveal would be my personal apocalypse. Instead, he was up there, fussing with his shirt, and I was down here, too far away to give his jaw a good jab.

"So, Helga, when did they open the portal again?"

"No one opened any portal, you smug bastard. I've been right here, living in Deerfield for most of the last ten years. Didn't you ever wonder, just once, what happened to Benjamin Stronghold's kids?"

"I didn't have to. I knew exactly where they were—I saw the Fae carry you through the portal with my own two eyes.

So you want to cut the crap and tell me exactly why they sent you over here? What do the Fae want?"

He'd thought we were already on the other side. He hadn't realized I was locked in the cupboard. The world swam for a bit. I hugged the trunk of a scraggly cedar, and rested my stinging eyes on my arm. All this time, I'd pinned the blame on him. Every time I'd seen kids waiting for a school bus, and known I had to stay in the apartment, I'd held him responsible. It was his fault. If he'd rescued me from the fire, my life would have been different. I don't know why I thought it would have, but I did.

I'd kept the memory of his betrayal festering, feeding it teaspoons of loneliness, mouthfuls of bitterness, and tidbits of self-pity every time the red-hurt began to flag, all because I was so unwilling to let that old grief die. Why? Brooding about the past wouldn't change it. Why couldn't I let it—no, *him*—go?

I gazed upward at him and saw the bright glow of him—the halo of light that deceived my eyes, and knew the truth. If I hated him and held him accountable for every piece of misery in my life, I could dwell on him. Keep the memory of him, beautiful and ten fingered, alive in my mind. Fantasize about the moment when we'd meet again. Why would I dream of even considering forgiving him? Resenting him was better than the fear of emptiness that would follow once I made peace with my losses.

"You still down there?" he asked.

I worked to keep my voice level. "You saw the portal?"

"It was hanging over the pond. Glowing lights. Pink fog. Smelled like flowers."

"Freesias."

"Like I said, flowers." He ran a thumb over the bristles on his chin, irritated. "I saw them carry you across, and then it closed. There was this god-awful sound as it did, like a—"

He *really* had been there. There had been a noise as the gates sealed—a horrifying wall of sound; terrible and frightening. It had been loud enough to be heard over the crackle of the fire eating its way through our kitchen. I'd feared the world was ending, had worried for Lexi ... "You saw my brother! Was Lexi okay?"

Trowbridge said slowly, "Lexi?"

"You didn't see the Fae carry me through the Gates of Merenwyn, you saw my twin, Lexi ..." Just saying Lexi's name out loud caused my throat to thicken. "We used to joke he'd sleep through the end of the world. He was asleep when the Fae broke in; he didn't have time to get to our hiding spot." A lie. There had been time—if his sister had gone and got him when her mother told her to. Goddess, was I even lying to myself now? In my mind's eye I saw my brother as he'd been that night, sweat-faced and defiant. "He didn't go easily—he fought back. I could hear the scuffles ... him cursing them out. They dragged him into the kitchen and then ..." Lexi had seen me hiding in the cupboard; I know he had. But he'd turned his head, and looked away, so they wouldn't know I was in our hidey-hole. "The Fae carried him out of our house, and I haven't seen him since." So inadequate. Such a terrible postscript to the worst night of my life.

I swallowed. "Did he look okay to you? Was he hurt?"

"I don't know whether he was hurt or not, all I could see really was the top of his blond head. One of the Fae had him wrapped up in a blanket. He was conscious though, judging by all the squirming." Trowbridge squinted and cocked his head to one side, obviously replaying the scene in his mind. "He was so little. I thought he was you."

"He was twelve." And small for his age.

"Well, you Fae are pretty small."

The words slipped out, unbidden. "You could have saved him."

"You've got this fixation about me saving people," he said. "There were five of them. All armed. Besides, I was hunting something else." He brooded for a bit, while I paused to stretch my sore calf muscle. "So you've been here all this time. The Fae didn't reopen the gates to Merenwyn?"

"No."

He lifted his nose and took in a long deep breath.

"You're trying to scent a lie, aren't you, Trowbridge? It

doesn't matter if you're standing on two feet, you Weres really are nothing more than—"

"Ah, ah, ah." He shook his head reprovingly. "Don't say something you'll regret."

"How's this, then? You're a total bastard, who has turned out to be a disappointing drunk. I can say that without a shred of regret. So why don't you take in another snootful of air, and test that statement for a lie?"

Merry moved against my chest, showing the first signs of life since she'd clamped herself around her buddy. She disengaged one of her twining stems from the ball to reach for my bra cup. I helped her in, fighting another surge of terrible fatigue. I leaned against a cedar to rub my eyes again. Some hero I was turning out to be. I wanted to just stop it all—smack the pause button on the timer ticking inside my head nattering at me to hurry; Lou was waiting, hurt and frightened. *Move,* I told myself, *you've only got another couple of feet and then you're over the hump. Back on level ground.*

Trowbridge folded his hands over his stomach. "So where have you been all this time?"

"A nice man let me live under his roof."

"Human?" His scent drifted over the lip of the hill, subtly altered—now it was hotter, muskier, somehow speaking of spice and complicated emotions; one of which my Were recognized as a predator's red flag.

"Yes."

"You were what? Seven?" His tone was casual—the type of strained blandness that never really deceives the listener. "There's an oak tree root a little bit farther to your left." He watched me fumble, and then asked, "Did he abuse you?"

I almost laughed. "No."

And just like that, the smoky heat in his scent signature dissipated. "A little more to the left. There. Just follow the roots up to the top. Should be easy enough." He got out of the car and stretched. "Even a nearsighted Fae could do it."

"I'm not nearsighted." I felt for a handhold at the top of the hill.

"Stronghold."

I squinted up at him, and discovered that my vision was almost back to normal, save for the fact that his halo hadn't dimmed. Trowbridge sat on his haunches, gazing down at me with a look that some dim-bulb might think bordered on friendly. "Give me your hand." When I didn't offer it, he reached down, grabbed the collar of my shirt and started hauling me up like I was the piece of luggage with the "heavy load" sticker on it. I was hanging from my collar, suspended from his iron grip. I coughed and spun, and tried to find another toehold.

"Stop wiggling, you're heavier than you look." He grabbed the seat of my pants and hefted me over the lip of the ravine. My feet found the ground, just in time, as the last two buttons holding my shirt together popped off, one after the other. The back of my shirt went over my head and then the rest of the garment peeled off my torso until it came to a wet, wrinkled mess on my forearms.

"Oops," he said, letting go of the collar.

"Oops?" I covered my chest. "I only had one shirt, idiot." I turned my back, lifted my hands, and tried to shimmy-shake the whole sodden mess down the length of my arms.

Trowbridge did a poor-assed job of smothering a snort.

I glared over my shoulder at him. For the first time he resembled the kid I'd had such a crush on. He grinned down at me, his wet hair partially screening his gleaming eyes. There was a bona fide Trowbridge-the-devil smile breaking out on his mouth.

"Turn your back," I said, taking a step sideways.

"Not on your life, kid."

The first attempt to swing the wet, scrunched shirt back over my head was a face-griming disaster. Part of me wanted to stamp my foot and cry. This was *so* not the way I'd planned on meeting Trowbridge again. I was *supposed* to be thin, wearing a kick-ass dress that screamed sex and seduction. Yeah, maybe the style of my gown kept changing in my head—sometimes it was long and body hugging, other times it was skimpy and short with a flirty kick-pleat at the back; but it was always black, and droolworthy sexy. And my hair was wrong—I'd envisioned it as being gloriously blond, not mouse-colored, and wavy, not hanging in limp strands around my flushed face. I'd be wearing a touch of makeup. Definitely no glasses. Plus, I'd *planned* on being in control of the moment—hell, I had clever comebacks worked out for every feeble excuse he summoned. My voice was going to be cool and detached; almost indifferent. My hands were going to be steady as I . . . aw, for Pete's sake—I was *supposed* to have a gun.

You'd think Karma would throw me a bone. I plucked at the rolled shirt, vainly trying to find the end of it.

"As much fun as I'm having watching you, I think you should let me help you." I could hear the smile in his voice. "You're going to have to lift your arms for a sec," he coaxed, coming up behind me. Glumly, I raised my arms and saw his hands over my head, reaching for the shirt. "Better duck your head," he said.

I did.

He rolled the shirt down my arms, and pulled it down across my back. Then his hands smoothed the wrinkled front down my sides. And that's when he stopped breathing. I could tell. He was right behind me, his hands were still on my waist, and he had forgotten to exhale.

What was it? Merry? She was mostly hidden beneath the lace cup on my left boob, with the exception of the tip of one gold leaf peaking through a scallop. My dangling glasses filled in my cleavage.

My boobs had definitely enjoyed reverse gravity and were now very eager to pour themselves into any open palm. There they were, Hedi's twin peaks, eager and nipple-hard, doing the boob equivalent of "look at me, look at me." He let out his breath in a long, slow hiss. I know I'm not Were thin; I know that put beside one of those leggy stick figures, I'm Betty Boop. Or better yet, Betty *Boob*. There'd been no miraculous makeover for me when I hit puberty. I'd gone from butterball round, to round with an exaggerated dip in the middle for my waist, as if someone had taken a ball of dough and squeezed it. My breasts were too large for a girl with short legs. My hips were too padded, and no matter how I tried, I always had a rounded belly, not a flat one.

There was a flush on his cheeks and an arrested quality to his face, as if he'd always been a fan of peanut butter sandwiches, and had only now discovered he preferred his peanut butter with a bit of jam. He reached around—my own breath got caught in my lungs—and tugged my glasses away. Merry's chain hung in a long twisting rope of gold that kissed my cleavage and led to the soft white hill of my breast.

And for the life of me, I forgot where I was. Only for a second or two. Because his eyes, they were . . . smoldering. How could arctic blue blaze like that? Maybe if it was blue steel, and it was heated to the point of melting . . . At that, my Were-bitch placed a paw on my spine. "Let me out," she whined. I silently shook my head. An undisciplined brain will get you into trouble. That's what Lou always said, usually when she was looking right at me. I took a few steps closer to the edge of the ravine, and pulled the edges of my top together into a knot.

"You've ruined my shirt," I muttered.

He stared at me thoughtfully for another moment, before he blinked, and then he was back to being Trowbridge, all irritated Were, who never knew when to give an inch. "I'm standing in everything I have left, thanks to you."

"Not my fault."

"Well, Heloise, it seems to me I was under their pack's radar until you broke into my room to steal my amulet." He slipped my glasses into his shirt pocket.

"You stole the amulet from one of my kind; I simply stole it back."

"I don't need to steal anything. I'm the son of an Alpha, for Christ's sake. It was in the mud by our pond—"

"*Our* pond."

"It was *our* pond." He led with his jaw. "Because every rock, tree, and shrub in that town belonged to the Alpha of Creemore, which made it my dad's pond. Every person who lives in Creemore is a tenant, not a landowner. You kids took over that pond like it was your own personal swimming hole—"

"As if Weres could swim. What good would a swimming hole be to one of the pack?"

"We choose not to swim. Swimming is for Faes and trout."

I limped toward the car.

He followed slowly, hands tucked into his pockets. "Interesting you call yourself Fae when your father was a full-blooded Were. You're part Were. You going to kick that under the carpet?"

He kept pushing, never letting me rest, probing and stirring up things better left sleeping. I paused in my tracks and stared ahead; seeing nothing in that dusk but encroaching darkness and road that twisted its way to a place I had no map for.

"I don't want this thing inside me," I whispered.

"You think you can cut the Were out of yourself? Because I've got to tell you, I've tried and I couldn't do it."

"Tell me, Trowbridge." Merry shifted inside my blouse, one tendril seeking the growing heat collecting at my throat. "Where were your kin the night my father called for help? When he lay dying on our kitchen floor with his guts all torn up, where were they? When the Fae came and executed my mum? Where *were* they? No one came. No one except you . . . and you left us there."

He'd grown still. "You weren't there. It was just your mum and dad . . . I'd have . . . I thought they'd taken you to Merenwyn."

I whirled on him. "I was there, Trowbridge. I *saw* you. Mum had hidden me in the kitchen cupboard—the cream-colored one on the wall right behind you. We used to tease her . . . she called it sacred wood, but it was just some old pine cupboard from a farmhouse kitchen. When the Fae came, she shoved me inside it, and set a ward." I wrapped my arms around my middle, suddenly feeling cold. "It had two sides, and a heart cutout on each door. Our spy holes. But Lexi said he'd grown too big and that he was never going to climb inside that box again." Bitterness climbed to my throat. "You came through the smoke, all bent over, like a hero out of an action movie running through a hailstorm of bullets. Blood all over you. You had your shirt wrapped around your bleeding hand. I thought you'd battled your way through the Fae to get to us."

"I didn't know you were there," he repeated through his teeth.

"Your father was supposed to protect us, and he let them slaughter my parents. He let them take Lexi over to Merenwyn." My anguish was bubbling up, tearing at my control. I flung my hands out in frustration and shouted, "Why would I *ever* want to be a Were?"

He jabbed a finger at me. "You know nothing about my father."

"I know his word was *worth* nothing," I spat back.

Trowbridge didn't speak for a moment. He was still looking at me, but he wasn't seeing me anymore; he was examining something else—something deep inside him, turning it over in his mind as if he were seeing it truly for the first time.

"His word meant *everything*," he said finally, in a deadly soft voice. "He died because of his word. They all died because he got our pack tangled up with the Fae. You know what the price was for protecting your family? My family. My father. My mother. My brother." His mouth twisted and a look of haunting loss swept over his face. "My wife . . . You weren't the only person to lose a family that night."

"Who killed them?"

"I don't know." His eyes were flat. "But the pack thinks I did it."

I hate thinking. I hate remembering; memories are worse than dreams. With dreams, you can be on guard. Vigilant against a sappy moment. But memories are sneaky. They slide into your head when you aren't paying attention. You reach for a can of soup at the supermarket and you remember. The picture was the same—the summation of my heartbreak as witnessed through a heart-shaped hole—Dad's splayed legs, the new smile line cut into Mum's throat, Trowbridge crouched beside her. But now, my treacherous memory added sound. A much younger Trowbridge holding my mum's hand, his voice breaking, as he pleaded, "Who killed them? Just tell me who killed them."

I did the math. He would have been eighteen then. Four years younger than I was now. He didn't kill his family—he'd been searching for their murderer. Probably still was.

I did not want to feel like this—like Merry's chain after a bad night's rest; tangled and knotted.

Trowbridge was silent, his mouth pulled down, as he twisted sideways to fight with the seat mechanism. I studied his right hand: his last two remaining fingers were curved around the steering wheel. The nub finger and one-jointed finger didn't have anything to hold on to. They stuck out. The battered gold ring jammed on the nub on his ring finger caught my eye; I looked away.

Why hadn't he died? He'd married right after graduation. He still wore his wedding ring, even if it was on the wrong hand—how come he wasn't dead if she was? That was part of the mating deal, wasn't it? She dies; you die.

"Would you have left me there if you had seen me?" I asked.

"Of course not. You might have known something about the wolf who murdered my family . . . That's all I wanted. The wolf that killed them. I wanted to rip him apart with my teeth. You weren't even on my radar until I tracked his trail to the Fae portal. Anyone who could lead me to them—"

"Was important to you," I finished. "That's why you tried to pick my mum up and carry her out of the house."

"I didn't realize her throat was cut. I saw the blood, but when she was lying there, with her hair all over her neck, I didn't see the wound."

"So you put her back down again."

"It was too late to save her."

He'd been very gentle. He hadn't shaken and cursed her like he had Dad's body. He'd smoothed her hair back, and attempted to read her lips. When she tried to tell him about us with her eyes, he'd looked over his shoulder, puzzled. His own eyes had been red. Teary red.

"You said a wolf killed your family. How do you know for sure?" I asked him.

"From the wounds and his tracks," Trowbridge said. "I woke up maybe fifteen minutes after he ambushed me. My hand was hurting, and there was blood everywhere." He gazed ahead into the dark night, his eyes hooded. "That's all it took. Fifteen minutes. Dad's body was in the living room, on the floor by his chair. My brother's was on the stairs." He slowly shook his head. "There's no way a strange wolf should have got the drop on either of them. Not unless he was some-one they knew and trusted . . . I tried to find the wolf's scent, and that's when I realized . . . the bastard hadn't left one." He slanted his eyes toward me. Fierce, blue. "It's impossible. Ev-erything has a scent."

Except me, I thought. *Or a Were who'd visited Merenwyn.*

"The bastard used my own blood to frame me. There was some of it in the hall, on the stairwell, on my brother's face . . . One day, I'll hurt him for what he did to them." A horrible smile, white teeth against the dark night. It faded slowly. "He planted my fingers under my brother's body and upstairs . . ." A pause during which he stared blindly at the gearshift. Then he continued, his voice a monotone. "I picked up his tracks outside the house, but the trail died out on the side road—too much gravel—so I backtracked them to the fairy pond. What's the name of that flower?"

"Freesias," I said softly.

"You couldn't even smell the pond over it. I counted five fairies crossing back to their own side. Two of them had a Stronghold kid between them. As soon as they were through, I went down there. The fairy portal was still floating over the water . . . I'd thought I'd seen a lot of shit in life, but nothing like that. I couldn't find any more tracks from the wolf; his prints seemed to start at the water." He inclined his head to-ward me. "I found yours and your dad's there too. A minute later, I found the Fae amulet caught in some bushes nearby. Then I saw the flames shooting out of your window."

He lapsed into a brooding silence.

I shivered. Trowbridge reached for the heater control and turned it to high. A tear dribbled down my cheek.

He turned the key in the ignition. "Do not start crying. The time for that is long gone."

"I'm not crying; my eyes are burning again."

"Here." He tossed my glasses in my lap.

I started looking over my clothing for a dry spot.

Trowbridge glanced sideways at me. Then his lips thinned. In what? Frustration? Exasperation? "Jesus," he snapped, jerking the gearshift back to neutral. He took my glasses out of my hands, pulled up a corner of his shirt, and started cleaning them.

"I'm twenty-two, not seventeen," I protested.

He rubbed the lens harder, gave it one last polishing swipe before passing my glasses back to me. His skin brushed mine as I reached for them.

And then I flared. *Oh Sweet Stars, no, not him. Not now.*

"Shit," he said. "Your eyes."

Instinctively, I slapped my hands back over them.

"They're glowing green," he said in awe. "I can see it right through your fingers."

Yes, of course my eyes were glowing green. I'd waited all my life for my first flare—that pivotal moment in life when everything shifts, and you accept the full weight of your destiny. For some Fae of noble birth, it happened when their magical talent kicked into high gear, for others their flare sparked at the sight of the child, the grandchild . . . their lover. It was that instant in time when you realized your one true thing—the thing you were born to do. I had flared. I'd finally done it, and the bright light beaming from my eyes wasn't Mum's cerulean blue, nor even Alpha-dog blue. I lowered my hands. Oh Fae Stars, the inside of the whole car was lit neon green.

"Only Alphas have the flare," he said slowly.

"Well, as it happens, so do Faes, born of royal blood." I turned to him. "I am Fae. See me flare."

As soon as my eyes locked on his, an answering white-blue flame deep within his eyes sparked to life. Wicked light, seductive and abrasive. *Yield,* it demanded. I stretched my eyes open, and held them wide, resisting the gut-deep urge to let my gaze drop before his.

I'd wasted too many hours coming up with words to describe just what shade of blue his eyes were. Mediterranean blue is how I remembered them. Deep set. Surrounded by a thick ring of stubby black eyelashes. They weren't Mediterranean blue; they were Trowbridge blue. Right now, they were lit with the Alpha-blue flame of his blood kin, and were beyond my ability to describe.

A stupid exercise, description. It's a memory game for a yearning, dreaming heart. It's something you play, waiting for a light to change, trying to find the right word, as if that would somehow return you to that moment, help you live that feeling again. Maybe one day, I'd go back to finding the right word, but right then, caught in the heart trap of pure feeling, I was only aware of what the blue flame in his eyes meant to me. It was power, it was desire, it was a fight and a promise.

It was everything.

My gaze dropped.

Chapter Nine

"Do all Faes have the flare or just some?"

"Don't say that," I said sharply. "Don't use the term 'the flare.' It's a very personal thing to a Fae. It's wrong to hear a Were say it. Just wrong."

He'd taken my chin in his fingers to examine my eyes. They'd stopped burning, and I was fairly sure that they'd stopped flaring because the interior of the car was dark again. Trowbridge had lines around his eyes, and a blue vein under his skin, right on the top of his cheekbone. That's the sort of stuff you wouldn't normally see in the dark. My eyesight seemed keener than before.

"Put your glasses on," he told me, putting the car into drive.

"Where are we going?"

"Toronto." He glanced at his side-view mirror. "It's damn hard to track anything in the city. Not impossible, but it will take them some time and a lot more trackers to find us."

"I don't want to go to Toronto." Maybe it wasn't so bad. Maybe I flared because he was *part* of my destiny; not my "one true thing"? Perhaps he'd been sent by the Goddess of Fate to help me find Lou? I tested the thought, feeling a little relieved. Surely, rescuing a fairy princess had to fall under the title "Great Destiny Options for You"?

"You don't have a choice." He hit the accelerator and the

back wheels spun on the gravel, shooting up a spray behind us.

He drove well, but too fast. It made my Were-bitch restless. I kept changing positions in my seat as she squirmed inside me. Trowbridge rolled down the windows and turned off the heat, which cheered my Were. Her general-doggie-happiness sent goose bumps popping up on my arm. There were other physical differences. My spell-casting hand wasn't crispy, and it should have been, considering I had propelled a commercial washing machine across the floor. My fingers felt fat and sore, but not sausage-fat and third-degree-burn sore. More like the sore you got when your hands froze slightly, when the blood came back. I held them to my nose. Definitely no scent of recent charring. No scent at all, except swamp, and the lingering woods-and-whiskey scent of Trowbridge still marking my hands.

I'd released my inner Were, and she was making herself known. Healing me, while Merry was busy cuddling up to her boyfriend. But for my Were, life was all good, right? Open window, open road. Prime mate material by her side. Free at last. There was a flutter, a stretch, low in my belly as the Were-bitch tested the walls again.

I turned sharply to him. "You said that my Were 'answered.' That means you called it. Stop calling my Were."

"Trust me, I'm not calling your Were." His voice was clipped, but a smile played at the corner of his lips. "Weres don't call to Faes. And by the way, that's a personal thing, 'answering the call,'" he drawled. "It just feels wrong to hear a Fae say it."

That's an Alpha thing, isn't it? Calling to the Were?

I touched Merry, and then jerked my hand away. Wrapped around the other amulet, she was twice her usual size, and foreign feeling, contaminated by the heavy, dead weight of the other amulet. The other didn't have her suppleness, or the intelligence that I always sensed when I held her. I don't know how she could stand being twined around it, her stone pressed hard to its center. Was she so lonely for her own kind that she was willing to spoon with a corpse?

* * *

The highway was better lit. I could see every nuance of expression on Trowbridge's face. "Tell me about the Treaty of Brelland."

He turned to me sharply. "How do you know about the Treaty?"

"That's what the Fae said before he executed my mother," I said. " 'Roselyn of the house of DeLoren, we have found you guilty of breaking the Treaty of Brelland.' "

Trowbridge shot me a look out of the corner of his eye. "So she was in on it. She took a Were to Merenwyn."

"My mother would never have done anything to endanger us. We meant everything to her."

He didn't appear convinced about that. Silence filled the car, except for the windshield wipers slapping away at the rain. He merged into traffic, encouraging a less confident driver into yielding. "It's a treaty written hundreds of years before you and I were ever born," he explained. "In the beginning, the Weres and Fae shared the same realm."

"Here or in Merenwyn?" *Weres once lived in the Fae realm?*

"Merenwyn," he replied. "They'd been fighting for God knows how many generations. Blood was being spilled by both sides; a lot of it—to the point where more people were being killed than being born. Then it stopped being a race war, and became an economic issue. Declining population meant less people to work the fields. So, the two sides brokered a deal. Three of the four kin packs negotiated with the Fae for safe passage to this world. In exchange, no Were from those packs, or any of their succeeding generations, would be able to use the portals to pass back to the Fae realm. To back that up, the Alpha of each gave a blood sample, which the mages used to alter the portal's magic. From that day on, so the story goes, no Were could either call or cross the Gates of Merenwyn. But something changed. Ten years ago, a Were did pass through the portal, and after he'd butchered my family, he was able to change into his mortal shape, and melt away." His eyes narrowed to little squints. "One day I'll find him."

"Why didn't the Creemore pack hear the portal open?" I said. "Why didn't they feel the earth tremble?"

"That confused me. They should have sensed the passing of the Alpha, before that . . . I tried to use my phone to call for help, but it wouldn't work. I sent up a howl, but no one came. It was like I was inside a bubble that broke once I left the property. The only logical explanation for that was someone had set wards. Around the pond, and your family's place." He shot me a speculative look. "Someone with some magic."

"It wasn't my mother, Trowbridge."

"Weres can't open a portal on their own and they don't have the magic to set wards. So who set a protection spell around the Alpha's house and the pond? It wasn't a mage or a witch. I would have scented that. It needed to be a Fae familiar with the pack. There was only one Fae woman who fit that bill."

"It wasn't my mother," I repeated hotly. "Don't blame her or the Fae for it, Trowbridge. It wasn't just any wolf that came through the portal. It was one of yours."

His skin released a surge of angry Were musk. It filled the car and tickled the hairs on the back of my neck. "Explain," he bit out.

I told him about seeing the wolf come through the portal. About the confrontation on the beach. About the scentless Wolf running up the hill toward the Trowbridge house. About Dad dying and Mum being executed. I used small words and no adjectives. I didn't cry.

"Why didn't your dad *just shoot* him? Just pull the fucking trigger when the wolf leaped through the portal?"

"He was a friend."

"What was his name?" His voice was low, focused.

"I don't know." I lifted my shoulder. "But I'd seen that wolf before. Sometimes he'd come during the moon time. He'd stand at the edge of the forest and wait for Dad. Not very often. But some moon runs he would wait for Dad." I rubbed the mud off my hand onto my thigh. "I don't think he was supposed to run with my father. Just a feeling. My dad would never answer any questions about the pack."

"But you saw him. Describe him to me."

"He was gray. Big." I made a helpless gesture in the air. "He had a white streak in his fur."

"Where?"

"On his shoulder. High across a shoulder." I brought to mind the image of the wolf, waiting for Dad, at the forest's edge. "His left shoulder."

Trowbridge grew so still, that even the air around him seemed to freeze.

"You know him." I sat up tall in the seat. "Tell me his name."

He was studying his hands on the wheel, all the skin on his face so tight that those fine lines became slashes. Then he shook his head, once, and then once again, both times so slowly, I could have said, "What? What?" but I was afraid to break the silence. Afraid to move. He kept driving, sitting right beside me but a universe apart from me as he worked something out in his head.

With dull eyes, I watched the cars as we passed them. All those unknowing drivers heading for their destinations, all so unaware of what can happen in just a few minutes. There are no guarantees in life. None at all. My head felt like someone had split it down the middle with an axe.

My ride-along companions weren't happy either. Were-bitch had finally stopped moving, but she kept dribbling more anxiety into the stress pool I had swelling in my gut. And Merry kept moving, back and forth, rubbing a tendril along my skin, like I was the dry twig, and she was the person intent on starting a fire. I knew she was hungry. I touched her with a finger, grimacing as I felt the hard, cold metal of the other amulet entwined with her own gold. *I will find you food soon,* I silently promised. She wrapped a tendril around my thumb, and I felt a burst of warmth, a feeling of almost comfort.

My eyelids suddenly felt heavy.

"You know what you should do when a whole pack of Weres are after you?" he asked, startling me out of a near-doze. "Run. Just keep chewing up the miles until you're out of their territory." He glanced in the rearview mirror an instant before maneuvering out and around a slower-moving vehicle. "Do you have any friends? Friends from out of town? Casual ones, ones that you haven't mentioned to anyone around here?"

"Why?"

"They're going to be searching for people who know you and places you frequent. They're probably at your apartment right now, going through everything you own. They'll look at every piece of paper, smell every sweater, interrogate neighbors, run down people you worked with. They'll search until they find you or you're out of their territory. Their Alpha is strong and motivated, and he's got a lot of foot soldiers." A muscle moved in his cheek. "He's got some excellent trackers." He glanced at me, quickly, his eyes a flash of that crazy bright blue under a fringe of black, before returning his gaze back to the road.

"But he won't go beyond his territory," he continued. "Not now. It's too hot out there for him. So, this is what you need to do. You need to give him what he wants, and make tracks. FedEx your amulet to Creemore. Then get out of the province. Or even better, out of the country."

They'll interrogate your neighbors. *Bob.* I fumbled for Scawens's cell phone.

"What are you doing?"

"I have to warn Bob," I said, fitting the battery back inside the phone. "I have to tell him to not go back to the store."

"Put the phone away. They've likely already found him," he said. "You have to think of yourself as a Rogue now. Just cut the ties. If your friend's still alive, calling him may put him in more jeopardy." His musk was an invisible pungent cloud around us that sharpened and grew hotter with every word he spoke. "If you care about him, the kindest thing you can do is head in the other direction and never look back."

I ignored him and started punching in the store's number. His hand whipped out, and crushed mine on the phone. "Turn it off," he said, "and take the battery out of it. They can track you through the GPS."

I gaped at him, momentarily speechless. Then I took the cell apart, shaking my head as I did so. "This is beyond paranoid."

"You want to call the guy? Fine. I'll find you a pay phone, but don't you use that phone until you're miles away from me." He glanced over his shoulder, cut into the slow lane, and took the next exit off the highway. To the right was the suburban sprawl of Mississauga: miles of curling residential streets all sucking you into a labyrinth of more curling streets. To the left was the industrial park, low flat buildings squatting in the dark.

He turned left.

Chapter Ten

He had a nose, all right. He'd driven us, tight-lipped and brooding, through the dark streets of the industrial park and found me a phone.

"A strip club?" I eyed the sign mounted over the doorway of what could have been a mom and pop restaurant except for the fact that there were no visible windows. The blue and pink sign flickered and the words "girls, girls, girls" were replaced by three images. What bright bulb had thought up three strippers posing in a martini glass?

"It's a gift," Trowbridge said, pulling the car into a parking spot. "It doesn't matter where I am, I can always find a drink when I need one. It's not the Ritz, but my options are limited." He pulled his shirt away from his body and inspected it. The sleeve had a hole in it, and a long darkened patch where the blood had stained his gray shirt dark maroon. "I've got an hour before closing time, and I need a drink," he said, ripping the sleeve off. He wadded it up and scrubbed the dried blood off his bicep. His skin had healed. There was just a suggestion of pink where the bullet had torn his flesh.

"I'm not going in there."

"I didn't invite you." He tore the other sleeve off and frowned at the result. He wound a finger around some of the threads and broke them off. "There's your pay phone." He

jerked his thumb at the curb. "And this is as good a place as
any to part company."

The Taurus subsided with a grateful rattle. During the
silence that followed, I counted the beats of the song playing
inside the club. There were no discernible lyrics. Just thumping bass.

"Are you going to kill the scentless wolf?"

His voice was hard as whip. "Kid, a platoon of Rogues
wouldn't stand a chance getting close enough to kill him."

"Then I'll kill him. Tell me his name."

"You listen to me." He looked at the blue and pink neon
sign blinking over the door. "You don't need to know his
name. You forget all about him. You don't stand a chance of
pulling it off. Do you understand? You'd be dead three seconds after thinking it." He released his breath, slow and con-
trolled. "Forget about revenge. Right now, you have other
problems. The Alpha of southern Ontario wants that amulet.
He's a powerful man, and he's a stone-cold murderer. Don't
ever mistake him for anything else." He darted a glance at
me. "You're such a kid." He scowled at his hand on the wheel.
"For once, don't be a stubborn little girl."

"I'm not a little girl."

"Then behave like an adult." He was all sharp cheekbones and forced calm. "Think it through. Find a box, put
your amulet in it, and send it express to the Scawens family
in Creemore. It will find its way to the Alpha after that."

The club's blinking neon sign painted a wash of color
across his knuckles. It kept changing, now hot pink, now
electric blue. Would I ever understand this man? "Don't you
want to avenge your family?"

Trowbridge slowly tilted his head toward me—ear up,
head hanging to one side. A strand of his black hair swept
over his brow to shadow his eyes but within them I saw a
spark of blue fire. The flare was gone as fast as it appeared,
and then his eyes were dark, and perhaps a little sad that I was
still so young and dumb that I needed to pose such a question.

"Will it bring them back?" he asked quietly.

Maybe it was that all-knowing superiority that pissed me

off, maybe it was his patent indifference. I searched for a pointed stick and poked him with it. "What about Candy?"

Suddenly all the oxygen went out of the car, as if he'd inhaled it all, and processed it through his hot lungs, and thrown it back to me, except now the air was stinking of fury and some sort of sodden, mixed-up emotional mess that I couldn't understand other than its added weight made the air somehow heavier, and it hurt my ribs to suck it in.

"You don't speak her name," he said, through clenched teeth. There was a pause. A pit opened between us, and things fell into it. Things I wouldn't put a name to, but recognized so well. "You don't ever mention her name again."

He shoved the door open with his foot. Clean air spilled into the car. "I need my amulet now."

Merry was listening. Her temperature changed from cool to lukewarm. She was tired, I realized, touching her. Tired and hurting and something else. I closed my eyes, shutting Trowbridge out for a moment, and tried to search for it. Still desperate.

"I can't do that," I said, staring ahead. I wanted to remember him as he was in my mind. Buttoning up his shirt. Looking at me with lust in his eyes, and caution in his heart. I could remember that. Treasure it. Pull it out when the humans overwhelmed me. Examine it in the years that stretched in front of me . . . if I was lucky enough to live through the next few hours.

"Can't or won't?"

I stared sightlessly at the glove compartment. "Both."

"I can take it off your neck right now."

"Yes. You could try." The air inside the Taurus suddenly felt heavy, charged like the atmosphere before a thunderstorm. "But I don't think the two amulets will come apart."

"Try it anyhow."

"I didn't put them together. It happened when I put your amulet around my neck. This—" I went to touch Merry, but drew back my hand at the last second. "This is something I don't understand. I didn't glue them together." The heavy air was moving; I could feel it, prickles on my skin.

"Try."

"No," I said softly. Inside the car, the air got hotter, more layered with Were. It smelled like a wild, unmapped forest, before the crackle of the storm. Trowbridge gave an exasperated huff, and reached out for them. He flipped the pendant over, found a piece of the dead amulet sticking out and tried to tug it free.

Merry sent a lightning bolt of pain up the chain that circled my throat. My feet shot straight out and my head snapped back. The long thin trail of my cry ended in a whimper. The air still swirled. It wrapped around me, and felt almost soothing to my hurt.

Blue light flared in the car, and then subsided.

"Explain that," he said, when my breathing had returned to normal. His hand hovered near me, as if he wanted to touch me, but was afraid to hurt me further.

"She's Fae. She was just protecting herself." I cupped a trembling hand over Merry and company. "You're a Were, you can understand the need to protect what you have. She's incapable of beginning a fight, okay? She's not a threat, she's not prey. You wouldn't blame a rabbit for snapping its teeth at you as you bit down, would you?"

My eyes started to burn. "She'll die without me," I said, my voice getting high. "If you take her away, she'll fade away just like your amulet did. I feed her and take care of her. In return, she heals me after I've used my gift."

The air kept moving, but now it was stroking me, confusing me with each soft brush.

His voice was low. "You need healing after you use your magic?"

"Mmm-hhm," I said, looking down at my hand.

I heard his hair brush his collar as he cocked his head toward me. "You know I can tell when you're lying. I can hear when your heart changes. So I'm going to ask you some questions and you're going to try very hard to tell me the truth. How much Fae magic do you have?"

"Not much," I said. *Except that I keep receiving my aunt's dreams, and it's beginning to look like I'd pass any myst-*

walker exam with flying colors. His eyes penetrated mine. I willed my heart to slow. "Almost nothing," I lied. "If you're talking in terms of a real Fae. I'm limited to moving things. I've tried to do other stuff—mind magic and climate stuff— but I've never been able to do anything else. I think the Were blood in me keeps me from doing anything really great." I knew my smile was bitter.

He didn't smile. He didn't blink. He kept staring at me.

Ah, a loophole. Trowbridge can sense a lie, but not an omission.

"You saw me move the washing machine," I continued. "That's it. I can move a washing machine. It's the biggest thing I've ever moved. I couldn't even move the couch back at the apartment when Scawens attacked me. I had to use the television to stop him." The little line in between his eyebrows turned into a furrow. "I used my magic to make it fly through the air. Smacked him in the head with it. Down he went." And then, when that didn't satisfy him, I said in a little voice, "What?"

"Scawens attacked you in your home?"

I nodded.

"What did he want?"

"An amulet. He thought Merry was yours." I took my hand away and looked at the heavy knot of Fae gold resting on my heart. "I told him no Fae amulet will ever work for a Were. Do you think that was enough?"

"Maybe it will work for a Fae girl who works for a Were," he said slowly.

"I'll never work for a Were, Trowbridge. Not one of them lifted a finger as my father fought for his life." I kept my gaze fixed on the chain-link fence ahead. Damned if he'd see the hurt in my eyes. "And I told you. I'm not really skilled. I'm pretty limited. Until today, I've never used it for any serious harm. You don't want to screw up your Karma."

"Karma concerns from a Fae."

"It's all around you, Trowbridge. You've got to pay attention to it."

"That's all you can do, then? Move things?"

I nodded again, feeling the heat in my cheeks.

"How about my amulet?" he asked. "Can you use its magic?"

"It doesn't have any. I don't know how you stood wearing it around your neck all these years. Even when it brushes my skin, I can feel its—" I tried not to shudder, but the acid was in my mouth again. "Deadness."

The air changed again. Hot, but not in a good way. It lifted his scent and spread it on every surface in a thick, hot layer. I rubbed my hand against my leg and still felt the clinging tingle of it.

"I can't separate the amulets. If you take yours back, you'll take Merry with it."

"You call it Merry."

"I call *her* Merry."

He must have heard the words not said—the sisterhood; the unbreakable twining plait of dependency, love, and friendship I held for Merry. The windshield wipers kept swiping at the rain, never catching that spot in the middle. "Fuck it," he said to himself, staring ahead as if he saw something there that I couldn't. He bit the inside of his cheek. Once. Just a brief, meditative snack before action. "It doesn't matter," he said in a hard voice. "They're all dead. Keep the amulet. It never did much for me. Consider it a gift from a Were Rogue to a new Fae Rogue. If you can figure out a way to separate them, then you can use it instead of"—he glanced down at her—"*Merry*. Listen to me carefully," he went on. "You have the car. Drive it until there's no gas, and then ditch it somewhere no one can find it. The gun I took off Scawens is under the seat. Make sure you turn the safety off before you point it at anyone. If you do have to aim it at someone, pull the trigger. Don't squeeze the trigger until they're close enough that you can't miss."

"I've never held a gun."

"There's always a first time." He rolled his window back up. "Do you have some money on you? Enough to get out of town with?" When I nodded, he continued. "It's probably not worth telling you this again, but the smartest thing would be to put the car into gear right now and keep going." His tone was flat, carefully washed of any expression. "Don't call your friend. *Forget him*. Keep moving, that's the key for the first few months."

"I won't be here when you come back."

"That's what I'm counting on. Are you still going to call your boyfriend?" His cold eyes measured mine. When he read the answer there, he tossed his head, the way men do, with their chins, not their hair. "Never let me stand in the way of true love. Go ahead. Call Billy-Bob. Tell him to run." He leaned back to dig into his pocket and came out with a handful of change. "Here." He put a couple of coins into my hand. "Take my fifty cents."

I stared at the coins. They were dull, old, and had probably crossed too many hands to count. Trowbridge escorted me to the pay phone, and waited until I lifted the receiver off its cradle. He watched me, expressionless, as I pushed the coins into the slot. When the change fell and the phone chimed, he turned toward the club.

"Their Alpha wants the amulet to open the portal," I called after him. "You know that, don't you? He wants to send someone to the other side. I won't help him, but he'll keep on searching for a way. Do you know what will happen if he ever finds one?" I thought of the terrible cold fury marking the Fae executioner's face as he drew a line across my mother's throat. "It will be war if he finds a way. You should warn the other Weres about him."

"Your concern is duly noted." He looked over his shoulder at me. I could see the laugh line where it curved up past the whiskers on his face, stopping short of his eyes. "But it's not going to happen, is it? None of us are in any danger as long as the portal is closed."

"The whole world is falling apart," I heard myself say.

"It fell apart a long time ago. There's no going back," he said.

He was still close enough that if I reached for him, I could have put my hand over his heart and felt the blood surge in and out of it. "The portal is closed?" he asked. I nodded. He tilted his head and searched my face. His fingers touched my jaw and then slid down to my throat, where my pulse beat. "And you can't open it?"

I shook my head, feeling nothing more than the heat of his knuckles against my throat. Nothing else. Not the rain. Not the sadness uncoiling like a worm.

"You don't know anyone who can?"

"No."

His eyes were slits as they studied mine. No glow, no gleam, just Mediterranean blue studying cool green. Then a door snapped shut between us that I hadn't even realized had been open.

"So, no problem," he said.

"What kind of man are you?"

"I don't know. Maybe the answer will come to me over my second Jack." He gave me a smile that wasn't one.

"You're not the guy I thought you were."

"Nobody ever is," he said, turning away again.

"Bridge," I called.

He held up a staying hand, but didn't turn back. He pulled open the door to the strip club. The music swelled, and he walked out of my life for the second time: it was only after the door closed behind him that I realized I should have pulled out the gun.

Chapter Eleven

The rap artist knew what he liked—big butts. A round thing in his face apparently made him "sprung." It was hard to hear the lyrics over the pounding bass streaming from the club, but I got that. *Baby better have back.* I hunched my shoulders against the sudden cold. The rapper chanted on, each word spitting out the same message over a driving beat. Lust. Sex. Satisfaction. A simple enough equation. I wonder if the floor vibrated with it—if the tremor wicked right up the chair legs so that men felt it while they watched the girls who moved to the music and sprang things with their big, round bums.

I called the shop and got the answering machine. "Lou and I have stolen money from some drug lords," I said. "They'll be looking for anyone who knows us." I thought about what else I wanted to say, but the words dried up, and so I finished with, "I'll leave Bob's car somewhere the cops can find it." Someone picked up. I listened to their breathing, and then carefully replaced the receiver in its cradle.

Humans are more afraid of each other than the big bad wolf.

Stupid mortals.

The rain had gone to bed. All that was left was the smell of it, and the water beading up on the windshields of the vehicles in the lot. As I reached the Taurus, the door to the club opened. I spun around, ready to say something snappy like "Hah!" but the man exiting the bar wasn't Trowbridge.

The club patron stood for a moment, holding the door open, waiting for his eyes to adjust, or maybe just hating the thought of leaving. He was around forty, with a fat-blurred jock build that was starting to sag, and a certain vanity to his clothing and jewelry choices. He started for the cars, thought better, and detoured for the laneway. He unzipped his pants.

A thin stream of urine hit the bricks.

He shook it, zipped up, and went back to his car. Before he drove away, he checked the mirror and smoothed his hair. I stood, one foot in the Taurus, and watched until his taillights grew small, wondering if I was invisible, or just a witness to a future that pained me to think of.

My Were-bitch's anxiety brought a metal taste to my mouth.

I forced myself into the car. Trowbridge had left his mark there, adjusting the seat way back to fit his long legs. I hung on to the steering wheel as I felt for the handle. The second I touched it, the seat ratcheted backward another notch. *Damn Were and his stupid long legs.* I grimaced, and fought with the seat mechanism until my toes were comfortable on the gas pedal. I fixed the side mirror; checked the rearview one too. All I had to do was decide on a direction and turn the key.

But first, I had to come up with a plan for a Lou swap that didn't include offering my head as a bonus. The original concept of a "here you go" trade seemed wildly naïve now. Stone-cold killer, Trowbridge had said.

"Merry," I murmured. "I don't know what to do."

I rubbed the back of my neck and felt Merry's chain roll under my fingers. She was a heavier burden now, what with the dead amulet stuck to her. She'd found a place under the damp knot I'd tied under my boobs with my shirttails, having been forced to give up on her usual comfort spot in the left cup of my bra. Merry, I was okay with. Anytime, sister, cuddle in. But when she kept trying to drag the other amulet up toward that warm sanctuary? I'd pushed her away.

I brooded down at the lump that was Merry and "it." I gave a polite jiggle. "Can we talk?" Instead of emerging for a parlay, she huddled deeper under the scant warmth of the knot, tightening around it—him?—with another sinuous twist of her gold. Which, considering the fact that I was sitting in a station wagon outside of a strip club, listening to grind music and hoping the door would open again, just felt a tad insensitive on her part.

I jerked her out by her chain.

She brought him with her. The love-melded clump of the two of them bounced off my knuckles and slid with a rasp to the bottom of her chain. And there they spun, slowly, first his foreign side, then hers, then his. She surrounded him like a lover or a mother, or maybe a shroud—God knows which—but Merry was cleaved to him like she'd never let go. Stuck willingly. Obstinately. And for my sake, I hoped, bloody well not-everlastingly.

I stroked her with the tip of my finger, while I considered the bit of him exposed beneath her twined tendrils. His gem was surrounded by a fretwork of gold. I ran my thumb over its cool surface. The dead amulet was a he. No doubt in my mind now that I'd actually made a point of touching him. He might be pretty, but he was a male Asrai. Even his chain felt masculine. I flicked on the overhead light and took a good look. There was a faint similarity to the design between them, but a huge gap in execution.

Merry screamed knockoff while he purred designer goods. A disloyal thought, but, screw it, his chain was nicer. It was thicker, heavier, with doubled-worked links, giving it additional depth that spoke of money. Real money. As a rule, I approved of Merry's over-the-top styling. Nobody believed she was any more genuine than the two point five carat diamond on the grocery checker's hand, and that worked for us as we tried to stay under the radar. But this male amulet could never go undercover. His chain had a presence, an obvious, supple density that hers didn't, and there was no Woolworth's to him at all. And that was just his *chain*. How had Trowbridge hidden him all these years?

"Who is he, Merry?" I twisted the clump around so that I could examine him closer.

I felt my mouth drop open.

Okay, I knew that his center was blue—light blue from the photo—but colors are off in photos and really off on cell phone screens. I held my fist up closer to the overhead light, careful not to let him brush my knuckles again. His stone was icy blue. Pricey blue. Even in the dim light available, I could see that this wasn't a piece of amber, polished up for the pretty; this was a jewel, cut to make it sparkle. Set carefully in a piece of Celtic artwork. This guy was the real goods. Which made me wonder, what was Merry?

What would he do if I touched his center? I swiped my thumb over his heart. The blue gem didn't change color. Or heat or cool. Lifeless. Defenseless except for Merry, who was already stretching herself impossibly thinner in a futile attempt to keep my fingers off him. Merry gave off a warning burgundy flash. Crap. She couldn't even summon up enough energy to spark vermilion.

"Okay." I placed them so that she rested against my heart. "I'll leave him alone." He would be easy enough to give to the Alpha if I could find a way to chip him loose.

That thought started a string of maybes. Maybe there *was* another Fae in this realm—someone who'd let a Were take a paddle in the Fae Pool of Life. Maybe Lou was just a backup plan—a spectacularly weak one. Maybe this mystery Fae would make a trade of my aunt for Trowbridge's amulet. One corpse for an almost-corpse. Harsh words, even said quietly in my head. But that was the truth, wasn't it? People comfortable with deception recognize truth more often than those who never fib. We have to, so we don't trip over it as we lay down another layer of lies.

Lou was actively dying, fading at a spectacular speed, gone within a couple of months unless I found a way of healing her. There were no books for that—no titles in Bob's bookstore that read *Save Your Fae* or *A Guide to Better Health Among the Paranormal*. I'd checked with the witches: a bunch of mumbling losers right up there with the tree huggers. I'd spent some time in the graveyard, searching for answers. The spirits that didn't run were bores, and the ones that did were incredibly nimble. I'd come away from each expedition with diddlysquat, and so I'd watched, and quietly noted every change of Lou's downward spiral over the last nine months. Now I waited, and wondered how long, and sometimes, when all I could think of was me-me-me, I prayed that when she left, I'd wither as fast as she had.

She was going to die in this realm sooner or later. And at this rate, probably sooner. It would be easier this way. I could do what Trowbridge said: drive until the Taurus had no gas. *With a quarter of a tank left, I won't get far.* I snaked my hand down to the bottom of my backpack and pulled out my brown envelope and put the bills on the seat beside me. Six fives. Two tens. Two twenties. Grand total: ninety dollars. That was all that was left of my doomsday fund.

Doomsday had come.

I'll have to sell a Tear from Mum's bride belt when the money runs out.

Surely it hadn't come to that.

I stared at the needle on the gas gauge and pictured my life in the days ahead. Me sitting behind the wheel of Bob's Taurus, driving along the long, flat ribbon of the Trans-Canada Highway. The old wagon vibrating every time the speedometer hit sixty. Nothing in the seat beside me except the litter of old takeout meals. Merry and her boyfriend grafted into an unbreakable lump, a suddenly heavy and foreign burden between my breasts. Fear behind me, choices in front of me, loneliness a spreading pool all around me. Knowing nothing about my future except the fact that I'd be spending it alone. Always on guard against that casual human touch. Eating by myself while eavesdropping on the conversations around me. Making stories in my head about those people's lives and futures as I drove on through the night.

Half of me would always be waiting for the Weres.

Could I stand living like that? Or would I run out of gas like the Taurus? Find a town on the road to wait until they came to put me out of my misery?

I picked at the stitching on the steering wheel cover.

Maybe I could find a good place to hide. Somewhere they'd never think to find me.

A quarter inch of graying thread hung from the line of stitches. I tugged it, and it slipped through my fingers.

It would mean another cautious life. Holding myself in check until the inevitable explosion. And then I'd have to travel again, and find another place . . . not quite running, but something that felt close to it. Scurrying with my breath held, chin tucked in, eyes always scanning my surroundings. I knew that hunted feeling; it had been my constant companion the first dreadful year after the fire. Even after we'd settled in Deerfield and I'd relaxed into my life somewhat, there'd always been that residual tight sensation in my chest, as if Creemore's air were still stuck deep in my lungs. I'd been holding on to it for . . . forever. All this time, waiting for permission to exhale.

Ridiculous. I wasn't accountable to anyone anymore. No one except myself, and maybe some knee-jerk reaction to the crumbling honor codes Mum and Dad had woven into me when I was a kid. Courage, valor, and family all rolled up in one motto: Strongholds hold. They don't give up. They don't run. They don't relinquish.

I'm not much of a Stronghold. Given a choice, I ran.

But if I did a runner this time, Lou would die among Weres, frightened and defenseless, and I'd spend the rest of my life looking over my shoulder, worrying. Eventually, I'd die too. Maybe tomorrow, maybe in fifty years. Alone for as long as it took with nothing more than an amulet who seemed strangely fixated on the corpse of another amulet.

The knot in my throat swelled until it became a bulge around all the stuff I kept swallowing down.

So. No running this time.

Problem one: I didn't even know where to find Lou. None of her dreams had given me a solid clue, and it wasn't like we could converse when she was dreaming; I was just a receptor to dreams—the earpiece without the mouthpiece.

She could be dead already; she hadn't shared a dream in hours. No way to check unless—*Oh my.*

No way to check unless I went to Threall.

I'd broken my pledge—*"I swear, Mum, I'll never go to Threall"*—twice, both times quite deliberately. The first time the very same day Mum pried the promise out of me. The second had been less than a year later. It had been a bad day, followed by a worse night. I'd hit my bed knowing two things: Lou was never going to open a portal and I was never going to speak to my brother again.

Traveling to Threall meant shearing my skin from my soul.

Nine years ago, I was too young to appreciate or anticipate the full horror of the agony my body would experience. I'd lasted maybe six seconds, hands stuffed over my mouth to hold back the screams, before I'd fallen back into my semimortal body.

With that, I'd closed the book on Threall. But now, things were different. Back then, I'd had a child's body, and I'd been completely ignorant of the fact that Fae gifts don't come into full power until after puberty. Imagine my shock when my talent for magic doubled the day I had my first period.

I gave the hanging thread another savage jerk.

How long was six seconds?

One thousand, two thousand, three thousand . . . six. Surely I could endure six seconds? How much longer would it take to make it all the way to Threall? Twice as much? I could stand twelve seconds of anguish in return for a future of peace, couldn't I?

What had I told Trowbridge? I am Fae. My eyes flared and the interior of the vehicle turned briefly green as I remembered my announcement.

And today, I'd flared for the first time. If that wasn't my body giving me the green light to purchase a day pass to Threall, I was a full-blooded Were. *Enough.* I grimly booted thoughts of Trowbridge into the corner of my brain where I kept broken things. Threall had been the catalyst for my flare, not my troublesome meet-up with Trowbridge. Hell, I'd been thinking about the land of mists ever since Lou's abduction—no, even before that. A visit there had been in the back of my mind ever since I started receiving Lou's dreams.

I just hadn't got past the point of toying with the idea, to actually doing it.

If Mum was right, then I'd be the Mystwalker in that realm, capable of traveling deep into any Fae's drowsing mind. Once I found Lou, I could mine her memories for details of her capture and discover her location. I imagined hero-me using my Threall-gained knowledge to slither in through a conveniently open window, tiptoeing past a sleeping Were, rousing my sleeping aunt, and leading her to Bob's car.

I could go digging for other secrets too.

How to open a sealed portal.

How to find a long-lost brother.

I could be a twin again.

Basic Fae magic is simple, or at least it has always been so for me. I focused on a command—fetch, grow, squeeze, whatever—and then somehow that action verb became more than a word as my wish melded itself onto the ball of Fae magic resting in my gut. When I released my magic and told it to fetch, it was as if there were a layer of my will or essence thinly spread over the line of magic spinning from my fingertips. Safe to say, I extruded my magic. But going to Threall required the reverse action. First off there was no word for soul separation, and instead of unleashing my magic outward, I was asking it to turn inward—implode versus explode.

I breathed out, and in, short little breaths, and then I took one last huge breath, and visualized it sinking down to my lungs, and then going beyond that, right down to my stomach, where it surrounded my ball of magic and squeezed. *Take me up to Threall.* A flare of heat in my belly. *Let my soul fly free.* A quick stretch of my skin as my Were backed away from whatever she saw going on down there.

Up, I thought, imagining flight. *Up.*

Oh . . . I hurt. Like someone was pulling my head, and

toes, and my ribs were starting to crack, my ligaments starting to tear. My breath came out in short little pants. *Lexi. Lou. Up to Threall.* "Push," I said, through my teeth. My voice turned into a whine of pain, high through my nose. More squeezing, and then, the beginning of the rip.

There was a resistance, a grounding, tied to a piece of me that didn't believe I could do it.

Oh Goddess.

A slow laceration—like being caught in the ragged claws of a sluggish contraction—impossible to stand. I sucked in some air, and pushed. One last horrific sharp rending, and then . . . No sound. No scents. No sensation of pain.

Overwhelming terror.

I had no body. I was nothing but a mind . . . a soul . . . a thing.

A *floating* thing.

No weight of Merry around my neck. No Were warm in my belly.

Nothing to anchor me to either realm.

Oh crap.

Chapter Twelve

Time passed. Not like eons, or days, or even hours. Just time. Long enough for me to contemplate the awfulness of being neither here nor there. Long enough for me to understand that minus physical sensation, emotions are blunted and muted—no aching throat to deepen your hurt, no gooseflesh or hair rising along your neck to amplify your fear—a concept, versus that marvelous gift of spirit and mind connected. Theoretically, that should be good, yes? No needless suffering, no squeezing pain in your solar plexus because you grieved for something you could never get back. And yet, it was worse. Because with nothing to distract you, sadness lingered and pervaded. You couldn't self-medicate by feeding your taste buds ice cream or comfort yourself with the soothing scent of lavender. Without functioning eyes, you couldn't observe any other life than your own interior one.

Nothing to hide behind. Nothing to do but think.

I want to have flesh again. Fingers and hands. Tear ducts and snot.

And then, another stretching feeling, and a swelter of crushing physicality—skeleton and skin being sewn together, blood vessels and organs being added to the mixture . . . too much, too fast, the sudden heat of my blood, the grave weight of my flesh, the unyielding construct of my bones . . . I'd have screamed but I hadn't earned my mouth . . . a little more agony as details were added—pores and hair, teeth and lips . . . and then, finally, *oh bless you, Goddess, bless you.* My body was returned to me. I had a heart. It was beating too fast. I was facedown—my least favorite position—boobs uncomfortably flattened, but beneath my knees and hips I felt solid ground. Gratitude and quick promises welled up. *I swear I'll never curse my big butt again. I'll be thankful for everything I have from the swell of my upper lip to the dimples at the bottom of my spine.*

I cracked open my eyes. My hand lay in a patch of sunlight on a small hummock of moss. It was so good to have a hand again. I spread my fingers and watched the tendons flex as my thumb pulled away from my splayed fingers. What a marvel of engineering and beauty was the semimortal hand. I turned it sideways, examining my paw. It looked pretty much like it did in earth's realm, small and on the pale side. Except, my skin felt different here. Thinner, more delicate. It tingled.

It was the magic-tainted air. I could smell it, sweet as freesias. I'd caught that fragrance once before—the night a Were had leaped through Creemore's portal—and had always remembered it as a double whammy: not only a scent, but a skin-humming physical reaction. Perhaps I'd remembered it wrong? Overemphasized its allure in my memory? The sensation I felt now was milder, its impact reduced just to a mild tingle that my body was already starting to ignore.

I sifted the air through my nose, testing for other scents beneath that sweet floral Fae fragrance, but there were none. Threall smelled like . . . flowers, damp mist, woods, moss . . . and nothing else. No humans. No Weres. No living creatures, big or small. And yet, I sensed living things all around me, even if I couldn't see them—the instinct sharp enough to bring me up onto my knees. I looked around the empty clearing.

I'd materialized in a open space roughly the size and shape of one of Deerfield's hockey rinks—about two hundred feet long, and less than half as wide. My lips curved into a smile. Mum had been right in one respect: Threall *was* a land of mists, but in this realm, the haze was predominantly bluish,

not white, and it didn't hover like a heavy layer of fog, it
moved in streams. I watched a ribbon of blue haze drift across
the glade before it ran a sinuous finger of smoke up over the
sharp tangle of an overgrown hedgerow. My eyes followed—

Sweet Fae Stars. I sank down onto my heels in wonder.
The lights.

The sky was full of them. Soft hazy balls of gold light—
some sun-yellow, some as tepid as weak green tea, others
defiantly peach toned, and a few, a blushing primrose. There
were other colors too; shades of green-mottled blue, a pinch
of pink, and even some that were decidedly earth toned, their
faint amber glow almost lost beneath the soft blue smoke
of Threall's mist. Oh, even more lovely—in the far distance,
just where fog-wreathed land met horizon, a handful of counterfeit blue moons twinkled. I wanted to pluck those blue
orbs from the sky and pocket them like jewels.

My connection to this landscape was immediate. *This
belongs to me. Each and every light.*

I watched their glow for a while, my fingers curling into
fists, wanting to reach and touch. The sight of them roused an
instinctive sense of destiny. *Mine.* There were no attached
wires or electrical lines to explain their luminosity. The perfectly round balls—all of them roughly the same size, with
skins as translucent as vellum—either hung from a branch
by a strand of the same stuff covering their surface, or were
jammed into the fork of a fantastically old tree.

Those trees. Even without their glowing lamps, the ancient specimens were the stuff of fantasy. What mortal had
ever seen anything the size of these old elms? Their trunks
were wide enough to drive a Hummer through and still have
room to spare. There had to be hundreds of them. The vista
of lights stretched for miles.

*Mum was so wrong. This is where I belong. Watching
over these soft hazy balls.*

I took stock of my new empire. If the clearing was about
the size of a small ice rink, then I'd say I was near the
boards at the center line—at approximately the midpoint on
one of the longer sides of the rectangular open space. When

I glanced right, to the goalie area one hundred feet away, I got a quick impression of two enormous black walnut trees sitting in the shadows. I then turned to the left. That end of the clearing was better lit, and a great deal less green. A near vertical wall of sheer rock soared fifty feet into the sky. Above its cliff, the sky was purple-black.

Interesting. I returned my attention to the mossy meadow that surrounded me.

Someone had taken care to add a sense of symmetry to the field by planting two long rows of hawthorns, one on either side of the clearing. Back in the day, they may have been nice hedges, but now they were just a thick border of shrubs that had been allowed to grow into a dense line of ground-sweeping short scraggly trees. They were overgrown, but they still did their job of holding back the trees attempting to encroach on each side. They too were inner-lit, though their illuminations came from deep within the thicket, and were not as colorful nor as varied as the ones in the dark sky, and definitely not as accessible, thanks to the sharp thorns of the hawthorns. Their glows were golden toned, but—and this distinguished them from all the other balls I'd seen—their surface had been treated to a wash of red. The overall effect was watchful and brooding.

On the heels of that thought, a curl of blue mist emerged from the small gap in the row of shrubs. It wafted along the hedges' tangled top, skimming the curved thorns, until it found a clump of red berries. Then, with a pirouette, it disappeared deep into the cluster. Less than two seconds later, it emerged in another spiral of now mauve vapor, before it streaked down where the two enormous black walnuts—one nothing more than a wind-nibbled, dying husk and the other, a robust living duplicate of it—held court.

The stream of colored smoke vanished inside the healthier walnut's dense foliage.

Even as I told myself to relax, I felt the hairs on the back of my neck rise. That tree gave me the willies. How could a bunch of leaves and twigs arouse the fight-or-flight response? Yes, it *was* the biggest, baddest walnut tree I'd ever beheld—sky-tipping, with heavily foliaged branches stretching out perhaps sixty feet wide. And it *was* decidedly ugly; misshapen bulbous growth erupted from the knotholes on its thick trunk. Not only that, its light set it apart from the other specimens in the forest. It was purple—not violet, or velvet pansy hued, but a deep eggplant with a throbbing blob of red in the middle of it. That freaking globe didn't just glow, it glowered.

Yep, all those things were grab-Toto-and-run scary, but there were *worse* things down at that end of the clearing than an evil walnut.

I may have left school in sixth grade, but I've been selectively self-educating since then through Bob's no-fines, no-jailtime lending library. Thus, I knew that before Columbus proved them wrong, those dumb-ass mortals had thought the world was flat. Hard to believe anyone could be that stupid. Almost impossible, unless you were standing where I was, looking at flat-earth evidence with your mouth hanging open in disbelief.

The world I'd been born to was round. Which meant, there was always a horizon. It's one of those laws of nature you take for granted. But here in Threall, that cardinal rule did not apply. Where I was expecting some sort of vista beyond those two walnuts—a forest, or maybe a babbling brook, anything to give you a reference for perspective—there was nothing. No sense of definition between ground and sky. The air between the almost-dead and living tree was flat as flannel, and gray as a banker's suit. Featureless—a backdrop of seething gray.

Not something you turn your back on, or for that matter, get too cozy with. What I meant to do was sidle away from it, but what I did was lurch. It took a few steps before I got my center of gravity realigned. It was almost like I was too light—I paused, stricken, and touched my stomach. There was no answering quiver from my Were.

I was empty. Gutted and tenantless.

It had been a long-held wish: the total exorcism of my Were-bitch. *Had I willed her dead?* I froze, both hands pressed hard on my belly, my breath suddenly caught in my chest. *Or was she alive and well in my mortal body, down in earth's realm, thoroughly disgusted by the scents emanating from the strip club?* I didn't know, but I kind of wanted her back, just to check.

I might have stood there for quite some time, my worry split between the walnut's malevolent ball of light, and the fact that my canine nature hadn't made the boat to Threall, but someone issued an invitation.

It was a single chord.

Soon followed by a single note, plucked by a string instrument that thankfully bore no resemblance to a harp. Two more notes. Plaintive. Then those unseen fingers delivered to me a song. Simple in construction; its melody climbed upward, took a half step backward, pressed on for a higher note. Lazily played and melancholy too, as if the song were a line drawing, hastily sketched in by an artist puzzled by something he couldn't figure out.

By the time the musician had played the final chorus, I'd pinpointed the location.

I started toward the wall of rock about a hundred feet to my left and as I did, the mist moved away, as if saying for all the world, "Clear the way, here comes the mighty Mystwalker."

Hard not to experience a little stroke of pleasure at that thought.

As I got closer, it parted and revealed the presence of yet another ancient tree. Great effort had been made to keep this elderly beech safe. From what danger, I wasn't sure, but it had been protected by a fence of sorts, fashioned from various lengths of branches. Someone, or several someones, had dug a trench, and then rammed branches into the exposed earth at a forty-five degree angle, one piece on top of the other. The end result was an intricate puzzle of forked branches and straight ones, bristling with pointed edges. The barrier curved completely around the elderly beech, serving as a six-foot-high impediment to anyone who had a pocketknife and a desire to carve their initials. I don't know who the hell would love that tree enough to go to all that trouble; it was as ugly as sin too. Its thick branches had grown twisted, so that the overall visual was tortured wood, as viciously gnarled as an old lady's arthritic knuckles.

Quiet from the center of the branch barricade. A listening sort of stillness.

There was no entrance that I could see. I walked around it until I found a peephole in the fence, and took a peek.

Well, hell. The last thing I expected to see was a teenager reclining on a silk divan, plucking a mandolin. She had an arresting face, much like the girl in the art book Bob had never been able to flip. I'd spent a lot of time studying that image, caught by the thought that the girl looked somewhat like Lou. And here it was again, another version of that the same autocratic face; long nose, shapely chin, eyes made compelling by the measuring look under their half-mast lids. Except this girl was far younger—in her late teens—and her hair wasn't dark like Lou's but blond, so pale it was almost silver. It fell past her shoulders and rippled down her back. Her dress was gentian blue, the vaguely medieval bodice and waist fitted to her slender body. The rest was long and predictably flowing. Fairy-tale fashion by way of Disney. The robe was a little too overdone in the embellishments, I thought, not much liking the embroidered silver flower design that ran up her sleeves.

Mum had been a prettier Fae.

Her eyes slanted toward me. Brown, not blue. She played a few more chords on her mandolin, and then asked me something in—ah, for crap's sake—Merenwynian.

"I don't speak Merenwynian," I said glumly. That response prompted another stream of lilting gibberish from the girl on the divan. "Like I said, I don't speak Merenwyian," I repeated very slowly, in that same earnest manner foreign-born people repeat things to us Canadians, as if saying the same thing louder and at a snail's pace would somehow improve our comprehension.

The musician's fingers kept moving over the mandolin

strings, but she spared me a hooded, annoyed glance from under her lashes.

"Goddess," I said in exasperation, turning to glance back at the black walnut and the dark ominous gray behind it. "You don't know how much I wish that you spoke English or that I spoke your language." I forced myself to tear my glance from the ominous canvas. Gave her a rueful smile through the fence. "It would make my trip to la-la land so much easier, because if there was ever a time I needed a spirit guide, this would be it. You see, I . . ."

My words petered out.

By all the stars in earth's heaven, I'd just spoken the last sentence in my mother's tongue. I opened my mouth to test this sudden skill—

"It's near dawn in Merenwyn. He is taking a chance sending you so late," she said in English. She softly played a few opening bars of what sounded like a Baroque piece. "Or did he think that you'd find me already sleeping?" She frowned at her long fingers on the neck of the mandolin and then carefully put the instrument down, so that its base rested on a rough rag rug that seemed mostly to be made of duns, browns, and bits of blue, and its short neck rested on a hideously ornate gilt table.

"Who *are* you?" I asked.

The blonde drew up her legs and clasped her arms around her knees. We exchanged a wordless moment through the crack in the makeshift fence. If I'd met her in earth's realm, on first glance she'd pass for human, just like Mum and Lou had. Her face was set in Lou's calculating coldness, and yet, I fancied that I caught that distinguishing otherworld quality; some of that river-old sadness Mum's face sometimes wore when she looked out our kitchen window.

"What is your message?" she asked eventually.

A trifle snappishly, I replied in my mother's tongue, "I don't have a message."

It seemed to me her chin sharpened. She released a knee and placed a hand on the fissured gray bark of the old beech beside her, but the movement looked odd to me; done in the same manner one half of a couple might do to catch their mate's attention. Uneasily, I squinted up into the foliage. Green ovate leaves, lots of twisted branches, and nothing else I could see except the obligatory ball of light. It was the hue of an overripe mango: orange bleeding into crimson.

"We have a challenger," the girl said.

I did a quick left/right with my eyes. The space inside the ring of branches wasn't that large; really, just enough space for the person contained within its circle of debris to pace in a figure eight around the two pieces of furniture and the massive tree's trunk, providing they were careful not to stumble over the twisted worm pile of its partially exposed root system. As far as I could tell, she was the sole occupant. I looked over my shoulder and surveyed the clearing and its parameters behind me. Nada in the open field around me. Though now that my gee-this-ain't-right instincts were roused, the surrounding woods appeared a trifle more mysterious, the cliff face a fraction more massive and impassive, and the blue-fogged hulk of the black walnut down at the other goal area even more horribly creepy. As for that long dark flannel screen behind it . . . *Don't stare at it. Don't beckon the things in that gloom to come into the light.*

I cleared my throat. "I'm not here to challenge anyone."

"What shall we do?" asked the girl of the tree. A pause during which I heard nothing except my breathing—there was just so little ambient noise in this world—as she waited for an answer. "Yes, we *have* been bored. And the other one hasn't spoken in such a long time." Above her, deep in the foliage, the light ball in her beech friend flashed; dash, dot, dash. She frowned at me in a appraising manner. "She's older than we have seen before, and has not as pleasing a countenance as our last guest." She pursed her lips. "No, she is not unappealing. Her hair is neither sun nor shadow, though her eyes are the green of the Chiron House. And she is . . ." She tilted her head back to get a bigger picture of me through her viewing hole. "Well shaped."

Unbelievable. I was standing on an astral plane, getting Joan Rivered by a fae nut-job.

"DeLoren." My tone was stiff. "My eye color comes from the house of DeLoren."

I think Loony Tunes heard me, because she gave a light huff, but she didn't lift her head from her communion with the Almighty Tree Spirit.

She's as mad as the proverbial hatter.

Mad-one nodded once or twice as she listened, and then she patted the trunk, obviously in agreement with the game plan.

Then her unfocused eyes sharpened, and pinned me.

"Are you a mystwalker?" I asked bluntly.

"We are disappointed." She sniffed. "Return to your mage." A little pause, in which I was probably supposed to genuflect and then disappear. When I didn't, she emphasized her point with a grand "away, beggar" wave before adding, "Inform him that you are not worthy of our time."

I raised both brows. "Just in the interests of clarity, who's 'he'?"

That question made her chew on the inside corner of her lip. Then she tucked her chin in and said sotto voce, "She pretends not to know of whom we speak. I said as you instructed, but she is *still* here."

"Hey, tree." I waggled my fingers at the beech.

Mad-one turned her head very slowly in my direction and studied me briefly, her hand still flattened on the fissured bark, before she smiled. As smirks go, it was akin to the wolfish appreciation a Were pays to a tray of thick juicy steaks—a mental tabulation of what was going to taste best as it went down.

"It is possible I'll have to deal with this one," she said.

"You know what? I'm good," I said. "I know what I'm looking for. You just stay there, and talk to your tree pal, while I wander around." I gave her a Starbucks smile through the crack in the barricade. "Won't take more than five minutes, tops."

Her brow had creased as I'd begun speaking, but that had cleared somewhere in the middle of my dialogue. Now, her head tilted to one side, she examined me like I was someone very dim. As she did, her fingers continued to stroke the rough bark.

"I *will* have to deal with this one," she told the tree. The interior of the ball caught in the old beech's thick branches flickered, more orange than yellow. "You are safe," she said softly, though I took that to mean the old beech was safe, and me, not so much. "I won't stray far. It will not take long to attend to this problem." Her gaze was upward, directed at the ball of light over her head. "I will be safe," she said, a lover's smile on her face, both rueful and affectionate. "Do not worry. We'll be together when daylight comes."

Oh . . . It clicked. Bats-in-the-belfry wasn't talking to the *tree,* she was conversing with the lightbulb nested in its leafy arms. I'd thought of the glowing orbs as simply pretty lights, set there by the Mystwalker to keep the dark away. But now, as I let my gaze wander over the sea of bright balls glowing in the deep purple sky, I remembered something. *"They say a part of every Fae lives in Threall, the dreaming portion of us,"* Mum had told me that late winter afternoon a decade ago.

But not as bodies, Mum, I thought. Not as people in corporeal form. The souls of hundreds of dreaming Faes were all around me. Indeed, Threall's night was gleaming with the glorious illumination from their soul-lights.

Like most things, simple once you understood. Each tree carried a soul. And to talk with one, all you had to do was touch its trunk.

Yes, so freakin' simple.

All I had to do to find Lexi and Lou was touch a few hundred trees. It hurt my head just thinking about it. I rubbed my temple. It would take forever.

A scrunch of fabric, as Mad-one left her silk divan, and then, suddenly, she was right on the other side of the divide, staring at me through the crack in the fence. Not a single blemish or wrinkle marred her petal-soft skin. Despite that, an absolute conviction came to me suddenly that she was as old as her gnarled beech. Tired too, I thought. And what? Sad? Weighted? Bound?

Her forehead creased. Whatever weakness had been exposed during my study was wiped out by the sudden anger that tightened the soft skin around her eyes.

I stepped back sharply, as did she, though neither of us broke our stare fest—maybe dominance through eye contact is something understood by all predators, not just Weres. Her slumberous eyes narrowed to slits. Then she lifted her chin and clapped her hands into a prayer position. With a small wait-till-you-see-this smile, she opened them. As her palms spread wide, the topmost branch of the barricade rose, and moved aside. The one below that followed, and then all of them shifted, so quickly that the movement was a visual blur, lifted up and away. Their branches hung in the air, trembling slightly above the arched doorway she'd created.

She stood one hip cocked to the side, her head tilted to the other, possibly considering what to do next. In my experience, churning minds usually herald bad things to come, so I put a few feet between us, and kept a keen eye on her hands. As she passed the threshold, the arch of branches trembled against each other, chittering like bones rubbing together in a grave robber's satchel.

Spooky, but not *half* as chilling as what was happening down at ground level. Mad-one didn't walk, she *glided* above the clearing's floor.

She kept coming and I kept backpedaling. I spared a quick glance behind me and realized the bitch was herding me toward the seething dark end of the clearing. Screw that. I altered my course to take me back toward the hedgerow.

"You know, I think there's been some confusion." I did a backward jog around a tree stump. "I'm not a challenger. I'm here strictly to find someone, and then I'm gone."

Mad-one replied in a perfectly pleasant voice—almost normal, considering she was moving over the ground like a wraith as she followed my retreat. "Then perhaps you wish to learn from me? I can teach you many things. How to breathe a whisper of doubt so softly they don't even know it's from your lips. How to change a dream from sweet to sour. How to plant a seed of craving that they cannot quench. You can stay and be my new chosen companion. We can be friends."

What happened to her last one?

"Who is it that you seek?" she asked, gliding closer.

As if.

She must have read my mutinous mug like I'd read her mad-ass, crazy face, because she made a lunge for me. Happily for me, it was evident she'd never had a twin. Her fingers harmlessly raked the air where I'd stood a second before. Child's play. I'd been ducking incoming G.I. Joes since Lexi's hands were large enough to hold a toy.

She was going to have to be faster than that.

As Mad-one recovered her balance—*aha! She's not impervious to gravity*—I cut loose and hauled ass, looking for a gap in the line of hawthorns. There! I surged through the first hole large enough to accommodate me. A thorn dug a furrow along my spine as I tunneled through. I felt a tug on one shoe, and let Mad-one have it—*why the hell am I always losing my shoes?*—scooting on hands and knees through the short passage as fast as a fox with a trail of starving hounds behind it.

I emerged and kept going, my steering still set for a full-speed-ahead crawl, not stopping until I was well past the border of shrubs and could go no farther, stymied by a minigrove of sumacs. I scrambled to my feet. This side of the clearing's woods wasn't civilized and cultivated, like the forest of ancient elms beyond the other row of hawthorns. It felt . . . wild. Blue fog silently snaked through the tall trees and saplings. Multihued jewel-toned lights glittered above. No pearly peaches or primroses in this misted sky.

I breathed through my mouth, waiting for Mad-one to come shooting through the same tunnel from which I'd just crawled. But she didn't. Once again, we stared at each other through a chink in a barricade.

She beckoned. "Come to me."

Why didn't she scoot through the tunnel? Or glide over the top of it? What was holding her back? Obviously she didn't have to worry about gravity. When I didn't emerge from the tunnel, she rose in the air, until her face hovered ghostlike above the line of hawthorns.

"Did the Black Mage tell you nothing of the things in these woods?" she asked. Her tone was bland, but her eyes were sharp as they calculated the risks of the thorns and the narrow gap between a nearby maple's low-hanging branches and the hedgerow top.

She's afraid—no, leery—of the hedgerow, I thought.

Wondering how much time I had before she overcame her distaste for some overgrown shrubs, I searched the area around me for a stone or a broken branch, but all I could turn up was a shred of old parchment—just a brush of my fingers, and someone's broken memory streaked through my being— and a handful of moss. "I told you before, I don't know what mage you're talking about."

Mad-one exhaled through her nose sharply and then she did something I hadn't anticipated. Her hands flattened into a prayer position again, but this time, when they parted a fire- ball erupted between them. I ducked behind a tree. I should have just let her hover there, holding her fiery handful of snap, crackle, pop, until her skin turned black. But curiosity got the better of me, and so I peeked. She'd been waiting for just that and she threw. Not at me, or at the spruce whose protection I was leaning away from, but at the section of hedge in front of us. The fireball tore a wide, burning path through the shrub- bery, but didn't cut a trail completely through the thick vege- tation. Instead, it got lodged three-quarters through, caught in the forked branch of an elderly hawthorn, where it smoldered a few inches from the overgrown shrub's soul-light.

No, don't. My hand crept to my mouth in horror.

The stubby branches cradling the hedges' spirit-ball burst into flame. I watched, sickened, as tongues of heat delicately licked at the parchment. With a sudden whoosh, it was con- sumed, and the soul was left naked—a glittering light burn- ing too bright for my eyes to look directly at it. I covered them and watched through my slitted fingers, as it danced an ago- nized jig in the heated air. Beneath my bare foot, the rough earth trembled. The soul-light flared once. Then with a pop, it was gone.

The hawthorn's roots wept as the rest of the shrub burst into flames.

Run. She'll be through the gap in the hedge in a moment or two.

While the fire devoured its meal, I slipped deeper into the woods the Mad-one seemed so reluctant to enter. *It's dark in here. Focus, you've got a witch on your heels.* I flitted through the trees, searching for a place to hide, and found it. *There,* I thought. *She won't like their light.* I dashed to where the two pines grew side by side, so close that their separate trunks had almost merged into one. Their brilliant glow dispelled the shadows. Behind them, the forest was tangle-thick, shrouded in mist.

Time for a last stand. I stood under the lights of their soul-balls, half frightened, half resolute as Mad-one glided our way.

"You murdered that soul," I said, when she came close.

"It was its time," she replied with an indifferent shrug.

"But you *chose* its time."

"I am the Mystwalker," she replied coolly. "It is my duty to guard this realm. Life or death, terrifying dreams or naught—it is to me that those decisions fall in Threall."

"It was a *living* soul." I shook my head. "No one has the right to make those choices."

" 'It' was nothing more than a guard, who could not keep you from these woods." Her voice grew hard. "The punishment for that failure is death."

"And you're the executioner."

"Killing one to protect many is not a difficult choice. A mystwalker's first duty is to protect the Royal House from those who wish it harm. You seem lacking in that training." She cocked her head, her brows furrowed. Then, decision made, she said, "Wind."

No hand gestures this time to give me warning.

The resulting blast of air hit me square in the belly. Even as her Fae-invoked chinook pushed me backward into the trees, my mind was spinning—*she can harness the wind? How'd she do that? Could I do that?*—and then my leg hit the bark of the smaller of the pines, and suddenly . . . *oh Goddess*. Sensation shimmered up my shin. Pleasure. Sweeter than maple syrup, more exciting than boosting a shiny silver ring.

My spine melted against its rough bark as the wind died around me.

I was in someone's mind. Deep within. No walls to repel me. My curiosity, always such a besetting sin, came boiling up within me as urgent as the need to drink, to eat, to think. I dipped into a soul's mind—not a dreaming one but a sentient being on the edge of waking.

Oh my. Mad-one's lip curled into an addict's knowing smile as I tipped my head back in near rapture.

The soul inside the pine is open for my exploration. My vision faded. *Wondrous.*

She was so different from me. Whole, not fragmented. She didn't live under a deluge of questions, or wade daily through a muddy stream of doubt. This Fae soul lived for the field, for the family, for wide-open spaces. Layers of scent delighted her, and each one she greeted with a gourmand's appreciation. Oh my, I thought, digging deeper. So sure. So steady. She was satisfied, and yet not self-satisfied.

Is this truly how others felt? Safe?

Excitement and pleasure streaked through me. It was the best type of stealing: I pocketed her memories like they were diamonds, chuckling at the things she found funny, marveling at the things she held dear. Grubby children and the grizzled face of an ugly man; all made beautiful by the way she loved them. Ah, that was it—the essential difference between her and me—she loved in the present tense. More stunningly, my dreamer knew herself to be—yes, there's the source of the biggest warmth—loved. She accepted it, without inspection or question. I followed the thread of that warm comfort, and found "him" everywhere and yet nowhere, until . . . ah, there . . . yes, there. Her soul was wound around him like Merry was wound around that cold, lifeless amulet.

And then, my eyes were open, and I found myself staring at the bleak weight in Mad-one's eyes.

"The first time you touch a soul," said the Mystwalker, "you begin to understand the possibilities of your gift." She spread a hand. "Here, as long as you fulfill your duties to the Court, you may live any life you choose. You can discover every secret once thought well hidden. Without ever leaving this realm, you can experience every sensation, every adventure. If you're gifted, you can alter souls and destinies.

"The Old Mage would have taught this. He would have trained you, and you would have understood that you have been given the great honor of serving the Court, and that your sacrifice protects those who need the most protection. But you were trained by the Black Mage, who taught you only what he understands—deception and guile. His skills are weak, his knowledge of Threall ever weaker, but his desire for power strong. Consider very carefully his instructions to you and your allegiance to his service. And think too of this. If you live past the dawn, I can show you so much more. If your wish is to plunder, I'll show you where to find the sweeter trees. But now, you must come away from this place. These woods are not safe for our kind. Things wander here in the daylight hours."

I pushed myself away from the dreaming Fae soul and felt the pang of disconnect when my fingers left her callused trunk. Alone again. The loneliness that I wore like a cloak was wrapped tight around me once more.

Mad-one sidled up to me, but I didn't flit away from her this time. I didn't fear her anymore. If anything, I felt—

The Mystwalker leaned past me to place her fingers on the ridged bark spine of the fir. Her eyes slanted into slits of purring pleasure as she invaded the other spirit's mindscape. "You didn't leave a sign that you had passed." She shook her head reprovingly, her eyes glassy and unfocused. "You must always leave a mark. Your purpose is to search for agitators and impose the will of the Court." Mad-one reached out to briefly touch the adjoining tree. "They have been together a long time, these two." She raised her head and looked upward where the balls of light were almost melded together. "True soul mates. They believe themselves above our command." A quick inhale, followed by a tiny smile. "This creature has never felt the touch of a mystwalker before. She's a moment from waking. She's trying to evade me." The ball of light above her flashed a bleat of stark yellow.

Both arms wrapped around the tree, Mad-one leaned her cheek against the rough trunk, and spoke. "He lusts for another. Someone younger and more beautiful. He sees her in his head, every day. He yearns for your death so that he can be free to go to her." The corner of her lip lifted. "When you wake, he will be gone."

The Mystwalker of Threall waited another beat, then stepped back, satisfaction twisting her youthful features into a smile that turned my stomach. She wiped her cheek clean with her hand before dragging it across the shining blue fabric of her gown.

Heartsick, I touched the pine whose sweet spirit had just been marked. Inside that near-awake mind, I could feel the dreamer's hurt, cold and numbing, spreading outward from that wound of doubt. My jaw hardened. I put my lips close the fir's bark, and concentrated. "He loves you. He always will. He dreams of no other. This was nothing but a bad dream."

"You dare challenge my mark?" she shrieked.

Kind of reminded me of the Wicked Witch of the West, the way Mad-one's voice rose, and damn me, if I didn't taunt her with a smile. Unfortunate choice, that. Suddenly, we were face-to-face, our breaths mixing in the close air between us.

"You will regret your actions." Her eyes were slits. "This is my kingdom."

"Go ride your broom," I said through tight lips.

With that, she put her hands on me. I felt her cold fingers bite into my shoulders.

But her mind. It tried to *invade* mine.

"What are you? " she asked, deeply puzzled.

Same song, different singer. I curled my fingers into a fist with the thumb on the outside, just like my brother had taught me, and bopped her hard, square on her freaking, long, aristocratic nose.

She cupped her snoot with a shriek.

Who's top dog now, Mad-one? I stood firm, both fists clenched, ready to give her another poke.

"Is this how the Black Mage chooses to provoke me? He sends me a creature such as you?" Mad-one said, winding up on a rant. "Who believes me to be no more than a lowly witch? Riding a broom of twigs?" Oh yeah. She was pissed. One arm up, one knee bent up, the Mystwalker levitated skyward. She hovered ten feet above me, hair floating in an eerie nimbus around her head.

And then she did something truly horrible.

She glided over to the male tree's soul-light. Her fingers stretched for its tether.

"Don't," I said sharply.

But she did. She tore the glowing ball from its berth, and held it tightly under her arm, pressed close to the ribs that protected her frozen heart. Then she glided downward and away, heading back toward the hedgerows and the clearing.

Two feet lower and I could have snagged her foot. I lifted a hand to send a stream of magic at her, but . . . what could I use? There were no convenient broken tree limbs on the wood's ground. No rocks, no stones. Just moss, blue haze, and soul-balls.

I ran at her heels, calling, "Give him back, bitch."

Her head turned, her hair sliding over her shoulder. She smiled. "If you wish to save this soul, then you must follow me out of the wild." She glided through the gap in the hedgerows, indifferent to the smell of smoke, or the thorns that tried to catch her gown.

She glided faster than I could run, with one shoe.

But when I cleared the hedge—another streak of blood marring my arm—I found Mad-one hovering, halfway to the safety of her branch barricade. She sank slowly to the ground, her attention focused on the sky above the black walnut. It looked . . . pinpricked. Natural light glittered through each tiny point. As I watched, a section of the gray canvas tore. Just a small rend, which widened until it was a jagged smile of blue, through which bright white light streamed.

"Daylight comes," she said flatly.

A streak of sunlight fell on her face. She lifted her head for a second to absorb it, looking young and unblemished. Her mouth parted slightly as she watched another tear appear in the heavens. Sunbeams streamed across the clearing's carpet of emerald moss. The transition from gray-shrouded night to sun-dappled day happened very quickly. In a matter of moments, every bit of pewter had been banished except for one dark cloud. The sun—or whatever was the source of the daylight—hid behind it.

But Threall still supported the flat-earth theory. Where a gray blanket had obscured the hypothetical division between land and sky, now there was only cerulean-blue heaven. The land past the walnuts looked like a precipice to an endless plunge toward . . . what? Earth? What would happen if I walked over to the edge of Threall's world? What would I see? While I speculated over that, a plume of white materialized. Like a rocket's vapor trail, but completely vertical and alive like water—it streamed upward, disappearing into the heart of the dark cloud.

"What is it?" I breathed.

She stroked the ends of her long hair. "The passage to Merenwyn."

"A portal to Merenwyn?" I frowned at her. "I thought they were all closed?"

"Are they?" Then with a small lift of her shoulder, "Such things matter not to a mystwalker."

I slanted my eyes toward the soul-ball tucked under her left arm. *Yeah, it looks like a lot of things don't matter to a mystwalker.* Casually, I took a step closer. Then, I pointed to another, much smaller, thinner stream of white that had sprung out of the central plume. It forked in two, and then folded back onto itself, so that its end was nothing more than a hook. "And that?"

Her fingers paused, mid-rake, in her hair. "An endless hell

for the wrong traveler. False trails such as those emerge from the portal walls. They are traps for the unwary or unschooled." She pointed to the hook at the end of the stream. "Observe how the false trail has turned back onto itself. Very soon it will collapse."

Creeping horror. "What happens to the people inside them?"

"They become part of Merenwyn's portal. Their essence is absorbed into the fabric of its walls." She stared at it for a bit, chewing the inside of her lip. "You can hear their cries some evenings." Then she looked at the soul-ball as if she had forgotten it was there and bent to place it by my feet. "Your Mage did not call you home," she said. "You should find shelter. They will be mourning the loss of this one and searching for its killer."

She started walking toward her beech, before I could ask her who "they" were.

I crouched for the soul-ball—*oh Goddess, he's awake and calling for his soul mate*—and tore after her. "Come back!" I yelled. "It's not dead yet!" I ran after her, holding the pine tree's spirit gingerly in my grasp. We caught up to her before she'd reached the sanctuary of her enclave. "You have to put it back where it belongs," I demanded. "You can't leave that woman to mourn."

Mad-one turned around, much too slowly and deliberately. "It will serve as a lesson to her."

"What, for cruelty?" I held the ball tighter. "Because I can't see any other lesson she'd learn."

She dipped her head toward the soul-light. "He has the instincts of an agitator. With his absence, she will spend every waking moment caring for the crops so that she has food to feed her children. She will have little time to ponder his political views. I made a balanced decision. She has her children and the rot of his destructive thoughts has been cut away."

"You don't know her." The soul inside the sphere was worried, deeply so. "She'll grieve herself to death."

"That will be her choice. I gave her a choice." She shook her head, and looked past me. "Do you find it beautiful?"

I cast an anguished glance at the soul-light. "Yes."

"But you can't reach it."

I looked up, confused. Her gaze was fixed beyond me, to the blue sky and its plume of white. "You behold the passage to Merenwyn and you wish it possible to slip into the sky and retrace your passage home, as safely as one of its portal travelers. To forget about Threall. To go back in time, to a safe place, when all you understood was the comfort of your home, and the warmth of its hearth. But it is a thing a myst-walker can never do. We cannot turn back time. The first thing we are taught is not to grieve."

Mad-one shook her head, and walked toward the trembling archway of branches, holding her long skirt aside with one pale white hand.

"You're everything my mum said you'd be," I shouted after her. "Soulless and mad."

She turned, her eyebrows raised. Then she said, "Wind."

A split second later the soul-ball and I were skidding across the clearing. The nails on my free hand made a furrow in the moss. I made a lunge for the sharp end of a half-rotted stump but overshot. The soul-ball and I did a tandem bounce off its crumbling remains and then we were in the arms of Mad-one's wind, the landscape a blur around us—gleaming lights, dark forests, and wind-whipped walnut trees.

' I closed my eyes—*please, Goddess, save me or make it quick*—before we sailed into the blue void.

Thud.

My back hit the half-dead walnut's bulk in a breath-catching smack.

We ricocheted off that dead branch, were shoved by the force of the wind straight through several broken boughs—*ow, ow, ow*—until we smashed into another that didn't give under our weight.

But on impact, I did the unforgivable.

I dropped the ball.

As per my prayer, salvation came for one. No help was granted for a soul-light that was nothing more than a bit of parchment over a brilliant sphere of light. So light, so flimsy, so fragile. It got caught on a cradle of foliage at the end of a mostly dead branch. I stretched for it, feeling the strain in my gut and my shoulder. My nail pierced its thin skin—*he's wailing, he's wailing*—then the net of greenery holding it parted, and the ravenous wind plucked it from me.

The soul sailed off the ends of Threall, its inner light bleating, straight into the restless, white plume of air. A noise splintered across the clearing. Horrifying. Screams. Not one from one voice, but from many. Aborted and choked, but I heard them.

I swear I did.

I buried my head in my arms.

"I will find your soul," called Mad-one into that hollow silence. "The Black Mage's spell of protection will not keep you eternally safe from me. When it wears off, I will search for your tree. But first, I will find those that you hold precious. The first soul I will feed to the wind will be a friend. Then I'll find a sister, a brother, perhaps a lover. I'll cause pain and grief to every person you hold fondly in your heart."

Lexi . . . Lou.

"You are not worthy to call yourself one of our number." Her voice climbed. "A true mystwalker is trained and educated. But it is evident by your speech, and your graceless manner that you have never spent so much as a month in apprenticeship. What were you? A farmer's daughter? A miller's child? One with a set of doting parents who kept your gifts well hidden? Though something happened, quite recently, did it not? Somehow your weak spark of talent was discovered and you were taken to the Black Mage. Did he promise you freedom if you traveled to Threall? Did he tell you his wards would keep you safe? Did he instruct you to hurt me and those I guard? You shall not. I am *always* on guard. The Black Mage lied and abandoned you to my care—a provocation one day that he will rue. As will you—before I grant you death, I will make you grovel in grief and mourning." Mad-one clapped her hands together. The branches held aloft by her magic began shuffling back into their places, until there was no crack in her barricade. From within it she said, "There is none to keep you safe from my wrath."

I pressed my cheek against the walnut's deeply furrowed bark.

I want to go home.

I said the last thing inside my own head. I know I did.

The mostly dead walnut replied, "All you need do is wish for it."

Oh crap, I'm one freak out short of a twig fence and tree conversations.

A dry chuckle. In. My. Head.

I've got to get the hell out of here before the munchkins start singing.

"Wish for it," repeated the nut tree.

I feel sheepish about the next bit. I didn't spare time to wonder why the tree was talking to me. I didn't search for its ball of light to check to see if it was scary looking or benevolent. I didn't ask it a single helpful question—for example: Do you know where my brother is?

Instead, I curled my legs around the branch and put my hands together in a prayer position. I thought of where I wanted go. Not to a dreary apartment, or Bob's car, or even to Creemore. I thought of a person, instead of a place. Someone who made me feel like I could have a home. Yeah, I know. A tad on the hopeful, mad side. But hell, I was already listening to a mostly dead tree's travel advice.

Then I said, "I wish to go home." And holy crap—suddenly I was falling, wingless and sharp—the same sort of sickening jolt you experience when your body drops off to sleep before your brain does, except in this case it was a longer fall. I had mists to breeze past, clouds to tumble through, and gray-blue sky to plummet from before I landed in the real world, hard enough to knock me out cold.

It's getting tedious, waking up confused.

Could have sworn I landed hard and went splat. And yet, here I was, standing upright in the strip club's parking lot, knees wet, hands stinging, my fingers wrapped around the handle of Trowbridge's gun. The rain must have started again while I was soul-traveling. I wiped a bead of it off my chin.

Bob's Taurus was five feet behind me. The strip club's door perhaps less than that. Disorienting. I thought I'd left my body in the car.

How'd I get here?

I looked down at my shoes.

My feet were pointed toward the club's door.

Another rap song ended. The new tune's beat was more seductive, less in your face. A woman could move to the song. Sway to it like a cobra as men with glazed eyes and bomber jackets a size too small watched with appreciation that never peaked and never waned.

"I want to go home."

Faced with a decision, I usually choose the most obvious solution.

I followed the direction of my soles.

Chapter Thirteen

Suzy-Q swung around that pole like she was weightless. I might be able to do that, maybe, if someone showed me how. And if I had zero body fat. And if my hands were as strong as vise grips, and I wasn't weighed down with clothing. Maybe if I wore a sateen string bikini top, a pair of abbreviated boy shorts, and a G-string, I could do it.

Maybe.

The club was a mixture of dark and light. The walls were black, and the furniture was drab colored. What light there was had been planned, thought out, and directed. Electric blue LED tubing outlined the bar and doorway to the can. Yellow beer logos flickered on the wall. A long bristling line of spotlights ringed the stage. They bathed the dancers' flesh in a film of red.

The bouncer was arguing with a stripper about VIP room tips. They didn't turn, even as the cold air wafted into the hallway with me. I snuck up behind them and tucked myself into the shadow behind the fake fig tree by the doorway. Then, I slid sideways, hugging the back wall until I hit the end of the bar.

It took a moment to get my bearings. The girls on stage had bills tucked into their string bikini bottoms, sticking out like frills on the sides of their hips. Most of the men wore baseball caps they hadn't bothered taking off. I wondered if their necks hurt, staring up like that—I hoped that Trowbridge's did.

I checked the profile of each upturned face. Old and wrinkled, average and not, young and groomed, just-plain-ugly, not-so-ugly, ugly and fat, bored and not-so-old. None of the faces was his.

A brunette was leaning on the bar, her arms folded, her bottom sticking out, talking to the guy sitting next to her. She wore a mostly see-through top that looked like it had been savaged by a T. rex. Her hair was tousled, a lot—the effect you get when you tease the shit out of it, hang it upside down, and spray it with half a can of hair spray.

"You going to buy one of those for me?" The stripper may have been skinny, but the heels made her Amazonesque in height. I couldn't see past her. She did another head toss, sending a waft of sweat and oversweet perfume my way. I rubbed my nose. He was here. Nearby.

"Yeah, sure," said my childhood crush.

There he was—just past the skanky brunette. The only guy *not* facing the stage. His head was bent over the three shot glasses lined up on the bar. "One for the lady," he said, lifting his eyes. Though he'd tipped his head sideways in the stripper's direction, his gaze hadn't moved toward her booty or the barmaid's belly ring. He was studying his own reflection in the mirror behind the bar. Maybe she-with-the-tits-and-hair wouldn't recognize it, but I, with the encyclopedia of Trowbridge facial expressions stored in my brain, knew what that blank stare meant: baby was feeling bleak. *Good.*

I tapped the lap dancer on the shoulder. She had two deep lines running like brackets on either side of her mouth, and a pair of drawn-on eyebrows that were as mobile as her lips. The brunette looked down, took in the full glory of me and smiled.

"Beat it," I said.

She laid a talon-tipped hand on her chest. "Excuse me?"

"I need to talk to him. Go away."

Skanky-ass parked her butt on the edge of the barstool.

In the instant it took to turn back to him, Trowbridge's

features had fallen blank. No "you're back!" welcome on his lips, no heavy frown either. His face was stupidly still as he stared at me, like he'd been caught by a thought he hadn't expected to reexamine and needed time to think it through before he made up his mind.

He lifted one eyebrow just slightly.

And with that, the world fell away. Yeah, yeah, the bar was still there—the bass-heavy music thumping loud enough to tickle my feet; the bar's belly-twitching stink of sex, sex, sex, a loathsome miasma all around me, and somewhere beyond the golden glow surrounding my tousled-headed Were, I knew Suzy-Q was still twirling around her slick man pole— but we—Trowbridge and I—we went into that mortal world between worlds, where all the other irritants disappear and there's nothing more than two thumping hearts, and souls singing.

I can see you, Trowbridge. Right through your eyes. Pain and want. *If your soul was mine to protect, I would hold it so tightly in my hands that even Mad-one's couldn't pluck it free.* Irises rimmed with a ring of midnight blue. *You're as sad as me, as lonely* . . . Oh my. I don't know what he was reading in my glittering green eyes, but his pupils dilated, dark and wicked hot with what . . . I leaned in. *What?*

And maybe that's what did it. I got too close. Before I could figure out what message had confused the hell out of me with its throaty whisper, the idiot made up his mind. First, he bit down hard on his back molar, enough to make a muscle ugly-flex in his jaw, then he blinked.

That's all it took. Good-bye, Cupid.

Trowbridge's glance was quick and comprehensive. "A Barry Manilow T-shirt? Where'd you come up with that?" he asked me.

I yearned to sink my teeth into his wet lower lip till he howled for mercy.

"The car." I lifted my chin. "Bob likes to be prepared. Do you want to talk here or outside?"

The lights on the stage behind him turned from red to purple-pink. "The discussion's closed." He jerked his chin in the direction of the shadowed doorway. "Take off, kid. You should have been long gone by now."

"How about that drink, honey?" said the brunette.

"Go away or lose those extensions," I snapped.

"Give us a minute, will you?" Trowbridge sent her a brief smile. *Oh yeah, send a smile out to the cheap seats.* "Then I'll see about buying you a drink." Even her ass looked sulky as she left.

"Okay, I've been thinking," I said. A lie, I'd been soul-traveling. *But I'm always doing that, aren't I? Lying to Trow-bridge. Dropping balls.*

Trowbridge had gone back to studying the line of drinks in front of him. "It's always good to try something new."

New is not always good. I briefly closed my eyes, and banished Threall. When I opened them he was studying me with his head tilted to one side. "I've been trying to come up with a plan that solves all my problems, but you know what? I'm not good at that. I'm good at finding things. Food. Jobs. Money for the rent. I haven't had time for plans. I just run from problem to problem, plugging up holes the best I can. This time running isn't the answer, and stealing isn't going to work, be-cause I don't even know where to find Scawens's Alpha." I swallowed to loosen the knot in my tight throat. "Help me, Trowbridge."

"I have helped you." With a small frown, he reached for the first of the three shots of Jack lined up on the bar. "You're alive, wandering around the world spreading some more Stronghold bad luck. This is the last time I'm going to tell you. Get a box, put the piece in it, and send it to Creemore. Then take your round little ass as far away from here and me as possible." He raised the drink in a salute and downed the glass's contents in one gulp. "I'm done. You're too much work. I've lost my invisibility, my van, and most of my cash. I'm down to my last pair of jeans."

But he still had his soul.

"You keep showing up at the worst times of my life, but you never do much good, do you? You just take in the scenery and walk out again. How's that feel?" I inhaled slowly through my nose, and steadied my voice. "I need help, Trowbridge. I need someone who can guide me through this. Someone who understands the Creemore pack intimately. Someone who knows the Alpha, and the way his mind works, and is strong enough to stand up to him."

The thin blue vein pulsed under his eye. Its beat was the only thing he couldn't control. His mouth, his eyes, even that telling muscle in his jaw, they had shut down, but he couldn't control the flutter of the pulse under his skin. "Do I look suicidal? Give him what he wants. That's all you can do."

"I can't." It came out the way it felt: near desperate.

He toyed with the second glass, spinning it in a circle, before he asked, "Why not?"

"Because he has Lou!" I said, sharper than I meant to. I put a steadying hand to my stomach. Fire. My stomach was on fire.

"Lou? I thought his name was Billy-Bob?"

"I can't give the Alpha what he wants. You told me he's a stone-cold killer, and that means he won't make a trade. He'll just tidy up the scene. I'm not ready to die, and I'm not ready to give up Lou. There's got to be some chance of a rescue without both of us dying. You know the Alpha. You know the pack. You've spent all those years watching your father guide it. You'll know what to expect, and you can help me come up with a plan."

"And why would I do that?"

"My family was innocent and I hold your pack responsible for their deaths." My Were shifted closer to my spine. "You owe me justice."

"Grow up. Your father and mother's union was an abomination to the Weres. You're lucky no one tried to take the family out earlier."

"No. We were under the Alpha's protection. You said so yourself." I studied his unyielding face and then said in a hard voice, "If you can't be Robbie Trowbridge anymore, can't you at least be Jacob Trowbridge's son?"

"Get out."

A less desperate girl would have stood back from those

eyes, would have noted the tension in his pose, and taken herself right out of that bar. *"Strongholds hold."* I was Benjamin Stronghold's daughter and I wasn't folding. I leaned into his personal space, and made it my own. "You want to explain your eyes? Huh? The whole Alpha thing? You flare Alpha blue. Only the Alpha is supposed to do that, right? You're a bloody searchlight of blue. Your body knows what you are, Robson Trowbridge. It recognizes you. You're the true Alpha of Creemore. When are you going to recognize it?"

Deliberately, he washed any emotion from his eyes— *you're too good at that, Trowbridge*—and reached for the last shot. "I was stupid to ever come back."

"Then why did you? Just to catch up with old friends? You're sitting alone in a strip bar and the thing you're ogling isn't a pair of tits—it's a row of shots."

"I'm not going to lift a hand when that bouncer throws you out." He tipped his head back and swallowed. "I have a life, a job, a business outside of all this. I've built something. I'm sitting in a strip joint because it's handy, not a habit."

"Are you sure about that? That it's not fate," I said, staring hard at his face, his stubborn, remote face. "Fate that you walked into my Starbucks just when I needed you?"

He gave that upward half-sided jerk of the head that looks like someone's just pulled his ear. "Look, I don't believe in fate and fairy ta—"

"Don't say it."

"I'm not a prince who'll fix everything with a sword and kiss." He lowered his voice to a growl. "I'm Rogue. I like it that way. I'm partial to my neck, and I'm not going to risk it rescuing another one of your boyfriends. I'm sorry, kid, but sometimes you just have to accept your losses."

"Lou isn't my boyfriend. Lou's my aunt."

His expression froze. "Your aunt," he repeated, in a hiss. "She's Fae, isn't she?"

"Yes."

"You told me the portals were closed."

"They are. I wasn't lying about that." He'd gone Were

again. If he had fur, his ruff would be standing up around his ears. "Aunt Lou was still in this realm when the Fae slammed the Gates of Merenwyn shut. She tried to go back, but she couldn't find a portal that would answer her call. When the mages sealed the entrances to their world, they locked her out."

Blue lights were starting to glimmer in his eyes. "And it never occurred to you to tell me this before?"

"You would have thought she was guilty of something, and she's not," I replied, trying not to blink.

"Let me guess: she wouldn't ever endanger you."

"She wouldn't have done anything to hurt my mum." A wash of heat warmed the base of my throat. "They were sisters. Close."

"Close enough to tell each other secrets?"

"Will you just try to understand? Just for once, don't go all Were on me." My amulet protector stirred against my breast. "Not *now*, Merry." I took a steadying breath, and continued, "You've got to understand. She found me that night. I can't leave her. She's dying."

"How powerful is her magic?" The lights in his eyes were no longer glints; they were spinning little spits of electric blue, sparking in the gloom.

I broke eye contact. Over his shoulder a girl was hanging upside down from her stripper pole; the only thing keeping her airborne was one crossed knee. "All her talent, everything she had; it's all gone."

"Can she open the portal?"

"No!" At my sharp reply, Merry started to pull herself up toward the opening of my blouse. I gave her a not-so-delicate push back into my cleavage and fixed Trowbridge with a glare. "She couldn't do it even when she was strong and had access to my amulet. She tried. Lou dragged me from portal to portal for days trying."

"Unbelievable," he said. "You realize that you just admitted to me that you know all the portals in the Alpha's territory? Do you know how lucky you are that you spilled that information to someone who doesn't give a shit?"

I stared at him for a second and then said, "You're flaring, Trowbridge."

He squeezed his eyes shut for a couple of seconds. There was a ripple over his body, and then when he opened them again, his face was set, and his eyes were Trowbridge blue. "We can't take another war. Forget the death toll, the fallout will be worse. It wouldn't be long before some yahoo with a cell phone saw something he shouldn't, and posted his clip on the Web. Enough of those videos stirring up fear, and it would be back to the Dark Ages. Except this time the assholes will have guns." He brooded at the men ringing the stage, his mouth turned down. "It wouldn't be the odd nutjob either. It would be everyone. We'd be hunted again with everything from BB guns to AK-47s."

"I'd steal Lou back if I knew where she was," I said in exasperation. "I thought all the Alpha wanted was the amulet."

"Which is why you came looking for me." He leaned back in his seat. "How'd you know I had one?"

"You had it around your neck when you came through the kitchen door. You were still wearing it when you walked into my Starbucks. Who was the geezer with you?"

"You were at Starbucks?" There was a screw-you glint in his eye, before he lowered his attention to the empty glass in his hand. He spun it. It made eight revolutions before he came to a decision. "All right, I'll take care of this. Give me the amulets."

"No," I said.

"It wasn't a question, it was an order."

I expressed my utter terror with a smothered snort. "And what will you do with them?"

He pushed out his chair. "Destroy them."

"I don't think so." *He'll thank me for saving his soul later.* I let the gun hang from my fingers for a moment, acknowledging its weight. Blew some air up at a strand of hair tickling my cheek. Then I stepped back from the bar, and pointed it at him.

"You can't have Merry and you need to come with me." I

felt my eyes flare and knew them to be flashing sparks of green fire.

"Jesus, you don't bring out a gun in a—"

"Gun!" shrieked Legs.

"It's all right, it's all right," Trowbridge said, holding his hands up. "She's going to put it away and leave." He whipped his head back to me, and lifted up his eyebrows in inquiry.

"Make me."

Which, as it happens, is the wrong thing to say in a strip bar.

Chapter Fourteen

There had been an instant, before flying fists turned into flying bullets. Just a tiny instant when my hand was caught in the nest of the brunette's hair, and I had glanced up, and saw him. Not as Robbie, or the Were. Not even as Trowbridge. Just a beautiful man in glorious prime, who was weaving effortlessly around the bouncer and some other guy who had stepped up to get an ass whipping.

"Come on, you slow bastards." He caught my gaze, just after his head had tilted out of the way of a blow. Over the bouncer's shoulder, he grinned. A flash of white teeth in a pirate's beard.

Happy. The stupid man was happy until some movement over my shoulder caught his attention. His face changed from happy to furious. That fast. The stripper with the bar stool never got to use it on my spine. He was there, and then she was flying through the air. And then he glanced back at me with a look I knew very well.

I was so surprised, I shot him.

"I didn't mean to," I said. "The gun went off in my hand."

"That's what they always say," said Trowbridge sourly. "'Officer, the gun just went off in my hand.'"

"Why don't you save your breath to heal?" I tenderly touched my head. Winced. "Why's it always my head?"

"You're lucky," he replied. "It's the hardest part of you."

"That's why I aimed for your ass," I snapped back. He narrowed his eyes on me. He did that a lot, training his eyes on me like I was some sort of prey. I bent my head and stared at him through the open car window. "Why aren't you healing? You were shot at the Laundromat. That bullet didn't cause you this much trouble."

"The last slug just blew through me. In and out of the soft tissue. This one hit the bone. Feels like it's stuck."

"Oh."

"Yeah, oh." He tried to shift positions in the car seat. He stifled a groan for my benefit, just because I was vertical and he was mostly not. "Okay, dial the phone and then pass it to me."

"I could speak to her," I asked, spinning his coin in my fingers. He still wouldn't let me use the cell.

"Just dial the numbers and pass me the phone through the window." I did both, slapping the receiver into his outstretched palm as the call went through. I folded my arms and leaned against the phone box. I could hear the steady drip of the coolant leaking from the Taurus. And his breathing. And our hearts, beating. Slower now, and thankfully, still completely out of sync, not even close to the perfect, thudding, heart-harmony of two mated souls.

"Cordelia?" His deep voice was roughed by pain. "We need help."

He'd grunted, "Fifteen minutes," after passing me back the phone but Cordelia was late. We sat for twenty-four minutes, parked right by the pay phone (which I found and which did not have a nearby strip club), and I was getting tired of his remarkably effective stifled groans. You'd think he'd just heal and be done with all the twitching, and distended neck tendon stuff. It was tiresome and repetitive.

Almost as repetitive as the tape that replayed in my head. It didn't matter how I played it; backward, forward, slow motion, or fast. The sequence always ended the same. First Trowbridge dodged the fist, then he grinned at me like we

were the only ones equipped with swords in a rigged gladia-
tor match, and then his face grew savage. He sent my
would-be assailant across the room like a double D weighted
paper airplane. Then he looked at me. There it was. That
look. The one that said "all mine."

Dad used to look at Mum like that.

Part of me was doing the hallelujah hand jive and part of
me was searching for a manhole cover to dive down. Did he
know that he'd given me "the look"?

"Your uncle can't keep my aunt," I said, trying to change
the direction of my thoughts. "It's wrong."

"I'll make a note of that." He ineffectually smothered a
hiss as he repositioned his leg. "While we're on the subject
of Faes and bad stuff, give me the amulets."

"Uh-uh."

"Do you know how many times you've defied me?" There
was no anger in the comment; his question had been delivered
with the same tone one might use for asking, "What year did
the Maple Leafs win the Stanley Cup?"

"Lost count."

He blew some air through his lips and I caught a little eau
de Jack Daniel's. "A team of crack Were guns for hire couldn't
liberate your aunt, right now. He'll have her surrounded by
layers and layers of people. She'll be deep in his territory."

"Don't you have a way of sneaking in there?" I asked with
a frown.

He didn't even bother to open his eyes. The guy who'd just
given me "the look" pulled his lip down and let it stay that
way.

"What were you doing here anyhow, if you have a job and
life elsewhere?" I played with the brunette-colored hair ex-
tension. "Don't tell me sightseeing. You came here without
an invitation for a reason."

Trowbridge's eyelids lifted, and for a moment the interior
was illuminated with a bit of an electric-blue fire before he
shut them again. He fumbled in his pocket, but as he was
reclining sideways in the passenger seat, with his blood-wet

jeans clinging to his right hip, it soon became a battle of will to pull his wallet free.

My Were-bitch was unhappy. Deeply unhappy. If she could have pissed on me she would have. I'd hurt him. This, evidently, was a very bad thing.

"Let me help," I said, reaching for him.

"Back. Get back." He slapped his perspiring hand at my own. "Back in your seat. Just stay there." He finally got his wallet out. His fingers were bloodstained, but the gouge on his knuckles was filling in. His thumb left a big wet spot in the middle of his credit card. His fingers kept slipping off the piece of plastic he was trying to pull out. "Shit." He sighed, and passed me his wallet. "Behind the credit card, you'll find a folded piece of paper. Bring it out."

Trowbridge had a credit card? He had to be in really, really bad pain. He'd just given me his wallet. Who was the clever Were now? I unfolded the paper. It was a one-line e-mail from Rachel Scawens, dated one week ago: "I need your help." I read it again, this time silently. "Rachel? Wasn't that your sister's name?"

His face was paper-white. "If you think the kid's a jerk, you should meet my brother-in-law."

"I thought all your family was dead." Then I winced, because that sounded harsh and unfeeling.

"Rachel was already living out of the house with Scawens."

"Then why are you Rogue?" I frowned at the large thumbprint of mustard on the edge of the crumpled paper. "I thought the pack chased you out. She could have vouched for you."

"The pack *did* chase me out of the territory." A pause. Then softly, "But first she told me to go."

My Were took umbrage at that. I could feel her swell inside me. "She didn't believe *you* had something to do with killing your family."

"It looked bad," he said with a shrug.

"So, she believes you now? Will she vouch for you? Tell them that you're innocent?" I refolded the paper, and put it back in among the seventy-five dollars he had left. "You could be celebrating Christmas with the pack." He didn't seem overjoyed at that. I thought a bit, and then asked, "This e-mail . . . it's not a trap, is it?"

"That occurred to me. So I called someone who I figured I could trust, before I went to Creemore."

"Geezer-Were," I said.

"Huh? Oh." He grimaced. "You saw him with me. Anyhow, I found out what she wanted."

"What?"

"Stuart," he said with a huff of laughter. "She wanted me to take her son away from a bad influence."

Impossible not to start grinning with him. "What bad influence?"

He bit the inside of his cheek before he said, "My uncle Mannus, the Alpha of Creemore."

"And you're giving me a hard time about *my* relatives."

"Shut up, Stronghold," he said without any heat.

"Back at you, Trowbridge." But my voice had grown soft. Don't be a sap, I thought. Only an idiot would allow a man to court her with insults.

The Taurus was getting cool. Thirty-two minutes had elapsed. He was still hurting and flaring Alpha blue whenever he opened his eyes longer than five seconds. He'd refused to wear Bob's wraparound large sunglasses because of their smell. He had no problem, however, confiscating my own glasses.

And then, to make my evening complete, Lou came calling. A slip. A suck. A slide into her world.

Mannus Trowbridge's shoulder-length gray mane is combed straight back. His clothing barely registers on me, other than it is comfortably rumpled. The calculation in his faded blue eyes is at odds with lips that seem permanently set on the edge of a smile.

Time hasn't been kind.

He approaches at a slow amble, his mouth moving to an

audio I can't hear. I sit behind Lou's eyes, and feel her fas-
cination and trepidation stir as he comes closer.

He puts his hand on her arm, hands that have never used
a shovel. No calluses. No roughness. Square-shaped, with
nicely proportioned fingers. The middle-aged skin is smooth
and unmarred except for the ink spot staining the pointer
finger.

That ink-stained finger can't seem to rest. It moves on her
skin, stroking in a circular pattern that soothes the craving
and adds to the ache.

And then the quality of the touch changes. She looks up at
him. His mouth is still moving, still talking, still wheedling.
But I can feel her fear begin, just a tiny spark of it, low in her
belly, as the nail on that finger begins to elongate and sharpen
on her arm. It keeps moving, in the same circuit on her pale
flesh, but as it turns it leaves a trail, first of skin whitened,
and then of skin brightened by blood.

Fear turns to terror.

"Kid?"

I could feel her scream bubbling up in my throat. Run.
Escape!

I shoved the car door open, and streaked across the street,
completely ignoring Trowbridge's command to stay. Someone slammed on their brakes, but I kept going, even as Trowbridge yelled, "Jesus, you almost got nailed! Come back here,
right now." I skipped over the road like a squirrel trying to
outrun a semi, and I didn't stop until I found a stop sign to
hold on to.

I could feel the ground under my feet again. Oh Sweet
Heavens, Lou's dreams were getting sharper. What if there
was a hole in one of them? I'd find myself yanked straight
back to Threall. I tightened my hold on the traffic sign. I was
safe. The post quickly heated against my bare hands. *It's the*
iron in it. My lids drooped. There wasn't enough ferrous in
the steel to make me ill, but the alloyed metal made me
feel—I cracked a huge yawn—like I'd swallowed a sedative.
A snooze-coaxing one at that. *I should let go.* But no . . .
clinging grimly to that pole, with my feet sunk deep into this

world's wet soil reminded me where I was. Earth's realm. *Here,* I wasn't going to find myself stalked by a morally bankrupt mystwalker. *Here,* I was safe. I pressed my forehead against the rain-beaded sign.

Stay far from me, Mad-one.

"Stronghold, get back here now!" Trowbridge roared.

I lifted my head.

There was a burned-tire smell coming from the white 4x4 Jeep that had skidded to a stop dead center on the road. A tall woman got out of the vehicle, and I had a quick impression of shoulder-length red hair and a thin build stacked on a pair of heels. My nose crinkled at the scent of her—Weres mixed with Obsession. Her back was to me as she leaned into the Taurus, revealing a bony ass that I wanted to kick. I straightened my spine, and scowled. *Turn her back on me as if I didn't count?*

She looked over her shoulder with a severe frown and then said something to Trowbridge in a low, husky voice, before she straightened up, adjusting the hem of her jacket.

How many women truly sway? Trowbridge's Cordelia did. She didn't walk, or mince: she slinked, weaving like a vertical cobra, across the street, her silver slingbacks clicking on the pavement, and her head held strangely immobile and high. Not a drunken sway, no: a graceful, hip-generated one that said the owner of the shoes had all the time in the world, that nothing, short of breaking one of those glittering three-inch heels, would make this woman lose her grace or composure.

I'm a girl, I couldn't help it. I checked her body over as critically as if she were Miss Southern Ontario and I was the squinty-eyed judge with a cellulite issue. Okay, she had me on height—who didn't? But I won in the curves arena. Trowbridge's Cordelia was a thin rectangle on very long legs. Her boobs looked wrong. Silicone, I thought, feeling a small measure of good will.

Had he ever given her *"the look"?*

The closer she got, the more my eyes started their preflare burn. I pulled Bob's wraparounds off the top of my head and slapped them on as she reached my side of the street. Ice-cold eyes stared down at me from a fifty-year-old face. The owner

of those eyes had made an attempt to hold back the evidence
of time and gender with a careful application of thick founda-
tion and liner.

"Bridge wants me to collect his Tinker Bell," she said in a
carefully throaty voice. The redhead studied me briefly, one
side of her mouth pulled down. "If I don't come and bring you
back, the bloody man will drag himself across the street.
Let's hurry, shall we? It's beginning to rain again, and my hair
will get wet." Her head turned before her hips did. And then
Cordelia, who had possibly been born Carl, swayed her way
back to Trowbridge. She stopped, perhaps unconsciously,
right in the middle of the golden circle provided by the street-
light, and turned to flick me a glance over her shoulder. Her
penciled-in eyebrows rose as her lips pursed. "Well? Chop-
chop."

I didn't chop, but I sure as hell followed. It was too damn
delicious.

Cordelia didn't ask a single question. Not one. Not how Bridge
got shot, or who I was. She had bony hands, with three blue
veins and large knuckles that looked strange with the nail extensions and French polish. But everything she did with those
hands was graceful. She brought out a blanket, which she
passed to me. She lowered the seats in the cargo area, and
then snapped her fingers for the blanket. I put it in her bony
paw. With a flick of the wrist, she covered the back with the
blanket, and then went to gather up Trowbridge.

She pulled his arm over her shoulder and helped him to
his feet. "You in first," she said to me. "Cradle his head, and
keep him from rolling about in the back."

I tried, but Trowbridge passed out on the fourth pothole
on the Gardiner.

"Look, darling, I'm sure you think I can carry him up all on
my own, but this is Ann Taylor, and you're wearing rags, so
will you put your bloody back into it? Help me with him.
Hold up your side while I get the key in the door."

We'd helped Trowbridge into the elevator, steadied him

as it shot up to the eleventh floor. We'd got him down the corridor to the door of her condo. What we couldn't do was to get him to go any farther. By that time, he was all Were and irrational man. The closer he got to passing out again, the more adamantly he held on to the door frame.

"I refuse to fight with him," she said. "He's all yours. I need to find some tweezers and plastic anyway. Drag him down to the dining room when you can."

I put two hands on his back and shoved him into the apartment. Trowbridge's shirt was mostly wet. Rain had done a bit, blood had helped, and sweat had taken care of the rest. All I wanted was to rip that torn, stained shirt off. It offended me, somehow, deep inside. The sight of it and the long, sleek muscles standing out on arms that were beginning to tremble, plus the stench of his spilled blood tainting his signature scent of the woods and wild; all of it bothered me.

I urged him a little deeper into the apartment then closed the door behind us. He'd gone from clinging to the outside door to clinging to the hat rack. Cordelia liked hats. Bridge's fists were crushing the wide, soft brim of a bronze chapeau more suited for the Kentucky Derby than church. A veritable concoction of netting, faux roses, feathers, and ribbon. Who wore that stuff?

I tamped down on my irritation. "Come on."

"Can't go with her," he said to me, through his teeth.

"Isn't she safe?"

"I can't control the flare in my eyes." He ground the offending orbs into the crook of his arm. "They're going off like sparklers. I don't want to—"

"Let her see," I finished. "Can't you just keep your eyes closed? Maybe pass out again?"

He shook his head. A wet curl got caught up in his bristles, and stayed there, hanging onto his chin.

"The bullet is working itself out the wrong way." Cordelia came out of a doorway with her hands filled with first-aid stuff. Bandages, scissors, long tweezers, and a knife. "Traveling up through the bone, rather than out of the flesh. Femur, I think Bridge said. That happens sometimes. The bullet will have to work its way through the hip. Painful, and sickening, if it's silver-tipped. It wasn't, was it? I've spread some plastic out on the table. Bridge, I'll help you to lie down."

I found myself stepping in front of him. One of his hands left its death grip on the hat rack to squeeze my shoulder. I had to spread my legs to keep from buckling.

"Bathroom," he said into my ear.

"Trowbridge, I don't want to help you—"

"He's not asking you to hold his dick to pee, darling; he's asking you to take him somewhere private to heal." Cordelia approached us slowly, her knowing eyes sorting and calculating. "Well, well, how totally unexpected."

"What?" I asked, looking between the two of them.

"Bathroom," Trowbridge said, sounding sour. He nudged me to the door on the right, three feet down the hall. He had lousy balance, and I ended up being his two-legged walker aide into Cordelia's tastefully gray-blue bathroom. It had a lot of shiny things in it: sparkly mirrors, and a glinting silver soap dispenser.

Cordelia placed the first-aid stuff on top of the granite counter. "Does she know what to do? She has to be very exact with the knife. Extracting a slug from a bone without causing more damage is not an easy task. " Her mouth thinned to almost nonexistent as she moved the white towels out of our way and looked around her spotless bathroom. "I should have brought the plastic in here."

"Do?" I asked. Trowbridge was holding himself upright with a bloodstained hand on the wall. He'd gone from white to the type of gray that spoke of imminent collapse. I took a step backward just to be safe, but his fist was clenched on my Barry Manilow T-shirt. "What do you mean 'do'? The last bullet came out on its own."

"The last bullet? Bridge, what *have* you been doing in the past few hours?" Cordelia's gaze flicked to me. "How are you with a knife, darling?" She smiled, a patrician effort that didn't warm her wintry blue eyes. "I can stay, Bridge. I can help you through this."

He shook his head.

"You can trust me." Some of her confidence slipped. "You have to know that."

As Cordelia read his face, her mouth twisted. She turned away. I noticed the skinny white skunk line near her scalp as she bent over, searching for new towels under the sink. She passed me some ratty beige ones and a bottle of bathroom cleaner. "I want every bit of his blood cleaned up, afterward. And don't touch the white towels." Then she spun on her slingback silver heels and left the bathroom.

"Lock the door," Trowbridge said. His head was tilted back against the wall. He was bracing himself with his good foot against the tile. "Hurry up."

I turned to do so, and so I missed seeing his long slide down the wall. I heard it, as did the Were-bitch inside me. I could feel her twisting inside me in agitation. I stared at my fingers on the lock, until he let out his final grunt of pain. Then I slowly spun around.

He was lying on Cordelia's white tile, his head near the toilet and shower enclosure. His bad leg was stretched out, but his good one was bent at the knee. He still had my glasses on. One lens was smeared with a thumbprint of his dried blood.

I knelt beside him. "We don't need glasses anymore." I took off my pair and reached for the ones covering his eyes. His hand caught mine. Warm. Hard. A little bloody, which generally would have made me puke, but it was Trowbridge blood, which made it precious as well as horrible. The gouge was still there across his knuckles from when he'd missed the bouncer and got the pole instead.

"I can't stop flaring," he said in a tight voice. "I can feel it."

I picked up one of her white towels, rolled it into a long snake, and jammed it against the bottom of the door. "Flare, then." I eased the glasses off his nose. He opened his eyes, and blue light, soul-searing, shone from them.

My own Were seemed to swell under my skin, making it feel tender and tight.

"You're going to have to help me, if the bullet doesn't

change course. God, I'm so hot." He grabbed the front of his shirt and gave it a good yank. The last of its buttons went rolling onto the floor, chittering like skittles on the ceramic. "Test the knife on your thumb. Is it sharp?"

"You're asking me to use a knife on you?"

"As long as this is working its way through me, I won't heal. Do you want me to be weak? In my uncle's territory? Now?" His neck muscles moved as he swallowed. "I can't protect you or myself. You wanted Lancelot, now be Guinevere."

"I've seen *Camelot*. She ended up being stuck in a nunnery, while he swanned off to France." I hooked my finger under the strand of hair stuck in his beard, and gently tugged it loose. "What would you have me do with a knife?"

He mustered a shaky grin. "First promise me that you'll leave me with my balls."

"You got it."

"Good girl." His lips were bloodless. "God, I'm thirsty."

I filled a glass with water, and brought it to his lips. He gulped it down, tipping his head back and breathing through another spasm of pain. "Get me out of my jeans, and then we'll talk about what I need you to do," he said. "Hurry. Just split the seams with the blade."

Something rippled under his skin, right near his cheekbone. Then, another ripple, over his brow. There was a sound, like the chatter of teeth, but Trowbridge's were clenched. Oh God, his bones were moving. My Were was howling inside of me. Howling, like a dog shut up too long in its crate. "Son of a bitch," he managed to get out.

"Trowbridge? What's happening?"

"Fuck, I feel like I'm changing."

"What do you mean, 'feel like'?" My hand hovered in the space between us. "Don't you know when you're going to change?"

"I shouldn't be able to. It's too early in the lunar cycle. There's not enough moon to make me . . . Oh son of a bitch." His back arched. "The bullet's moving again . . ." He gasped twice. Two sharp wrenching inhales in between backbreaking contractions. "Hurry up with the knife. You're going to have to cut down to the bone."

I ripped away what jean material I hadn't cut away and poised the blade's tip over his hip. I could see his skin stretching and thinning.

"Whatever you do, don't be afraid," he whispered. "Don't be afraid in front of me, okay, Tink?"

"I'm never afraid of you."

"Liar."

"Mhhmmhh," I said. My eyes were hurting, burning fiercely. He was in pain, my Trowbridge. Horrible pain. And the answer seemed to be right there. *Yes,* my fur-girl said. *Guide him.* "Trowbridge, change."

"I can't." He rolled his head on the tile. "I won't. Not now." His ribs flexed and I watched the skin sink in between them as he took a deep breath.

I watched his leg muscle ripple. "You'd heal as a Were, wouldn't you? Faster than as a man?"

He gave a rough nod.

"Then change," I pleaded.

"I can't. It's not a choice. It's not time."

"Well, you better get yourself a new moon calendar because you're changing. I can see it. Your bones are moving. I can hear them." It was an ugly sound, but I didn't want to tell him that. "If I cut you down to the bone with a fillet knife, it will be horrible and bloody and more than a little aggravating to your Were." I paused, studying him. "Oooh, you should see what just happened to your jaw. Look, pain is triggering your change anyhow. Let it happen. Otherwise, I'm the girl with the bloody dagger facing a pissed-off wolf."

"You talk too much." At least that's what I thought he said. His vowels were changing shape along with his jaw.

"Sometimes." I reached out to brush back his hair, as if I had every right to do so. If I was going to die, fate should at least hand me that cookie crumb. While he was on the floor, writhing, he was mine. Just for a bit, before he turned all ugly and furry, and possibly throat-ripping-outish. "Trowbridge, change."

"Can't. Control. It." He took a breath and then spat out, "Might hurt you."

"Yeah, but I'm the one with the knife." I put a shaky grin on my face, as I cut the rest of his jeans off. "Do it."

"Throat." The ripples were constant and ugly and made his words come out as mumbles. "If I attack. Push in deep. No—"

The room went blue.

In the end, he didn't change fully. He changed just enough to scare the shit out of me, and maybe it was that—the stink of my fear in that small bathroom—that made him pause halfway. Could he do that? Even for me? I don't know. Maybe all the shifting of bones, the snapping and crackling, the stretching of skin and tendon . . . possibly all those horrifying body adjustments was enough.

Trowbridge stopped, hovered and held, halfway between man and wolf, and then with a terrible howl that belonged in neither the world of beast nor of man, he pulled himself back from the brink. My bullet, flattened and twisted, pushed through his flesh and fell into my waiting palm.

The rippling under his skin stopped. The noises reversed. Pops gave way to sound that made my stomach turn— somewhere between the noise an ocean makes and a slurp. There were a few more crackles, one long stretch of sea-slurp, and then he was Trowbridge again.

Wet with sweat. Stinking of pain. And strangely, mine.

Other women say "I do" when they're wearing white and their groom is wearing a new haircut and tie. My man was wearing a torn-up shirt and his old wedding ring. He was lying on blood-smeared tiles in a bathroom that smelled vaguely of Pine-Sol and Obsession. But he was mine. My Were-bitch had always recognized him, even before I'd recognized her.

I might not be his One True Love, but he would always be mine.

Now I understood the terrible burn in my eyes at the sight

of him. Why my flare reached for his. The reason my mother had given up her princess crown, her family, and her future. I saw the yin and yang of it all. The yearning and regret. The instinct battling the common sense. Mum had said that she knew when she found her love, and that one day I would too. She hadn't told me I wouldn't be able to keep him once I did. I felt my eyes burn, but it was different pain. Not across my eyeballs, but deep in my tear ducts. I'd seen Mum cry twice. The first time when she and Dad had a fight of epic proportions and the last time—the image of which I'll never rid from my memory—a minute before she died. I knew what was coming. I waited, fists on my knees, breath caught behind my teeth. My tear ducts filled and stretched. The agony of passing my first real Tear made me suck in my belly and bow to it. I whined, high through the nose, as it fought its way out.

He reached out to my face, and knuckled away the thin stream of blood trickling from my eyes. "Stronghold?"

My nails dug into my palms. The Tear squeezed out and hung, pink-glazed on my lower lid, before it fell.

"Shit." His eyes opened in surprise as its wetness bit through the almost healed skin on his knuckles. "It burns," he said in a hushed voice. Bitter as acid, cold as ice, my Tear glittered and rolled off his hand, leaving behind a residue of splintered diamond chips that shimmered through the red glaze of his fresh blood. He wiped his hand on a towel, and watched me with a frown.

Another one rolled down to my chin and hung from it.

He caught it in his palm.

Pink water turned to brilliant white ice. It shone as bright as the brightest light, lit from the fire of love and pain, before turning hard. He let it roll in his palm. "Tink?"

In his palm lay a small pebble of perfect diamond, truly tear-shaped.

"What—"

"Fae Tears," I whispered.

I needed to be clean and alone—for once I needed time to think—but I only got clean. Trowbridge had his shower first, and I refused to get into it, even when he smiled his most devilish smile, and cocked up his eyebrow. That wasn't the only thing that had been all cocked up.

I tried not to look, and failed.

He left the shower curtain open. When my socks were wet from the growing puddle, I rolled another of Cordelia's white towels into a footrest. His head pivoted with my movement, and for a second the air was perfumed by a scent I began to pinpoint as "me-predator."

He didn't say anything though, and went back to soaping his chest. I didn't say anything either. Too much had gone on, all of it silently, before he'd gotten up and turned on the shower. We'd rested quietly on the floor, leg to leg, hip to hip, and had given ourselves a mental time-out as his body fully healed. I'd shifted my leg away from him and his had followed, searching for my warmth again. I'd concentrated on breathing, and studying Cordelia's shiny soap dispenser between taking glances at him underneath my lashes. He hadn't rolled his head in my direction. Not once. But there had been a faraway expression on his face as he'd rolled my second Fae Tear between his fingers, like it was one jewel too many on a long string of worry beads.

Once the water had warmed he said, "You first." But I'd just shaken my head wordlessly and he'd stepped in alone.

Still now, he wouldn't go and leave me, not even after he'd showered and rinsed the conditioner out of his hair. He sat on the seat of the toilet, the towel wrapped around his narrow hips tenting at his groin, watching me as I stepped fully clothed into the humid shower.

There were questions coming, and worse, answers that had to be created out of half-lies and half-truths. I thought I needed time alone to figure stuff out, but maybe it was better this way. With him here, I couldn't think of anything else but what I wanted and why I shouldn't take it.

I pulled the curtain over, and adjusted the tap, and waited at the dry end of the tub for it to feel warm enough for my Fae skin's comfort. I didn't know what to do about Mum's bride belt. There weren't many places to hide it. After a bit of indecision, I took it off and hooked it over the shower rod, as far away from the wet as I could get. I'd trusted him so far with my life; I could probably trust him not to snatch my mum's belt.

I hoped the steam cloaked me in invisibility as I unzipped my pants and dragged the sucking length of them down my legs. Water was running in two dirty streams from my bare feet. I pulled off Barry Manilow and threw him on the tub floor. Panties or bra next? Bra. I turned my back and took it off. I hooked my fingers on my panties, feeling the elastic stretch like my good intentions. My panties landed on top of Barry, and I spent a nanosecond thinking, *How perverse was that?* before I got under the spray.

My ride-alongs were deeply divided. Merry was stiff, even under the warm spray of the shower, and my Were-bitch was feeling like hot spice rubbed into my skin, but from the inside. I turned my back to Trowbridge, but there was no keeping him out anymore. He was in my head as surely as Lou's thoughts, as surely as the Were-bitch who wiggled against my vertebrae. He was there, everywhere.

His eyes were obviously open, because his side of the curtain was lit by pulsing blue. My own eyes were reacting to his; the tiles around me were bright with my flare. But he'd changed even that, hadn't he? My Fae light had flavored itself with Trowbridge blue. What had been green ice was now the color of the Caribbean. Inexplicable.

I want him. My body knew it. It was welcoming him already; breasts swelling, skin growing taut and sensitive, feminine core turning slick and heated.

I had always wanted him—the girl in me had burgeoned, hovered at the threshold of womanhood, just by inhaling his aroma and observing his body as it flexed and stretched. My uncharted desire had recognized him. Known him in a way that was not of mind but of instinct. Goddess, every time I spied upon him, I'd fancied that I'd developed a scent of my own—musky and heavy, as tantalizing as his.

I would always want him. My yearning for his body

couldn't be extinguished by self-will. He'd been the bare-chested hero of my dreams; the man with the simmering glower in every romance novel I'd ever read, the body I'd superimposed over any male substitute that had ever caused my vagina to twitch. Goddess knows how much I had tried to shed this longing. But it was part of me, as if somehow my settings had been permanently fused to his, the dials frozen in one position, so that no other creature could ever call to the sexual urges buried deep within me.

Thinking about how much I burned for him was like conjugating verbs, except figuring out French tenses wouldn't hurt this much. I closed my eyes as I washed my hair. When I opened them I could see a spotlight of blue focused bust level on the plastic liner.

Merry was quiet. Too quiet and too dull, but for once, for one bloody minute of this last terrible day, I wasn't going to think about her, or Lou, or the whole yawning hole of stupidity of a Were/Fae union. I had twigs to ferret out of my tangled hair. I had some serious scrubbing ahead.

"You about done?"

"Soon." I picked up the soap to rewash every part that hadn't been washed twice already.

"I'm hungry. We should raid Cordelia's kitchen."

"Do you think she has any chocolate?" I ran my fingers over my scalp, searching for any seeds I'd missed.

I heard him pull in some air through his teeth.

Suddenly the curtain was pulled back. Trowbridge stood scowling on the other side. He turned the water off, and yanked a towel off the rack with enough force to make it shudder. He sucked in another hard breath, and his towel fell to the floor, and then I drew in a deep breath of my own. The bride belt slithered off the rail and fell, landing in a heap of gold at his feet. He picked it up, and held it out to me. When I didn't reach for it, he shook his hair to one side, and bent to fasten it around my waist. His fingers were trembling.

He clumsily patted me dry with the towel before he picked me up. Not the pretty way. The efficient way, because he was not only a man in motion, he was a man on a mission. He grabbed my midsection and the back of my legs and hauled me out of there like I was a three-year-old ready for my nap.

Trowbridge fumbled for the door with one hand, and then we were out of the bathroom, and making good time down the hall. To where, I couldn't tell. I was too busy cataloguing things, like how it felt to be skin on skin (the underside of my arm against the top of his shoulder) or to smell him so clean and so near (goddamn aphrodisiac, they should bottle it) or how tiny he made me feel (a freakin' princess in his arms, no less).

The apartment was dark. I got a fleeting impression of light off stainless steel as we booked it past the kitchen. Trowbridge was comfortable in the apartment. He knew enough to veer sharply left when we hit the living room to avoid the side table, and he knew where the sofa bed was. He hesitated before lowering me to it.

Music played in the apartment behind Cordelia's closed bedroom door. A man's voice, bluesy and sad, singing about his Little Valentine.

"I want you," he said in a harsh whisper.

"I know."

"I'm going to have you." His voice was firm, but his smile was tentative.

"I know."

"Tell me you're not a virgin."

"Oh Fae Stars." I raked my fingers through his hair, and pulled it backward until his head was tipped back. His lips curved. "Do you always talk this much?"

He laughed, and I did too, even though I was in midair, and the towel was parting from my body. There was a brief moment where I was naked and needing, right before his body met mine.

Skin to skin. I know they write poems about it, but they really should write more. Long stanzas about the sweet friction of woman-skin sliding against man-skin, words woven into blushing praise about the steely slopes of strong man's muscles, perhaps a few short ditties about the sweet roughness of callused fingers against a breast.

He touched me. With gentle fingers on my jaw, and the backs of his knuckles on my cheek, stroking, feeling, imprinting me forever. My inner Were was rejoicing. Yes! There would be no man but this man. And no moment but this one.

He kissed me. Soft lips for such a hard man. Soft and quizzical, testing and urging, pleading for me to follow. He sucked in my lower lip, and I fell. Crumbled and fell.

Kiss me forever. Just kiss me forever.

His hand drifted down, and left a trail, hot and his, along my collarbone, along my throat. His lips followed; each kiss repeated by the soft echo of his hair. I was liquid heat, and unthinking, until he did the unthinkable. He opened his mouth and said something dumb.

"I can't do this with that thing around your neck." He gestured to Merry. I sat up and covered my swollen breasts with my hands.

"Thanks for bringing up the issue of our total incompatibility," I said, feeling my lip turn mulish. "I can't say much for your timing, but I guess it's better late than never. You're right; we shouldn't do this. You're a Were, and I'm a Fae, and we shouldn't even contemplate having sex. What was I thinking?" I reached for the folded blanket on the bottom of the sofa bed, deaf to my inner Were's whine of distress.

"Stop." He caught me by my shoulders and held me there. He put his teeth to the part of my neck that was connected to my shoulder. The traitorous bitch in my belly shivered with delight.

"Do not mark me," I said.

"Never crossed my mind." He kept nibbling and sucking on my flesh, right there. Right where some part of me had been standing waiting, tapping its toes and scowling at its watch.

I'll count to forty and stop him then.

He had Merry's chain in his hand in five. He eased her over my head by seven. He put her on the side table by nine.

And then his tongue moved over the spot he'd been tenderizing, and my toes curled. Toes do that if the right man is sitting behind you, with his legs wrapped around you and his hard cock pressed against the cheeks of your butt.

He slowed time down with Trowbridge kisses, and Trowbridge fingers. He stroked and sucked, and licked and turned my leg this way, and moved my hip that way, until I was weak and oblivious to anything else, not reason, not my soft belly, nothing else but the need to reach for him and lick him too.

The music was louder. Much louder. Someone's heart was breaking somewhere, but for once it wasn't mine. The taste of him. Salt. Woods. Man.

There reached a point where I got an opportunity to take a good look at him. *That* part of him. I mean, he was in my hand, and my face was just there, and I couldn't help but take his measure and starting thinking real hard about the moment coming up. Would it fit?

I didn't have a chance for doubt to turn to trepidation. He pulled me up his long, hard body, drugged me with a few more kisses, and then he rolled me onto my back. His cheeks were flushed as he propped himself up on his elbow and let his gaze roam over the feast of Hedi. Instinctively, my hands flattened over my stomach. He growled, but I don't think he meant to, because there was a hint of cover-up to the mocking "tsk-tsk" he uttered as his maimed hand lightly captured fluttering ones. With a hint of Trowbridge twinkle, he gently lifted my arms over my head, and pinned them casually there, not savagely, or hurtfully, more like someone unsnapping their folded napkin before they set down to the business of consuming their meal.

I sucked in my breath, and held it there, maybe a little longer than I should have, but I couldn't have exhaled in that moment for the all the green tea in China, because he was suddenly studying me in a way that made me want to arch my back and preen. Gone was that annoying, light bantering humor that had marked his face just two seconds before. It had been stripped away, and replaced by a far deeper one of intent. Yes, his gaze was a little possessive—but not in the

"I shall stalk you" manner, more in the helpless "touch her and you die" way. And yes, I could see something else—an essence both primal and instinctive. It called to my Were, and she told me to bend one leg, and lift my chest a little higher. Feral heat simmered between us. Cheeks flushed, he brushed his knuckles down my neck and then those skillful fingers uncurled to slip sideways down the valley between my breasts. They slid under one silken mound and cupped its weight as if testing a peach for its juiciness. I thought it filled his large paw quite nicely, and he must have arrived at the same conclusion, because he held my breast for another beat, his eyes mere slits, before his hand slowly opened—fingers to cradle its weight, thumb to stroke its nipple. *I am woman. I am Were.* My head tipped back in pleasure. Who knew happy breasts could cause such a savage ache down there? *Crap, I'm a string on his violin. Pluck one end, and the other part quivers.*

"God," he said, sounding one notch away from stunned. "I love your skin. When I touch it . . ."

Pleasure bubbled up, champagne bright and light. "What happens?"

"I can feel your magic hum." He traced my collarbone with his finger. "I can sense your Were."

Fear melted away.

There was more stroking, and sighing (that would be me) and heavy breathing (him), and then we reached the point of no return. He was poised over me, his face gorgeous with the strain. His shoulders were a poem to male beauty. I could feel his erection, heavy and hard against my thigh. *I did this to him. I reduced him to this—trembling, sleek muscles covered in a faint sheen of sweat. Half wild. His hungry wolf glittering from behind his narrowed blue eyes.* Like to like—the thought shot a lick of fire right down to the heels I'd dug into Cordelia's percale. I opened my heart, then my legs. Curved my arms around his neck and lifted my pelvis to his. *At last!* bayed my Were.

His heat slid through my wet folds and met my personal pearly gates.

I winced and scooted back a millimeter.

He muttered something I interpreted to mean "I worship you." *Oh Trowbridge . . .* I pulled him closer and he surged for the goal.

And with one thrust, my accord with my inner Were was torn.

Pain. Hot, nasty, and unforgivable. He filled me up, and still he kept going. Stretching, changing the shape and history of me. Thick. Large. *Penetrating.*

"I change my mind, I change my mind," I said, scooting.

"Jesus, Mary, and Joseph," he said, following on his knees. "Easy."

"Don't easy me," I hissed. "That hurt."

"Shhh, I can make it better." His lips dipped for mine as his hand slid over the slope of my stomach in the general direction of my happy button.

"Make it better?" I howled, slapping his big paw away. "It's too late for that."

He took in a shaky breath and hung his head, exhaling slowly through his teeth. A curl of black silk floated in the air between us, got afraid, and flew back to the safety of his tousled mane. "Okay, Plan B. I'll pull out. Don't move."

And of course, I moved. It was hard not to.

"Son of a bitch." He shuddered. "You're making it impossible to pull out. Just stay like that for a second, or you're going to trigger the Were—"

"Trigger what?" I shrieked, and shimmied up the bed until my head hit the wall, and still I kept going north, even though I was dragging a six-foot-two piece of Were with me.

"The mating knot," he said, with another intense shudder.

I put both hands on his shoulders and shoved. Which is when I learned that Weres' penises are not exactly like human penises, not that I was any authority on human penises. Immediately his member swelled inside me. It didn't precisely hurt, but it didn't feel right.

But worse, far worse, was what happening inside me. Sure, my Were might not have been able to do anything about my sudden change in the game plan. She could control neither my thoughts nor my tongue. But she was real familiar with the territory down south. And for the record, she was not agreeable to this sudden, unexpected course adjustment. Outraged with frustration, she doubled in size, deluging my interior with her ho-hormones. My body's response was to swell certain intimate channels. I mean *swell*.

"You're getting bigger," I said. "Take it out!"

He curled in his stomach muscles, flexed his hips a smidge, and hissed when my nails scored twin lines down his back. "I can't," he spat back in frustration. "It's no good. You've inflamed the mating knot." There were no words for what I was feeling and so I settled for trying to melt him with my death glare. "Don't look at me like that. I am *not* the bad guy. You wanted this as much as me. You *said*, 'Oh Trowbridge!'"—*I said that out loud?*—"When I asked if you were a virgin, did you say, 'Yes, Bridge, I am a virgin.' No! No, you did not. Did you in any way, give me an indication that—"

"Would my virginity have made a difference?"

"Yes," he said, through his teeth. "It *would* have made a difference. I would have slowed down. Given you a chance to accept it. Taken longer—"

"But you wouldn't have stopped?"

"I would have stopped the moment you asked, just like I have now. But it wouldn't have stopped me from trying to change your mind, because you're fucking Fae catnip to my Were. I smell you and I want you. I touch you and . . ." He lapsed into silence. "Whatever. Listen. I'm not taking the blame for this. You're as responsible for this *situation* we're in as me."

Another splatter of sweat on my breast.

"I don't have a scent." Okay, maybe I had one now. Fae blood had been spilled and the bed smelled a bit like cinnamon.

"You do for me. You've always had a scent to me."

I stared at him. "Well, I am *not* respons—"

"Your vagina is clenched around my dick like a fist," he said flatly.

Oh hell. He *had* noticed.

For a second we studied each other, before my eyes slid from his accusing ones to examine his scruffy beard with acute dislike. *I am a needy fool,* I thought. Was I so anxious for another's touch that I lost any sense of discrimination? *Look at him, Hedi. He's a gorgeous skirt-sniffing dog with the homing instinct of a grazing water buffalo, and don't you forget it. Use your brain. Just once. Think.*

Maybe he saw something in my face that I hadn't seen in his. In a softer voice he said, "There's nothing we can do except wait it out. Eventually it will ease."

Just what every ex-virgin with a serious case of remorse wants to hear. "No wonder birth rates for wolves have plummeted," I muttered. "Does this happen every time you have sex?"

"No," he said.

Too fast and too evasive. "Then why did it happen *with me?*"

"I don't know."

His shuttered gaze was fixed on the hollow of my throat. *Fine.* I chose another focus point—conveniently, Cordelia had an étagère filled with rhinestone crowns—and started counting. One crown . . . two crowns . . . three crowns, four ridiculously cheesy coronets . . . five . . . Very hard to think when you've got a male's weight over you. Six diamond diadems, seven—*Goddess, this is going to take forever.* I should have let him "make it better." I thought about that for a bit. It *had* been very nice when he did that thing with his mouth, even if I did feel a bit awkward with my legs splayed open like that. Well, he couldn't do that right now, not without breaking his spine, but he could lavish some effort on my boobs again. I poked his chest with my finger. "Hey," I said, trying to sound conciliatory.

He looked down his long nose at me.

And pfft, there went my Trowbridge-love. "It's occurred to me that maybe we're in this position because you didn't do it right," I drawled.

"Kid," he growled. "I'm well past wanting to do this right."

"Fine. How much longer?"

"A while," he said through gritted teeth. "Stop talking, I'm trying to think of something else." A bead of sweat rolled down his jaw. My eyes followed the droplet of perspiration as it coursed down his neck. It hung on his collarbone for a second, and then fell on my boob. With a grimace, I wiped my breast dry with my finger. "How. Long."

"Keep talking, Tinker Bell, and it will take a year." He looked more in pain than when the bullet had been chewing its way through his femur. Back then, I'd felt remorse for my twitchy trigger finger, but then again, back then, I'd been admittedly weak in my helpless attraction for my childhood crush. Now, not so much. I flinched as he shifted his weight on his palms.

"Seriously, a minute or two or three?" I asked. Then with dread, "Fifteen?"

No answer.

"Trowbridge?" The sweat was beading up on his throat again. I blew some air on it, hoping it would evaporate.

"Stop that!" He took a deep, steadying breath, then let it out in a slow puckered-lip whistle. "I'm not sure how long it will last," he said, somewhat savagely. "I've never had one before, all right?"

He'd never had a mating knot before? Not even with dandy Candy? Well, well, well. I bit down on the instinct to give him a teeth-baring smile. Pleasure spread through me, sugar-sweet and warm. *Never, huh?* My inner Were—usually so slow to take advantage—took note of my ambiguity and immediately started some flexing of her own.

"Oh, that's better," he moaned.

I allowed her to do it again; fascinated by how his eyelashes fluttered with each faint squeeze.

"That's so . . . good," he said huskily.

She did it again—squeeze, squeeze, pulse—while I just lay there. With every contraction, he looked a little more tortured . . . and intent. Just who was he rallying here for? Hedi? Or her Were? *Like to like.* What if it was just me? No Were.

No Fae skin. Just me. Mortal-me—the person sitting on the bleachers watching all this go down. *Just who are you making love to, Trowbridge? Me, or my inner Were?*

See me, I wanted to howl.

I shut down and allowed his cock and my inner Were-bitch to take over at that point, since it was obvious all other union negotiations would be acrimonious.

It pumped and she squealed. Enough said.

But for me, the semimortal Hedi-me? I felt splintered and detached. I stared at the ceiling while Trowbridge grimaced over me. Yes, my skin goosefleshed as his head snapped back. But who put that look of ardor on his face? Not me. I watched the blush bloom on his throat and chest. I observed his strained neck tendons; heard him grunt low. Felt the gush of warmth inside me. *If I have a litter of puppies, I guarantee he'll never get a chance to experience another mating knot.* I turned my head and closed my eyes.

Silence.

Hot breath on my shoulder. More stomach-quivering shivers of delight from my inner bitch before she sank into her sex-satisfied stupor.

Ho.

Trowbridge pressed a kiss on my brow. On my eyelid. On my nose.

"Hedi?"

I squeezed my eyes so tight the tear that had been looking for a way out threw up it hands in disgust, and trudged back to my cramped ducts.

He ran a gentle thumb across my tight lips, before he pressed gentle coaxing kisses on them. "Tink," he said softly as he threaded his fingers through my hair, brushing the sensitive pointed tips of my Fae ears. He cradled my head, then leaned his forehead against mine. His long nose against my short one. Our breaths mingled.

A minute and three seconds later, the knot eased. My satiated bitch yawned, gave herself a celebratory shake, then subsided into a snooze.

I rolled to my side.

I heard a sigh. The singer was still lamenting his lost Valentine.

I reached for Merry and put her around my neck, then curled up in a ball and wondered if there was any Kleenex nearby. And somewhere between my stratagems for wrapping the blanket around myself and going to the bathroom for another shower, I fell asleep.

I didn't even wake up when two warm arms pulled me into their protective cradle.

I didn't feel him tug the covers up over my chilled body. I didn't notice how easily his bristly chin found its place by my pointed little ear.

No, instead, I slept.

And prayed that I wouldn't dream.

That's my story and I'm sticking to it.

Chapter Fifteen

Something tried to claw its way through the door, which is dumb, animal dumb, because anyone with any sense would realize all that frantic scratching would only lead to nails worn down to the nub. The door is steel, set in a cinder-block wall. With its covered round rivets, it's like a fire door—the type you find at the bottom of a staircase, under a sign reading EXIT, except in this case there's no bar to push on and no handle to turn.

People kept on this side of the door are going to stay there.

Someone had customized the door, adding a small viewing window about the size of a book, at eye level. A screen of metal mesh is positioned over it. Thin strips of screw-studded metal secure it. The walls of her prison are gray cinder block, distressed by claw marks and pockmarked by gouges. Ugly. The poured concrete floor has a drainage hole in the middle of it, covered by an iron grate.

Lou backs away from the iron grate.

There's nothing else in the room. No blanket, no window, no bed, or water. Over her head is a false ceiling, made of the same wire mesh used to protect the glass window. The real ceiling is a foot beyond that, and unfinished, exposing the wooden joists and subfloor of the room above it. A single-bulb light fixture is screwed into a beam overhead.

The ceiling cage seems like a thin protection. One good

swipe with a Were paw and it would come down. Unless, of course, it's—

Lou reaches for the dull gridwork of mesh covering the glass window with one long white finger. She strokes it, her finger growing more languorous with each swipe. There are few things that make her languorous in this world. Maple syrup, a wad of cash, and any one of the oldest of the old—gold, platinum, or silver.

Silver. The dull mesh isn't oxidized metal. It's tarnished silver plate.

She fits both hands in the area, positioning them so that each fingertip is on a different welded join of the gridwork. There's a moment's pause as she gathers up the remaining essence of her gift. She flattens both palms hard across the mesh.

Her mouth's calling to Ebrel, Fae goddess of the Seven. She keeps her eyes on her hands. The Fade has reduced them to nothing more than tendon and bone.

The color of the mesh changes from uniform to mottled as the grid sweats pinpoints of shiny liquid silver. Her hands quiver as the mesh becomes slick with a top coat of the precious metal. It's hers, now ready for the taking.

One dot of wet silver begins rolling toward her fingers, pulled by the magnetism of her call. Drips turn to rivulets. The silver rolls in a thin molten river, following the path laid by the trail of her fingers. Down the smooth surface of the metal door. A leap in space, before landing with a wet splat on the floor into a pool accumulating by her small feet.

Stupid, ignorant Were fools.

They had put a Collector in a room fortified with silver—debilitating to Weres, but utterly harmless to the Fae.

Can she hear me? As I hear and feel her? I can't just be a spectator to her dreams anymore, they were too dangerous to me. I call to her. "Where are you, Lou?"

She raises her eyes, and considers the mesh-covered ceiling.

"Soon," I hear in my head. "Wait."

* * *

Even in my sleep, I was so tired I could barely move. That struck me as funny in a sad way, though I couldn't figure out why. Another wave of lethargy swept over me, and my dreams twisted from Lou's to my own. I was no longer standing beside her in that prison. Instead, I was on a raft, drifting down a stream, sloth happy in my nakedness. The sun was warm on my skin. I could feel it right over my breastbone, lulling me into a deeper sleep.

Then a flicker of irritation intruded. Something was jiggling my raft. I was no longer drifting, I was being bounced. There was an annoying babble in the background. And the sound of water. Falls? Were we going over the falls? I turned my head from it all and tried to find a way back to that warm peace of indifference, but the stupid raft kept bouncing and shaking, and the annoying dribble of words was getting louder and louder.

Words sharpened. Turned into sentences and opinions.

"Darling, I've heard of difficult women, but really, gloves?"

"Get the water ready."

My Were-bitch was with me on the raft. She was whining because she didn't like the rough water. I could feel my jaw opening to echo her cry, but all that came out was a low broken mewl.

"Okay, on the count of three. One."

Heat was on my breast. Almost too hot. Just in one spot. Right over my heart. Hot. I twisted my head, and felt the burning around my neck. I was going to drown going over the falls. I was too tired to swim.

"Two."

So hot. Burning.

"Three."

"The thing's dangerous," said Trowbridge.

Water was dripping off my chin. "Give Merry back right now, or I'll hex you and you'll never turn into a wolf again."

"Stronghold, I know when you're lying."

He was holding Merry by her chain with one pink rubber-gloved hand. Cordelia's arms were crossed, but the dripping pail she'd used to douse me was right beside her on the dining room table. "The thing is dangerous," he repeated. "I shouldn't have to use a pail of water to wake my lover."

"Merry is not an 'it.'" I was wet, naked, and furious. And kind of shaky on my feet. "Your amulet may be an 'it,' but not Merry. She's a soul, Trowbridge. She's a thinking, feeling being. She needs to be around my neck. Without me, she'll fade and die. I haven't given her a real meal in twenty-four hours, and she's done a lot of healing over the last day. She's worn herself down trying to revive your amulet." I yanked the blanket off the floor, and wrapped it around myself. "Take a hard look at that thing she's clinging to. You starved it to death. That's what happens if you don't feed a Fae Asrai."

Merry had thrown caution aside. Resolutely hanging on to her corpse-friend, she kept throwing charges up the chain, while she tried to haul both of them up the chain to get near Trowbridge's fingers.

"You let this thing feed off you?" His eyebrows arched in disbelief. "Like a freaking parasite?"

"Don't call her that." My eyes were starting to flare.

"*My* amulet—"

"Stolen Fae amulet."

"My former pendant," he continued, "never did anything except hang around my neck." He gave her chain a violent shake, and Merry fell back down to its end. She extended two thin strips of herself and latched onto her chain again and started, once more, painfully, to pull herself up, but the other amulet's weight seemed to be draining her. "It's like a freakin' bug. It was over your heart. It was throwing colors and I swear it was throbbing. You were whimpering in your sleep."

"Merry doesn't feed off me. She's never fed off me. Fae Stars, she's a vegetarian." I stopped as his eyebrows rose at my lie. "Okay, she needs and prefers the taste of plants and trees, but she can borrow from me in a pinch. It's only happened twice before. Both times, only because it was too difficult to get to a food source, and I offered. And she only did it because I insisted. I *offered*, Trowbridge. She'd never feed off me in my sleep."

"She did this time." Blue-white lights were beginning to spin slowly around his pupils. "You wouldn't wake up no matter what I said or did. It was like you were drugged. Your breathing slowed until your chest was barely moving. We had to douse you with a pail of water to wake you up. Look at you now, for God's sake. You can't even stand straight. You've got one hand on your blanket and the other holding on to the wall. All I'd have to do is blow, and you'd fall down."

Just to prove how wrong he was about my general wobbliness, I removed my hand from the drywall, and reached out for Merry. "Give her to me, Trowbridge. For heaven's sake, you don't need a pair of gloves."

"You didn't see it when it was feeding on you," he said. He shook her down again and put her into a white pillowcase. "You have a hammer?"

"In the kitchen, bottom drawer," said Cordelia. Her gold earrings brushed her shoulder as she tilted her head toward the doorway behind her.

"Don't do this, Trowbridge." I followed, tripping on the blanket.

Trowbridge was "au natural" except for the pink rubber glove on his right hand. Cordelia's head swiveled to watch his ass as he stalked into the kitchen. I pushed past her. He was crouching by the drawer, rummaging beneath the Tupperware.

"What are you doing? You know you can't break Fae gold." He shot me a thunderous glance. "I need you to calm down. She wasn't going to truly hurt me, she—" I ducked as a plastic container went flying past my shoulder. "Trowbridge, stop." I touched his shoulder, hoping to calm him, but contact seemed to make it suddenly worse. He shot to his feet, holding the hammer in a murderous grip. My words dried up, and without thinking, I took a step backward.

He laid the writhing bundle on the black granite counter.

"Four dollars a linear foot, I don't think so," said Cordelia, pulling out a chopping board.

He was *not* going to pulverize my amulet in front of me. I ducked under Bridge's arm, and covered Merry with both my hands. "She's been my friend for a long time." My voice was steel. "I'll protect her against even you."

The hammer was poised high.

"The only way you can kill her is to starve her," I continued, speaking slowly. "And if you do that, you'll not only kill her soul, but you'll do something to mine." In the shelter of his arm, I could feel the heat of him. Merry tried to curl a finger of gold around my thumb through the cotton pillow-case.

He breathed hard over my head. "It was *feeding* off you."

Out of the corner of my eye, I could see the glove, the bubble-gum pink stretched to soft rose where it pulled over his knuckles. The pinkie and the ring finger of the glove stood out empty.

"She is important to me. A friend when I had none." I looked up at him. Jaw, stubble, tight mouth, and a cheek muscle that kept flexing. A quick dip of his chin, and a flash of blue as he returned my gaze. I could feel my own eyes burn, and knew that they had begun to glow. I kept my gaze even, neither demanding nor yielding.

I waited, holding my breath until my chest felt tight.

Some of the wildness went out of his eyes. He lowered the hammer slowly, but even so, with his Were strength it landed with crack. A tiny piece of silica chipped up and landed back down askew on the resulting divot.

"You bloody girl, see what you've done," said Cordelia, sounding a lot like Carl.

I let out my breath slowly through my nose. I could feel his warm chest against my arm.

"I'll fix it, Cordelia," he said.

"Yes, you bloody well better," Cordelia said. "You might want to rethink your girlfriend material. This one's the plague." She turned on her heel and left us alone. A few seconds later a door was pulled closed. Obviously it hadn't made enough noise, because it was opened and pulled closed harder the second time.

Alone and naked again.

Trowbridge rubbed a finger into the gouge on the counter.

He'd had a Coke; I could smell it, and us, mixed together, on both our skins. "Why can't you give up on this stuff?" he said in a low voice. "Destroy the amulets. Let your aunt go. You're as much Were as Fae."

"I need to see Lou one last time."

"Doing that will get you killed. For what? She's going to die anyhow. You've got to harden up, Stronghold. Cut your ties."

"How do you live like that?"

"You just do." He took the granite chip I'd been using to finger-skate over the counter, and put it back into the divot. "You can't stop people from dying. The only thing you can do is fight to stay alive."

"What if she's innocent?"

"Let the Weres decide for you."

"No," I said sharply. "I'll decide for myself."

He stepped back from me and went to lean against the kitchen doorway, to study me with a set expression.

I put my hand up when he opened his mouth to speak. "Lou didn't have to come for me. She didn't have to feed me or keep me safe all these years. For that, I owe her. It would be wrong to let her die alone and frightened. I don't want to live with the guilt of that. I don't think I can."

"Sure you can," he said in a hard voice.

Oh shit.

I might as well have asked him point-blank how he could bear to live after his mate had died. He read my mind, and gave me a smile that wasn't one, before slipping away.

Merry started winding around my finger the moment he cleared our space. "Let go, Merry, so I can get you out of the bag." I opened the pillowcase to peer inside. Her stone was dull; the residue of her fear had left a faint brown streak in the middle. "You need food."

The sun was rising. I rubbed a hand over my eyes as I came out of the kitchen, Merry and her pal curled in the palm of my hand.

Trowbridge was leaning against the dining room table, gazing out the window.

"I'm sorry," I told him. "I didn't mean to say—"

"You need to feed that thing now?" He pushed himself away from the table with a slow flex of his hips. "You want a plant or a tree? Take your pick." I followed the direction of his eyes. Cordelia had a green thumb. There was a bowfront window area, beyond the curved back of the upholstered dining room chair. In it was her garden: a lot of potted plants in all the same stone bisque-colored containers, two shrubs that flirted with the idea of being trees, and three potted orchids on a small table positioned out of direct light.

"Won't she mind?" I asked.

He shrugged. "Most of them were presents from me. I'll buy her new ones tomorrow."

I laid Merry down on the top of the orchid's roots, and then stood, in my blanket, with my arms wrapped around myself as the pink-shell sky tried to turn blue. "Don't you ever get cold?" I asked him.

"Were blood." He raked both hands through his hair, his thumbs curling to tuck a heavy wedge behind each ear. "We're always warm."

My mouth had gone dry. "And naked, mostly."

"That too." He went into the kitchen. The tap ran, and he returned with two glasses filled with water. "But this time, I have an excuse. I have no clothing left." He passed me a glass. "Cordelia is going to get us some this morning."

"She won't be in a hurry to do that. I think she's enjoying watching you walk around buck naked." I chugged down the water. "How do you know her?"

"There are a lot of Weres out there who couldn't fit in. Things were hard for Cordelia. My dad found her a safe place while she healed. I always liked her. She was so different from everything in Creemore. I always admired the way she wouldn't bend, you know? Though she was too smart to put on a dress when she was around the pack, she found subtler ways to flaunt her femininity. She didn't just grow her hair; she styled it . . . she'd come to a meeting in a peach-colored shirt, and a sweater only a girl would choose." His lips curved into a bittersweet smile. "I think she probably always understood how it was going to go down, and yet, she wouldn't change for anybody. She knew who she was. In her head, she was always Cordelia. I kept in touch, and when I was in need, she answered. She helped me get back on my feet. We're business partners now. And friends. She knows that I spark sometimes," he said, pointing to his eyes.

"Then why wouldn't you let her see them flare last night?"

"I don't know. I only felt right with you being there." He rubbed the back of his neck. "But I do trust her."

Music started again.

"Who's that singing?"

He shrugged, crinkling his eyes against the sun. He must have done that a lot because the sun had left its mark. He had three lines running across his forehead, and a fanwork of them radiating from the corner of each eye. His skin was too naturally golden for him to appear off-color, but there were blue smudges beneath the sooty line of his lower lashes. He didn't wake up with flyaway hairs and rooster bed head. He woke up looking pretty much as he went to bed, with Pre-Raphaelite curls and scrub of beard. But the daylight showed what the night had hidden: the glints in his dark hair weren't from the sun.

"After Candy died, I never thought I'd see another spring. That night, when my sister told me to run, I went, not because I was afraid of dying, but because I wasn't going to let the pack take me out for something I didn't do. If I couldn't pick the time, I'd pick the place. I went to the mountains and waited for the mate bond to take me. But I never got sick . . . never got weak. I was as strong six months after her death as I'd been the day I married her.

"Candy and I got married the first Saturday the week after high-school graduation. That's what we Weres do, isn't it? We marry our boys off young, hoping the mating bond will bind us to the pack." He lifted the glass to his lips, took a long swallow. Wiped his mouth with the back of his hand. "It works for most people. And my parents were good about it. They saw that I liked Candy, and they encouraged the match, even though her line wasn't known to be prolific breeders.

Too much intermarriage. Fertility rates were really low. Marriages that led to more than one child, like my parents' match, were rare. Sometimes I felt like I was hitched to a post in a stable, waiting for my turn to buck and fuck. Not a Were. Not a wolf. Just a small cog in everyone else's plans." The sun was creeping up over the top of a distant black-lined roof. It peeped at us, winking, sending fingers of light toward him.

"So I married her. And she loved me. Right away. Sometimes I wondered why. How can you love someone so easily?"

I pulled my blanket closer.

"I liked her. A lot. At first, we just had a lot of fun. Most of it in the sack." He grimaced and rubbed a hand over his belly. "But . . . well, you know how we do the civil ceremony for all the humans, and do the mating ritual later in front of friends and family? Well, we did it. I said the words. She did too . . . But something went wrong. It didn't take. I didn't feel any different and I don't think she did either, because she looked at me like I'd . . . But everyone was smiling at us, offering me a beer, so we didn't say anything. " He didn't turn. He kept studying the sky ahead of him. "Candy didn't want us to tell anyone. We kept going, day after day, like everything was perfect . . . She kept hoping . . . But it was me. I couldn't stick, you know? I always felt like I needed to roam. That there was someplace out there calling to me. And I wanted to be a musician. I loved playing the guitar. Wrote a few songs. Thought myself a fine little rock star." His voice turned hard. "So that was where I was the night my family was being butchered. I lied to my wife and family, and drove myself into the city. There was a band looking for a guitarist. In my head, I had it all worked out. I was going to blow them away with my music, and Candy and me would hit the road with the band. I put my cell on silent, and then I went into the bar.

"Joke was on me. The band sucked." He tipped his head to the side. "Maybe I did too. Too late to know. So instead of going back, I thought, 'Hey, I'm here, I might as well have a good time.' The band left, but I stayed, talking to the bartender, and drinking and flirting with a girl who thought I was hot. Getting away from the pack, being in the bar—it left me with a taste, you know? A taste of how it could be. I thought about it a lot as I drove home. Didn't look at my cell until I was at the lights on Main and Water. There were six missed calls from Candy. I was already thinking up a lie as I drove up the drive.

"I didn't smell or see him. I didn't hear him until it was too late. When I came to, the house was dark, and silent. My fingers were missing." He stretched his right hand and held it up, holding back the sun. "That seemed like a big deal, for a second. How could I ever become a rock star?

"And then I smelled the blood. Their blood." He paused, looking blindly ahead. "I found Candy's body in our bedroom closet. I pulled the cell phone out of her hand, and put her on our bed.

"You're supposed to die. Mates are *supposed* to die. That's what I was thinking as I ran away. That maybe the mate bond had taken hold of us, and I had been too shit-stupid and stubborn to recognize it. That I wouldn't have to live with the shame long, that I'd just die. But in the end, I didn't do that either." He turned to me, watching me from under hooded eyes. "Here I am. I didn't die—I just got old before my time."

Blue sparks around the swirl of light in his eyes. "I'm not sure if I'm capable of bonding. But I do know this. I can't stand to see harm come to you. I can't bear to watch you hurt. And I want you. Even if our first time sucked, I want you. There's something about the scent of you and the feel of your skin."

He frowned. Blue sparks faded. His eyes turned back to Trowbridge blue.

"I'm not much of a bargain, Tink." His gaze flicked away to linger on Cordelia's plant collection. "I keep telling you that I'm tired of saving you, but I'm starting to think you believe the shoe's on the other foot. I'm not looking to be saved. I am what I am. It is what it is."

The orchid had shriveled up, its flowers soft and spent. I picked up Merry and put her on the next one. The sun was warm on my shoulders, and I did something I never thought I'd do. I let go of the blanket, letting it pool by my feet. There I was. All ins and outs. Naked as my jaybird lover, standing in front of a full-length window in the light of day. Seeing how he'd bared his soul with his life story, I'd thought the grand gesture warranted another one, but now I felt exposed and I didn't know what to do with my arms.

I said, "Fae Tears are probably like the first time a Were changes. It's a rite of passage. I wish Mum had told me how much it hurts. I would have been a better kid." I reached for the small pouch dangling from Mum's bride belt, loosened its ties and spilled out a few pink diamonds into my palm. With a finger, I sorted them. "These two are our birthstones. This was after a fight between Mum and Dad. This was when Lexi was lost, and your dad brought him back. This one," I said, pushing one that was longer and thinner than the others. "This one was her last Tear." I felt a chill, remembering why she cried it, and the expression of despair and futility in her eyes as it spilled. I turned away.

Trowbridge came up behind me, putting his arms around my waist. I felt his chin brush my hair.

"But this one." I held it up to the light so that we both could see it. Pink-white light. Perfect in shape. "This was her first. She said when she cried that tear, she knew." I turned my head slightly so that my forehead rested against his neck. "She called it Dad's Tear."

I held up the new one, custom made by my own tear ducts. "This one is yours."

He liked that. What had been semisoft went rigid. "My eyes always burn when you're near, Trowbridge."

His hand began to move.

"Make love to me," I whispered. "Just me this time."

Our heads turned together when the bedroom door opened. Cordelia stood, keys in hand. Her hair was held by a headband, a shoulder bag swung over her thin shoulders. She lifted her chin. "Can the fornication at least wait until I'm out of the bloody apartment?"

It did. Fornication waited until much later, but making love started the moment the door clicked closed. Different somehow, now that truth lay in bed with us.

The only pain was the need.

"Do you see me, Trowbridge?" I held his face between my hands.

"Yes," he said.

Kisses. Touches. Small noises that led to bigger ones. Want displayed. Trust offered. Self-awareness fading to focus on touch, on sensation, on the growing urgent need. His breath, my breath, merged together. Body-slapping, sucking noises. Rocking.

"Easy, sweetheart, it will come."

Searching for it, waiting for it, straining for it.

And finally finding it.

He sighed. "I'm almost afraid to ask you, but what are you thinking?"

"About when you almost changed into a Were. That was pretty strange. I thought you needed the moon to transform into your wolf. Ever heard of it happening before?"

He concentrated on untangling a knot in my hair before grunting noncommittally.

"Have you?" I insisted.

He caught my hands and laid them flat over his chest. "There are folktales, I've heard, about one or two Alphas being able to do it long ago. But that was back in the Stone Age, and I never believed it. The only Were I knew who pulled it off was the scentless one."

"So what's your explanation?"

"Fairy juice," he said with a ghost of laughter in his voice.

"You hadn't squeezed me by then."

"Maybe just being in a small room with you was enough." He was studying our two hands; mine were small and white under his large one. "Anyway, I didn't completely change, did I? It stopped. I'd need the moon to turn full wolf."

His nails were chewed down to the quick. I couldn't imagine him gnawing on them, but by the same token, two days ago, I couldn't imagine being cuddled by a naked Robson Trowbridge.

His fingers brushed a tender spot on my back. "Ow," I

murmured, too lazy to lift my head from the warm cradle of his shoulder.

"You've got a graze there. Did that happen in the bar?"

I turned my head but couldn't see much except my own shoulder, and his suntanned fingers softly stroking my pale skin. Kind of hypnotic to watch. Judging by his slitted eyes, also somewhat hypnotic to the touch. "Where?" I asked drowsily.

"Along your spine. Maybe three inches long."

How'd I do that? He never let anyone get near me in the strip club. Maybe when I was falling down the hill? No, that was hours ago; I would have healed by now. Suddenly, the memory flashed in my mind's eye, quick and hot. *Me on my knees, furrowing my way under the hedge in Threall, Madone on my heels.* I pressed my hand to my eye, and silently counted to twelve. Took a breath, to find the image of the crazed Mystwalker still crystal sharp. I counted some more, my lips moving silently.

"You okay?" he asked.

"Yeah," I said gruffly. There were salty beads of sweat under the thin mat of his chest hair; I rubbed his skin dry with my finger. *You're not in Threall now. You're lying in bed with your Were lover, wasting time when you should be looking for Lou.*

"You don't heal as fast as us, do you?"

"No." *Wounds received in Threall take longer to heal. I'll have to remember that.* I wished I had Were healing powers and strength. It made them indifferent to the prospect of hurt. And brave when they shouldn't be. Dad should have called for help. "Who was the scentless wolf who murdered my father?"

"My uncle, Mannus Trowbridge," he said, "present Alpha of the Creemore pack of kin."

There were noises. Traffic below. The ever-present hum of appliances and tick of the clock. But here, between us, not counting the uneven tempo of both our hearts, I heard only silence.

"Your uncle killed my father." There was a big hollow pit in my stomach. "Then he went and murdered his own brother?"

"Weres can be like that. Driven." Trowbridge drew long fingers through my hair. "Mannus saw something he wanted, and he found a way of getting it." He curled a strand around his thumb and considered his hair-wrapped digit for a moment before he resumed speaking. "My uncle wanted to rule the pack, but he had a few obstacles in his way. My dad was never going to bequeath his Alpha flare to his brother, not when he had children who had a right to it. A stupider man would have taken all but one of us out that night, and then offered a choice to the last survivor—his life for the crown. But a massacre like that would have resulted in a Council inquiry. For him to get away with the murders, the passing of the title had to look organic, like it was a gift from one dying Alpha to the Were of his choice. So he needed a scapegoat for my family's murders."

"You," I said softly.

He nodded. "Me. But before he could slaughter my family he had to figure out how to get enough power to flare like an Alpha. There's only one place he could have got that from."

My gut squeezed. "Merenwyn."

"Weres can't travel there alone, even if they want to break the Treaty. Someone had to lead him through the Gates. It's not like—"

"Walking through a door." I listened to his heart thudding in his chest.

He tilted his head at me. "That's what I've heard." His other hand went back to his second-favorite resting spot—my breast. Cupping it, he said thoughtfully, "Only those Fae-born can pass through the portals, and few of them have been taught the way to this realm. Somehow, my uncle met someone who knew the route, and was willing to lead him to the Pool of Life. He probably used some of that charm he was always spreading about when I was young." Bridge's lips turned down. "He was always smiling . . . always promising things he'd never come through with . . . Maybe he fell in love with . . ."

The pause grew until I filled it. "Lou."

There it was. The shadow I'd kept behind me. When I was

small, *it* had been small, but I'd felt its presence, and had been careful not to turn my head. But it had grown as I had grown; lengthened and stretched with every rationalization I'd manufactured. I didn't need to turn my head to see it. Past the landscape of his chest was a window. And past that was a postcard-pretty spring day, with blue skies, and puffy clouds. But inside the apartment, the shadow of my aunt hung over my shoulder.

"I don't know how she did it. The portals aren't supposed to recognize Were blood, but somehow she found a way. She took your uncle to Merenwyn." My voice sounded thin. I made it stronger. "She was the Fae that broke the Treaty, not my mum."

"Yes." His scent swirled in an eddy around both of us. "Who else could it be?"

"For the longest time I thought it was another Fae. He didn't have a face; he didn't have a name, but it had to be him. Not my aunt Lou." My mouth was too dry. I bit the edge of my tongue and waited for saliva to ease the ache. "I didn't want to know. If she was responsible . . . what type of daughter would that make me? Didn't I owe my family more than to go with her, and call her aunt? I had doubts, but I didn't know what to do with them. It was so much easier to believe that she was guiltless. I was twelve. All I could think of was who was going to take care of me. I rationalized every doubt away, and kept doing it. Even later, when Lou got weak, and I was the person bringing home the food and paying the rent, I didn't leave. I could have walked out the door, but I stayed. I told myself that she found me when I needed her the most and I owed her my loyalty. She found me, and took me away from the fire. She could have left me to the wolves, but she didn't. It had to be another Fae that set that first domino to fall."

I shook my head. "Even now, I don't know what I am to her. Does she love me because I'm her sister's kid? Or am I her burden of guilt? Her redemption? How can someone be both sides? The good and the bad?"

"It happens all the time."

I looked over to Merry, hanging off the edge of the

lampshade where I'd put her after she'd taken the juice out of every living plant in Cordelia's home. Other than some squirming—no, not squirming, more like two lovers adjusting to each other in bed, everything a sensuous ripple of gold—she hadn't moved. Not only that, but she hadn't spoken to me since I had made love to Trowbridge. No flashes of color. No soothing brushes of Fae metal against my skin. Another bridge had been destroyed; my stomach clenched at the thought. Everything seemed different in this new day's light.

"The amulet that Merry's wrapped around was Lou's. It's how she got back and forth from one realm to another. She must have come that night hunting for *it*. Not me."

"Some sort of portal key," he said.

"I wonder if this is what it felt like for Lou." I shifted away from him, but he moved his leg to breach the gap. "Your uncle used her like a pawn."

"No. They were equally guilty." He released the strand of hair twined around his thumb.

I tossed my head, and rolled on my side. The pillow smelled of him. "So why aren't you doing something about it?" I asked, staring at the *Vogue* magazines stacked neatly on Cordelia's side table.

"Who says I'm doing nothing about it? I'm not stupid enough to go in there on my own, but I've learned patience. There's more than one way of killing him." For a moment neither one of us spoke, both wrapped up tight in our own individual hells. Then he sighed, and slid behind me. He pulled me close until we were as tight as two spoons nestled in the same drawer. "The worst is over. Not knowing for sure—that was the hardest part. The questions, the guessing . . . that's done with now."

"I'll never see Lexi again." *Or visit Threall.*

He held me tighter and rubbed his chin on my shoulder. "Probably not."

The pain was sharp. It took me a couple of minutes before I trusted my voice. "Lou loved your uncle, Trowbridge. I could see it in her thought-pictures."

"Thought-pictures?"

I told him. Somewhere near the end of my explanation, his two fingers bumped into my ear. The peak of it seemed to fascinate him. I put a hand over his to stop him.

"Does it feel bad?"

"No, it feels too good. When you touch me there, it's hard to think. It's easier just to feel." He kept running his finger over its curved tip. I felt my distress easing.

"Can you see into my mind?" he asked.

"No." Oh, how I wished I could. "You're not Fae."

"Let's run away," he said in his husky voice.

"Where would we go?" I closed my eyes and thought of places we could run to. New York, Paris, London, maybe—

"B.C. I have people who owe me there."

Oh swell. *Let's go live with a bunch of granola-eating, tree-hugging, let's-recycle nut-jobs.* But I didn't say that. Thinking back, I probably should have, but instead, I asked, "You think humans can protect me against Weres?"

"Not humans. Weres in B.C." His fingers momentarily stopped stroking, and my tension started building. "There's a bunch of them out there—all free-will Weres. It's pretty out there. There aren't many rules, like there are here. You don't have to work for any of the Alpha's approved companies; you can take any trade you want. We've got everything there, from artists to road crew to Internet geeks. Every four months we all pitch in and raise enough money to keep the Western Council off our asses, but for the most part, we're too far north in the bush for them to bother with us. The town's run more like a pirate ship than any Alpha pack. Some of them are a little rough around the edges, but they're good people. I'll take you there."

Wasn't that a cheerful thought. "They'll send me back to Mannus in a box."

"I'll shred the neck of the first Were who threatened you." His skin released a small scent-bomb of possessiveness.

I felt my stomach get tight. "I don't want to live among Weres."

He thought about that as he resumed his sweet caress of my peaked ear. When my eyelids started to droop, he murmured, "Then I'll find us another place, somewhere remote, where you'll feel safe."

A long thin streak of sun had laid a path of gold along the carpet. Another finger of light was reaching for Merry. I felt that squirm I got when I thought I was doing something right, but instinct was howling, "Be careful, danger is all around us."

"What's wrong?" He inhaled then his hand went to rest over my heart. "You're hiding something."

I killed a soul today. Not with my own hands, but it amounted to the same thing. If I hadn't dismissed Mum's warning about mystwalkers, those entwined pines would still be growing arrow straight, their two soul-lights safe in their boughs.

"What is it?"

I shook my head. "Nothing."

"If it's about your aunt, you need to tell me."

I pushed his paw off me. "Why?"

"This is bigger than us." He sounded like the Alpha he was supposed to have become. "The Gates to Merenwyn have to stay closed. The Council needs to know what my uncle is trying to do. When they find out that Mannus has the last remaining Fae in his possession, they'll send a small army to kill him." He rolled onto his back and stared up at the popcorn ceiling.

I did the same, flopping on my back, but I chose to tilt my head to watch the morning light stream through the window. "And Lou too."

"She should have stayed in Merenwyn."

"I'm half Fae," I said, feeling suddenly cold. "What do you think they'll want to do to me?"

"You're also half Were. I won't let them harm you." Exasperated, he pulled me toward him again.

I lay there, but I didn't let myself melt into that boneless Trowbridge-let's-make-love-again ooze. "What am I, then?"

He didn't answer. Seemingly preoccupied by my hip, he ran his finger along the slope of it, like a kid playing with his toy car, and then he tried to lay his palm flat in the dipped valley at my waist but it wouldn't lie flat. His hand was too large, and my curves too serious. "I love your skin. No one has skin like yours." A study in contrasts. My skin, whiter than white, blemish-free except one small reddish freckle. His broken hand, sun-kissed, missing fingers, with a crosshatch of pale white scars decorating the knuckles.

I insisted. "What am I?"

His voice was reflective and sad. "Addictive."

"You can't keep me safe," I said.

"I can try."

I asked quietly, "Until you feel like you're trapped?"

A flush crawled across his cheekbones. He raised his glittering eyes to mine. Underneath the cold set of his features, I thought I saw something vulnerable. "I give you my word, as the son of Jacob Trowbridge, that I will protect you, Hedi Stronghold."

I bit my lip and nodded, and then leaned my cheek against his shoulder.

He hadn't answered directly. "Addictive" is an adjective, not the pronoun I wanted most. And protection doesn't mean lifelong devotion. He sealed my mouth with his and stroked my ear, and muttered things into it that were neither verb nor noun. And for the moment, I chose to believe that when I looked at him, and thought "mine," he did too. I chose not to think too deeply, because that would lead me out of his arms and into a cold scary place.

We made love again. Slowly, achingly beautiful. When it was finished, I wound a finger in one of his curls and laid my head to rest against his chest.

"Robbie, I—"

"Don't call me Robbie."

I lifted my head, and gazed at him, disappointed. "I can't call you Robbie?"

"No."

"You're destroying a childhood dream," I said, feeling my lips turn into a wistful smile. "I always wanted to kiss you and call you my Robbie. I don't want to call you Trowbridge for the rest of time."

"Robbie Trowbridge is gone." His face was sad; the lights in his eyes extinguished. "I'm Bridge now."

"Bridge." I kissed him and stared deep into his eyes, hoping they'd spark again. But they didn't, and after a bit, I said, "They call me Hedi Peacock now. Helen Stronghold died in the fire."

And then I put my head on his chest again. Pulled my hair away so I could feel his flesh under my cheek. He began to finger-comb my hair, slowly, from my temple to its tip, each gentle tug weighing my eyelids until they drooped. I was tired. So tired. I closed my eyes as I felt his arm tighten around me. I would not count the minutes. I would just yield, and take this memory, one for my own—one that no one would ever share. "My Robbie," I mouthed silently against his skin.

I'm a thief, so I did what I do best: I curled into my lover and stole some time.

Before time ended.

Chapter Sixteen

Trowbridge's arm fell off my shoulder and I woke with a start. And then she pulled me. No slip, no slide. Lou put a hand into my brain and yanked me into hers.

She's waiting.

For me? No, not for me. Waiting for something else.

"Lou," I say. "Where are you?"

I can feel her impatience. And then she surprises me. "Quiet," she says, quite clearly, with an authority I hadn't heard in months. So I watch silently, and realize she's in the same room as before, but now I'm seeing it from the vantage point of the floor.

The door opens. One of them walks in. Young. Strong. Enemy. His footsteps are confident.

Stupid.

He uses his boot to roll her over onto her back. Stuart Scawens stares down at us. His mouth opens to say something. I can't read his lips, but it doesn't matter, because he suddenly stops mid-breath. His eyes widen and he takes two stumbling steps for the door.

Too late. The crudely shaped spike catches him mid-chest.

An expression of horrible surprise flickers across his face. Stuart bends his head to gape at the silver sticking out from his breast, and then he wilts, sinking to the floor. Lou clenches her fingers, and turns her fist sharply to the right.

Stuart's face contorts as the spike rotates deep into his body. She smacks her fist down on her open palm. His legs jerk when she splays her fingers wide. The silver spike melts into his body. Pure agony twists his features. His eyes roll as he convulses on the floor.

Lou walks past his body to the door. Up the basement stairs, straight through to the kitchen. Pauses to lift the keys off the brass key rack that had four running wolves over four hooks. She pulls open the door and takes a moment to scan the backyard. Fir-dotted hills are in the background. The yard is outlined with a line of straggling pines. She gets in the truck, and turns the key. Then, my sick old aunt, who loathes driving, puts it in gear. Her hands are rigid on the steering wheel as the car begins to move.

"Where are you going, Lou?" I ask her. "Show me."

The dream speeds up. I see a sign on the corner. Airport Road. The back of a truck. Signs overhead passing. Barrie. Highway 400 South. Cars speeding past hers. Highway 401. Then she's in Toronto, driving down city streets. The pedestrians change from business people to students. She makes a left and a right, turns onto a short street, filled with Victorian houses mixed with small towers. Her gaze is constantly moving. Street. Pedestrians. Left. Right. Then she sees the sign: PUBLIC PARKING. *We pass another sign,* ROTMAN SCHOOL OF BUSINESS, *before she noses the car down into the underground lot. She stops on level three, pulling the car into a slot in the middle of the empty parking level. Her hands are shaking as she turns off the ignition.*

"Come," I hear her say, loud in my brain. "I am waiting."

"I know you're awake," he said. "I can hear the gears in your brain turning."

"Go away, Trowbridge. I'm sleepy." *She's waiting. "Come and get me,"* she said.

"Get up, Tinker Bell, we've got to get going."

"Where?"

"West, Tink."

But Lou was northward. She'd run the same dream sequence in my head for the two hours I'd slept, until it felt like a new scar. I knew where to find her. *She knows I can dream-walk or, at the very least, she knows that she can speak to me in her dreams. Can she use it against me? Keep me captive to her needs?*

I'd never escape her. She waited for me on the outskirts of every dream, hovering over me in the daylight hours, ready to slip her dreams into my mind the second I had an unguarded moment, or an instant of unfocused thought. A fear had grown inside me that even death wouldn't be able to stop her. An echo of her soul would stay in this realm to haunt me, until there was no peace in sleep, and no comfort found with daylight.

I'll go mad if she doesn't drag me back to Threall first.

If I abandoned her and stayed with Trowbridge, what would happen? Would his attraction fade as my own brain started to soften under the weight of Lou's madness? Just how much of an aphrodisiac is it to watch your girlfriend babble about dreams? Could I ever tell him about the dangers of Threall? And even if Lou died, and left me free, there was the other problem. Could I hang on for that day he says, "You know what? I've changed my mind. I'm real keen on Faes. And by the way, I love you."

I don't have that type of stamina.

I rolled over stiffly. Fifteen minutes ago, Trowbridge had moved from sitting and staring at me from across the room, to standing over the bed and staring down at me. I had a leg cramp from not moving.

"Don't you ever sleep?"

"Not until I'm sure that Merry's not going to feed off you again. We're going to have to come up with another plan because I can't share a bed with her." He sat on the edge of the mattress, cradling a glass between his hands, staring at her hanging from my neck. "Want some apple juice?" He frowned and touched my chin with the back of his knuckles. "Your skin's all irritated."

I put a smile on my face. "You're going to have to choose, Trowbridge."

238 LEIGH EVANS

He took a sip of his juice, his hooded eyes intent on mine. I felt the chill of it, and changed my question. "Me or the beard."

He quirked an eyebrow. "Cordelia's coming," he said. A few moments later, I heard the sound of heels along the outside corridor. A key turned in the lock. Cordelia went straight into the kitchen and dumped the bag of food in there before coming into the living room. I pulled the sheet up higher. She tossed two bags onto the end of the bed, and then turned to open the windows to the cold spring air. She stood stoic and proud, beholding the graveyard of her plants for a moment.

I felt a flush of deep shame. "I'm sorry."

Her spine stiffened.

"I'll go out today and get you new ones," Trowbridge said.

She spared him a thin-lipped smile before she turned for the privacy of her bedroom and her record collection. Chet Baker started singing about his Funny Valentine again.

Trowbridge opened one bag, and said, "Oh shit." He pulled out a pair of fitted black pants and a silver-gray dress shirt. A pair of black loafers were at the bottom of the bag. Then came a nice pair of sexy black briefs. A white T-shirt. A black belt with a silver buckle. There was even a leather tie for his hair.

"Hello, *GQ*," he muttered under his breath, examining the tag inside the pants. He dumped the stuff back into the bag, and stood. "Don't worry about the plants. I'll get her a whole bunch of new ones, plus a tree. Okay, I'm for the shower."

"You like the water too cold. I'll join you in a couple of minutes." He studied me for a moment, and then leaned over to kiss me. When our lips parted, he spoke, his breath moving into my mouth. "Don't wait too long."

I picked up my bag. It was lighter. A pair of cheap black leggings, some pink flats that were stamped "genuine imitation leather," and a size twelve plaid shirt with a $4.99 price ticket hanging from its sleeve. No underwear.

"Trowbridge?" He was already halfway down the hall. He turned, his hair sliding over his shoulder. That was the picture I'd carry in my heart: his brows raised, his shoulder bare, the sun from the east window painting a rectangle of light on his naked foot—not the brooding, slightly soiled man at the strip club. No, it would be this image I'd remember. Standing tall. Pure. Beautiful to my eyes. "Finding a bar is not your gift, okay? It's your curse."

He frowned at me before turning away. One hand was pulling his hair back off his face as he walked down the corridor. He had beautiful arms and a fluid walk that spoke of grace and power. "Hey, Cordelia," he called, as he passed her door. "You got any fresh razors?"

"Left-hand drawer. There's an electric shaver in the one beneath it."

I put my stuff into the backpack. The shoes were ruined, and Barry Manilow could stay, but the pants and underwear would dry.

Cordelia walked back into the living room as I finished pulling up the leggings. Her gaze flickered over my breasts and Merry while I did up the plaid shirt and rolled the sleeves so my hands were free. She handed me an elastic band for my hair, and watched with cold, old eyes as I wrapped it around the end of my braid. I picked up my glasses and put them on.

I could hear the sound of the shower running over the *brr* of the electric razor.

I am what I am. It is what it is.

I slipped on the pink flats. They fit perfectly. I tilted my head toward her in inquiry. She smiled. That smirk changed to a frown when I walked to the hall closet and pulled out her leather jacket.

I will not be torn.

I slipped the jacket on and then stood staring at the door handle.

Four out of five people I love are Fae. Lexi, Lou, Merry, and me.

He'd probably hear the door close and then all my noble decisions would be for nothing. I could say I tried, that I opened the door and he stopped me. Not my fault. Would that be enough? Could I live with the lie that I knew what the right thing was, and was going to do it, but he stopped me? Would that satisfy Karma? Or would that vengeful Goddess know, and somehow up ahead I'd find myself revisiting the moment I'd stood by this door, knowing that he could save me from a hard decision.

I heard Cordelia shift, followed by the hollow tap of her acrylic nails on a button. She pressed down, and the blender churned into life with a high shriek.

Taking the cue, I opened the door. Closed it softly. Waited for the elevator. I rubbed my arm, checking to see if my Were-bitch's anxious struggles were making my skin ripple too.

My forearm was smooth and pale. Hairless like all Faes'.

The doors opened, and I got on.

The stone steps were cold on my ass. I'd never given enough credit to the thermal qualities of nylon underwear before. Without it, the cold leached right through my skin to my bone. I waited for a bald-headed dog walker to pass. His bichon kept snapping her head back to check on me as she pranced after him. He turned around and glanced at me, but saw nothing out of the ordinary.

Just another student.

The hidden courtyard seemed to have periods of flow, like traffic lights. Quiet and then the doors would open and a stream of students would flood past us.

The sun was heating up the patch of grass in the middle of the square, casting shadows of green and dark where the ground was uneven. As courtyards go, it was pretty large. Twenty-seven tall trees, a lot of stonework, and a few shrubs. Peaceful. Secluded and hidden in the center of two joined buildings. The gray stone blocks some poor bastards had hewn a couple of hundred years ago had weathered nicely. The arches and columns had absorbed grace and stood strong, indifferent to the passage of time. The whole damn building was pretty in a fanciful, arrogant way with its carvings and curlicue embellishments. Someone should slap a knight's standard on the top of its fairy-tale turret and be done with it.

It was the best I could come up with because I had something to do before retrieving Lou.

I thought about asking a student for the name of the building, but they were in a hurry, hats pulled low, heading past the courtyard without even a glance at the trees. They were my age, a thousand years better read and yet, somehow, a thousand years younger. They'd graduate with a diploma from the University of Toronto, and anyone who scrutinized it would know just how bright and learned they were.

What did they learn here? The trees were moving to the wind's whim. With no fluttering foliage to hide what's happening underneath, you could see how the early spring breeze flailed the thinnest branches. No pity there. Bend to the wind or break. I'd never make it a day in the classroom. I'd be looking outside the window, watching the trees, thinking the wind was cruel.

"I'm sorry but I really think your amulet friend is dead," I told Merry quietly. I could feel her listening. She made a movement of denial, the points of her ivy leaves scratching Cordelia's jacket. I'd placed her on the outside of it, turned toward the square, so that she could see what I saw. "I know you want him to be alive, but that's a dream, isn't it? He feels dead. He doesn't move. He doesn't change color or temperature. He doesn't throw sparks up the chain. Can you prove differently? Because now's the time." We sat there, watching the bobbing backpacks pass by. The heavy oak door closed behind the slowest-moving student, and then we were alone with the squirrels and trees.

"Dreams won't keep us alive."

The stolen bolt cutters that I'd palmed in the hardware store were tucked into the waistband of my leggings, but they were heavy, even if they were only slightly larger than my pockets. I had to keep a hand pressed to them so that they didn't fall.

"Your friend was in the hands of a Were for too long." Her stone turned an ugly red. "I know you hate Trowbridge for that, but he didn't know any better." My throat was tight. I had to work my jaw to loosen it, before I continued. "He's not a Fae. He didn't know how to care for your friend. We won't be seeing Trowbridge again. So you can let your resentments go. It would be better for both of us if we let the past go.

"I'm going to get Lou now. She's waiting for us, just up the street."

The wind was whipping the trees again, churning through the branches, impossible to please.

"She can't know about your amulet friend. Ever. She'll start believing she can open the gates again, and we'll be back going from portal to portal, watching her sing herself hoarse as she tries to summon one. If there's any shred of life left to your amulet, she'll drain him dry. You don't want that for him, do you?

"This is a nice place. It's got a lot of trees, with deep roots. They take real good care of it. It will be pretty here in the summer with the ivy. We can bury him under that big oak. If I'm wrong, and he has some life deep down inside, then he can feed off the roots of these old trees and get stronger. Maybe we can come back and check in a couple of years. If he's healed, I promise I'll find a way to get him back to his own kind."

I blinked, seeing the future. "If I can, I promise that one day I'll try to get you back too. But right now, that's all we can do—take a chance, and hope for the best.

"Give him up, Merry. If I let you keep hanging on to him, you'll die too. There's no honor in two deaths, just because you think that fantasies can come to life. They never do. In real life, there's always someone following the Prince's white horse with a bucket and a shovel.

"Besides. It just won't do. If I let you keep hanging on to his body, you'll keep on pumping your essence into him until you fade like Lou."

I fingered her chain.

"I've been falling asleep on and off since you grabbed him. I don't like sleeping because I'm afraid of the dreams. You know that. But here I am, falling asleep in the middle of stuff that should be turning my hair white. And I'm thinner. Mum's belt is hanging on hip bones I didn't even know I had."

I watched a black squirrel lying on a swaying bough, his tail twitching and whiskers bristling as he watched us. "You've been feeding off me for him. I don't know what to say about that, except this: don't ever do it again. I don't want to look at you one day and hate you. I don't want to have to leave you in a forest and walk away."

I pulled out the cutters. "Here's the deal. I'm going to make it easier for you. I'll cut him away from you, and then you won't have to worry that you didn't do your best." Her chain started to heat. "You can burn me, and I'll heal, and I'll try again. You can throw as many thunderbolts as you've got left, and I'll wake up and try again. You can try to protect him, but you're not big enough. There's always some part of him left exposed."

A student in a peacoat, her phone jammed to her ear, shouldered through the exit of the building behind us. I waited for her to cross the courtyard and reach the heavy, double wooden doors that led to the student lounge. A burst of noise, and then silence. "You have no choices, Merry."

I let the pincers open wide. I'd have to start with the little parts of him first. The collar on Cordelia's soft leather jacket started to smoke.

"It won't hurt for long, Merry. I promise."

Chapter Seventeen

My spoon snapped in half. I turned it around and started using the sharp end to gouge furrows into the hard-packed soil. The gravesite I'd chosen was under the canopy of an old tree, just on the edges of it, where the afternoon sun would have a chance to warm the soil. The tree of choice wasn't the biggest one, nor the fullest, but it was the one that smelled the least of dog pee. It had a white scar on its trunk that made it appear diseased, but when I put my hand to it, and felt for its essence, it felt strong. Scarred but healthy. It seemed a good choice.

I stopped, mid-rake, as sensation rolled over me.

Trowbridge was coming.

The prickle of awareness grew into a pull, as if he were north and I were the needle. My Were lifted her head from her paws and sat up. We could hear him, outside on the street, the distinctive click of his heels along the sidewalk, getting louder and faster as if he'd felt the pull too. I shouldn't be able to hear him. Not through the stone walls, the classrooms, and the long oak-wainscoted halls. Certainly shouldn't be able to distinguish his footsteps from all those treading feet. But I could. To my ears—Fae pointed and usually human deaf—his were the *aha!* of footsteps.

Look what happens when you accept your inner Were.

He paused at the exterior stone steps, and then ran up them lightly, as lightly as all those long-legged lean Weres do. I heard him manhandle the door, and then the first shock wave of his rage came rolling down the corridors and through the walls, past the oblivious students, to nudge and bite at me.

The hair on the back of my neck stood up.

I listened as he walked past other people down the marble corridors—their footsteps were just noise to me, forgettable—listened, air caught in my lungs, as he kept coming in a straight unhesitating line, closer and closer, until my heart, my blood, and my skin knew he was on the other side of those heavy glass doors.

Oh Goddess, I can feel him.

My Were was happy. Relieved. All would be well.

Stupid bitch.

Trowbridge pushed open the door. I watched him stalk toward me, the dark outline of him glowing against the contrast of the dark passageway. His halo wasn't as bright, but I could still see it—a thin edge of golden, white light softening his outline. Someday another woman, a Were-born appropriate one, would see that and think it cause to claim him. I tested the thought and discovered I was almost numb.

"You left me." His voice was lethal soft.

"Yes."

"No smart comeback?" He leaned against one of the arches cut into the passageway, with his arms folded over his chest, deceptively at ease, except his chin was up and his cheekbones seemed sharp and unforgiving. He'd had a chance to work on his beard before he discovered my absence. The edges were tidied into crisp outlines, and the rest was thinned down until it was a two-day shadow on his chin. There was a flush of heat across his cheeks and his eyebrows were drawn tight into those flying vees. He was holding it together, but he was on simmer.

I was right. He is handsomer without the beard.

All the noise faded away. It was just the two of us, in a courtyard for fairy-tale princesses and dispossessed princes, alone with frozen squirrels and muted trees.

Just two hearts.

For all its simmering anger, his heart rate was steady,

maybe pumping a hitch faster, but still even—purpose driven, blood rich, a deep bass thump in his chest. Rage must be easier to contain with its edges and margins.

My own half-breed Fae heart was skittering about in my chest. It felt like a pinball ricocheting off the posts, fighting gravity and trying not to fall into the hole waiting at the end of my run. Love, ping. Fear, ping. Sadness, ping. Yearning, ping, ping, ping.

Say the right thing, Trowbridge. Find the right thing to make me stay.

"You led a trail straight to the subway. It took me three trains to find the one you took. That's all. Three trains. It didn't take any effort to track your scent from the Internet café to here because you pushed the button on every fucking light pole." His voice was too low, more growl than human. "You didn't clear your browsing history. Do you know how damn stupid that was? A few clicks and I knew exactly where you were going. I didn't even have to follow your trail. I've been on the campus for less than ten minutes. That's all it took to find you."

Gravity always wins. The pinball slipped off the last lever, missed the grabbing hook of hope, and fell, plop, into the hole.

I turned the broken utensil in my hand. "No one could have found me except you, Trowbridge. I don't leave a scent trail."

"To me you do." He exhaled his tension through his nose. A little bit more Were smell permeated the commons. The black squirrel abandoned his perch and scurried for refuge on the adjacent pitched roof.

"Besides, Cordelia does, and you're wearing her jacket."

"You want the jacket back?"

"Don't be stupid." He came out of the shadows and crossed the landing to the stairs. He had on Cordelia's slick shirt and sharply pleated pants, but he wore his own scuffed-toed boots. The untucked shirt was hanging on to him by two buttons, exposing the white T-shirt beneath it.

"You think I'd let you wander off, Stronghold? You're just a baby; you don't even know what's out there."

"Mortals and Weres. I'll survive."

"You've just been lucky."

"Lucky." The spoon slid off something hard in the small hole I was digging, grazing a white line across its muddy surface. I used my fingernail to pry the something out. A pebble. Worn and smooth. I tossed it on the pile I had growing by my knee. "Yeah, I guess I've been real lucky."

"Will you stop digging?"

The only answer to that was to put a little more juice into my excavation.

He walked across the grass until he stood beside me, his booted foot sinking into the turf. The soil hadn't dried from last night's rain. I could feel it clammy wet, soaking through my leggings. I shoveled another handful of dirt into my palm, and tossed it onto the molehill of dislodged soil. A clump of clay bounced off his toe.

"Stronghold, knock it off."

I stabbed harder into my little pit. Faster, channeling a little bit of Norman Bates, and a little bit of Glenn Close from *Fatal Attraction,* and a lot from every other person with a battered heart and no hope left.

He crouched beside me, his thigh brushing my hip. I leaned away from him, and kept going. I could hear the *huh, huh, huh* of my breath coming out of my chest. I could hear the scrape of the metal on the red clay. I could hear his breathing, steady beside me. He waited until my *huh, huh, huhs* started to slip into cracked *he, he, hes* before he caught my hand with his. Held it, bruised and shaking, in the safe cage of his own.

Not mine. Never mine.

I curled my bleeding knuckles into a fist. "Let go."

"Stop, Hedi." His voice was soft. "You're hurting yourself."

"No." I yanked my hand out of his. "Why do you have to make this so hard?"

"It doesn't have to be."

"Yes it does." I pressed my hand against my chest, and felt Merry. She was still warm against my fingers. "It's always been hard. It's never going to be easy. I left you, why'd you have to come find me?"

He rubbed his chin and turned his attention to the hole. "How deep does it have to be?"

"I have to find a bigger root. These small ones aren't good enough."

He picked up the bolt cutters. "I can dig faster."

It was ungraceful work, chipping away at the hard-packed earth. His short, hard jabs were more effective than my scraping, so I sat back and watched as the small grave grew.

"Is this good enough?" Trowbridge asked.

I tested the cavity he'd created beside a taproot the diameter of my wrist. "No. It has to be wider. It's got to be big enough for both of them."

He tilted his head at the hole, and then at me. I hated the compassion I saw in his eyes.

"Don't. Don't you dare pity me."

He made the hole deeper, and wider, and then sat back on his heels.

"I couldn't do it," I said, staring at the bolt cutters in his hand, telling myself to get it over with. "I tried. I thought if I took those cutters, I could clip him away from her, like he was some sort of vine wrapped around her. But *she's* the vine, holding on to him.

"I can't hurt her. She needs to go in with him. That's what she wants." My throat seized up in pretear pain.

I lifted Merry over my head.

"Are you sure about this? It doesn't have to be both of them," he said. "I can pull them apart. You can keep Merry."

Merry and her lover swung like a pendulum from her chain. She wrapped around him; he nestled within her embrace. I cradled them in my palm. "No, I can't." She sent some warmth into my hand then shot a starburst of orange-red from deep within her amber heart. I told myself to remember the last sunset I'd ever hold in my palm. I knelt to lay them in the hollow. Him first, her on top.

My face would be the last she'd see.

The Fae Tear I'd been holding squeezed out through my tear ducts, and ran a straight course down my cheek, and fell, glittering as it went, to land in the middle of her stone. As I knelt there, watching it harden, Trowbridge's hand found a place on the small of my back. He backed away as I filled in the hole, and patted the ragged circle of sod flat again.

It took no time. None at all.

I left the two lovers in the root embrace of a hundred-year-old oak, covered by a layer of this realm's dirt. It wasn't good enough. It would never be good enough. But it was the best I could do.

There were a couple of wooden benches overlooking her grave. I made my way to them with the slow steps of an old woman. Sat, held my stomach and rocked a bit against the pain.

He watched me, his hands jammed into his pockets.

"I've got a Were loose inside me. I don't think she'll ever go back to sleep again." I waited for the numb to come back. "I used to think of myself as a Fae, but I'm not, am I? I'm both."

His boots left a dew trail on the grass as he came to me. He considered me, and then his face softened. "You are what you have always been."

"Is that supposed to cheer me up? I'm part Fae. And when I'm around you, I feel like I shouldn't be. "

"I didn't mean to make you feel like that."

"Tell me that everything is going to be different." I crossed my arms under my breasts as if I were cold, but I wasn't. A tearing hurt was deep inside, and it was spreading . . . oh Goddess, it was filling me up. "Tell me that we're not going to be destroyed because we want to be together. Tell me that you can make it hurt less."

"I can promise that it will be different." He sat down beside me, carefully, like I might bolt or hit him. Slowly he extended his arm until it curved around my slumped shoulders. He pulled me to his chest. Hesitated for a second, as if he were selecting a choice from a new menu, before he settled on stroking my back. "I can promise to kill any Were who wants to hurt you."

I could hear his heart beat in his chest. Thump, thump against my ear.

"Does it hurt less now?" he asked.

I shook my head, and felt his designer stubble catch in my loose hair. "It hurts worse." His hand paused mid-stroke as I sniffled. "I don't want to fall in love with you."

"Then don't."

"You suck as—"

"A therapist. I got that." He turned me to him. Bent his head so he could gaze directly into my eyes. I'd never seen his face so quiet, and I wanted to put my hand to its nakedness.

"Stay with me."

The black squirrel chittered a warning from the tree, but I couldn't tear my eyes from the pull in his. "You're making it hard again."

"Stay."

His expression softened as he read the warring want in mine, and I thought for a dreadful second he was going to say something wonderful. Instead, his hands left my shoulders and cupped my face. His lips settled across mine, as if they'd been born to land there. Cherish and worship there.

Oh Sweet Stars.

"I know what will happen," I mumbled, turning my head, three kisses too late. "The Weres will—"

"Shut up," he said. Four more kisses. Sweet to the soul. Acid to the conscience.

Just tell him. About Threall. About your doubts. Instead, I said, "I know where Lou is."

He pulled his lips back from mine, pausing to breathe. "I know." He caught the wisp of hair that kept straying across my lips, and tucked it behind my ear. "I was pretty sure you knew where she was before I went into the shower, but I was going to give you time to tell me on your own."

"I'm going to save her."

"I figured that."

I frowned. "How would you know that?"

"You ran." He brushed his thumb over my lower lip. "What we have is . . . unique. I don't think you would have left if it hadn't been for a prior obligation."

So he thought what we had was special, did he? It was kind of drugging, that thumb of his on my lip. "I won't let you give her to the Council. I'll nurse her right through to the end of her fade."

"Okay." He leaned in and kissed me again.

I felt tears burning again, which interfered with my breathing and sort of took away from the whole wonderfulness of the moment. He kept his warm lips pressed to my brow as I cried human tears into his jawline. Messy. A whole lot of snuffling, quite a bit of dripping, and one or two shudders. Trowbridge bore it well. He never stopped stroking my back, and he let me cry without once shushing me, even though he grew a little rigid when my sniffs into his collar turned into wet sniffles. I pulled away to wipe my nose clean on the sleeve of Cordelia's jacket.

He pulled me to his chest again, and then tunneled his thumb up underneath the mess of my straggling hair to find my ear. He found the point of it and started to roll his thumb over the peak and down, and back up, over and over again, until my breath settled, and my eyelids fell to half-mast.

His voice was whisper-soft. "Promise me I won't ever come out of a shower to find you gone again."

"I'll never leave you while you're in the shower again. But how can I be sure that I won't wake one morning and find you packed and gone? We should both be required to pledge that we won't leave, without . . ." I shrugged, and stared sightlessly at my knee. "Without saying good-bye." I raised my head, and searched his face.

A flicker of a smile crossed his lips. "It's a deal."

We sat for a while without talking.

Finally, Trowbridge twined his fingers around mine and pulled me to my feet.

I'd say the earth moved, or something equally grand, but my moment of revelation was smaller than that. I looked up at him and saw the truth. His hair was too long. A piece of it was flying across his cheekbone, flirting with the wind. He was too tall for me. I'd always have a crick in my neck just looking up at his beautiful face. He was prettier than me, and no man should be prettier than his girl. His track record as suitable mate material was disastrous.

And he sucked at declarations. Let's face it, "Stay with me" does not equal "I worship you, my beautiful Princess, and claim you forever as my mate."

It isn't even close.

He would never fully appreciate the splendor of my Faeness. It would never be easy. The Weres would still come gunning. *He may never say he loves me.* But here's the thing: even habitual liars get tired of the habit of lying. It was time to admit a piece of self-truth that the twelve-year-old Helen Stronghold had understood without question.

He was nonrefundable. I'd claimed him twice. Once when I was a child, and the second time on my knees in another woman's bathroom. It was a done deal.

"You're probably going to break my heart," I said, craning my head back to look up at him.

"And maybe you'll break mine." His eyes were somber. "Are you ready?"

The stinging wind was at it again. It blew cold air over Merry's grave and brought moisture to my eyes. I nodded.

"It's time I met your aunt Lou." He pulled me toward the courtyard's exit.

"Be nice."

He didn't say anything, but he did do that one eyebrow lift thing. He waggled them, and I found myself smiling into his eyes.

"I mean it, Trowbridge, you can't kill her."

His eyes went from playful to alert in the space of half a second. He cocked his head to listen. I strained my ears a moment longer and then heard it too. Running feet. Staccato taps more than heavy Were thuds. We turned in unison across the commons, toward the same set of doors that Trowbridge pushed through.

A Were was coming. Trowbridge lifted his nose to the air, and tested it. He pushed me behind him.

"What is it?" I asked, trying to strain to see beyond his wide shoulder.

"Trouble."

The heavy mullioned-glass doors opened for Cordelia, who, it turned out, could actually run at a pretty good clip in two-inch court shoes. She skidded to a halt and thinned her lips at the sight of our joined hands. "They're coming. Mannus is right behind me."

Chapter Eighteen

Trowbridge slid a glance toward Merry's grave and said, "We've got to lead them away from this place. Now."

And then we were running—sprinting across the flagstones, down another set of stairs, steeper and shorter. I felt a shiver of cold as we ran past an alley. We entered a cloistered passageway. He pulled open the first of several heavy oak doors lining the cloister and then snapped a quick question to Cordelia. "How many?"

"Mannus, two pups, and a young bitch," she replied, catching up to us.

"No adults?"

She shook her head, her mouth curled. "Not a one."

If my mate had planned on taking us to a large classroom, he was out of luck. Behind door number one was nothing more than a small stairwell. In front of us were eight steps, each riser's edge capped by metal, leading to a three-foot linoleum landing and from there on to another set of stairs that ended at the second floor. Trowbridge put a hand on the creaky, wooden banister and cocked an ear to listen. "Where the hell are all the students?"

"Over there!" shouted a Were from the quad.

Trowbridge's head whipped around. He stared out at the courtyard, and then yanked the door closed. His eyes were feral slits. "There are too many," he said to Cordelia.

"I'll slow them down," she replied. She turned and took a position at the foot of the staircase.

Trowbridge grabbed my hand, and then he propelled me up those narrow stairs at a reckless speed, pulling me hard with his hand and his will. I glanced behind us in time to see Cordelia pocket her earrings. Her shoulders were braced.

There was no choice but to turn right at the top of the second floor. A squeak of hinges echoed up the stairwell as the outer door opened again, and then I heard Cordelia drawl, "Hello, darlings," followed by that first smack of flesh hitting flesh.

Trowbridge yanked me down the short corridor. On the right, two small classrooms, on the left a series of doors with names on them. He booted open Dr. Reznikoff's office door with one kick.

I had an impression of books, papers, and shelving, and the stale smell of old sweat. There was a high-pitched scream from downstairs, and Trowbridge brushed past me to struggle with the window. When it didn't slide up, he leaned back and kicked it to pieces. Wood and glass flew.

There was another scream, this one as piercing as my father's cry when the wolf slashed his belly, followed by the sound of people running up the stairs.

Trowbridge looked at the door and then at me. Blue lights spun around his pupils, then his jaw hardened. "I'll find you."

"What do you mean?" I asked, but he already had his hands on my waist and was lifting me to the window.

"No!" I locked my hands behind his neck. "I'm not leaving you."

But his hard fingers plucked them free, and then he picked me again, saying grimly, "Yes you are."

From behind me, I felt something sickening—waves of freezing air were coming through the doorway. Numbing cold.

"Trowbridge?" I asked, suddenly feeling faint.

"I promised to protect you, remember?" he said, the blue comets in his eyes sharper and brighter than ever before. "Put your legs through the window, sweetheart."

Now he calls me sweetheart? Now?

I lost myself for an instant. Lost myself to disbelief and the arctic air that kept coming, now harsher, more bitter. Trowbridge took advantage of my hesitation. I found myself hanging from the window, held there by his grip on my wrists, with my feet scrambling for purchase and the ground too far below.

I looked up at him, suddenly terrified that I'd never seen him again. He gazed back at me and winked.

Then he let go.

I met the copper roof of the cloister passage with a thump, rolled, once, twice, before I felt myself airborne, and thought, *This will hurt*, all in slow motion.

It did.

It wasn't far to go, really. Maybe ten feet, but I landed on those uneven flagstones that I had admired, left foot first. I heard the snap before my body registered the breaking of my bone. I may have shrieked.

I went beyond my body, beyond sensation. My heart and eyes were on Trowbridge. He was bent in half, with one leg out of the window, one hand on the remaining upper frame. Someone grabbed his trailing foot. Another pair of hands took hold of his pants and started to pull him back into the room.

He's mine.

I pointed my hands at the window and closed my eyes, visualizing the inside. Papers, a pen-littered desk, lots of heavy books. I called to my magic and hoped that it heard me past the anxious panting of my Were.

My power burst from my core, poured itself into my veins, surged past the Were, plucking parts of her rage and anxiety as it shot past her. Glee. Joy. Up it came, like a drug, past my shoulders, down my white arms, bursting through the tight channel of my wrists. My blood was Fae blood. My blood was Were blood. In that moment of desperate need, the two became one.

Hedi's boiling blood.

There was no pause for my talent to build.

It was my birthright, it was my magic, it was my will.

"Attach." It jetted out of the tips of my fingers, not in bursts, but in a long malicious whip of evil intent. There was no miscalculation of aim. Past my love's head, through the glass window, straight to the long wall of books.

Learn this. Do not hurt what is mine.

I didn't seek a contact point. I took the room. The magic streamed from me, and instead of splitting into separate strings of Fae power, it became a wet sheet that stuck to everything in my mind. Books. Fat unreadable tomes; the heavier and denser, the better.

I whipped my right hand in a vicious swipe.

"Storm."

The books shot off the shelves, like academic projectile puke. As the first book left the oak trim, I began to rotate my wrist, fingers curled. It felt strange, moving that wet sheet of power. At first it was jarring, uncomfortable and wrong. But as I got my balance, it got easier.

Move it in a circle, watch it twist like a rag in the sink full of water. It answers my call. It is mine.

It felt good. So good. Giddy again. I shivered.

The Were let go of Bridge's jeans. Now free to move, he twisted to kick the other guy in the face. Four kicks, it took. And during it all, I kept up my maelstrom of book retribution.

The anticipation of their pain made me forget my own, and caused my lips to twist in pleasure. I was beyond such mortal things. Now re-formed, and conscious only of my own lust for vengeance and power.

My mate didn't lose his balance when he fell the distance between window and tin roof. He landed like a cat, twisting in midair.

Not a cat, silly, a Were.

That struck me funny, and I threw my head back to whoop at my brilliance. Wondrous to release the full promise of my Fae nature. Magnificent and glorious.

I called deeper, and knew myself to be strong as I stood and arched my back, and felt no misery except the blissful, burning rush that poured from me. The shelves were moving, tearing themselves off the wall, and they were striking the targets.

I heard yelps, and a cry.

A loud belly laugh of happiness escaped my lips.

Trowbridge leaped from the roof, and landed the right way.

Strong. Beautiful. Mine. I should share my power with him. Yes, what a good idea.

I reached my left hand for him, feeling my back arch and my buttocks clench. *I'm an electric wire. Hear me sing.* Even my abdomen felt tight as a drum skin. I was all bone, all skin, no fat or soft tissue. A new Hedi. A Fae-Were hybrid of blood and bone. Incendiary. Burn it all up.

I was—

Trowbridge hit me, square in the jaw. My head snapped back, and my brain screeched to a halt, and the magic line snapped, and I collapsed, suddenly empty.

He put an arm under my back, and as he did, my spine screamed. It felt broken, stretched beyond possible. I pushed away from him with my hands, and that hurt more.

Trowbridge didn't stop. He put his other hand under my legs and lifted me, and I thought I was going to pass out. He spun on his heel, and then we were moving Trowbridge-speed. Past a student cowering in one of the hobbit doorways, past the line of silver, circle-topped bike posts that made me think of Celtic crosses jammed into the ground, past the woman—*oh, Cordelia, what have they done to you?*—lying bloody and splay-legged in the passageway.

Past columns, too fast and too many to count. Toward the alley.

I could hear them coming.

They were coming, they were coming, but where were we going?

Not the alleyway. Something was wrong with that dark

passageway. What? I couldn't remember. It was from before I had become what I was.

But what am I now?

My temperature began plunging. No longer fevered. Cooling, cooling.

There were decorative gates between the two buildings, stretched across the alley. Medallions of something bright suspended between brackets of dark wrought iron.

My teeth began to chatter as icy fear slid along my spine.

He put a hand to the gate and shook it, and grabbed the steel padlock fastened through the lock and yanked it hard. It bent but didn't break.

My chest felt heavy.

The Weres were close. I could smell the wrongness of them. Were and something else. I rolled my head away from the specter of all that black wrought iron.

Had he forgotten the Fae of me?

There was no time left for the lock. No time left to pull open those hideous gates. The Weres were here.

"Shit." Trowbridge cursed.

He let me go, and let me slide to the ground, and then, oh Goddess, oh Goddess no, he rested my back against the wintry-cool, sickening iron and turned to face the Weres at the mouth of the alley.

I didn't cry out. That would have taken too much air. From my throat came a rattle—a strangled exhalation of lungs squeezed tight by fear and poison. He turned. "Hedi?" Then he was on his knees again, saying, "Shit, shit, shit." Pulling me away from the hideous metal gate, curling his arms around me protectively. Over his shoulder, I saw Stuart Scawens smile and take aim. What did it take to finish that bastard?

Stuart-the-unkillable threw something at my love's unprotected back. It was pointed at the tip, this thing that meant to torment my mate. Like falling from the roof, I knew it would hurt.

Lou's silver spike whistled through the air, and then

Bridge's head flung back with its impact. I felt the echo. The unity. His anguish muted but real, right between my shoulder blades. Pulsing. His thoughts with mine.

Get it out, get it out.

My mate didn't let go of me. Didn't let me fall back against the decorative gate. He held me tighter and said, "Shit," one more time. He didn't tremble so much as shake, and with each tremor I could feel it: the strain, the poison.

Stuart was beside us, looking happy. With his gloved hands, he pulled Lou's silver spike out of my mate's back. I almost thought for a second, *I forgive you.* Perhaps he saw the entreaty in my eyes; he bared his teeth and plunged it back in deeper. Lower this time. In the lungs.

And we both screamed. We both shook, and clutched each other, and then our limbs weren't our own. They were something else, jumping like attached to electrodes, jerking like they were overstretched.

Agony.

"Stop." It was an old man's voice. Thick. Furious.

Stuart's gloved hand was still on the handle, I could see that. Saw him turn his head.

The old Were snarled. "Can't you ever follow my orders?"

I heard footsteps, and knew my enemy came closer. I would not look into Mannus's eyes. Not as the poison sucked the Fae from me. He'd see the hate in my gaze. He'd know that I lusted for his blood, that I craved to make him writhe and suffer. He'd boiled me down. Down to pain, and hate, and fierce retribution. He'd caused the end of my first life, molded the second, and now was there at the melting point of my third.

There would be no kindness, no hesitation when his time came.

"Take the spike out of his back, but keep it close. Put it in his pocket. We want him weak, not dead." I could feel his gaze on us. "Be careful with the girl. She's not one of us."

The wrong-Were smell got closer. I didn't want to gag. Show no weakness, I told myself.

"What about the fag?"

"Bring it too."

They pulled us apart. The wrong arms cradled my broken back, and let my broken foot brush against the iron gate. That was the last I remembered.

Please, Goddess, don't ever let me remember more.

Chapter Nineteen

But I do remember.

Some part of yourself allows you to forget the details—the little stuff that niggles you afterward—because the weight of the absolute horror would flatten everything else into unrecognizable roadkill. And so, there's much I have forgotten: blurred scent memories and warm-up details to the horror, but there's one thing I'll always remember.

The first of the worst.

I gave up Merry when they held the knife over the last remaining finger on Bridge's mutilated hand.

I woke to a room that smelled of blood, Weres, hamburger, and dope, feeling iron-sick and battered. Hands, face, ankle, ribs, heart. They all hurt.

"Biggs, tell the witches to hurry with the wards. I want this place sealed tight in under an hour."

I fought to place the man's voice as I struggled up from the swampy pool of not-here, not-there semiconsciousness.

Mannus's goons had propped me on a chair. I tried to move, and discovered my body had been played with. My arms felt constricted. My legs awkwardly splayed. Worse, there was something tight tied around my neck, securing it to the high back of my seat. My chin could move a few inches up, a few inches down, and another few left and right.

I blinked to clear my eyes, and started with down. Silver duct tape had been wrapped around my torso, binding my arms to my ribs. My shirt was open and bunched up under the tape, exposing my left nipple, in all its beaded worry. I rolled my bare feet and felt the pressure of bindings around my ankles.

I was in the living room of a house I didn't know. There was a set of long windows to my left flanked by dark blue curtains that hung perfectly straight in the stale, airless room. A brass lamp sat on a spindly side table and cast a golden circle around Mannus's easy chair.

The girl from the Laundromat cocked her head. "Her eyes are open," she said to her Alpha. Mannus nodded. Beside her, Stuart leaned against the fireplace, still wearing gloves, drumming his leather-clad fingers against his thigh.

My mate's scent called to me, but its rich copper smell had been altered. I rolled my eyes to the source and found devastation.

Goddess, what have they done to him?

Trowbridges's head was slumped down on his naked chest. Dried blood had glued a few strands of his black hair to the side of his face. He'd been secured to his kitchen chair with lengths of chain wrapped around his chest, thighs, and ankles. More of the same bound his arms behind his back. Scawens had made sure his chair wouldn't move by driving nails through each chair leg straight into the plank floor. Someone had cut Bridge in several places: just above the chain on his chest, below it on his belly, and across his thighs. Straight lines, no hesitation, just pragmatic prep work for more chains—these thin and filigreed, the blood-glazed silver set like a natural seam of the precious metal running along the crevasses of these wounds. The Weres had used padlocks to secure his ankles to the chair legs. His foot was naked again.

I worked some saliva into my mouth. "Trowbridge?"

Don't be dead.

I tested my bonds. At the slightest movement of my hands, pain came in nauseating waves, so unexpectedly savage that my shoulders hunched against it. I counted to eight real fast—just enough to hold back the panic—then peered down. My left hand resembled raw meat. The right hand was worse. A piece of skin hung from the thumb.

I was crispy again.

And misfiring. Where was my magic? It should have surged up from my center like venom, but it hadn't. I probed inside. It was usually right there. Almost tangible to feel. A little ball low in my gut that sparked if probed. There was no ball. No sense of being. Empty.

My Were shivered near the bottom of my spine. *Don't panic. Keep breathing. Count to yourself . . . one thousand, two thousand, three . . .* Impossible. Panic stampeded through the thin barrier of my self-control and took with it every shred of common sense. I flailed. I wriggled. I tried to run, but that was useless, because I was bound to a kitchen chair, and four wooden legs never work as well as two human ones when terror tells you to flee. My frantic thrashing sent my chair crashing to the floor, and once there, it seemed to poltergeist on its own across the oak floor to my mate.

"Where do you think you're going, you ugly, little half-breed?" Scawens's heavy foot came down to pin my chair in place, two feet from Bridge. The young Were smelled worse to me. More musk, more dope, more anger. What happened to the silver spike that Lou had melted into his core? How come Scawens was hale and hearty, and strong enough to pin me to the floor with his stinking boot?

The girl beside him said, "She looks like a rabbit on a spit."

Scawens stared down the length of his nose and smiled as I fought for my breath. And for a bit, that's close to all we heard in that room. Me rasping away on the floor like a fat girl at a cycle spin class, and crickets doing the mating call somewhere outside.

"Pick her up," ordered Mannus. The tape bit into my flesh as Scawens righted my chair and positioned me to face the Alpha. In real life, without the gauzy filter of Lou's dream recollection, my enemy's jowls were longer, and his nose a little more bulbous. For an Alpha, he wasn't even that big.

I'd have called him rawboned, except for his waist, where he had the obligatory middle-age paunch. The flare in his eyes was low and weak, like a blue flicker around a gas element just before it goes out. The handsome peacock of Lou's dreams had aged into an unremarkable man, except for the intermittent glint in his eyes.

"Robson is alive for the moment." Wrinkles hung in crepe folds over Mannus's eyelashes. He tested me with a little flare, a feeble flash of turquoise blue, translucent, almost spent. Returning his gaze, I felt a light tug, a little over-here, a soupçon of down-on-your-knees. I'd spent the last twelve hours flare-sparring with a natural-born Alpha. Mannus was no Trowbridge.

I shifted my gaze to the bookcase behind him.

"Well, that would be the Fae in her, I guess," he murmured to Stuart. "Her mother never knew her place either. Look at me when I speak, Helen."

One shelf on the bookcase was devoted to books about music. Theory books, music books—Stuart's hand lashed out before I could steel myself for the blow. Pain bloomed on my mouth; hot and savage. I stuck the tip of my tongue out, and tasted blood.

"Slow down," Mannus said. "She hasn't got the stamina of a full Were."

Chains chimed as my mate stirred. Trowbridge lifted his head, and then shook it, slow like a stumbling boxer who'd gone one round too many. He worked his jaw, then spat out some blood, but his lip was fat, and the spit didn't clear. It ran down my mate's lip to his chin, and then hung for a moment, a glistening tear of red, before slipping to join the other splatters on his chest.

"Hedi, don't talk." Trowbridge tipped his head back, and I swallowed a gasp as I took in the full horror of his misshapen profile. His straight nose wasn't aristocratically straight anymore, and the eye closest to me was bruised and swollen. He cleared his throat. Spat some flux out again. "Don't say *anything* to him," he said in a stronger voice. Then my Trowbridge turned his chin in the general direction of Mannus and said relatively clearly, considering the state of his lips, "Fuck you and fuck the entire pack."

Scawens coiled a fist.

"Stuart," said Mannus. "When will you learn that you can't squeeze anything out of a corpse?" The Alpha pointed a finger at me. "Yesterday, you offered a trade: an amulet for your aunt. Stuart claims he saw you take the Royal Amulet off Robson's neck. Which was interesting, as we've checked you over very carefully, and we can't find it." He crossed his leg. "What have you done with it?"

"I don't make trades when I'm tied to a chair."

"Does it appear that we're negotiating?" asked Mannus.

"What do you *want* from us?" I cried. "Can't you see Lou's dying? Whatever you think she can do for you, she can't."

"Louise is not dying." He held up a hand. "Yes, she is weak, but that will soon be fixed. And you're partly to blame for that. You've let her get into a terrible state. You should have come to me the moment she started to fade."

"Excuse me for not dialing 911-Were, but I had reasons. Like maybe we've spent ten years *hiding* from Weres. Or how about this? Lou *hates* Weres. And here's the kicker—I had this crazy idea that Weres were bloodthirsty and prone to violence. Reality sucks, eh?"

"Lou hates Weres," he repeated. "Why don't I send someone to fetch her, and she'll tell you how she really feels about our kind?" He said to the girl from the Laundromat, "Dawn, go tell my mate that her niece is awake." As Dawn turned for the stairs, he added, "And this time, find something for her to wear before she comes downstairs."

Mate? "Lou would never mate with a Were." But what if she had? *She wouldn't. She's hated and feared Weres for as long as I've been with her. She's loathed the fact that Were blood pulsed in my veins.* But the little niggle of doubt grew. I thought back to her dreams, and the young predator who'd stared at the Pool of Life as if he'd soon own it.

"You're so sure of yourself, aren't you? Youth," he mused. "You think you know everything when you're young, but you don't. You think you have all the time in the world, but you don't. Things happen. Choices are made."

"Like marrying a Fae?"

"Oh, I didn't marry a Fae. That's for romantics, like your father. You don't need to be married to choose your mate. The mating rites can be done within three minutes, maybe two if you're in a hurry. You don't even need witnesses. I don't think more than four people knew that I was mated to Louise."

I wondered if my mum and dad were two of those people.

"It was a dumb idea, but I was a kid, and I thought I could turn it to my advantage. But it wasn't as easy as I anticipated. We fought a lot. We've been mated for twenty years, but if I stopped to add up all the days we've lived together, I doubt they'd total more than a week." He brooded at the family picture on the mantel. It was too dark for me to make out the details, but it appeared to be a wedding photo. The girl in the center wore a long white dress. "One week in twenty years. When it's your turn to choose your mate, Stuart, weigh the pros and cons, and then weigh them again, because your fate will be tied to hers for the rest of your life. Even something that looks good on the outside can come back and bite you on the ass. I thought Louise's life force would keep me strong for another hundred years. I never imagined she'd go through an early fade."

Mannus ran a thumb over the sagging skin at his jaw. "I was fading as fast as she, and I didn't even know it. It didn't matter how much sleep I got, I never felt rested. My joints ached. Food didn't taste good anymore." He glanced at Scawens. "For a while I wondered if I was being poisoned." The Alpha studied his second for another beat. "Then one evening, in the midst of explaining to me why we needed to consolidate the pack's debt, Roy Talbot keeled over. He was gone in two minutes. By the time the cops came searching for Monica Talbot's next of kin, we'd already dug two graves. It's our way. One goes, the other follows."

Mannus watched me over the rim of his mug as he took a

sip of his peppermint tea. "That's what I was thinking as I watched the cops go back to their cruiser. And then—bam! Just like the proverbial bolt of lightning, it hit me. Louise was dying." He made a face. "Which was a bit of a pickle, because as far as I knew, my mate was still in Merenwyn. Had been, ever since the night they closed the gates."

Mannus put down his cup and blotted his lips with the side of his hand. "I thought, 'This is it, this is where you lose everything. The pack, the future, it's all going to go and there's nothing you can do about it.' All the sacrifices I made, all the plans—it amounted to nothing. No matter how much land I bought, the humans were squeezing us out of our own territory. I'd emptied our bank accounts trying to match the offers developers were throwing at the locals. Bills were mounting. Everything was turning to shit just because my mate was in Merenwyn being forced into an early fade and I had no way of getting to her."

"That makes no sense, even if I believed you," I said. "You can't connect my aunt's illness to your financial issues."

"You have your father's belligerence, do you know that?" Mannus smiled at me, but there was a bleak edge to the set of his lips. He made a vague motion with his hand. "My mind was clouded, and I made some bad decisions because of all of the—"

"Confusion," I supplied, unimpressed. "We lived in the same apartment since I was fourteen. You guys can track a deer over kilometers, but you can't track down one dying Fae living in the suburbs?"

"As I told you, I didn't know Louise was on this side of the portals."

I pointed out what seemed obvious. "Mates don't lose track of each other."

"You have an idealized concept about mates," he said shortly. "Louise and I argued, and we separated. She was in Merenwyn when they closed the gates."

Now that was interesting. How'd he known she was in Merenwyn? She could have been anywhere, couldn't she have?

Some of my disbelief must have shown. He raised his brows. "I didn't know that she'd found a way over," he said. "The last time I saw my mate she was in Merenwyn. I have heard nothing from her for the last ten years until a few days ago. I had no idea she was in this realm, or that she'd spent ten years hating me . . ."

It was starting to sound more like my aunt. It explained the bitterness, the fear of Weres. But why? I asked him, and to my surprise, he answered.

"Because I left her in Merenwyn, when I had to." He saw my reaction, and his lips firmed. "We were discovered in the Fae realm and it came down to my wolf's choice . . . if I'd been fully human, I wouldn't have abandoned her." His face lost expression, as his eyes unfocused, remembering. And that scared me even more, because there was truth, not deception, in the way all those smile-induced lines, now empty of manufactured mirth, scored his face with deep slashes. "We were at the Pool of Life. I'd become wolf, and you just don't think the same when you're in your moon-called nature, as when you're fully human. Particularly over there. I felt more wild there, less mortal . . . The guards shouldn't have found us. We'd taken so much care to be stealthy. We'd made it to the Pool, and were sure no one had seen us. Lou stood guard as I walked up to my neck in their sacred water."

He grimaced. "It took some courage to dip my head under the water, but I did it. And that's pretty much all I remember. I came out of the Pool as a wolf, and saw the Royal Guards riding hard through the forest. So many of them. Armed with bows and arrows." The corners of his lips drooped, and his eyes grew sad under his heavy brows. "If they captured me, it meant a life of enslavement. For her, not much more than a public censure, and maybe a week or two in the tower. They don't hurt their own kind . . . so my wolf chose. We ran for the gates and left Lou to the guards." His restless eyes kept returning to the photo on the mantel. "I'll always regret that. But my other nature saw the hunters with their weapons, and instinct is so hard to deny. If it had been just me, in mortal form . . ." He shrugged after a moment of reflection, and gave us a self-deprecating smile. "We've gotten off track somehow. You asked about the pack's financial issues."

His sigh was lengthy and somewhat overdone. "In some ways, I hold myself to blame for all the debt incurred. I should have just calmed down and waited for the powers that be to bring forth a solution. I've always known my destiny was to rule this pack. But things had gotten so bad . . . and I didn't know that Louise was here, right under my nose all this time. If I'd known that . . ." He spread his hands. "I'll never doubt my fate again. The universe has returned my mate, and soon I'll have the Royal Amulet. She'll call the portal, and a new chapter will begin for my pack."

"We have friends," I said, flexing my feet against the tape's hold. "People will be searching for us."

He uncrossed his legs. "Your aunt never mentioned your bounty of friends. Should I be frightened? Summon the pack to protect us from a horde of your friends?" A fragrant curl of steam rose from his cup of tea. "Here comes my mate."

Lou entered the room wearing a shapeless gray T-shirt, and a pair of yoga pants; an incongruous clothing selection for my haughty aunt. The overlarge T-shirt hung from her shoulder, exposing her collarbone, sharp and thin as the wing of a primed crossbow. She shuffled in, and picked a spot on the carpet between me and Mannus.

Yes, I should have spat at her. I should have denounced her too. Instead, my eyes watered at the sight of her. "Oh Lou."

She didn't rush to me, arms outstretched, seeking assurance. Nor did she gasp at the sight of me silver-wrapped, and bound to a chair. Lou didn't do much except stand there, her face devoid of expression—no tears, no sorrow or fear. The canvas of her lined face was flat, except for the spark in her eyes. Though her flare was little more than a fleck, I could see it clearly in the gloom—a tiny flash of amethyst fire deep inside her brown eyes. Her first flare in months.

The Were part of me noted something else. She'd presented her back to our enemy.

"You *are* mates," I said. Feeling sick, I turned over cards that had always been facedown, and tallied up their values. "That's how you got a Were through a Fae portal. It sensed your Fae blood in him and let him through."

Chapter Twenty

I don't know what happened after that. Did I lunge for Lou? Did I lunge for Mannus? I was on the floor again, panting like I'd hit mile twenty on a marathon. The chair and I lay sideways. Stuart didn't need prodding. He dragged me and my chair back to upright position and stood, too close for my nose, behind me. "We should have nailed her chair to the floor," Stuart said.

"Or maybe just her feet," said Dawn.

Mannus said, "What did she mean by the gates recognized your blood in mine?"

Lou rubbed her ring with her thumb before she turned to him. "The child has always been obsessed with blood." Hands clasped, thumb pressed hard on the emerald, she radiated innocence as she lifted one shoulder and said, "The gates do not recognize one type of blood from another."

I felt like pointing a finger and shouting *"Liar!"* but I didn't. She was playing a deep game, but I couldn't work out what it was and how I figured into it. But one thing was clear: Mannus didn't know that touching her ring allowed Lou to fabricate on the spot. She stood easy as her mate cocked his head to listen to her heart. After a beat or two, he said, "You speak the truth." And just like that, her hastily crafted fib went sailing over the finish line, with a jaunty, "gotcha fool" flag fluttering from its mast.

Mannus said gruffly, "You can have your five minutes with her. After that, she's mine." He went to the desk and opened a drawer. I swear to the stars that I could literally see the cold air pour out. What the hell did he have in there? Mannus reached inside and brought out what appeared to be a short piece of leather. Not that scary. He tossed it, and it landed with a thunk on the dusty desktop. I felt another shudder of cold. *Is it a whip?* My skin did an obligatory crawl at the thought. *They're just trying to soften you up with your own fear.* If so, full marks for them. *Go ahead and label me intimidated.* I'd have sold my soul to know exactly what artifact from hell he'd summoned from the bottom of the desk's drawer. I was frightened but not in terror. But you see—I still didn't fully believe that Lou wouldn't step up, at the last minute. That everything wasn't just a whisper away from destruction.

"Where is my Royal Amulet?" Lou asked in a querulous tone. When I wouldn't lift my gaze past the logo on her shirt, her dry fingers touched my chin. The tape tightened at my throat as she lifted my face till I got the full impact of her little flare. "Tell me."

"Tell me." I felt the long familiar suck of depression just taking in the greed in her eyes. "It's been the pattern of our life together, hasn't it? Do this. Do that. Don't cry. Don't ask questions. If you're frightened, count until you're not. Stop sulking. Come find me. Does that sound familiar? It should, because I came running. But you were never in danger, were you? Scawens never got staked with a silver spike and you never were held captive in a room lined with silver. It was just another fabrication. You've been feeding me a buffet of lies as long as we've been together."

"I warned you to stay out of my head."

"Then why haven't you stayed out *of mine*?"

"I am dying here. I need the Royal Amulet to open the portal and return home. I can't die here among . . ." Lou paused, and reconsidered her word choices. Then she cut to the chase. "Tell Mannus where it is."

"You know, that's the part that really kills me." Bitterness made my jaw ache. "You *can't* open a portal. You tried. Remember? Over and over again. We spent weeks traveling from place to place, trying to summon one. Can't you get it through your head? The gates to Merenwyn are closed!"

"Not to one who summons it with the Royal Amulet. And Mannus has made a pledge to me—"

"Do you actually believe—"

"If you tell him what he wants to know," she continued, as if I hadn't spoken. "He will release you. You may carry on with your life."

"And what about Trowbridge?"

Her eyes turned scornful. "He is one of them."

"No." I stared her down. "He's mine."

Trowbridge shifted. The padlocks swung and sent a thread of his scent to my nose. "Don't, Hedi," he said. "You don't know what he's capable of."

"This is going nowhere fast," said Mannus.

A familiar expression flitted across my aunt's face as she examined me. "You smell like them now," Lou said with deep disdain. Her eyes sparked purple, a quick hint of amethyst before fading to flat brown.

How quickly love turns to hatred. Think of a way out of this. Think.

Someone knocked on the door. Scawens inhaled through his nose and said, "Biggs."

"It better be good." Mannus folded his arms. "Tell him to enter."

I recognized Biggs as the dark-haired Were from the Laundromat who'd been reluctant to join the fight. He had clever eyes, and a flat mouth, but his most noticeable feature was his height. By human standards he was diminutive, by Weres' he was Lilliputian. *Help us,* I silently pleaded. Biggs's face didn't soften, but his lips got thinner.

"What is it?" asked Mannus.

"The witches won't accept the check," said Biggs.

"Tell them there won't be any trouble with this check."

"I told them that, but they're insisting the outstanding balance be cleared before they set the final ward on the eastern end of the property." Biggs's eyes roved from Mannus to Dawn, Scawens to me, and then back to Mannus. What he didn't look at—didn't even glance at—was Trowbridge. "The coven wants to speak to you and only you."

"Without that last ward, I'll be up to my ass in Weres as soon as the fairy portal's scent floats over the pond." Mannus scratched the bristles on his chin. "It always comes down to money. My kingdom for a stack of bills." Suddenly his fingers froze mid-scratch. His head slowly pivoted to me. Turquoise lights spun slowly around his pupils, like blue comets with tiny green tails. "Dawn," he said in the same sort of voice I'd use if I found twenty bucks in my winter jacket. "Bring me the thing you took off the mutt's waist."

Bile rose in my throat as Dawn pulled Mum's bride belt off the shelf. Mannus took it from her and untied the pouch's soft leather fastenings. He peered inside. "So," he said, pouring the Fae Tears into his hand. He held them under the lamp's light. Six stones winked from the wrinkled plain of his palm. Mannus settled on one—the smallest and brightest—and put it aside. He let the others roll down the funnel of his fingers back into the soft leather pouch.

"How priceless is priceless?" He turned the Tear I'd shed for Trowbridge between his blunt fingers.

"The witches will recognize its value," said Lou, in a flat voice. "They'll pretend it's almost worthless, but they will want it enough to agree to anything you request."

His face turned sour. "I hate wasting resources." He stood. "My patience is almost gone, little mutt. I'll settle this and then I'll settle you."

There would be no "settling" of me. A cold thought, but a clear one, cutting through all those half-formed expectations based on a relationship that has expired. Once he came back, I had no future to moon over. Lou wasn't going to help me. Hell, there was hardly any present left. My heart turned as hard as the stone inside his fist as the Alpha walked to the door with my Tear in his hand. Just the thought of a witch reaching for it. Fouling it with her touch.

Fury.

"Don't you remember the old Alpha?" I shouted in defiance. "Trowbridge's father flared electric blue. Bright blue. Just like Trowbridge does." I was bulletproof in my rage. "Mannus doesn't flare like a Were, he flares like a mated Fae. He's nothing more than the second son of an Alpha who had to trick a Fae into believing he loved her, just so he could go to Merenwyn to steal some power and a blue-green flare."

"Shut up," said Mannus.

"Trowbridge's got jack in his eyes," said Stuart to Biggs. "He doesn't flare."

"That's because you're poisoning him with silver," I said. "Real Alphas have a pure blue light, not a green-blue one. Can't you see you've got the real Alpha chained up? Ask *Trowbridge* who killed the old Alpha."

Mannus grabbed the leather thing from the desk and started over the bloodstained floor in my direction. I spat out the rest rapid-fire. "It was Mannus. I saw his wolf come through the portal—" Mannus pressed the thing in his hand against my skin. It was colder than the Atlantic in January. Cold enough to feel like a flame.

Oh my Goddess.

I looked down at my chest. Held flat against my flesh was a leather dog collar, and from it hung a long bell of iron.

I screamed.

"You bastards, you bastards," I heard Bridge hoarsely shout.

The lights went out, and I was walking the dark halls of my mind again, calling for my Trowbridge, but finding nothing except dark curtains waving in a cold killing wind.

Weak. I'm so weak.

Fingers pinched my chin. My head was wobbling on my shoulders now, no longer held immobile against the high back of the kitchen chair by a choker of duct tape. That had been torn off, and tossed to the ground, replaced by a length of leather that Mannus had fastened around my neck. The dog collar's iron pendant rubbed against the hollow at the base of my throat—right in the place Trowbridge had kissed with soft lips near dawn. My shoulders jerked against the cold burn of its contamination.

"My father made this collar," said Mannus. "He told my brother and me if we ever saw a Fae, we were to trap it and collar it. I should have put it on you the moment we had you in the chair. How does it feel?"

I took in a careful, shallow breath.

"When I talk to you," said my torturer. "I expect an answer, even if it's just a nod."

I opened my eyes and found Mannus's face was inches from mine.

"Do you know what the worst type of Alpha is?" he said. "A nice man. I am not a nice man. I can't afford to be."

"She's a Fae!" Trowbridge's voice was rough, almost shaky with desperation. "No one will believe her. You don't have to kill her."

Mannus's full lips hardened. "It doesn't matter now, does it? The walls have ears. Even if I ordered Biggs to be silent, I can't be sure that someone else didn't hear her. They're always listening, waiting, and judging. Besides, it will make what happens next easier for them to understand. Once they know that I've already been to Merenwyn once, and nothing happened the last time I broke the Treaty—"

"They came over and executed my mother," I shouted. "Because of what Lou did. What you both did. You're both traitors to your kind."

Mannus straightened and wiped his fingers on the soft corduroy of his trousers. "I'm *not* a traitor. None of you know what I've given up for this pack or what I've had to do." He went to the fireplace, and lifted the framed picture from the thick slab of pine that served as a mantel. Examining the photo he said, "My brother got to be a nice man. He loved his family and cared for the pack, in his own way. But he couldn't see past the old ways into the future. Humans were coming for our land. I warned him of the danger but he wouldn't listen."

He wiped the mantel clean, and replaced the picture.

"It has always been my destiny to guide the pack through

this threat. I understood that and knew what had to be done."
He moved closer to Trowbridge—close enough that he could
have touched his matted curls. "I executed my brother for
the good of the pack. Then I killed his wife and his second
son. I even killed your Candy. She didn't even fight. She just
closed her eyes."

"You bastard!" Bridge roared. He planted both feet on
the floor and tried to stand. The chair creaked, and lifted an
inch, but the nails held, and shone like gray teeth in the gap
between chair and floor.

"Do you think their deaths didn't hurt me?" Mannus
roared. "He was *my brother*."

"He was *my father*!" It was howl of grief and fury.

Mannus turned to Biggs. "You know in your heart that I'm
right. Developers and cottage people keep chewing up our
territory with their earthmovers and chain saws. It won't be
long before one of them uses a cell phone to film a moon run,
and the video will go . . . what's the word again, Stuart?"

"Viral."

Mannus sat down heavily. "I can't buy all the land we need
to keep us safe from the humans and their cameras. I've tried,
but with every purchase, I drive up the land values. I can't
force fealty on the hundreds of humans who want to Jet Ski
on our lakes. They just keep squeezing us north." His voice
turned petulant. "It's not right. We belong here with the land.
We are pure—"

"Weres," I said. "Just men that turn furry at the moon. Big
deal. You share the world with two-legged mortals, and a
couple of beat-up Fae. What makes you think you have any
more rights than anyone else?" My split lip burned. "Trowbridge, show them," I pleaded. "Show them who the real Alpha is. Flare."

"Yeah, show us your flare." Scawens pulled Bridge's head
back, so that his profile was exposed to the white glare of the
halogen light. "He's the big Alpha, right? Well, I don't see
any flare." He moved his fingers to either side of Bridge's
face and then crooned, "Come on, buddy. I think you need to
show your lady your flare." And with that, he put everything

into his punishing grip and forced Bridge's head to turn my way.

I gasped.

My mate's blue eyes were covered by a thick grayish-white film.

He was blind, my Trowbridge.

And he was going to die. The blue vein high up on his cheekbone had turned silver-gray.

"Do you need another demonstration in Were endurance?" Mannus said to me.

"Lou, please," I whispered. "Take the silver from him."

"It is in his lungs," she said, as if that were enough.

"Lou . . ."

"You have always been too sentimental. It is your greatest flaw," she said. "A trait that would not have served you well as a mystwalker."

I started to cry. Not even Fae Tears. Just hot, wet, salty ones that tasted human.

"Most people have ten fingers, you can take your time, give people a little time to think between amputations." Mannus settled deeper into his easy chair. "But as you see, my nephew doesn't have much in the way of fingers left. Perhaps it makes the ones he has left all the more precious."

Stuart ran his tongue across his upper teeth.

"Last chance," said Mannus. "Why not tell me?"

Crying is for people who still have some fight, some sense of injustice, some faint hope that their tears will change the thing that they dread. When you know it won't, you weep.

Mannus snapped his fingers at Stuart.

I wept as Dawn dragged a table over to Trowbridge's chair. Helpless tears dribbled down my cheeks as Trowbridge fought to keep his arms free and lost. I watched as Stuart kept them flat on the table while Dawn wound a thick chain over them and under the table, and then did another circuit, just to make sure. She tested its tightness then crouched to hook a padlock through the links. I heard the snick of it closing, and felt another wave of dread.

"You son of a bitch, I'll fucking kill you. I'll—" Trowbridge didn't get the rest out, because Dawn took a knife and deftly sliced open the wrist on his bad hand. Blood welled. Stuart handed Dawn his gloves and a small box. Impassive as a surgeon, she slipped the leather over her hands, opened the lid and pulled out another silver chain, which she wound around his bleeding wrist, pulling it tight, so it sank deep into the channel of her cut. The table's wooden legs knocked against the floor, like a shutter rattling in a storm, as he struggled against the effect of the silver slipping into his bloodstream, but eventually the room turned . . . quiet, except for my tears, and the sound of Trowbridge breathing hard through his teeth. When Trowbridge's hand was limp on the table, Dawn spread his fingers out negligently, as if she were inspecting worms for the hook.

Then she stepped back for Stuart.

Bridge turned blindly in my direction with his milky silver-poisoned eyes, and gave me one last order. "Stay strong. You hear me, Hedi? It doesn't matter what they do to me." And there it was. Just under the bravado of his words. He'd kept it in check by resisting and feeding his rage, by swearing and promising them murder, but as Stuart dragged the sharp point of the knife teasingly over the back of his mutilated hand, I felt the bitter bite of my mate's fear. Inside me. Right in my core. Right where my Fae ball used to roll.

"Not so brave, now, are you?" Stuart taunted.

Robson Trowbridge didn't beg for mercy, not even when the Alpha's second slowly sawed through the skin and tendons of his finger. Whatever illusions I had about humanity died in the moment Scawens leaned into the knife to cut through the gristle and sinew of the joint. While Trowbridge bowed his head, fighting hard to keep his agony in his chest, I cried out. Lower and louder than I'd ever done before, more animal than my mate.

I trembled on the edge of capitulation, told myself not to, and did it anyhow. The words spilled out. "Please, stop, just stop."

"Don't you dare," Bridge said between his teeth. He sucked in a shuddering breath. "Don't you do it, Hedi."

My chest shook with sobs. "I can't watch this . . . I can't do this."

"He'll start a war if he goes to the other side. One we can't hide or win. Weres must never go to the other realm. Not ever."

Mannus sat on his haunches to inspect me. "You can stop this." He waited until my sobs were broken hiccups, and then he said in his deep, fatherly voice, "All you have to do is tell us where the Royal Amulet is. You know where it is, don't you?"

Stuart used the tip of the knife to push Bridge's finger off the table.

I wept, shaking my head "no," snot running down to salt my lips, until Mannus put a hand on my knee and said, "It's time to tell me."

Stuart looked up, and waited. The faithful collie waiting for the Frisbee to be sent in the air again.

Mannus watched my face and said, "Stuart, go ahead."

That's when I gave up Merry.

Chapter Twenty-one

Mannus called someone on his cell. He kept prodding me for more details. What was the name of the building? When I couldn't answer straight, Biggs carefully closed my shirt, and buttoned it up to my neck. The back of his hand brushed against the underside of my chin as he centered the iron pendant gently on top of the plaid shirt, creating a barrier between the metal and my skin. His gaze ricocheted off from the condemnation he found in mine.

Five minutes later, again the questions. Which building? What side of the commons was the grave? I answered as best I could, and eventually, the Were on the other end of the phone was dispatched to unearth Merry.

"Come, mate," Mannus said to Lou.

She stood, without needing any help, and straightened herself stiffly as he put his hand on the small of her back. I watched her walk away, back held regally straight. Our gazes caught, but didn't hold, as her eyes slid from mine. He guided her out of the room, and I heard his heavy tread follow hers up the stairs.

Before he'd collapsed into himself Trowbridge had moaned, "You shouldn't have done it." I'd said, "I've saved you." But he shook his head and said, "No." It sounds like a small word.

Two letters. The easiest thing to learn, that word, "no." Mum said it was my first word.

But the way he'd said it.

No.

His eyes were half open, but he still hadn't rolled his head my way. His finger had stopped dripping. The sound of it had near driven me mad. Toronto to Creemore is eighty miles. How fast could Mannus's minion find Merry on the campus? How fast could he drive back to Creemore? How much time did we have?

Open your eyes, Trowbridge. Open your eyes.

Stuart and Dawn had been left to guard us, not that we represented much in the way of a threat. I was duct-taped to a chair, Bridge was chained to his. Stuart collapsed on the couch while Dawn inspected my stuff. First, she picked up my glasses and entertained herself by examining her hand, the newspaper, and finally, me, through the finger-smeared lenses. Next, she sat down with the bride belt. She ran a nail over the metal embellishment on the leather pouch.

Biggs snapped on the overhead lights. "Would the Alpha let her touch that?"

Stuart rolled his head and said lazily, "Did anyone ask for your opinion, Biggs? If she wants to play with the mutt's stuff, she can." He stretched his arms over his head and yawned. "What do you want?"

"Paul has to leave." A flush crawled over Biggs's face. "He wants to know what he should do about the other prisoner."

Stuart stuck his finger in his ear, and dug out some ear wax. He examined it, and then flicked it off his fingernail. "We should just put it out of its misery."

"Was that a direct order from the Alpha?" asked Biggs stiffly.

"Tell Paul that you'll watch over it."

"I can't," Biggs said. "The Alpha's given me another job."

For a moment, Stuart did nothing. Then he tilted his head to the side so that Biggs could watch Stuart's outer cheek pulse as he thrust his tongue inside it in a crude mimicry of fellatio.

The flush on Biggs's cheeks grew fiery.

"It must really piss you off," Stuart goaded. "As long as he rules, you've just got to bend over."

Biggs's gaze slid over the things in the room, and then clung to the shotgun mounted over the hearth.

"Go ahead. Take it down," Stuart said. He smiled slowly. "Aw, that was mean, wasn't it? You'd need a stepladder to get it down from there. You know what? It's still loaded with silver." He made a gun with his fingers and aimed it at Biggs. "Bang. Bang."

Woodenly, Biggs asked, "The other prisoner?"

"Bring it here."

Stuart waited until Biggs had backed out of the room, before he gave a curt nod to Dawn. "Leave that stuff alone, babe. Let's not screw with the Alpha right now." Dawn made a moue with her mouth, but she put the pouch back on the table.

For another beat or so of my heart, we all stared at each other. I wished my heart weren't beating so fast. I wished Trowbridge's were beating stronger.

Stuart smoothed a hand over Dawn's shoulder. She giggled and popped her shoulder free from her shirt. He bent his head. I averted my eyes and let them rove over my surroundings. The overhead light made it easier to see the details.

The room was large, built with the standards and space of the last century. It had high ceilings, and honey-colored, oak-framed windows and doorways. It felt like a frat house now, but once this house had been a home. The outdated couch had big flowers on it, and exaggerated overstuffed armrests. Mannus's easy chair had chintz fabric, a sunken seat cushion, and dark stains on the armrests. The ashtrays were full.

There were bloody footprints circling Trowbridge's chair.

Stuart stopped worrying Dawn's shoulder, and went to open the window. Night air seeped into the Were-hot room. It brought other scents with it. Essences of ponds, and hills.

Fir trees and pine mulch. Aromas I hadn't caught in such a nostalgic bouquet in eleven long years.

Creemore.

I looked around me again. The long windows with their faded blue curtains. The birch tree outside. The music books on the shelves. They hadn't brought us to any house in Creemore, they'd brought us back to the Trowbridge manse.

Oh, Trowbridge.

The picture that had fascinated Mannus was back on the mantel, a little off center. Bridge's family was caught frozen in time, smiles wide, wearing their best duds, all lined up beside a wedding cake. Four months later, they'd all be dead, except of course, Mannus, and the supposed traitor in the middle of the photo; the groom with an easy smile, and tense eyes, who was marrying his Candy.

A visual reminder of loyalty and treachery, I guess.

Biggs returned, huffing as he dragged Cordelia into the room. He propped her in the corner near the television. I would have taken Cordelia for dead, what with her head tilted to one side, her mouth open, and a silver knife jammed in her gut, if not for the slow rise of her chest. A big wide red oval stain circled the impaled blade, forever ruining her Ann Taylor shirt.

I strained to listen to her heart. It was there, weak and sluggish, but there.

Her hands lay open palmed on the dusty wood floor.

Another broken soul.

The iron was making me sleepy. I kept jerking my eyes open, and each time they blearily refocused, they landed on the Trowbridge family photo.

Somewhere in the house, a cell phone rang. Mannus returned holding his cell a few minutes later.

"Got it." The Alpha snapped his phone closed. "They're on their way."

Mannus walked to the window, absently kneading his lower back with one hand while he inspected the sinking sun. "Your kind made my life hell. I thought I got rid of the lot of you." He grimaced. "Do you know the pack still talks about your family? They think you haunt the pond, because they never found your body. Every so often someone thinks they caught a glimpse of a little blond girl in a white night-gown playing by the water with her brother."

Mannus's lip curled in a sneer. "A few years ago a bunch of kids got brave and brought their sleeping bags to the fairy pond. They came running home with their tails between their legs, claiming they saw purple fog and lights over the water. I went there the next night, but I never saw any fairy lights. Stuart, how many days did I make you patrol the fairy pond?"

"Thirty, Alpha."

"And you never saw any lights or fog. How about you, Dawn?"

"No, sir." She picked at her fingernail.

"The young ones still talk about it, though, behind my back. Little bastards." He focused his gaze broodingly at Stuart. "Society is going to hell. We've got to start over." He let out a deep sigh and collapsed into his chair. "I've passed through that portal. Felt the taste of its mist on my tongue." His fingers drummed the armrests. "Someone is trying to open it. I thought it was Louise, but now I know that she's been here ever since they closed the gates." He formed a steeple with his fingers then studied the half-assed church made by them. "Tell me, Helen, where is your brother?"

I had my teeth clamped so tight, my jaw hurt.

"Do you really want me to hurt your mate again?" Mannus sighed. "Someone rouse Robson."

"Lexi's safe in Merenwyn," I said.

"Then he's the one trying to open the gates."

I felt my lips tremble and tightened them into a thin line.

"See, Stuart? I told you the Fae were coming. We're only just in time." Mannus chewed the inside of his cheek. "It's beautiful over there. Fields and forests as far as the eye can see. I'd never felt stronger or more alive. It was . . . I don't know how to describe it." He rubbed one of his swollen knuckles. "Their Pool of Life does something to you. It takes the magic you were born with and I don't know . . . magnifies it somehow. I changed into my wolf, right there under their sun. I didn't have much of a flare before, but after that—I was Superman." The memory made him smile. "I felt like I had two beams of light coming from my eyeballs. I was twice as strong and doubly as handsome."

Mannus was lost in reverie and totally oblivious to the way Stuart had suddenly stiffened after he'd dropped the "flare" bomb. "Once we have the Royal Amulet," he continued, "my mate and I are going to swim in that pond again. And then, we're going to hold the doors to Merenwyn open and let my people come."

So that's the game Lou was playing. She was going to lure him into the portal and then lose him on the way to Merenwyn. A little smile creased my lips.

"You find that amusing?" Mannus snapped. "What exactly do you find amusing?"

There's times when you have to use a little crumb of truth, to hide a much bigger chunk of fact. "Lou won't do it," I said evenly.

"Lou won't do it," he mimicked. "Louise wants to go home. She'll take me."

"Going through the portal will break the Treaty," I said, thinking of the Weres he would have led into Merenwyn. "The punishment for that is death."

"That would be important only if I wanted to negotiate. I told you, I don't negotiate. It will be war. We have surprise on our side, and access to something they haven't had to worry about in fifty years." He walked over to me and touched the dog collar around my neck, and then leaned down to watch my face as he said, "We have iron." Using his thumb, he rolled the hanging locket up so it burned the underside of my chin. His eyes creased into slits when I flinched.

"One pound of iron filings in the royal house's well and they're done," he said. "That's just the beginning. When I'm finished with them, there won't be a single living Fae left in Merenwyn."

* * *

A car pulled up outside. Biggs opened the front door to shepherd in a tall, nervous Were still in his late teens. From the way his gaze darted around the hallway, I figured he thought he'd finally made it to the big time. He didn't quite genuflect in the presence of Mannus, but he did perform an uncool head bob as he wordlessly passed a Ziploc freezer bag to his Alpha. Then he further solidified his geek status by jumping out of his skin when Dawn touched his sleeve to lead him to the back of the house.

Biggs sat on the bottom stair. His clever eyes watched us through the railings.

"This can't be it," said Mannus, looking at the large lump in the bag.

Lou had come down the stairs a few minutes ago. Whatever they'd done upstairs had made her a little stronger, and a lot less wraithlike. And that, somehow, was far worse. She stood beside her mate; anticipation contorting her face into a mask of greed and excitement. Under the hall's light, she seemed even thinner, as if all the fat and muscle had been burned off until all that was left was bone and sinew. Combine that with the crazy-lady intensity, and . . . I wanted to cover my mouth at the awfulness of it, but couldn't, so settled for sucking my lips inward and biting down on them.

"It has to be," Lou said sharply. "I can sense Fae gold."

Mannus swung the bag out of her reach. "Not till we're at the fairy pond."

"It's the Royal Amulet. Ebrel can feel it."

"Put your hand down. I don't want Ebrel calling to it."

She looked impatient, but she tucked her calling hand into her armpit. "Let me see." She paused and then added, "Please." Mannus dug in the bag and brought them out. He hung them off his finger so that they pirouetted in front of us. Lou inhaled sharply and then turned slowly to me. "You let your pet attach itself to my amulet?"

"What?" Mannus said.

"Her mother's amulet is wound around the Royal Amulet."

He frowned at them. "I'll rip it off."

"You may damage the Royal Amulet." Lou's voice developed an edge. "Leave it for now. I know how to get it off."

"Is her mother's amulet of any use?"

"No. It was keyed to my sister's blood, not mine." She sniffed. "Without my sister, it's no more than a child's pet."

"I don't like it," said Mannus. "Take it off."

"I need to be at the Pool to remove it."

"We'll see about that." Mannus held them in front of me. The amulets rotated in the space between us. First a view of Merry. Then a view of the Royal Amulet. First her, then him.

My throat felt raw. I opened my mouth to say something to Merry, to explain, to say "I'm sorry" and discovered that there was nothing I could say beyond "Forgive me." And how useless was that? I closed my mouth and watched her rotate until her spins petered out, and then she just hung there, facing me. Mud was embedded into the filigree of her gold. A fat streak of it dulled the smooth belly of her stone.

"Did you do this?" Mannus said.

My gaze rested on Merry clinging to the Royal Amulet. "I did."

"Undo it. Now."

"Can't." I looked at him and tried to smile. "It's a done deal."

They didn't kill me. Or pull out the knife and start on Bridge again. I got another bruise on my face, but that was from Mannus doing the eyeball-to-eyeball flare thing. He seemed big on grabbing chins and squeezing them as he stared into your eyes.

"You said you'd stop that," Lou said, from over his shoulder. His head turned, and I was treated to his profile. "I know how to remove it. I can do it at the pond."

"It better be all right." He slid them back into the Ziploc bag, and stuffed it into his pocket. Then he stepped behind me. His knife blade pinched my cringing back as he sawed through my duct-tape bindings.

"Now," he said, into my ear, in his soft, lethal voice.

"You're going to come with us to the fairy pond. And if there's any problem with these amulets, I'm going to personally cut my nephew's throat while you watch." He paused to let me absorb that. "Then we'll start on your fingers. You got that? Stuart," he said. "Bring Robson."

Chapter Twenty-two

There was still light outside the Trowbridge home, but it was dying light. Grayed down except for the western sky, where the sun was now turning an unlikely pink-red. Shutting the homestead's door, Stuart said, "Alpha, what do you want done with the fag?"

Mannus gave an indifferent shrug. "It's no longer useful." His attention was on the sweater he was fussily draping over Lou's shoulder.

Stuart said to Biggs, "Take care of it. Then come down to the pond to help watch the prisoners."

Kill the prisoners, I thought.

Biggs disappeared into the house.

Trowbridge was crumpled on the paint-blistered porch, unable to stand after Dawn teased the silver chains from his wounds when it'd become evident that he was too weak to walk on his own and too much of a silver-festering problem to carry. She'd got them all, except the one across his belly. There the skin had tried to knit itself whole, burying the silver chain under a scarred seam, and had mostly succeeded, except for a place at the right edge, where his flesh had refused to bond. It had left a small weeping hole. Blood and pus oozed from it, dyeing his shorts' once-white waistband.

He was so weak.

They kept us apart, which angered Dawn, as it had fallen

to her to look after me. I wasn't that difficult to guard. I'd stopped weeping. I stood, head slightly bowed, hands hanging limply by my side. Frightened to my core.

"It's going to be a beautiful night." Mannus pulled Lou's arm through his. He gave her a quick charming smile. "Perfect for travel." They started across the lawn.

Scawens cupped a hand to call. "Kid!" When the teenager appeared in the doorway, Stuart cocked a thumb at Trowbridge and said, "I'll need help bringing this prick down to the pond."

Dawn pushed me forward.

Trowbridge's dad would have never recognized his property. When I had been a child, the home's landscaping had been fastidious, and in my personal opinion, fussy. Sometime since, the pack had stopped using the mower and now the once carefully tended lawn was hinterland, filled with the disorder of prickle weeds and the pod-stippled stalks of last year's milkweed. Scawens and the kid hoisted up my mate, and I followed them as they led the way across Trowbridge's lawn, all of us funneling into a single file, picking our way through the nettles toward the line of trees that marked the beginning of the untouched forest that ringed the Trowbridge home. I knew, even without looking up, where we were headed. But I did glance up, and felt another dribble of dread. In the waning daylight, the path to the pond seemed like a dark tunnel, the trees black and forbidding over it.

Bad things waited at its end.

"Let's go," said Dawn to me.

I fell down, elbows first, healing hands tucked protectively into my chest. Dawn grabbed my shirt and tugged me back onto my feet. I took a few more weaving steps across the weed-choked lawn then sank to my knees. Her boot hit my ass. I curled up into a defensive comma. She hit me again. It struck me on the third kick that I was doing a pretty good job of looking ill. It wasn't that difficult—every time the iron touched the hollow of my throat I had to swallow down bitter bile. And truth be told, it didn't hurt much. Somewhere my body had cut the ties to the neural pathways, overwhelmed by the horror and cold conviction that if I walked into the throat of the forest with the iron bell tinkling at my throat, I'd never walk out again.

"You stupid bitch," said Dawn. "Stop doing that." She grabbed me by the hair and pulled upward. I felt my eyes slit as my skin stretched.

"Take her collar off," Stuart said to her. "She's slowing us down."

Dawn sneered. "She's just pretending."

I brought a hand up to my mouth and gave Stuart a guileless look.

"Take it off," he said. "I don't want to miss anything."

Her fingers fumbled at my neck and finally I was free. I hid my relief with another feigned fist-covered burp. She grunted, irritated, and gave my shoulder a shove.

A gnarled root snaked across the path of beaten earth. I hesitated and was rewarded by another hard shove. Fear ahead, and fear behind. I inwardly shrugged, and took my first step into familiar woods. Ten years of absence collapsed under a deluge of memories. Once, I'd wandered here at will. I'd learned which branch of the track led to the field where the pack gathered for their moon runs. Memorized which turns would take me to the crop of sunsweet berries. I'd spent hours on this footpath, trailing after Lexi, half listening to his boy-proud boasts.

I'd claimed these paths as my own, but had I ever really seen them? Had the forest always been this beautiful? Had the air always smelled this good?

Dawn leaned in and said, "Welcome home, mutt."

Ahead of me, Scawens and the kid sweated as they half carried, half dragged Trowbridge between them. It hurt my eyes to see him suffer while I walked free.

I concentrated on the path. It was narrower, and not as often used as when I was young, when the earth had been worn smooth and the leaf mulch broken into tiny fragments that felt soft under the feet. As I listened to the hollow echo of our footsteps, I imagined moles and mice, scurrying down dark passages beneath our feet.

Run, little animals. The wolves have come.

Too soon, the forest starting thinning. The setting sun sent streaks of light between the well-spaced trees, brilliant gold. My mouth got drier. I could smell the pond.

I don't want to die.

My feet slowed as we passed the last cluster of trees. "Hurry up," said Dawn, pushing me into the small clearing at the top of the Trowbridge ridge. Everyone paused, as Mannus walked to the edge and brooded at the pond below.

He turned and gave Lou a bittersweet smile.

She didn't return it.

I forced my gaze past her to search for familiar things. Trowbridge's favorite tree was still there, but the worn spot beneath it where he once strummed guitar was gone. Missing too were the twin pines that had hugged the edge of the cliff. Mannus turned from the pond, and our entourage followed. But as we made our way to the rock-studded trail that twisted down the hill, I glanced quickly down over my right shoulder to the pond, and found it too altered. What did I expect? Nature never stops to mourns us. It carries on, conscious only of its own cycle of growth and death. The thought slipped in, unwanted. *Where would they bury me?*

A finger of cold ran down my spine.

Three Weres waited by the pond. Young. Muscled. Shifting on their feet with badly disguised anticipation. I revised the bad guy count to six Weres and one old Fae.

Oh Goddess, we didn't stand a chance.

"The last part's too steep for you, Louise," said Mannus, sweeping her off her feet. Lou turned her head and looked at me, expressionless, as he carried her down the cliffside path.

At first I thought it was blood.

The pond water was red. Not all of it. Just the part near where I stood.

I studied the oily rust-colored film polluting the water. The pond smelled wrong. Metallic, and somehow cold. At the marshy edge, the bulrushes' submerged stems were stained brick red.

I drew in a sharp breath as I realized what it was.

Iron. Bleeding from the ferrous-rich rocks that the new Alpha had used to make a retaining wall for his hill. It had held back erosion, but poisoned the water.

I could feel the cold pull of it.

The sounds of animal life—birds tweeting, frogs croaking, ducks quacking, all the stuff that belonged in the pond trailed off into silence as Mannus walked over to its edge. He stood facing it, his lips pulled down.

Lexi would have been pissed off too. The northern end of his watering hole had been taken over by his personal bêtes noires, lily pads. In his absence, they'd spread out, leaf over leaf, crowding each other so that their fat saucer leaves tilted sideways. The only thing that had checked their proliferation was a half-submerged log—the last visual remnant of the tree that had once grown at its edge. All that remained of the once-tall pine was its toppled trunk, bark stripped and sun bleached. It floated at the pond's midpoint, still anchored to the land by the weight of its twisted roots.

I wanted my brother beside me so bad, my knees felt weak. *Don't look. You won't find him there.*

I couldn't stop myself. I turned my head toward the opposite ridge, half expecting to see some part of our old home still standing. There was nothing for my eyes to linger on. The gray-shingled roof was gone. Whatever walls had been left after the fire, had fallen. The hill path had been overtaken by an infestation of cockleburs.

My brother didn't stand under the tree, beckoning to me. Scabby kneed, and twelve.

It was all gone.

Even the clearing that we'd affectionately called the beach had been swallowed up by nature, shrunk until it was little more than a foot-wide strip of pebble-embedded mud.

But near it, I finally found one surviving relic of our past.

Lexi's pirate rock sat where the last ice age had left it. Five feet high and almost as wide, it had withstood everything nature had thrown at it. When we were finally allowed to roam free, we'd done so, both with our minds and our bodies. And then, we'd discovered the rock. Something larger than my brother. Harder than his sharp nails. With his usual blithe insouciance, Lexi began his summer siege, determined to wrestle dominance from a hunk of granite. At first it was enough to just climb to the top. We'd jammed our sneakers' toes into the crevasses and pulled ourselves up, fingers scrambling for handholds, and for the space of a week had thought ourselves both very fine, sitting high above the dragonflies. But that had paled. And then it had become a prop for Lexi's stories. For the rest of the summer we'd been pirates. Explorers sometimes too, as we pretended we stood on the deck of a tall-mast ship. Our marine battles had been long and bloody. Together we'd withstood sail-tearing storms and grapeshot. We took turns dying; being the victor and the victim—mock battles with broken hockey sticks and horrific injuries that were painless and invisible.

There was a twin of the boulder beneath the pond. We'd found its rounded edge with our toes. Lexi had grinned. The pond had no secrets left for him to uncover. The siege was over.

By the next summer, the boulder sat alone. No children to crow from it. Abandoned not by youth's natural transition from fascination to boredom, but by the fact our childhood had been broken, cut in two in one terrible, bloody night. Yet, the rock still stood, silent witness to what once had been.

The keening sense of loss rubbed against me, painful and invisible.

Trowbridge grunted as they let go of his arms. Dawn checked my instinctive start as he fell to his knees. For a moment my mate just rested, slumped on his heels. Then he lifted his head. His nostrils flared. His battered face turned in my direction. Higher went his nose. He pinpointed Scawens. Another head tilt and he'd fixed Mannus's location.

"Where do I have to stand?" Mannus asked, reaching into his pocket for Merry's Baggie. "Here, wasn't it?" He checked himself against the landmark of different trees, shuffling until he was about mid-center on the beach, a foot back from the water's edge.

"I must wear the amulet to summon the portal." Lou cast him a sideways glance from under her lashes. "The amulet and the caller must be one."

"Don't try anything rash, mate," he warned. "Open your hands." He tilted the bag and spilled the golden mass into her waiting palm.

Her mouth became a thin slash as she inspected the contents of her hand. "Think you're clever, do you? Twisted yourself around the Royal Amulet, did you? Ugly thing . . . useless, cursed thing," she said, poking Merry. Lou's lip lifted in the way it did before she did something cruel. "Bring me some pond water."

"Don't, Lou," I whispered.

The kid brought her some red-fouled liquid cupped in his hand. She dampened the sleeve of her sweater with it, and then held it, poised over Merry. A long tear-shaped drop hung and then fell, splat, dead center on Merry's belly. She cringed, spat a defiant spark of purple and wove her vines tighter around the Royal Amulet. Lou smiled. With casual cruelty, my aunt swiped the sodden wool over Merry's belly, laying another thin layer of corrosive water over my amulet friend.

A tiny rivulet of the ferrous-strong water trickled into Lou's palm. "Yes," she said, with a horrible teeth-baring smile. "It burns, doesn't it?"

"Stop it," I pleaded.

"Let me do it," said Mannus, in irritation.

Lou turned away from him, hunching her shoulders over her prize like a truculent child. Her blistered fingers found a weak strand. She pinched it. Tried to use a nail to pry it up. Then she took another dollop of water, and let it sit. "Patience," she said to Mannus, watching the shuddering ball in her hand. Suddenly Merry exploded in a flurry of awful contortions, colors sparking from her center. Red. Purple. Blue. "Now, watch." And then my aunt succeeded in accomplishing something I thought could not be done. With a smile to match her twisting fingers, she broke a strand of Fae gold in two. What followed was a quick ravishment, an unleashed spit of Fae cruelty.

And finally, when tiny splinters of broken gold lay glinting at her feet, my aunt stopped. Lou extended her open hand to the Alpha, imperious and proud. "I told you I could do it," she said.

What had been one clump, was now two.

Frowning, Lou lifted Merry by two fingers and then dropped her, as if she were a soup bone that had lost its flavor. She placed the Royal Amulet's heavy chain around her scrawny neck. Her voice was reassuring. "I don't think any harm has come to the Royal Amulet."

"It doesn't look right."

"It is fine," she said. With tender care she inspected her pet. "Yes, it is well." Her shoulders were relaxed. She had what she wanted. And true to form, she cared little of the destruction she'd left in her wake.

It was her way.

I watched with lowered eyes, and hatred seething and churning, as Merry stabbed two torn ends into the soft ground, and painfully pulled herself toward the sanctuary of the tall weeds.

"I will summon the portal now," Lou said, and stepped to the edge of the pond. She shook the tension from her hands.

How many times had I watched Lou perform her precall rituals? Each time, hoping as hard as she, that she'd find a way. That the gates would come. That I'd find my twin.

One last open-squeeze session with her hands before she raised them chest high.

Goddess, I loathed the sight of her now. Hated her for what she'd done, hated the pitiless hunger in her eyes. *Take a good look, Hedi. That's Lou's true face.*

She stiffened as Mannus put his hands on her waist. Then she tossed her head and opened her mouth to begin. The rite always started with a seven-second hum, followed by the first real note, so low it sounded like a moan, and then on the same breath, the low flat would climb, and the true melody would begin. She'd sing in the language of her home, which sounded nothing like English, or any other language spoken on Earth. It was a difficult dialect to decode; capable of sounding harsh and heated when she said it under her breath and sometimes, when I'd done something stupid, relentlessly hectoring. But when she sang for the portal? I wish I could call it something else. Ugly. Horrible. Discordant. But it wasn't. The melody was haunting—perhaps because as she sang, Lou's voice softened from her usual grievous tone. The sound that spilled from her mouth was sweet, tender, and yearning. She'd lift her voice to the wind and patiently repeat the song from beginning to chorus, and all the time, her hands would be outstretched, as if she were hoping to absorb energy from the air. She could do it for hours. She *had* done it for hours. She'd warble until her hands trembled and her voice was gone.

But this was ten years later, months after the start of her fade. Would her voice crack? Falter?

At eight seconds, she abandoned the warm-up and went for the first low note. It was too much of a temptation for Scawens and Dawn. "Watch them," Scawens said to the kid, as they turned in the direction of the pond, transfixed, like the other Weres who stood in a ragged line around the pond; their eyes were trained on the pond as if they expected the portal to suddenly appear with a flourish of horns.

The kid cast an anguished glance toward us. As his eyes met mine, I lowered my own submissively. I kept my head down and watched his feet, and then when those size elevens finally turned in the direction of the pond, I held my breath and soundlessly backed away.

Four steps, five steps. Each one taking me farther away from Bridge, but one step closer to Merry. The kid never turned around. I let out my breath, and kept going, my eyes darting between three compass points. Trowbridge in the east. The kid in the north.

And in the south . . . Merry's muddy trail.

Her painful retreat had dredged a path between the weeds and left a wavering line into the shrubbery. It disappeared under the base of a dogwood. I knelt, and parted the low branches. In the gloom beneath the shrub, I searched for the gleam of her gold in the dark, and couldn't find it. Where *was* she? I sat back and looked for another trail, some indication that she'd only stopped here for a moment, before she'd crawled painfully to another spot. But there was nothing. I roughly parted the branches and scanned the area again . . . and . . . Oh Goddess . . . found her. *Oh Merry-mine.* She was a ball of brown. Mud-streaked, dull. Covered in swamp slime that camouflaged her gold, and muted her amber warmth. Quivering against the trunk of the little shrub. Naked. One of her vines trailed behind her in the mud, like a small bent root.

"It's me," I said. But she flinched under my gentle touch. Shivered and tried to pull that trailing vine up to hide her nakedness. "It's *me*." I touched her just with my knuckle. She shivered under it. "Let me dry you," I said. "It will hurt less." She allowed me to scoop her up from the dirt. Oh Goddess, she was trembling in my palm. I blotted up every drop of that water I could see. Blew tiny beads of it from her crevasses. Gently patted as worry swelled. She was too dull. Too unresponsive.

Pain could do that. Grief and shame could too.

I went to put her inside my bra and realized all over again that I was equally naked beneath my plaid shirt. She hung for a moment, limp and unresponsive between my breasts. Then she moved. Closer to my skin. Huddled against it, as if she could suckle from its warmth.

I tied the shirttails into a knot, welcoming the pain in my hands as I did so.

And as I did, Louise sang on.

The three of us had to get out, now, while the Weres were spellbound by Lou's performance.

I felt corrosive hurt just by thinking the word "Lou."

I looked for something that could be used to our advantage. There were a lot of rocks, but they had iron in them, and I doubted my Fae talent would agree to attach itself to any of those ferrous-contaminated stones. But there was a small chunk of granite near the big pirate rock that had been there for years. I could use that. Providing I was healing fast enough to have some magic. I rooted around my insides and checked. My magic was pebble-sized in my gut. I rubbed my thumb against my finger pads, using friction to roll off the dead skin. The layer beneath felt new-tender but not charred. I was healing. How many repetitions of the song before they got restless? I needed time. Just a little more time to think out a plan. A course of action that wouldn't leave us all dead.

Bridge took matters into his own head. Literally. He surged from his knees, and head-butted the kid, causing him to fall ass over kettle. "Go, Hedi," he yelled as he turned, head lowered and shoulders bunched.

I didn't get farther than three feet toward that rock before Dawn tackled me. "Ooof."

"Run!" Trowbridge said. Running sounded good, since Dawn was smacking me around, left-right, left-right, not holding anything back. Lou didn't lose a note, not even as Dawn punched me in my gut. I could hear her warbling in the background, as I fell to the ground.

I let out a grunt on impact, and my mate called, "Hedi?"

Stuart hit him. A one-two in the kidneys, and down my lover went. Scawens's face twisted into a savage scowl as he reached for a rock.

I screamed, "Trowbridge, look out."

Stupid right? He was blind.

And then Dawn said, "Something's happening!"

The male duck suddenly broke into a skimming flight, his feet dragging on the surface of the pond as he herded his family to the shelter of an overhanging shrub. The rock fell from Stuart's fingers. Goose bumps broke out on my hairless arms.

Lou had called, and the portal had answered.

Chapter Twenty-three

Cold horror, born of the gut and the mind, tightened everything into a moment of awareness—that little hiccup of breath that freezes in your windpipe when you realize you really haven't lived your worst moment yet. It was coming, and when it hit, oh Goddess, when it hit.

The air moved the way it does in a heat haze. The pond rippled and bubbled as if a bait ball of fish swarmed beneath. And there was a smell that all the Weres raised their snouts to. They might not know the name, but I did.

Freesias.

White vapor came next. Not like fog, more like someone had dropped a dollop of whitewash into the air, just so our eyes could track its sluggish rotation. The patch of swirling air grew. Pure white started to pinken, then became ruddy, until the mist was the color of a dark plum.

I thought, *That's not right*. But I watched with fascinated eyes as little specks of white-gold light, like fireflies on a hot summer night, started to glint in the deep purple air. The sparkling bursts of light increased, mixing in with the swirling air, until the whole whirling, magenta mass changed its aspect one final time. In one big gulp, the dark seething vapor swallowed all the fireflies, and presto.

Deep plum had become violet-pink.

Now *it's right*.

The energy ebbed. The top curling point of the spinning vortex slowly sank into the mass circulating below. The bottom flattened, and started looking solid, resembling a fog-coated floor; one that was five feet above the water, and had no discernible support, but still—a floor. As I watched, the air made one last sluggish rotation, and stopped altogether. The mist stayed, but now it rolled and twisted upward in two soft-formed columns, flanking a curtain of lilac mist.

"Bring it closer," said Mannus.

The melody Lou crooned changed from haunting to lullaby soft. The floating portal moved a few feet toward us, and as it did, that sensation ran over my skin again. Alive. I felt as if I'd only been half alive before, and just hadn't known it. The magic fragrant air made my skin hum and my body ache to open to it with crooning pleasure. I found my head nodding to the music, my own hands lifting toward the warmth of the portal, unconsciously mimicking Lou's. The slow glide of the portal stopped a couple feet north of the log that bisected the pond. It stayed there, hovering perhaps a yard above the surface.

"Why won't it come closer?" Mannus said.

It's the iron, I thought. *It's the iron in the water.*

Lou's thread-thin voice trembled on the last note then fell quiet. Her hands hung limp. She stood, staring up at it with a look of joy that stripped years from her face.

"Is that as close as you can get it?" Mannus stalked over to the water's edge, near the felled log, and frowned up at it, hands on his hips. "We'll have to use this to get to it." He tested the trunk's stability with his foot, then walked a couple of feet along its floating back before turning to his mate. "Come, Louise." He gripped her hand and helped her along the spine of the felled pine.

"So, it won't go any lower," Mannus mused, gazing up at the portal. He rocked into his back leg and then sprang to catch the floor's mist-shrouded edge with his hands. His back muscles flexed under his shirt as he power-armed up. From there it was short work to swing a foot up. He slithered up on to the portal's misty floor, and then rose to his feet carefully, as if he expected the ground to splinter beneath his weight. A moment to collect himself, and then he spun back to us with gleaming eyes. "Help her up here," he told Stuart.

Dawn flicked a censuring glance at the kid guarding me. "If she moves another inch, I'll take off your arm." The teen took my arm and tried to look fierce, but the hand wrapped around my elbow trembled faintly.

"It's been so long," Lou said, once she was standing beside him, staring up at the gateway to Merenwyn. "All this time spent in the mortal world, slowly dying."

"You'll be young and beautiful again. We both will. All you have to do is open the door," Mannus said. "Say the word to open the gates."

Her thin lips opened and she said three words—sharp, concise, full of authority. I heard a beautiful sound, like tiny brass bells dancing in the wind, as the opaque shroud between the two realms lightened. Mannus put a hand to touch it, and she said sharply, "No! The demons that dwell in the world-in-between wait for an opportunity to slip through the gates. Do *not* offer them your hand." With a frown, he shifted back and watched. His head bent as he tried to peer through the dissipating veil. It thinned until it was gone, and all that kept one world safe from the other was a round gate, its surface smooth and clear as window glass. Fog curled in a clockwise circle around its edge.

Such Fae deception. Here on earth's realm, the door to the portal was appealing and inviting, as nonthreatening as possible—hobbit-round, and charmingly wreathed by violet-pink smoke. Who'd think twice before stepping into it? Only someone who'd seen the passage from Threall would know it wasn't an easy step between this world and that, but a vertical plume of white smoke that pierced a never-ending sky. Only a person who'd witnessed its false trails and its appetite for innocent souls would hesitate before putting a foot through that doorway.

Merenwyn's daylight spilled through the gate, and the things it touched on our side—my aunt, my enemy, even the dark pond—were warmed pink-gold by its glow.

Incredibly tempting to the unwary. So close. One step through the gate, one short passage through the world-in-between, and the traveler would land on a strip of land, no more than ten feet wide, thick with natural grasses. A clump of them swayed in Merenwyn's breeze at the edge of a steep drop. Down in the green valley, the Pool of Life glittered; its water so very blue the cloudless sky appeared faded. But beyond that was the true prize: layer upon layer of virgin forests, green and untouched, rising with the swells of Merenwyn's hills all the way to the horizon.

Mannus cast a triumphant glance at his collection of openmouthed Weres. "Pass me something. That branch over there," he said. "Now, watch." He turned the length of sumac in his hands, smiled for his audience, and eased its pointed end into the gate's mouth. The stick trembled in his fist. With a magician's flourish, he let go. The gate slurped it inward. Then the bells—no, not bells, wind chimes—tinkled in an unseen wind. Beyond the gate's barrier was a tunnel of wicked updrafts, fierce enough to make the sumac dance in midair for a couple of beats before it shot upward out of sight. Far less spacious than I'd thought when I viewed its spiraling shape from Threall. In reality it was a narrow space, perhaps wide enough for four people, if they stood close and held hands as they were propelled toward the heavens. We waited. Two seconds passed, perhaps three, before the branch fell onto the grass in Merenwyn.

"Prepare yourself for that. You're going to feel like you've been sent to the moon on a rocket," said Mannus with a grin. His good humor faded as he held up his hand. "As much fun as it looks, there's a few things you need to know. Though it looks like it takes seconds, it feels more like an hour to get to Merenwyn. It will be dark in the chute, but you'll have some light from her amulet's glow. You may sense things in the shadows around you. Louise calls them demons, but there are no such things as demons. But you'll hear voices, calling to you in that fairy-shit language. Don't let them worm their way inside your head. Be strong. Hold on to my mate's arm. Focus on landing in Merenwyn. All you got to do is stay tight, and wait it out."

I shivered.

Mannus lifted his arms wide and stepped back closer to the gate. He didn't cross. Instead, he played with its pull again, tipping his head back so that his long graying hair flew up behind him, and his shirt fluttered, pulled taut across the soft bump of his belly. "It will be a new world. A new start." Mannus closed his eyes, and rolled his head on his neck, luxuriating in the sensation. "My mate and I will cross first. She'll return for each one of you, and guide you in turn, while I wait for you in Merenwyn. Make sure you have your vial of iron shavings in your pocket. And remember, getting to the Fae realm is only the beginning of the plan. Keep your mouth shut when you land. We don't need to advertise our presence until we've got the job done."

She'll never come for them, I thought. *And Mannus will have never been seen or heard from again.*

The Alpha reached for his mate.

Lou recoiled. "What do you think will happen to me over there?"

"You'll be my Queen." But his smile was quick and much too light.

"Can you protect me?"

"You can count on it," he said easily. He gave her a wink. *Stupid. Never taunt a Fae.*

She offered him her most dreadful smile in return, and then with a furious cry, shoved him into the gate's mouth. Mannus staggered back, arms windmilling, but all his aerobics couldn't stop his back foot from sliding into the gate's throat, and once that happened, he was the fish and the gate the reel. "You Fae bitch, I'll get you for this!" He leaned on his good leg, gritted his teeth and fought to free the other, but the gate's suction was indifferent to his efforts. It pulled him deeper into its maw and he promptly lost his ass. "When I get out of here, I'm going to—"

"Sy'ehella," said Lou.

If wind chimes sang when the gate opened, hell screamed as it closed. The first voice was young, broken, and plaintive. Another followed, sharp and harsh. Their numbers swelled—

hundreds of voices, crying, screaming, speaking in a language that sent another shiver up my spine—combined into a horrifying cacophony of pleas and moans that made the hairs on the back of my neck stand straight up. Lost souls, caught and forever tormented in the passage's walls.

The gate's misty edges started to thicken and creep inward, as the aperture pursed its lips on the struggling Were caught in its mouth.

The kid's grip on my arm became painful as he watched in horror. For his Alpha, there was no hope, because there was no solid door to grapple open; there was only a clouded circle of mist, inexorably tightening around him. It swallowed Mannus's wrists. Devoured his shoulders. As its toothless gums settled on his neck, Mannus thrust out his chin. "You bunch of sniveling ingrates! After all I've sacrificed for you? May the moon never call to you again! May you stay cursed in your mortal—" A look of surprise crossed his face. His mouth gaped, eyes bulged, and then his head dropped to the floor, neatly severed, as the door to Merenwyn sealed and smothered the clamor of those terrible cries.

Silence except for the oddly hollow sound of Mannus's head rolling across the portal floor. Lou frowned down at it, her face sour. And then she hauled off and kicked it. Her mate's think tank spun off the end of the portal and fell with a plop into the water below.

"She killed him," said one of the Weres.

Quick as a hiccup, the "Oh shit, I'm the deer" expression crossed Lou's face.

Yes, I thought.

Lou babbled the words to open the gate as Stuart's buddies swarmed for the portal.

The chimes tinkled, and then—

Crack!

An echo followed the trajectory of the shot.

"No one move!"

Bullet and voice put together totaled one hell of an attention-getter. All eyes turned to the overgrown path winding down the Stronghold ridge. Biggs stood, a head above a thicket of cockleburs, with a shotgun jammed into his shoulder. His finger was curled around the trigger.

If he says better late than never, I'm going to take him out, I thought, as he carefully made his way down the hill. Right on his heels followed a scrappy-looking guy, carrying what looked like a machete. And at the top of the ridge, just under the tree where Lexi used to plot our next great adventure, stood a tall redhead. True, Cordelia had an arm braced over her gut wound, but she was upright, and in my desperate calculations, upright was enough. Even as I thought—*maybe that'll be enough*—another shot tore over their growls. I saw a chunk of something fly off one of Mannus's crew. Flesh? Bone? Whatever, the bad guy tumbled backward into the pond. Where the hell did Biggs find another gunman? I squinted at the path and found the sniper: a middle-aged guy hidden among the weeds, halfway down the hill. His rifle barrel was steadied on a rock.

"George will take out the next man who moves, and he's aiming for the head." Biggs broke through the last of the waist-high weeds. "You want to chance coming back with scrambled brains, go ahead." Apparently no one did. All but Stuart retreated.

Biggs trained his shotgun on Lou. "Fae, take your amulet off."

Lou gazed at me across the pond, entreaty in her eyes.

"I have no problems taking you out," Biggs said to her. "Throw it in the pond."

Lou took the Royal Amulet off slowly, reluctance obvious. For a second she held it in her open palm and contemplated it with such sweeping sorrow that she almost seemed pitiable. Then with a venomous curse, she clenched her fist and hurled it. The Royal Amulet spun high in the sky, its Fae gold chain trailing after it like a comet tail. Comprehension hit most of Stuart's pals at the same time. It was too late, though, for those nonswimming Weres, even though a couple of them charged the water, and then stood there, frustrated, calf high. The rest of them watched the amulet's soaring arc through the air. My breath caught as it landed on the tight spear of a young lily pad deep on the northern edge of the water. It bounced off that to land on another lily pad's tipped surface, and fell, with a light plop and a slither of gold, onto its final resting spot—a flat, dry lily pad that had been so eager for the light that it sat a good three inches above the rest, floating on the surface of our old pond. A bit of its chain dangled off the end of it, swinging lightly, and then that too stopped. Merry started to heat on my chest.

I put a quelling hand to her. "Wait," I said in an undertone.

"Everyone get back to the land and then sit, hands clasped behind your head. You too, Stuart," Biggs said.

"See you found a stepladder to reach the gun," Stuart called to Biggs, nothing moving except his eyes. "How did you get through the wards?"

"Think back, genius," Biggs said. "Who told the witches where to set the wards? That's always been your problem. You're criminally sloppy. You give vague orders like 'Get the hags to set the wards,' and 'Take care of the fag.' As it turns out, Cordelia was very appreciative of the care I took easing your silver blade from her guts."

Stuart sneered. "I'm going to use your hide as a throw rug when I become the new Alpha of Creemore."

"We don't need another Alpha," said Biggs. "We've got the rightful one here, but he's got a shitload of silver in him."

Oh yeah, come to his defense now.

Biggs flicked me a glance, as if he'd read my mind, then said to Scawens, "If you want to challenge Trowbridge's birthright, you know what to do. Give us a flare. What did you say to Bridge? Oh yeah. Come on, Stewie, let me see you shine."

"I command you—"

"I'm tired of talking," Biggs said. "You've got nothing. You *are* nothing." He pulled the trigger. Stuart's body took to the air, flew off the end of the portal, and landed hard at the edge of the water.

"Stuart!" screamed Dawn.

Biggs swung the rifle on her and yelled, "Stay!" She took a step backward and furrowed her brow at the sharp dominance in Biggs's tone. "It's too late for him. He's gut-shot with silver; you know there's no coming back from that," he said to her. "Don't throw your life away after a loser like him." Then he turned the rifle back on what was left of Stuart. "The first was for Becci," Biggs said quietly, "but this one's all for me." He pulled the trigger and watched, resolute as a good section of Stuart's head splattered into the pond and the iron-rich water turned a little redder.

"Now, he's out of ammunition," said one of the bad guys. "They both are."

That's when all hell broke loose on the muddy bank where Lexi and I used to play pirates. Biggs tossed the weapon aside and met a larger Were's charge in midair.

The kid chose mutiny. He let go of my arm, and ran.

Chapter Twenty-four

"Trowbridge."

He was out cold, curled on his side on the wet, pebble-strewn ground, one arm wrapped around his head. I pushed him onto his back. "Trowbridge, wake up." Mud. It was on his hair, smeared across his forehead, slimed across those high cheekbones, even in his mouth. I swiped out his mouth with my finger and bent to listen. His lungs crackled. A wave of helplessness washed over me. I cradled his jaw and thought of a world without Trowbridge. "You listen to me," I said fiercely. "You are *not* dying here. *Not* by my pond. *Not* on this ground."

Trowbridge's eyes opened to half-mast. "I'm not planning on dying today," he slurred.

"Good, because the cavalry's come." My voice wobbled. "It's starting to look like we might get out of here."

"How many?"

I looked around and subtracted two. "Four."

"Help me up."

I tried, but he couldn't seem to coordinate his feet and leg muscles. We compromised with halfway. I kneeled behind and offered him the warmth of my body, holding him tight in the circle of my arms, while he cocked his ear to the danger around us. "They're everywhere," he said tautly, turning his head to track the noise. "You sure the cavalry's winning?"

I nodded into his neck.

"Harry's here?" His hand searched for something to use as a weapon.

My lips were pursing for "Who's Harry?" when the hair on my neck stood up. Danger's near, they informed me, which is useful and stupid all at once, because of course danger was near; it was all around us; Cordelia grappled with someone ten feet on our right, Biggs did the same with another Were not far beyond—for heaven's sake, we had blue level seats to a minor Were skirmish. But the way my hair prickled made me feel that this danger was a little more up front and personal. I sniffed and picked up a stream of concentrated venom. Over there, at two o'clock, according to my right nostril.

"Oh shit," I said.

"He's wrong," Dawn said in a queer, flat voice. Blood and bits of pink fleshy stuff daubed her shirt. "He is going to die today. I'm going to make sure of it." Her eyes glittered with tears that hadn't fallen, and probably never would, because as I watched, her face hardened.

"Get behind me." Trowbridge struggled to stand.

Fuck that. I lunged for Biggs's shotgun.

"It's empty," Dawn said tonelessly.

But it worked well as a cudgel. I swung the rifle stock at her, and cracked a couple of her ribs. On the next swing, she caught hold of the barrel. We did a couple of revolutions of Hedi the Flying Fae, before she let go mid-twirl. The world spun and when it stopped, I'd flattened a sumac, but I hadn't lost hold of the shotgun. She darted forward. Something raked down my side, from armpit to hip bone. Hot. A different type of pain. A trickle of blood ran warm down my ribs.

Dawn inspected my blood on her hooked fingers. "You've got such soft skin, I can tear it like tissue paper," she said. *She used her nails, that's it?* Oh Goddess, I was in such trouble. "You think I'll let some soft little Fae bitch have the life I was supposed to have?"

I blocked her next swipe with the shotgun. For that piece of dexterity, she made me dance—slashing left and right, never quite catching my skin, each one of her slashes driving me backward. A streak of fear cooled my spine when my foot sank into the pond. If the iron gates hurt just how bad would it be to have red iron slime coating my skin?

Dawn gave a knowing smile and slashed again. "I'm going to eat his heart," she said.

"You want my heart? Come and get it," Trowbridge shouted. He'd pulled himself mostly upright with the help of Lexi's pirate rock but he looked like he would go splat with the first gust of a strong wind. His milky white eyes shone through the tangle of his hair.

Dawn tilted her head at him and smiled.

Mine!

My Were's vehemence gave me a shove in the right direction. I stopped worrying about the iron muck. I stopped feeling terrified and helpless. I sloshed through the water, shotgun braced like a horizontal ram, and rammed into her. Agile as a gymnast, she twisted mid-fall. We rolled on the ground fighting, but she was better at the whole you-go-on-the-bottom thing. Within three rolls, I was pinned under her crushing weight, my arms squeezed between her bony knees. Those Were-bitches are heavy, for all their leanness.

What followed promised to be a licking. Three blows into my punishment, a weaving shadow blocked the light over her shoulder. A hand found a hank of Dawn's dark hair. I caught a glimpse of Trowbridge's thin lips set in a snarl as he peeled the murderous bitch off me.

And then his beating began.

Sacrificing a hunk of hair, Dawn spun to deliver a savage kick dead center on Trowbridge's weeping belly wound. With a guttural moan, my mate's head tilted down, and in graceless slow motion, he sagged to his knees.

No! My Were's rage poured into me. Foreign, molten hot. I could feel her in my head, in the tightness of my muscles. Worse, I could hear her. *Kill, kill, mine.* Oh Goddess, was this how a Werewolf really thought? In flashes of color and heat, and broken words? She had too much emotion. She saw things too simply. She didn't factor in fear or morality. *Mine, mine, mine. Kill.* I hovered on the edge of capitulation as her soul fought for top-bitch status.

Dawn giggled and pulled back her foot to lash out again.

Just like that, I went feral. Mortal wrath melded to animal rage, and as one, we turned to our ball of Fae magic sitting low and heavy in our gut and gave it a sharp nudge. *Mine. Ours. Kill.*

Yes, it answered.

My mother's gift burst free from its fetters, surged up my chest, and split sharply into two different streams at my breast. Fae-bred magic scorched down my arms and spilled into my hands. *Prey, hunt, kill,* it sang. It felt different. Bolder, sharper. Alive and aware . . . as if it were . . . thinking. With a malicious sizzle, it spread outward through my circulatory system, searching for every capillary. But now, it wanted all the territory. The skin. The will. The mind. I pressed the back of my throbbing hands against my temples. I didn't want this. Not this. Not both of them free inside my head, running riot through my blood. Oh Goddess, I wanted out of my skin. Away from this. Soul pain, horrible, disorienting, as if I were shrinking and swelling all at the same time. And then . . . no sound. No sight. No feeling. It lasted seconds and when sensation came back, I didn't hurt. I was apart, and part. Sensate and not. Aware that there were three souls alive in me, but no longer conflicted. Three souls in one body—

And all of them hated the creature named Dawn.

Twin lines of fluorescent Fae malevolence erupted from our fingertips. "Get her," I said. Our fat green pets rushed forward, questing, and found the dark-haired enemy hurting what was ours. They streaked through the heavy air and startled her with their kiss. Dawn froze mid-kick. Could she see the lines of magic spooling from our hands? We let our magic nuzzle her rib cage and slither around her hips. She gasped and ran anxious hands over her body. With a mewl of fright, she spun around, her hands still frantic at her waist; plucking at what could not be seen, tearing at what could not be broken. Whatever she saw on our face twisted hers into stark terror.

Behind her, our Trowbridge was on all fours. He tried to put a foot under himself, failed, and fell clumsily on his hip. His breath was noisy. Wet. Not right. Broken. His mouth was open. Our Trowbridge was broken.

We gave our hot hands a squeeze.

"God, what is that?" she screeched. "Stop it!"

"But we've only just begun." We levitated her flailing body high above what was precious and brought her forward for inspection. Ripe with fear, her scent was. When she was close enough to spit on, we smiled. "Maybe we'll eat your heart instead." And then we flicked our hands upward. The bottom of her soles danced over our head.

We towed her to the pond. Ancient instinct quailed at the iron, but our Were soothed the worry with a trickle of her magic. We drew a thoughtful toe through the wet membrane of scum sheeting the bottom. No pain. No dip in our well of talent. We were stronger when we were able to sip from the other two. We'd felt the surge in power granted when our mortal had released the animal. We waded in up to our knees. There was a drop-off in this pond, we remembered. A flick of our wrist sent Dawn skimming toward it. A good fight she gave with her kicking legs, and tearing hands. Fear and sweat and fury all mixed together in a foul-smelling brew.

"Like a chicken on a spit," I whispered.

We bent to plunge our hands beneath the water, and let the water soothe the heat. A smile tugged at our lips as our magic dived too, sinking under the oily surface with our prey. The surface roiled. A big fish, we thought with detachment. Dawn's hip crested the surface as she fought for air. We tightened our hands into fists and sank them deeper. "But so easily killed," we marveled, watching the animal spasm in our grip. A stream of bubbles, too small to sustain life, slipped from its gaping mouth. It gave one final, violent twitch and then fell limp. A great wash of fatigue swept us. We waited for the animal to breathe again. When it did not, our satiated magic slithered from our prey. They floated in the red water, twin serpents attached to the tether of our fingers, waiting.

So tired. We willed our legs steady as our magic waned.

Even as we fought the diminishment, we sank, small and tight, into the place our mortal sister kept us safe. Cocooned in the deep warmth of her belly, we took comfort from the feral presence curled around the tail of her spine.

Sleep. Yes. We'll sleep.

I was cold and soulless but my ears were working again. Mortal-me sat in the stinking muck at the water's edge. My throbbing hands lay limp in the frigid, red water.

"Let me go." Trowbridge's voice was harsh, desperate. A murmur of another low voice, soothing. "I don't believe you. I can't feel her. It's just like before."

I should go to him. But my legs felt heavy. My hands weighted. I blinked, once, twice, and on the third squeeze of my lids, the reddish haze blurring my vision cleared and my sight was my own. *Am I me again? Hedi, without any back-seat drivers?* I felt me, mostly. A little empty. Flatter somehow. I tested the odd, longing loss of that thought as my body started sending damage reports. Hands bad. Hip screaming. Ribs sore. Ankle throbbing.

Merry moved at my breast. One of her vines disentangled itself from the disordered nest around her amber-red stone. It stretched up for the chain, found a link and twined around it. She started the long slow climb to my shoulder. Once there, she perched on my collarbone and gave me a tentative pat with the flat of her leaf. She trembled there for a moment, while I breathed slowly through my nose, before she pressed herself close to the warm beat of the Fae-Were blood thrumming beneath my skin.

Don't blame her for checking my soul condition before cuddling up. I was asking myself the same question. *Am I me? Really me?*

My eyes continued their restless catalogue. A fairy portal hung over the lily-choked water. I studied that for a couple of speculative beats, before moving on. A girl's body floated facedown, near the old pine log. We killed her. No, I killed her. *I'll think about that later.* It looked like the fight was mostly over. Sniper-guy was walking around checking for life signs. Machete-guy was enjoying beating the last bad guy to his very last breath. *They're animals.* I listened for the unique beat of Trowbridge's heart. It was there. Uneven and too slow, but there. *Animals, yes. But what am I? Something worse. A hybrid Fae without limits.* Something tickled the back of my brain about being Fae. Some thought about water that seemed urgent to a problem at hand. *What was it?*

"I *said,* he needs you." I slanted my eyes sideways. Cordelia's bony knee showed through the tear in her skirt. How long had she been there? Her scent alone should have screamed "intruder." Perfume mixed with blood. A subtone of grief. "Get up," she said sharply. "And do something about those things." Her ringed fingers made a gesture to the two lines of green shimmering under the water. A light breeze licked the surface and gave them the illusion of scales.

"You can see them?"

"Of course I can." She grimaced. "Get rid of them before he sees them."

"He can't see them; he's blind." I bent my head to inspect my hands. Broken nails. Fingertips stained sooty black in some spots, weeping red in others. Ugly with heat blisters. From each, a line of magic streamed down to my two well-fed serpents. Their heads turned back to me as if seeking a command. "These are part of me."

"Hedi!" Trowbridge called. His voice sounded rough.

"You heartless fairy bitch, either you go to him right now, or I'll bloody well carry you there." Cordelia's nails were ringed with red. She curled them into her palm, but she couldn't hide the stain left on her by this night's evil. Her first knuckle was grazed and puffy.

Some things could never be washed clean. Like blood traces and kin.

A heartless fairy bitch . . . The wind from Merenwyn streamed through the portal's gate, indifferent to my mortal cares. Come to us, it urged with sweet seduction. Leave your mortal troubles here, it promised. There is sun in Merenwyn, it promised, and deep pools too, waiting to soothe your hurt.

Water to soothe your hurts. The kernel fell. Germinated and grew.

"He's dying," I heard myself say tonelessly.

"What?" she snapped.

"Bridge will die because Weres have no cure for silver in the gut." My voice was flat, rendered clean of hurt and want. "That's what Biggs said. No cure."

"Well, aren't you a bleeding heart," she said.

"And so . . . Bridge will die."

A pause. Her scent got sharper. Then, a rough growl. "Yes."

I lifted my gaze to study Merenwyn again. "But the Pool of Life would save him."

Another pause, during which her grief ebbed to let something warmer in. But just as suddenly, the warmth melted away and the scent of her grief returned, sharp as aged cheese. She said harshly, "It would break the Treaty. He'd never agree. He'd die first."

"We don't ask. We wait till he's hardly conscious." I kept my gaze on the portal. Merenwyn's daylight streaked a path of gold across the pond. "He needs to have my blood in his veins to pass through the gate. If he doesn't have it, the gate will reject him."

"What do you mean, 'reject'?"

"I think she would have lost them in the 'world in-between.' I know this—my aunt never had any intention of bringing Weres to Merenwyn. The only part of the pack she had to worry about was Mannus. He was her mate, and she'd brought him through once before." In my mind's eye I saw her rubbing a thoughtful thumb across her emerald ring.

"How?"

"She gave him her blood."

"The mating bond," she said, a faint thread of awe in her voice.

I watched one of my serpents roll in the shallow water. "When Trowbridge goes through the gate, he'll have mine in his veins."

"You can't make that choice for him."

"Watch me." I stood. "Cut," I said. There was a splash and then another, as I turned and walked to the mate of my heart.

Trowbridge was no longer beautiful. What wasn't streaked with blood and mud was tinged putty gray from the poison in his veins. No longer untouchable either. Scars had failed to crust over the residue of silver left in his wounds. He still bled, which Weres never do for very long, as witnessed by the thin line of red streaming from the gash across his abdomen. Trowbridge was slumped against my pirate rock, but as I walked to him, he put his good hand down for balance and rolled on his hip. His bicep bulged, but he couldn't lift himself to his feet. "Take it easy, Bridge," Biggs soothed. "She's coming."

He'd been beaten, broken, and yet not.

Mine.

"Is that you?" Trowbridge said as I knelt beside him. Merry slid into my shirt as his left hand searched for my shoulder. Long fingers slid up my neck, and wove under the loose strands of my hair. He pulled me close until our foreheads touched.

"It's me."

"I thought I'd lost you. I couldn't feel you anymore." His lips were a bruised purple-blue. I lowered my gaze, past his blood-speckled chin, down his muddy chest, all the way to his lap where his mutilated hand lay, palm turned upward. My eyes followed the blood-caked lifeline running deep across his palm.

"I'm sorry. I'm so sorry." His metallic breath warmed my nose.

"You have nothing to be sorry for."

Trowbridge's forehead grated against mine as he shook his head in denial. "Don't know why I didn't do it. I should have just done it and died with you."

"Done what?"

"Should have been there to protect you," he muttered.

"You did protect me." He had, in every way he could. "You were wonderful."

"Wish I'd been a different guy."

"I don't." I could smell death leaking from his lips. Hear it in the rail of his lungs; in the slowing thump of his heart. Through my numbness, a tiny spot of bleeding hurt bloomed. My voice dropped to a whisper. "Don't leave me here to die alone."

"Never again, sweetheart." His voice was tender. "Love you."

Tears welled.

His eyelids drooped to half-mast. "So tired, baby."

"You can't sleep yet. There's something you have to do."

"Just a little nap, Candy." His lashes fluttered close. "Just a little nap."

I stopped breathing, while the thinking part of me got caught in a loop, like a scratched CD that plays four chords before it skips, burps out some static, and then replays the same damn chords. Except, there weren't four chords. Just two syllables, *Can-dy*. Karma had waited until I believed myself too frozen to feel injury; too numb to flinch from pain.

Clever bitch, Karma.

Biggs was pretending he'd missed the exchange. Cordelia wasn't bothering to dissemble. I could feel her eyes on me, sorting and sifting, weighing and measuring.

I bent my head and hid my face behind a curtain of hair.

Then I started to turn the hand crank on my old friend, rationalization. It was a name. That's all. A name. He got confused. Trowbridge loved me, didn't he? He'd said so.

No, he hadn't. He'd said it to *her*.

And with that, a flood of hurt broke through the sagging levees of my self-deception.

Oh Goddess. I can't do it anymore. I can't keep reshaping sharp things into round things—refashioning hard truths into soft, palatable half-lies.

Trowbridge still loved her. Me, perhaps not.

Bitterness welled.

This was what all the last ten years had led me to? All that jumping from one wobbling rock to another, just to get back here? All those wasted years spent smiling to humans, hiding the tips of my ears, and steadfastly turning my nose from the sweet scent of fellow Weres? It had all boiled down to this moment *here*—on my knees by the fairy pond in Creemore. Losing again. But this time to a freakin' ghost named Candy.

There was something almost sniggerworthy about it, if I'd been a bitch named Karma. I felt a weak trembling of my lips and damned myself for it.

So how about it now, Hedi? Do you still want to give him your blood?

The alternative was to watch him die.

Could I do that? Add this loss to the others, and live with the sharp-clawed remorse tucked within my chest, nibbling away at me from the inside, without . . . without what? I wanted to say "without dying, too" but the word that sprang to my mind was "hemorrhaging."

It kept coming back to the blood, didn't it?

I considered my wrist. It was unmarred. Baby soft. Beneath my white skin, my Fae-Were heritage ran in a blue crooked line to the heel of my palm. It defined me. Neither Were nor Fae, but both. Was there enough Fae in it to keep him safe from the "in-between"? I thought back. Remembered, with an inward flinch, how I'd sensed that separate soul—curious, detached, and alive. Yes . . . I had enough Fae in me.

With a measure of my Fae essence pumping through his veins, Trowbridge stood a chance of making it to Merenwyn and healing. Without it? He would die here, slumped against Lexi's pirate rock.

A chance. Not a certainty. And if I gave it to him, and he died . . . the mate bond would claim its tithe. Could I risk my life on a nebulous instinct?

"Biggs, go watch the Fae," said Cordelia.

"Why?"

"Do it," she said sharply.

I looked away from her, thinking hard.

I'd claimed him as my mate. Said that I wouldn't give him back.

But that was twelve hours ago! Before I was old enough to comprehend that this mate thing was so much more than just desire and a promise to endure. It was a three-sided business—the good, the bad, and the oh-so-fucking-ugly.

I can't do this.

Yet even as I thought that, my ears were evaluating the wet rail in Trowbridge's chest. Counting the seconds between his inhales.

A movement out of the corner of my eye. Cordelia's hand touched the silver-hued vein on Trowbridge's face. Old hands, shaking like mine.

Two broken hearts, then.

I'll be old like her one day. Alone like her.

Cordelia and I reached for Trowbridge as he buckled over in a rib-racking cough. When his horrible, hacking spasms were finally done, and another splatter of something tarnished-black had been added to the blood-soaked ground, I touched his cheek with my charred fingers, and said, "Shhh, Trowbridge. It's going to be okay now."

My Fae-Were vein was a twisted road map along the inside of my arm.

Let it be enough.

"How is it done?" I asked her.

Cordelia's face was bleak. "He needs to bite you."

"Here," I said, pressing my arm to his flaccid lips.

"That's not how it's done." Cordelia pointed to my throat. "Pull your hair from your neck. No, the other side of your neck. You'll have to put this part—" Her nails skimmed the area just above my collarbone where my neck muscle was soft and tender from the attention Trowbridge had lathered on it, just twelve hours before. "Right up to his mouth. He'll bite down until he draws blood. As he draws your essence into his mouth, you have to say 'Heart of my heart. Mate for all my years. I offer you my life.'"

I gazed at her with agony. Not like this. Not in front of her. Wasn't it enough to read my face? For all the tears in heaven, I'd loved him since I was twelve . . . despite what

I thought he'd done. Goddess, even when I'd sworn to my-self I loathed his wicked heart, I'd never been able to scrape him from mine. Did I have to say those words in front her, kneeling in the pebble-strewn mud?

Yes, Cordelia's hard eyes said.

There was no choice. There never had been.

"Trowbridge," I said, as I pushed my hair back. I guided his mouth to the spot he'd tenderized the night before. "Take my blood." His lips softened into a kiss on my skin. "Trow-bridge, bite me."

But he wouldn't.

He turned his head.

"Bite me!" I said brokenly. "I can heal you. Take my blood."

He was dying. Thump, thump. His heart slowing. Thump, thump.

It was my father again. My mother once more.

Thump, thump.

No. I wasn't that girl anymore. Crouching in the cupboard again, watching everything that mattered to me slip away. I wasn't going to sit there and listen, useless tears dripping down my face, as the mate of my heart breathed his last.

I steal. It's what I do.

I wiped my face with my elbow. Cleared the hurt with a deep, shuddering breath, and then I found a spot: a silent, safe place inside me. I gathered up all that was left breakable in Hedi, and told it to stay there. Cover its ears and close its eyes. I'd come back for it. I'd come back for *me*.

Then I stepped outside of myself, and became what I needed to be.

Face shuttered, I softened my voice as if I were soft, and sweetened my tone as if I were as toothsome as Candy. My sooty fingers left smudges as I stroked his skin. "You never made me your mate." My throat—it ached. "You said that you wouldn't let me die alone again. Never again . . . Re-member? . . . You promised me."

His eyes were milky and blind, but his face—oh Goddess,

his face-brow pleated, lines bracketing his mouth, bruised and bloody—none of it was as bad as the look of tormented guilt I'd just carved into it.

"Wife?" he asked weakly.

"Mannus has come. Do it now." I bent closer and pressed my counterfeit flesh to his lips once more. "Make me your mate."

An endless moment before his mouth opened. His teeth settled on my tendon. He touched it once with the flat of his hot tongue, and then suddenly, I felt a tearing pain. Hot, burning, and fiercely welcome. He sucked my blood into his mouth, and I said the words, my eyes on Merenwyn. "Heart of my heart." . . . My Fae essence flowed into him . . . "Mate for all my years." A joy-filled quiver from my Were . . . "I offer you my life."

"Quickly," said Cordelia. "Take his."

I am a thief.

I set my teeth. I broke his skin. I swallowed his silver-tainted blood.

And as I drank, and felt a strange, soul-soothing warmth spread over me, Cordelia roused him back to consciousness and forced him to say the vows, giving him a pat of encouragement at the end of each one.

It was done. The heat inside me kept growing, growing. Were-hot, love-warm.

Trowbridge's face grew calm and peaceful. When he spoke his voice was so soft I had to ask him to say it again. "Don't know why . . . I waited."

"You're a stubborn man." I tucked his curl behind his ear. "Do you feel stronger?"

A pause. And then he said, "Yeah." This time I could smell his lie. His fingers reached blindly for mine. He twined his gently around my blistered ones. "Don't cry, kid."

And with that, his eyes closed one final time.

His grip loosened.

Thump, thump.

My fingers lay in the cradle of his open palm.

Those were his last words.

* * *

Little snatches of it will forever haunt me. Cordelia leaning down to pick up Bridge. Her red hair sweeping over her shoulder, her white face set as she carefully gathered him up. Trowbridge's limp form hanging from her ropy arms. His head thrown back, exposing his throat, vulnerable and naked, and the teeth marks I'd left on his skin.

The slow thud of his heart. So much slower.

We had so little time.

"Hurry!" said Cordelia, shifting him higher in her arms. "Biggs, grab the Fae!"

And then, indeed, it seemed we flew. Cordelia kicked off her shoes, clutched him like her baby, and ran. I followed her, Merry bumping on my chest, running for my life and his. Close behind us, Biggs followed, Lou thrown over his shoulder.

"George," he yelled, passing the sniper. "We're gonna need a hand."

The water sheeted over the floating log as the five of us peeled down its length. It started to roll. "Go!" said Machete-guy, bracing his hands against it. "I'll hold it."

We reached the midpoint. The portal floated over our heads. A hint of Fae magic streamed through the gate, ghostly and fragrant, carried by its soft wind. Strengthening me. Sharpening me. Could Trowbridge feel it too?

"You'll need to go up first," Cordelia said harshly to Biggs. "I can't make the jump with him in my arms. I'll pass him to you."

The diminutive Were emptied Lou into George's grip. Then he lifted his chin and squinted at the curling mist above him. What was Cordelia thinking? Biggs couldn't be strong enough to haul Trowbridge up. Why not Machete-guy or George?

Biggs rubbed his hands on his jeans, crouched, and suddenly sprang for the sky, arms flexed. Up he flew, light as a dancer, straight up and over the lip of the portal. Gone for a second from sight, and then his lean face appeared over the edge. He extended his arms. I watched, biting my lip, ears straining to measure the sluggish thumps in Trowbridge's chest as Cordelia gently lifted him high. Biggs caught my mate's shoulders, and hefted him over the ledge with supple, breathtaking strength.

Cordelia turned to me. "You next."

Her face was half man, half woman. Tired. The face of a fifty-year-old survivor who understood tomorrow she'd wake, feel the pain, and somehow, get out of bed, make the coffee, and go on. A life of compromises and buried dreams . . . "He knew," she said shortly, as if the words hurt her to say. "He knew it was you." Cordelia's eyelids dropped and her lips twisted. Then her hands bit into my waist, and I was tossed high. Biggs plucked me from the air, and deposited me on a floor that shouldn't have felt solid, but did. Mist swirled around my ankles.

I knelt, shaken, beside my mate.

Oh Sweet Fae Stars. The closer I was to the gate, the better I felt. Was it my imagination or was Trowbridge's heartbeat a little stronger? I flattened my ear on his chest. Yes, not by much, but perhaps by just enough. Merenwyn's wind reached for my hair, tugging it with coaxing fingers, urging me to turn my head and follow it to Merenwyn. Its touch enslaved. Seduced. Beckoned.

Merry made a sudden, sharp movement against my breast. A short spiked strand shot out seeking a handhold. She found it, twined herself around the rope of gold, and rappelled upward, frantic and clumsy in haste. "Careful," I said, reaching for her. She swarmed over my hand, evaded my grimy fingers, and scuttled onto my shoulder. I tucked in my chin and twisted my head, so we could be eye to eye, and then said, "We're going to make it. I can feel it."

The light inside her amber core flashed orange.

Danger. "What? Where?"

She stabbed a bristling leaf over my shoulder. I turned my head. Behind us, Biggs was crouched over, his hands reaching down for Lou.

My stomach tightened. "If I could, I'd kill her for what she has done to you . . . if I had ever thought she was that dangerous . . ." My voice trailed off. A lie. I'd always known she was deadly, but I hadn't anticipated her hurting me or mine. So I mixed a morsel of truth with a tidbit of false promise and fed it to my friend. "I can't do anything to her because we need her. Once we get to Merenwyn . . ." A weak threat. Lou would be stronger in the Fae realm.

Merry's ivy prickled needle-sharp. "Listen!" her body silently screamed. Her stone pulsated with hues. Red. Purple. Orange. A hysterical flurry of flash cards. Love. Pain. Danger. "Listen!" She gestured to the water once more.

My eyes searched the pond. Water, iron-tainted. Floating body. George staring up at us from the log. Lilies . . .

"Oh Sweet Jesus!" Biggs exclaimed, recoiling from Lou's limp body.

The mist licked over my aunt's torso, sipping at the Fae in her, but Lou lay quietly under its caress. She was oddly limp, her face frozen in an expression of fixed hunger. Her mouth slightly open, her eyes unblinking.

"What is it?" I heard Cordelia say.

No, no, no. My hands crept up to cover my mouth.

"She's dead," said Biggs. "I didn't do it! I put her on the floor and she . . . was just gone!" He touched her chest, his face appalled.

A sweeping tsunami of cold horror swallowed me whole. "She killed Mannus," I said, feeling the panic rise. "I forgot about the mate bond. I knew it was hurting her, but with everything that happened . . . oh my Goddess, I wanted her dead. I wanted to kill her myself. And now she *is* dead and she can't guide us." My eyes flew to the gate. "Without her, we can't find Merenwyn. I don't know the way. You have to know the way! The winds . . . we'll get lost in them." *"An endless hell for the wrong traveler,"* Mad-one had said. Those voices! Not demons from the land in-between, but lost souls screaming from within the portal walls.

Thump, thump. Thump, thump.

My mate's life was leaking away, right here, while I knelt beside him, staring in growing hysteria at Merenwyn's green fields. Yes, Trowbridge's pulse was a little stronger. His

breathing a little less shallow. But for how long? Not forever.
A little bit of fairy juice riding a current of air couldn't be
expected to support his life—and for crap's sake, mine—for
eternity. Its healing touch was ephemeral and unreliable; not
a cure, only a promise of one.

Merry stretched an insistent tendril toward the water.
"What *is it* with the freakin' water!" My gaze roved over it
and found the answer.

One Royal Amulet, floating on a lily pad, at the deep end
of the pond.

I raised my hand, pointed my finger, and said, "Up." And
nothing happened. "Up!" There was no itch in my fingers. No
exultant rush up through my veins. My magic slept. "He will
have to wait." Merry sent up a color flare of distress. "I don't
have any juice left, and he's safe enough now . . ." My voice
floundered. Merry jabbed at the Royal Amulet again. "I *know*,
Merry." Her jabs turned into stabs—furious, pointed, and urgent. "What do you *want* from me? Can't you see . . ." The tip
of her leaf touched my mouth. Lay there trembling, the same
shushing gesture she'd used to calm me when I was little. She
pointed to herself, then to Bridge, and then, finally, to the
portal.

Hope flamed inside me. "You know the way. You can
take Trowbridge to Merenwyn. You'll get him to the Pool of
Life . . ."

My words dribbled away, because a warning blip of purple began throbbing in her center. She turned a leaf flat to
me, poised it like a crossing guard's sign. Then very slowly,
she tipped the leaf toward me, and then down to the Royal
Amulet floating on his precarious leaf.

Ah. I saw it then. A trade.

"You'll do it if I stay here and rescue your prince." She
made a go-on motion. "Help him heal . . . keep him safe from
harm. Sure, Merry, I can . . ." I could hear myself speak. The
glibness. The quick assurance.

And something strange happened. It felt like I stood outside myself for a second, and saw all of us. My unmoving
mate. Cordelia's heavy frown. The gate's glittering vision of

Merenwyn. And me, the girl with the quick, meaningless promise, with an amulet perched on her shoulder.

And in so doing, I saw the thorn in me. The thing Merry already had recognized.

The balance of our future relied on the value of the one quality I'd forgotten I'd ever owned.

My word of honor.

My cheeks burned with shame.

"But for that to work," I said, quietly, "you'd have to believe that I'd keep to my word. That I'd feed him and protect him. That I wouldn't forget or rationalize that it was too difficult." I stared at Merenwyn, where all hope lay, but inside my mind's eye, I was seeing something far less pretty.

All the lies. All the twists from truth, and the quick-steps away from responsibilities.

"I know the difference between right and wrong. Sometimes I make the wrong choice, but it's never because . . . That's a lie, isn't it? I don't make decisions based on right or wrong. I always opt for the easiest thing." I touched my mate, and felt the coolness of his flesh. Then I slanted my eyes to my friend. "I've lied to you at least a hundred times. And to others, whom I love, I've lied . . . And broken promises more times than I can count . . . forgotten stuff I shouldn't have . . . but if you can tru—" I looked away and swallowed hard, but the burning ache in my throat didn't go away. I felt her heat warm my shoulder, encouraging me to go on.

It came out raw. "Trust me. Just this one more time. Please, Merry. Trust my word. I will rescue him and care for him as if he were my Trowbridge."

For the space of two of Bridge's wet breaths, she thought about it. And then from deep inside her, I saw a warm dark ember of red.

I held out my palm.

She crawled into it and curled a leaf around my thumb.

My chin crumpled.

And so, the last of the worst.

Cordelia cradled Trowbridge's head as I carefully drew

Merry's chain over his matted curls. I hid my sadness with lowered eyes, and nestled her in the hollow of his throat. A warm pulse, a little cradle to keep her snug as they soared to Merenwyn. She shortened her chain, and tightened her grip, twining her tendrils securing links of her gold necklace. *Seat belt on, ready for the perilous winds.*

I bent down to brush Trowbridge's lips. "Get to the Pool, no matter how you hurt." His eyes moved restlessly under his lids. "If you—when you come back, you won't find Candy. You need to know that."

I laid another kiss on my finger then brushed it across my amulet's amber core. "I'll keep my promise, Merry-mine. You know the way. Take him home." A tendril of gold briefly touched my finger in response. I smiled. A weak effort. "Remember to abandon ship well before he hits the water."

I've witnessed enough soul death this day, please let Merry remember the way.

Another loud boom made us flinch.

No more time.

I settled my sooty hands on his legs. Cordelia gave me a resolute smile, the type Daniel probably gave the lion. She placed her hands, one on his bicep, one on his hip. She swung her head my way, and raised her eyebrow. The wind whipped her hair off her face, stripping away her artifice, showing me her bones and grit.

How had I ever thought her plain?

She nodded to me, a silent signal that time had ended.

Together, Cordelia and I sent them to Merenwyn. The wind chimes tinkled their haunting song as the gate's mouth caught Trowbridge's feet, and sucked them inward. His fingers twitched as his torso was tugged across the threshold. I watched the last curl of his trailing hair disappear through the mouth, thinking, *Come back to me.*

Thump . . .

Don't die.

Thump.

And then my world and history changed, one more time.

My mate and friend flickered between this world and that, and were gone.

We waited. I found my lips moving on their own. *One thousand. Two thousand.* Nothing. Merenwyn's green field lay empty. *He's dead. It was too late.* A yellow wildflower nodded in its wind. *Twenty thousand. Twenty-two. It's been too long. What have I done? The land-in-between . . .* I took a step toward the gate.

"Wait, the bells are still ringing," Cordelia said. "Watch the surface."

The faintest ripple shivered across it. It grew, and bloomed, a circle within a circle, until the entire surface was distorted with concentric rings. Through them, I saw the broken image of a shooting blur of gray. The image lingered, frozen, as the gate's skin gave one last shimmering undulation before it settled.

He landed hard in Merenwyn, all four feet splayed in the grassy field. For a few seconds, Trowbridge's wolf just lay there, sides heaving. Then he lifted his massive gray head, and rolled onto his side. His ears twitched as he inspected the world around him. He tried to stand. Fell. Tried again and this time made it to his feet. A huge canine shake, from head to stern. Something bright gold flew off his neck and bounced into the grass.

Oh Goddess. That was Merry. How will he get to the Pool of Life?

His wolf's face was lean and angular, with darkly rimmed eyes set tilted in a white mask. The same black outlined his lips, giving him a clever, foxlike mouth. He had streaks of blood on his thick coat but still he was large and powerful, even listing to one side as he stood on his throne of flattened weeds.

His ears flicked forward as he tested the wind for its scents. Then, favoring a paw, he limped across the grass toward the gate. Closer and closer he came, stopping only when he was a few feet from the portal. Trowbridge's wolf made an anxious noise, part yelp, part yawn, followed by another sharp bark that made my Were tremble.

"Here," I whispered. His head snapped up. Then, his dark-rimmed eyes looked through Merewyn's gate, straight through one realm into another. There was intelligence in those honey-brown eyes. But they were indifferently predatory, until—

They found me.

For a breath his eyes remained golden. On the next they flared blue. The pure, clean fire of his Alpha flame tinted my face, reached into my heart and held it warm and safe. My eyes burned. My chin came up, my face softened, and I flared.

"Look at that!" said Biggs, as everything around us turned turquoise blue.

I was the one. *The* one.

But I'd forgot about Karma, hadn't I? She sat down beside Fate and murmured something in her ear. And then because there is a cost to every deed, Merenwyn delivered its final slap. A breeze ruffled the wolf's fur, slid over his snout, and slipped through the gate.

Trowbridge's scent was hot and layered. A wedge of love, a segment of pain, and a thick core of fury.

Cordelia's mouth barely moved. "We did the unforgivable when we broke the Treaty."

And I am not sweet as Candy.

The wolf took two steps backward. Three more, then another. Alpha proud, he painfully backed up, veering a little more to the left as he favored his right side. He sank lower, until he was crouched on trembling haunches. I saw his fierce blue eyes measure the distance. And then I realized with a sickening drop of my stomach that he was coming back. Without the healing. Without an amulet to guide him through the terrible wind.

"You're not strong enough to do it again. You'll die," I said, whisper soft. "We'll die."

His muzzle crinkled up into a snarl.

I'd learned some things over the last forty-eight hours.

How you can love, and be loved, and still not come out of it with a love.

"Sy'ehella," I said.

The pregnant hush of our realm was pierced by the pitiless screams of a hundred trapped souls from the land-in-between. In Merenwyn, his gray wolf let out a howl of pure rage.

And this time, without an Alpha to muck up the works, the gate did what it was supposed to do. Smoothly, without fanfare, its liquid surface clouded over and choked off those terrible cries. "Jump, girl!" Cordelia said as she leaped for safety. Biggs soon followed.

It would have been the smart thing to do.

But I stayed, believing the portal would linger as long as I knelt beside it and waited. Merry would find him. Together they'd make it to the Pool. He'd be back soon.

Heartsick stupid, that was.

The portal to Merenwyn didn't give a flying fig about my self-imposed vigil of penitence and woe. Around me, the high, shimmering columns slumped and flattened until they were nothing more than a lazy circuit of rolling, white fog sheathing the softening floor. Then the wondrous pink lights dimmed, one by one. The sky grew gray.

It wouldn't leave, it couldn't leave.

But it did.

When the gate was less than a transparent wash before my eyes, I raised my hand to touch it. It scattered like ash. *Gone,* I thought, as the floor beneath me fragmented.

I fell.

Were-sired, Fae-bred, mortal soft, I plummeted earthward. I felt the sharp streak of pain as my foot glanced off the log; another bone-crunching hurt as my hip smacked a moment later. And then—

I was plunging into the fairy pond's bitter cold, feet first, arms trailing high over my head. Past my knees, just an instant. Past my thighs, just a flash. Past my heart—

Oh Goddess, I still had one.

The iron scum on the pond's bottom waited. My pointed

feet sank into the mud, drilling deep through accumulated years of rot and slime, cutting like a butter knife through a bottomless layer of sludge and compost, until finally, my descent stopped.

I floated, feet caught.

The iron-poisoned sludge wrapped cold hands around my ankles and squeezed.

I was just mortal-me. No longer strong-by-three. I felt the cold creep up my legs, the burn in my chest for air, and realized I *am* going to haunt the fairy pond.

Enough. There was no plan. Just instinct.

Hedi chose life.

Four frantic backstrokes earned freedom for my right foot. I searched for a toehold and found one as my bare toe brushed against the soft, rounded hump of a large granite rock—the twin of Lexi's pirate rock; waiting for me where the last ice age had left it, patient, under all the lily pads and sludge, knowing that I'd find it again. I flattened my right foot on its rounded top, bent at my knees and shoved off.

Pop! The mud spat me free. Cheeks fat with souring air, I winnowed my way skyward. My head broke surface. My first breath was greedy and foul; a mixture of oxygen and swamp water. Coughing and spluttering, I dog-paddled my way to the log. Too tired to swim any farther, I stayed low in the water and wrapped a weary arm around the sacred old pine trunk.

I looked up into the sky.

What was left of Merenwyn's portal shimmered like a shred of white gauze floating on a zephyr of air. Then, in silence, it vanished as the sun sank below my horizon.

Gone.

Chapter Twenty-five

"Open your eyes, you bloody stupid girl." I was being smothered by a wet towel. "Don't make me smack you again.
Wake up."

I wish people would stop hitting me.

When I rolled my head away from the wet, breathing became easier. I coughed a bit, and felt a hand whack me on
my back again. My cheek stung. So . . . I could feel pain
again. I could sense when something was dry, and when
something was wet.

"Open your eyes," said the same throaty voice. "We're
not out of trouble yet."

I was afraid to open my eyes.

"They're through the wards." A different speaker; this
one much younger and male. "We're shit out of luck if she
doesn't open her eyes and flare. Do you think she can do it
again? We could really use an ace up our sleeve."

I was sitting upright, my back being supported by someone
who felt warm. My ribs and hips hurt, my hands throbbed.
A hand smoothed my hair back. Fingers briefly touched the
curve of my ear. "You can't let them win," she whispered.
I heard a sniff. Refined. Snot withheld. "Not now. Not after
what we've done."

I opened my eyes, and looked up into her blue ones. Not
Trowbridge blue. Not Mannus blue. Cordelia blue. The

cover-up had caked itself into the lines under her lower lashes. She had a smudge of mascara under one eye, and I could see one end of her false eyelashes had pulled away, and was coyly fluttering with each of my breaths.

I bit my lip until it hurt. "I closed the gate on him."

"You did."

Tears welled.

"None of that," she said. "Look around you." I turned my head against her bosom. Biggs was kneeling beside us. I didn't know how I felt about that, so I turned my head back to her bosom.

"No, over there," Cordelia said firmly, steering my chin upward. An outline of people stood on top of the Trowbridge cliff. Too many to count. "And here," she said, helping my head rotate toward my old home. More silhouettes.

"The pack," I said.

"They've just watched you and Cordelia shove their brand-new Alpha through the Gate," said Biggs. "You flared before, please tell me you can do it again."

"They don't want me; they want him."

"Yes, but as long as you're alive, and bear his scent, you're proof that he's living," Biggs said. "So, in the meantime, you're it. If you've got any flare that can impress the bejesus out of them, now's the time to put on a light show." Biggs still had clever eyes. "Anyhow," he said with a lopsided smile. "He'll be back. With his luck, he'll come back smelling like roses."

More like freesias.

"I'm not really his mate," I said.

"Yes you are," said Cordelia in a hard voice. "In every way."

"I'd feel it if he was dead, wouldn't I?" I asked her.

Cordelia thought for a bit, then nodded. "I think you would."

The first one down the Stronghold path was Geezer-Were.

"Stand up," she said. "Don't show any weakness in front of Harry Windcombe." Geezer-Were was Harry? My feet felt wobbly, and I couldn't seem to stop shivering, but I stood. Cordelia positioned herself close behind me, disguising the fact that the only thing keeping me mostly upright was her firm grip on the waistband of my pants.

I could smell her perfume, even through the swamp water.

Obsession.

I thought of him. I thought of me. And then I thought of that moment when our eyes had locked through the gate, before I caught the hot scent of his anger.

I flared. It was that simple. I felt its burn, let it go, and the light poured from me. I swept my eyes over both ridges, so that they all could taste it. Then I focused on the white-haired man who was walking down the hill in front of all the others. Geezer-Were stopped, mid-amble, and let it wash over him. He smiled, briefly, and I found myself thinking, *Now there's a man who doesn't smile too often.* But then he did something I hadn't expected. He lowered himself stiffly onto one knee. He bent his head over it, and kept it that way. And then, in the hushed silence of that moment, they all copied him. One by one, all those other Weres fell to their knees, toppling down like a line of dominoes.

It would have been a good time for a speech, but I was wordless. I let my flare burn until my eyelids felt like they were smoking, and then allowed it to fade away. "Was that enough?" I asked Cordelia.

There was a pause and then she said, "Yes."

"What now?"

"You have to choose your second. Right now, before they have time to think it through."

I leaned against her, suddenly weak. "I'm not an Alpha."

"You're his mate, which makes you Alpha-by-proxy." Her shirt was wet, but her inner heat radiated such tempting warmth, I wanted to press myself against it. "You need an enforcer."

"Alpha-by-proxy," I murmured. "I don't want to be Alpha-by-proxy."

"Well, you don't have a choice." I let my spine rest, just for an instant, against her knuckles. In response, her hand quickly twisted at my waistband, tightening her grip, and then she jerked me upright. "Now stand up strong. You can be a healthy Alpha-by-proxy, or you can be a dead half-Fae."

I squirmed and tried to plant my feet. Her grip relaxed, just slightly. "What do I do, just point?"

"I don't give a damn how you do it. I'm wet, I smell like a sewer, and I need a shower." A long fluttering strand of her auburn hair played shyly with my shoulder. "Just choose."

She was as tall as Trowbridge, as strong as any Were, but her aroma was different; female and not, animal and cosmetics, pain buried so deep under layers of other scents that it was almost undetectable. The decision was easy. "Well, you're my second."

"Poor choice, darling." But there was a softening in her voice, just a fraction. "Choose someone from the pack. Preferably one of the good guys."

"And I'm supposed to know who's a good guy?"

Biggs cleared his throat. Cordelia raised her brow, and made a swift calculation. "Windcombe would be the best of the lot. He went rogue rather than serve under Mannus's leadership. He's got old ties to the pack and he's naturally strong. Bridge trusted him."

I tried to pitch my voice like I was used to giving orders. "I wish to speak to Harry Windcombe."

Harry stood up, about as stiffly as he had sunk down, and slapped some dust off his knees, before he began picking his way down the path, taking his time, the placement of every step deliberate. I said to her in a low voice, "Are you sure about this?"

"Yes."

"Will you be my third?"

There was a long pause. I twisted my head to look up to her, and saw that she was staring at the air above the pond. "No, but I'll be your friend," she said, her voice soft and low.

With an oddly watchful smile, she offered, "If you'll be mine."

When he finally reached us, I realized that Geezer-Were was tall, really tall. His shoulder-length hair was wavy, and mostly white. He had a moustache that curled like a handle-bar, slapped on a face that was tanned and deeply wrinkled. Once he'd been handsome. You could tell. "You met Trow-bridge at my Starbucks."

His dark eyes crinkled as he slowly looked me over. "The little girl behind the big machine."

"Don't call me a little girl," I said. "I'm not little."

"No." There was no irony in his voice. "I can see that now."

"What did he want from you?"

"Help," he said.

"A little late, wasn't it?"

"Yes," he said. "I went and got some friends to square up the numbers, but by the time I came back here, I was too late. You might not want to forgive me for that." Harry had a way of looking at you as if he were asking questions and getting answers all without the other person having to say another word.

Trowbridge had trusted him. I lifted my chin. "Harry Windcombe, will you be my second?"

"It will be an honor." He bowed. "Mate of our Alpha."

"Until he comes home again," I added.

It was grave, his nod. "Until he returns to his pack."

The first order I gave him was simple. Harry hooked his fingers on his belt loops and rocked back on the heels of his Western boots before nodding. I wondered if he had a horse somewhere nearby. "Consider them gone, Helen."

I corrected him. "Hedi."

A few minutes later, both ridges were clear of the pack. I kept my knees locked during the reluctant exodus, but even so, Cordelia had to keep her grip onto my waistband tight, pulling it up so hard my crotch went numb. When there were no Weres left, but for her and Biggs, she let go. She caught me before I hit the ground and swung me up in her arms. She started toward the Trowbridge path. "No," I said. "I don't want to go near that house. I don't want anyone to ever go there again." Without a word, she pivoted, and headed toward the path Biggs had made down the Stronghold ridge.

She did smell like pond water.

Epilogue

You think you're going to die after living through your personal worst, but you don't. What's the alternative? I've met ghosts. Most of them are a bunch of losers, always moaning about what could have been or should have been.

So I had one more thing to do, and being near empty magicwise, I'd knew I'd have to do it the old-fashioned way. I had the thought I should do it on my own. It seemed perfectly plausible to me that I could man the oars with my crispy hands, hold the flashlight between my teeth, and steer the course to Merry's prince, without any help at all. Then maybe I'd sit there out among the lily pads, contemplating things, hoping to make sense of all that had happened.

That had been the pattern of my old life. My new one had unexpected hitches to it. Turns out the oars were really heavy, and the old wooden boat that Biggs and the other guy had brought me wasn't a hundred percent seaworthy.

And besides, Cordelia wasn't having it.

She sat beside me on the wooden seat and kept a steady beam of light on the lily pad. Biggs manned the oars, while Harry stood tall on the mud bank, waiting for us to return.

There seemed no end to this night.

"More to the left, Biggs," said Cordelia.

"Dude, it's harder than it looks."

"Call me that one more time and I'll cut your balls off."

"I'm the third," he said.

"I'll still cut your balls off."

"Leave it, Biggs," I said. "Her name is Cordelia. She is to be called by her name, and nothing else." I could hear her inhale of satisfaction. So to even it out, I said, "Cordelia, he is my third and that requires balls."

There: my first quasi-Alpha ruling.

They lapsed into silence as the boat reached the point where the portal had once floated over the lily pads. Biggs stopped pulling on the oars, and took that moment to bail out the bottom of the boat with an old yogurt container. But we all turned our gaze skyward. I don't know, maybe we thought the portal was still there, but somehow it had turned invisible. Or maybe some of us thought we'd have a fairy-tale ending. All we had to do was wish for it, and the lights would return, the wind chimes would sing, the air would be sweet—and he would be there, Merry around his neck.

Fantasy. But then again, I know there's a place up there, far, far north, past earth's moon and stars, where a half-mad Mystwalker protects a Fairy Royal Court. Would Trowbridge's soul-light be up there now? Spilling electric-blue light for the wonder of the woodland creatures? Or was there no forest-of-souls for the Weres in Threall? No grove of trees for the humans?

And what of me? Where did my soul-light glow?

No one said a word when I raised my hand to trail my finger through the night air where once the portal had hung. There was nothing there to grasp, like there had been nothing left here of him after the gates closed. Though . . . that's not the whole truth, is it? That's just part of the truth.

There had been something left in Creemore after he'd gone. A grieving redhead, blood on the ground, and me.

And there was something visible in the night sky over my head. There was a moon that would soon be calling, and stars that some lovesick fool would wish on, and maybe if I knew where to look for it, a hole in the Milky Way too.

There's always something there. It just may not be the thing you want.

Biggs picked up the oars and started pulling on them again, cursing under his breath as the blades got caught among the lilies' rubbery stems.

I moved to the prow as we drifted the last few feet. The starlight made the Royal Amulet's gold gleam in a way that Merry would have coveted. I leaned out to pluck him off his lily pad. As my fingers wrapped around his unfamiliar shape, I felt him move. Just a little quiver, perhaps a little start of fear as I lifted him off the safety of his lily pad. I turned him over. There was the tiniest blue fire deep in the center of his sapphire. Once his chain was warming on my neck, I hesitated, turning over the idea of tucking him inside my borrowed sweatshirt, close to my naked breast, but in the end, I let the Royal Amulet rest on the outside of my new hoodie. It reeked of Were, but he'd have to get over that. There would be no more hiding.

I gazed up at the ridges. Light streamed through the trees on the Trowbridge side. The last person to leave the house had left the lights on. Maybe tomorrow, I'd send Biggs to shut off all the power there. Close the curtains. Lock the door. Seal the memories away.

There was lots of activity up on the Stronghold ridge. A man was hanging a camp light from the lowest branch of our old maple tree. Some women were gathered in a gossip-sized huddle. More people were involved with directing the driver behind the pickup wheel as he slowly backed a trailer over my mum's old vegetable garden. I'm not sure he was paying attention to their comments, but it was worth a small smile, watching them flap their arms. The trailer resembled a big silver bug. I knew, with absolute certainty and a little inward squirm of cheer, that Cordelia would hate it. She'd moan and snarl and pout. But she'd stay.

I knew that too.

I scowled at all the Weres milling around up there. They were there to help, supposedly, but I could feel their eyes on me. They were curious, I guess. After all, I was supposed to be a ghost. But that's the problem with myths—they're never accurate. If you want proof that I'm very much alive, take a good whiff. It's not easy to catch, but it's there. Yeah, I smell a little like Trowbridge. I guess one day I won't even notice it. I can still feel him though. Inside me. Like I have two hearts buried under my broken ribs.

While he's gone, I'll stand in his place and learn the way of the Were. That might take some time, but time is something I'm banking on having plenty of. I'm twenty-two. With any luck, I'll figure out how to run a Pack before they realize I haven't got a clue.

But in the meantime, there are things to be done.

Somebody needs to feed me.

A cookie will do.